Blood Destiny

by Tessa Dawn

A Blood Curse Novel
Book One
In the Blood Curse Series

Published by Ghost Pines Publishing, LLC
http://www.ghostpinespublishing.com

Volume I of the Blood Curse Series by Tessa Dawn
Second Edition Trade Paperback Published December 03, 2013
10 9 8 7 6 5 4 3 2

ISBN-13: 978-1-937223-10-6
Printed in the United States of America

Author may be contacted at: http://www.tessadawn.com

This is a work of fiction. All characters and events portrayed in this
novel are either fictitious or are used fictitiously. Any resemblance to
actual persons, living or dead, business establishments, events, or
locales is entirely coincidental.

Ghost Pines Publishing, LLC

Dedication

To you – for surviving what few others could.

Acknowledgements

My thanks to all those who made this work possible: Reba Hilbert, for being such a delightful and talented editor to work with; Lidia Bircea, for bringing the Romanian language alive; and Greenhouse Designs, for another wonderful cover.

To my "sister" Monique, for stepping up when it was needed. My immense love to Kiana, Nashoba, and Angelina – thank you for your endless support. And to Steve, for being a lighthouse in the storm.

A Special Word to Readers

Dear Readers,

This book marks the second edition of Blood Destiny, reissued in December, 2013, after a wonderful, three-year run in circulation. The first edition was originally published by Charles River Press in December, 2010, and I am forever grateful to Jonathan Womack for believing in this project. Now that Blood Destiny has found a new home, I wanted to let you – the fans – know how much I appreciate your endless support of the Blood Curse Series. Your enthusiasm has been amazing. And I also wanted to let you what you can expect from this second edition:

It is essentially the same book as before – simply reissued with a new cover and minor, editorial updates. The only substantive change is in the Romanian interpretations that appear throughout the text: Following the release of book one in 2010, I began working with a new Romanian Interpreter on the series; and I asked her to go

BLOOD DESTINY

back and rework her beautiful, native language in
Blood Destiny as well. This reissued edition
reflects those updates; however, the story, plot,
and characters remain the same.

Prologue

800 BC ~ Romania

"Your punishment has been decided."

In the dark Romanian castle of their beloved homeland, the royal twins, Jaegar and Jadon, fell to their knees on the cold stone floor while the remaining males of their kind waited anxiously outside the castle walls to hear the edict. Their thick black hair fell forward, shielding their terrified eyes from their accuser, as torchlight cast eerie shadows upon the dank gray walls around them.

Their accuser was The Blood of countless victims.

Each one slaughtered without mercy.

The grim face of death eager to exact revenge.

"*Great Celestial Beings*, have mercy on our souls," Jadon pleaded as the ghostly apparition drew closer.

"You make me sick, brother!" Jaegar spat the words, unable to conceal his rage or his arrogance.

The shadow weaved to the left and then to the right like a phantom pacing.

And then it bent into a horrible arc of darkness, dipping down until, at last, it hovered face-to-face with the trembling men.

Oh gods...

Flushed and swaying, Jadon Demir reached out with a firm hand to steady himself against the ground. He cast a sideways glance at his older twin, who was now as pale as moonlight.

"From this day forward you shall be cursed! And your sons shall be cursed. And their sons after them...unto all eternity." The shadow drifted closer and a heavy mist settled on their skin. "And to make certain your suffering is inescapable, you shall be made immortal. Condemned to roam the earth in darkness as reviled creatures of the night. Forever forced to feed on the blood of the innocent to survive."

Jadon inhaled sharply, his heart pounding in his chest.

Despite his iron resolve, Jaegar collapsed on the floor.

The ghostly aberration continued: "As punishment for your unspeakable crimes against women, you shall never know the love or companionship of a female, nor shall you be capable of producing female offspring. Your sons will be born in sets of twins. Two children of darkness. The spawn of human hosts who will die wretchedly upon giving birth—even as the firstborn of the first set will be demanded as a sacrifice of atonement." The phantom glowered with fury. "Failure to yield the sacrifice will be met with a hideous and terrible death!"

The damp walls of the cavern creaked as if moaning beneath the pronouncement, and the torches flickered in and out as a deep red glow consumed the once-yellow flames.

Jadon Demir shook like a child unable to awaken from a nightmare. His chest heaved as he struggled for breath.

"I beg of you, grant mercy!" The words came out in a rush.

The phantom dipped and hissed, "Speak quickly."

Jadon cringed and averted his eyes. "I beseech you before all of heaven, before the Ancient Ones who came before us, and in the presence of the Celestial Gods: *Remove this curse upon my house and the house of my descendants.*"

The shadow stood still...listening.

Then all at once, Jadon's voice became a haunting song of sorrow, a sound so melodious that the room lit up, and the moon and stars dipped down to hear the beleaguered prince's words. Beneath a wind of grace and power, his plea took wings and flew...

"While I have walked among the warriors who have sacrificed our women, I have never taken life with my own hands. Although I have failed miserably to save the innocent, I have tried to convict the guilty. And while it is true I have enjoyed the privileges of the mighty, my heart has wept for the weak. Your wrath is deserved. Your punishment is just. But I

Tessa Dawn

beg of you: Search my heart…and have mercy upon me and my house."

Clearly disgusted, his older twin sat up and slowly turned his head to the side, his stark onyx eyes narrowing with contempt. He cursed Jadon beneath his breath and held his gaze in an angry glare.

"Remember your place, brother. That which curses us now is the blood of the slain, the wretched *females* we offered to the gods for our birthright: to be worshiped beside the Celestial Beings. Plead not with these *inferiors* for mercy. We are the strong. The powerful. What we did was justified. And I will not beg mercy of a female."

The room erupted into angry flames.

Sparks flew through the air like fire and brimstone.

A revolting abomination of heat licked at the brothers' skin, yet it did not consume their flesh.

And then the voice of the slain cried out from within the flames: "Ours was once a proud and noble race, before you led the corruption of our men beyond the abyss of evil." A blast of rage scorched the dark twin's eyes, turning his pupils from black to red as he was brought to his belly before his accuser. "In your thirst for power, Prince Jaegar, you have sacrificed the last of our females: our powerful sisters, mothers, and daughters. The keepers of the secrets of our race. *You have not achieved greatness.* You have brought an entire civilization to its knees! To the verge of extinction!"

The blaze then formed a halo around the body of the male who had pled so eloquently for mercy.

"And Prince Jadon, we have searched your heart and find your words to be true. You and your descendants—alone—shall be granted four mercies accordingly: Though still creatures of the night, you shall be allowed to walk in the sun. Though still required to live on blood, you shall not be forced to take the lives of the innocent. Though still incapable of producing female offspring, you will be given *one opportunity* to obtain a mate, and the sign of her arrival shall be heralded in the heavens.

BLOOD DESTINY

"Though still required to atone for the sins of your people, your twin sons will be born as one child of darkness and one child of light, and you shall be allowed to sacrifice the former while keeping the purer soul to carry on our noble race."

And so...

Banished from their homeland in the mountains of Eastern Europe, the descendants of Jaegar and the descendants of Jadon became the Vampyr of legend: roaming the earth, ruling the elements, living on the blood of others, forever bound by an ancient curse.

They were brothers of the same species, separated only by degrees of light and shadow.

one

Present Day

The dark woods were eerily quiet. Not a single sound invaded the night. Not even the soft hooting of an owl overhead or the faint rustle of leaves in the trees as an icy wind swept through the darkness. The ancient, circular clearing was on hallowed ground. A spherical graveyard surrounded by tall, looming pines and enormous, jutting rocks—the final resting place for the fallen descendants of Jadon.

Nathaniel Silivasi knelt before a perfect, lifeless body as it lay unnaturally still upon an ancient stone slab. His fraternal twin, Kagen, crouched down beside him.

His heart was heavy with sorrow—his grief overwhelming. The gravity of the loss was almost too much to bear.

It was still hard to believe that their youngest brother had fallen. *Shelby:* the last born of the five, a soul so full of mischief and humor. *Shelby:* vibrant, powerful, and gifted beyond measure.

Only five hundred years old, he had died as a mere fledgling. Just another proud warrior lost to the original sin.

Nathaniel cursed the heavens against the fate of their kind.

Like all descendants of Jadon, he was a being of both darkness and light, a powerful prince of the night, protecting the earth and its inhabitants from the darker demons of their species—the descendants of Jaegar.

He bowed his head in silent resignation, trying to accept what could never be changed: Shelby had failed to complete his destiny, to obtain the one human woman tied to his infinite soul, the only being in a lifetime of immortality who could free him from the ultimate claim of the Blood Curse.

With piercing eyes the color of emeralds and long black hair

1

that flowed like the wind, Dalia Montano's path had been chosen long before her birth. Chosen for Shelby and the future of their race.

It had been Dalia's fate to bear Shelby's twin sons: a child of light, who would forever lift the dark curse of death and spare his soul from eternal damnation, and a child of darkness, who would be offered in atonement for the sins of their forefathers.

Nathaniel trembled as the memory replayed in his mind.

Shelby had immediately recognized all the signs—just as he should have—the bloodred moon, the sudden appearance of his birth constellation in a pitch-black sky, even the matching birthmark on Dalia's inner wrist. But he had failed to consummate the ritual in time.

Wanting to make things easier on the beautiful human female who had turned his heart as easily as she had twisted his fate, Shelby had waited too long. And in doing so, he had created a lethal opportunity for one of the shadow descendants of Jaegar to get to Dalia first.

Valentine Nistor.

The true undead.

A living, breathing expression of evil itself.

As one of the oldest and more powerful of the Dark Vampires, Valentine had managed to take Shelby's life without ever lifting a finger—without ever drawing a single drop of blood.

Resentment stirred in Nathaniel's heart.

The Dark One was as cowardly as he was evil. He could have fought like a warrior, but he had chosen to go after his enemy by manipulating the Blood Curse instead. A descendant of Jadon was a very hard creature to defeat in battle.

Nathaniel sighed and resolutely shut his eyes.

He was fighting to keep his tears at bay, struggling wildly against the rage that was mounting in his soul. A single tear escaped, and he quickly wiped it away.

What difference did it make? What had or hadn't happened to Dalia? The bottom line was the same: She had not given birth to Shelby's sons, and when the Blood Curse had come for the unnamed one, without the sacrifice of the darker twin to stay his sentence, Shelby had died an agonizing death of retribution. Punished for a crime he had never committed.

Nathaniel set his jaw in a hard line. He refused to engage in *what ifs* and *if onlys*—speculating about the ancient curse or wondering what Shelby's life would have been if the damnable thing no longer existed. The Blood Curse did exist. And it would always exist for his kind. As sure as the sun would always rise in the east and set in the west. Like all vampires, Nathaniel had simply learned to accept it. It was an intrinsic part of their way of life.

Kagen reached out and placed a steadying hand on Nathaniel's shoulder, his dark brown eyes focused on the ground. "You know I share your pain, brother." His voice was a mere whisper. "Like you, I have lived long enough to know the deeper tragedy of this loss. So many proud warriors gone…and for what?" He shook his head with disgust.

Nathaniel swayed, feeling suddenly light-headed. "I never thought it would hit this close to home. How could this have happened, Kagen? *To Shelby of all males?*"

"One word," Kagen said, "*Valentine.*" He bit down on his lower lip, and his hand began to tremble. "But we cannot shed such tears, my brother. Remember, we must still guard our emotions."

Nathaniel knew his twin was right.

The force of such overwhelming grief spilling onto the earth from an ancient vampire could easily call forth an earthquake or command a flash flood. As it already stood, too many humans were going to die as a result of Shelby's passing, as a byproduct of the earth's grief.

Nathaniel nodded, his heart turning as cold and impassible as the stone slab his youngest brother now rested upon. He fisted his hands at his sides. Though he wanted to scream at the heavens, rage at the earth, weep until there were no tears left to cry, he knew he could not. His duty would not allow it.

His honor would not abide it.

Betraying no emotion whatsoever, he silently cursed his ancestors in the ancient tongue, daring them to retaliate, urging them to try and stake their claim on him before he could seek his vengeance for Shelby's death.

And he intended to seek his vengeance.

Kagen read Nathaniel's mind effortlessly. "You may not have a chance to impose your retribution, Warrior. Not if Marquis gets to the Dark One first."

Nathaniel glanced at his twin, noticing the subtle red embers glowing deep in the centers of his eyes. Kagen's own anger was scarcely contained.

"That might be true, brother, but if Marquis feels so strongly, then why isn't he here?"

"Nathaniel—"

"Do not excuse him, Kagen!"

Kagen shook his head. "I wasn't going to, brother."

Nathaniel sighed. "I know *exactly* what you were going to say, but that doesn't mean I understand..." His voice trailed off. "Nachari's absence? Sure. He couldn't possibly make it home in time, and Shelby's journey couldn't wait. But Marquis? He sits at home embracing the torment in his soul even as the shadows grow deeper within him. It isn't healthy. He needs to say good-bye."

Kagen frowned, his dark eyes filled with shared understanding. "You know he could not attend, Nathaniel. What did you expect him to do?" His voice held no hint of judgment. "The sky itself would have rained down blood and fire had Marquis been forced to place this blessed one in the ground. Marquis is too old. Too powerful. *Too angry.* I know he's always been the strong one, but I fear this may be too much...even for him."

Nathaniel rubbed his temples in slow, methodical circles, trying to ease some of his tension. Marquis was, indeed, having great difficulty with Shelby's death. "Has he spoken to you?"

"Briefly."

"And?"

"And he blames himself, Nathaniel. What do you think?"

Nathaniel shook his head. He knew that it was more than the injustice of the Blood Curse that tormented their ancient sibling, now fifteen hundred years old: Marquis was consumed with guilt over the *way* Shelby had died.

Kagen crossed his arms in front of him. "Marquis believes that the curse should have claimed him first. The Blood should have demanded a son from him long before it demanded one from Shelby. But it's the fact that Valentine got to Dalia—" He cut off his words the moment his voice began to quiver.

Nathaniel hissed beneath his breath. "None of us saw it coming."

"True." Kagen shifted uncomfortably. "But *Marquis* is the eldest, which makes him the sworn protector of our family. In his mind, he was responsible for the safety of his less powerful brother. As a male of honor, he should have seen to the safety of the human woman."

"It wasn't his mistake," Nathaniel insisted, knowing he felt guilty himself. "We all let Shelby down."

Kagen rubbed his eyes; he looked weary. "I know that. And Nachari knows that. But Marquis—"

"Will never forgive himself," Nathaniel supplied. He wiped his brow and shrugged his shoulders as if he could somehow lessen the weight of his grief with a gesture.

Kagen looked off into the distance. "Marquis will have to make his own peace with what happened in time."

Nathaniel hung his head. "Will you, Kagen? Will I?"

A long moment of silence passed between them before Kagen spoke again. "At any rate, Marquis is far too stubborn to take counsel from either of us. Perhaps Napolean can speak with him when things settle down...make him see that we are all equally to blame."

Maybe, Nathaniel thought. "He has to know that his leadership is still needed."

Kagen nodded. "More now than ever..." He cleared his

throat. "Nachari should arrive tomorrow evening. Being Shelby's twin, he was even closer to him than the rest of us. He is definitely going to need Marquis's support."

Nathaniel agreed, although he couldn't imagine anything that would ease Nachari's pain. "Perhaps they can console each other...now that they each walk the world *as only one*."

The slip was inexcusable.

Nathaniel immediately averted his eyes and bowed his head in a slight nod of regret: a warrior's apology.

It was rare for a vampire to refer to the missing twin of the blood sacrifice. It was simply understood that in every family, there would always be an odd number of sons—an eldest brother who walked alone, the firstborn of light whose twin of darkness had been sacrificed at birth. It was seen as rude to mention the one who had never been named. Impolite to even acknowledge his existence.

Kagen overlooked Nathaniel's error. "This won't be easy for either of them. I do not look forward to all the dark days ahead of us."

"Nor do I."

Nathaniel stood up then and drew in a long, deep breath. "It is time," he whispered.

Kagen rose to his feet and slowly nodded.

With a wave of his hand, Nathaniel gradually began to lower the heavy stone slab deep into the earth, the body of his beloved brother resting silently upon it, uncovered, so that the earth would embrace him.

Nathaniel spoke softly in the ancient language of their ancestors, offering a prayer for peace—a final benediction—and then he requested *safe journey* to the Valley of Spirit and Light, making an impassioned plea to the Spirit of Jadon himself to grant Shelby absolution for his failure to relinquish a son.

Nathaniel watched helplessly as his cherished little brother descended deep into the ground, never to rise again. Despite his best efforts, two burning tears escaped his eyes, each one instantly transformed into a single heart-shaped diamond: the color, crimson red.

"Travel well, my brother. Go in peace."

two

Jocelyn lifted the canteen from the weighty, navy blue backpack and took a long drink of water. She checked her compass once again, glancing furtively at the sky to determine the position of the sun. She was making great time. There was plenty of daylight left, more than enough to reach the cave before sunset. Placing the canteen back in the pack, she adjusted the weight evenly on her shoulders, her mind continuing to analyze information as she headed deeper into the forest.

Jocelyn knew that she didn't have permission to move on the tip her informant had given her. She wasn't supposed to be there. And if anything went wrong, she was on her own. But she also knew that it couldn't wait. *Human trafficking. Ritualistic killings.* The entire case was so bizarre.

As an agent of ICE, a highly specialized department within homeland security, Jocelyn Levi had been investigating one particularly shocking human-trafficking ring for months. Unlike more typical rings that forced young women into sexual slavery or sold children into forced labor, these victims were being taken for much darker purposes—to be used as sacrifices in ritualistic killings.

But by whom?

Jocelyn shook her head, carelessly tucking a handful of thick brown hair behind her ear. Over the last two months, her unit had discovered three freshly discarded bodies, each one showing signs of the same hideous brutality. The sight of the mutilated corpses had been abominable, but they were close to finding the head of the ring, or at least finding the man who was selling the women. Still, they had no idea who was doing the actual killings: what kind of cult could be behind such gruesome acts of evil. They had never managed to uncover an actual crime scene.

Jocelyn sighed, hoping that today would be a major

breakthrough. If the information her source had given her about the cave was correct, then she was about to make a huge discovery.

Her informant had assured her that she was not walking into a danger zone, that the site he had told her about was no longer being used by the ring. As always, they changed locations frequently, moving around to avoid detection by the authorities. Unfortunately, this meant that there would be no fresh forensic evidence, but the information Jocelyn hoped to uncover was of a different kind anyway.

Jocelyn slowed her pace as a series of tall, reddish rock formations appeared in the distance, strangely shimmering into view like a desert mirage on a hot day. An eerie chill swept through her body, raising the hair on her arms, and a deep sense of foreboding settled into her stomach. She shivered and stared ahead. There was something about the peculiar canyons that shook her to her very core.

Although most people would have turned back, most people would not have been there in the first place.

Jocelyn was not most people.

Solving difficult crimes was her life. Stopping the *really, really* bad guys. And she was very good at it. She had always had a sixth sense, an uncanny ability to stay one step ahead of the criminal mind. It wasn't like she was psychic or anything. She just had a way of *feeling* things. Walking into a crime scene and *knowing*. As if the very essence of the place whispered secrets to her of the people who had been there.

Now, after months of dead ends, she finally had a reliable lead; and she had no intention of letting the information go to waste.

Jocelyn drew in a deep breath of crisp mountain air, her lungs working overtime to adjust to the altitude of the Eastern Rocky Mountains. The beautiful, expansive territory ran along the Front Range of North America, full of hidden canyons, dense forests, and towering, majestic peaks; under different circumstances, it might have been an idyllic place to vacation.

Her sense of dread grew stronger with every step she took, so powerful that it almost felt as if there were an invisible hand holding her back, something warning her away. She shook her head in an effort to clear her mind as she pushed forward against the invisible barrier.

She had come way too far to turn back now.

The faces of the victims, their broken and tortured bodies, continued to replay in her mind like a gruesome, private slideshow, reminding her of just how much was at stake.

Picking up the pace, Jocelyn headed deeper into the canyon.

The oddly shaped underground cavity, at the end of a series of narrow limestone tunnels, was exactly where Jocelyn's informant had said it would be: beneath a thin-arced entrance at the back of the cliffs, just beyond a waterfall. Jocelyn wondered how something so beautiful could be used for something so evil.

It was well after sunset when she reached the cavern.

She had slowly worked her way through a long labyrinth of passageways, going deeper into the earth with every step, until she had finally emerged in a gigantic chamber with enormous cathedral ceilings and jutting white columns. The scattered limestone pillars were erected haphazardly, as if a divine hand had simply tossed them about, and there was a small pond of stagnant water toward the back of the chamber, just beneath a series of low ledges. The cave itself was eerily dark, humid, and chilly. The air was musty and damp.

Jocelyn abruptly shut off her flashlight as a faint sound caught her attention. She thought she heard an echo coming from one of the adjoining tunnels. It sounded like a woman softly moaning.

She instinctively crouched down, her senses fully alert.

She reached for her gun, removed it from the holster, and ran to the rear of the cavern. Then she quietly waded through the sulfuric-smelling water, slid down onto her belly, and crawled like a snake beneath an extremely low rock overhanging. She repositioned her slender frame in the tight space so that she could still see out into the chamber, and burrowed in as deeply as possible.

God, I hope there are no spiders or bats in here, she silently prayed as the sound from the tunnel grew louder. Whoever was out there was clearly coming her way.

It was then that she saw the firelight erupt—as if on its own—illuminating the entire structure like a dark sky on the fourth of July.

Crude, ancient torches were anchored into the limestone walls in perfectly spaced increments, running all the way around the structure in a flawlessly level circle, and Jocelyn almost gasped as her eyes took in the details of the ancient cavern for the first time. Fiery orange blazes illuminated every nook and cranny of the chamber, revealing carefully carved structures placed purposefully throughout the room. It was an amazing circular fortress, no doubt created naturally by the earth over centuries of dissolution.

But it had also been carved by human hands into a ceremonial hall.

Jocelyn held her breath, hoping she was deep enough into the crevice not to cast a shadow into the stagnant water. For the first time, she noticed that there were three ledges spaced diametrically apart like the points of a triangle along the cavern walls, and each one led to a steep drop. A certain death should anyone try to escape.

The thought was bone chilling.

In the center of the room, there was a large stone slab with a smoothed surface, much like a bed made of granite, and there were intricate carvings on either side, ancient symbols that Jocelyn didn't recognize. But the color at the top of the stone was unmistakable. Jarring and unsettling. Jocelyn cringed as she imagined its purpose.

The center of the stone was a deep crimson red, the obvious result of years of decaying blood that had crystallized into the stone's pores. This was clearly not the work of a serial killer or a regional group of fanatics. This chamber was ancient. And these crimes were generational. The room spoke of a hidden way of life that had belonged to a people—*a culture*—for hundreds of years.

Adrenaline coursed through Jocelyn's body as the horror of the chamber sank in.

She held her breath and strained to see more.

On both sides of the bloodstained slab, there were additional man-made structures carved into granite: a raised altar on the left with a small basin smoothed into the top, and a wide bench on the right containing a backrest with arm-holds for comfort. Each structure sat about three feet away from the head of the slab.

Jocelyn shuddered.

She could feel the darkness and the unspoken pain etched into the fiber of the chamber, and once again, her stomach lurched. The hair on her arms stood up.

It was then that they entered.

A tall, dark, heavily muscled man. He was graceful yet intense, striking but dangerous. He was definitely malevolent.

Not human.

And he carried a very pregnant woman in his arms, obviously the one who had been moaning.

Dear God...

Jocelyn didn't know how she knew the creature wasn't human. She just knew. He looked like any other man, except that he was far too stunning, handsome in a way that seemed impossible. His long hair fell just below his shoulders in perfectly groomed waves, and his chiseled features were flawless, as if he were a statue rather than a man. But what really gave him away were his eyes. They were vacant...empty...soul-less.

Dark as the night and just as lifeless.

They might have held a strange beauty if they hadn't been so...dead.

And the color of his immaculate hair was unnatural too: It was a deep raven black, interspersed with bloodred tendrils, highlights that had not been added with dye. Jocelyn thought it shimmered like the surface of a lake beneath the moonlight; it was almost beautiful...in a demonic sort of way.

She hunkered lower and held her breath as she continued to watch, mesmerized.

The pregnant woman's eyes were open, but she looked unaware, like someone in a trance. She appeared to be young, maybe nineteen or twenty, with beautiful black hair and stunning green eyes. Her pale face was etched with...something...like a frozen look of terror from a nightmare. Thank God she was so checked out.

With a wave of his hand, the chamber began to fill with the smell of incense, and a dense gray fog began to hover just above the ground. It surrounded the bloodstained slab in the center of the room, instantly adding a ghostly feel to the chamber. Jocelyn couldn't scoot any further back into the crevice, so she tried to make herself smaller, willing her physical body to disappear.

There would be nothing she could do if he saw her.

Somehow, she knew, even as she cradled her gun in her hand, fully loaded and ready to fire, that her fate rested upon remaining hidden. There could be no detection. Luckily, the creature appeared far too engrossed with the pregnant woman to scan his surroundings, far too confident in his overwhelming power to concern himself with checking the chamber for others. And the sulfuric water she had waded through was a powerful mask of scent. Or at least she hoped it was.

There was a strange exhilaration gathering around him now. A sense of great expectation. Power radiated from the male as if it were seeping through his pores.

He glided to the bloodstained slab in the center of the chamber and slowly laid the woman down on the pallet. For a moment, Jocelyn thought she saw a hint of tenderness in his actions until she heard a faint laugh rise from deep within his throat. A twisted cross between a leopard's snarl and a hyena's hackling that made her skin crawl.

"Dalia, awaken," he commanded. His voice was like a velvet

song, a rich cello from a concerto, as pure as the night and deeper than the ocean. He bent over the pregnant woman and kissed her. She awoke as commanded.

"Valentine, help me!"

She gulped the words in a desperate plea for mercy. Her eyes were wide with fright, and then, as she surveyed the chamber, a shriek of unbridled terror escaped her throat.

Jocelyn was not prepared for the sound that filled the cave.

The cry was so full of anguish that it momentarily stole her breath, even as it filled the room with electricity. It was unlike anything Jocelyn had ever heard before—the woman's misery was beyond comprehension.

Jocelyn had the sudden urge to vomit and had to struggle to remain quiet as her stomach protested, threatening to give her presence away. Fortunately, the agonized screams drowned out the sound of her gagging.

The woman was in labor, and something was terribly wrong.

She writhed and screamed. Tried frantically to crawl away. But the man simply leaned over her, watching with indifference as he placed one powerful hand against her chest, pressed her down, and held her to the stone.

Jocelyn shook her head and blinked several times, as if trying to wake up from a nightmare, hoping it was all a bad dream.

The pain continued.

The torture persisted.

The cries went on for what seemed an eternity, sweat pouring from the woman's forehead, her hands clenched in a contortion of anguish, as the dark male sat quietly watching the whole scene with a look of pleasure gleaming in his eyes.

The man shifted back and forth on the hard bench.

He appeared to be deliberately controlling his breathing, and there was an erotic quality to his movement. It was as if he were deriving sexual pleasure from the woman's suffering, struggling to restrain himself from touching her while she labored.

Unable to bring his excitement under control, he bent over and pressed a hard kiss against her mouth as she moaned in pain.

It was beyond sociopathic.

And then, what happened next was so shocking that it left Jocelyn both hypnotized and repulsed at the same time: The creature's perfect lips drew back like a predator's snarl, and his canine teeth slowly lengthened into two razor-sharp...*fangs*. And then he scraped them back and forth over the woman's neck—again and again—leaving deep, jagged gashes in his wake. Groaning in a low growl of ecstasy, he finally sank them deep into her flesh, his body shuddering with pleasure as she cried out in pain.

The entire scene was unspeakably brutal. Jocelyn felt like time was standing still as she lay motionless on the floor of the cave, desperate to conceal her own presence from the monster.

Helpless to save the suffering woman.

And then the woman's struggle reached a fevered pitch. Her cries grew so forlorn that Jocelyn actually considered drawing her weapon and revealing her own presence just to end her suffering.

There was no time.

Muscles began to stretch. Bones cracked and ribs popped. As a terror that could only be described as unholy rose in the form of a plaintive wail from the woman's throat. The baby was not moving down through the birth canal, but up...*up*...into the chest cavity. Jocelyn fought to hold back her own terrified scream, and her mouth fell open in horror as the woman's rib cage exploded outward. Fragmenting as it burst open, it exposed her heart and lungs.

The dark creature sighed in contentment.

He stood up over the broken body, reached into the gaping cavity, and lifted out what appeared to be *two* perfect newborn infants—both males—with thick, raven black hair. Hair striped with demonic strands of crimson red.

When the creature strolled to the raised altar, he seemed to falter for the first time, like he was struggling to remain in control. He placed the firstborn of the two sons gently into the basin, pausing only long enough to stare into the child's eyes and place a soft kiss on his forehead. It was as if he knew he couldn't keep the child. The tenderness was bizarre.

Instinctively, he held the remaining infant close to his chest and moved back from the altar. He watched the abandoned baby squirm, and his eyes became as cold as ice.

The dark fog moved then.

It swirled, becoming increasingly solid and thick.

It took the form of two long arms with extended, skeletal fingers as it reached and grasped. Moaned and wailed. In a shrill, high-pitched cry of victory.

The wail became louder as the fog swirled closer to the altar, where the child lay waiting.

And then Valentine's muscles clenched. His forehead wrinkled with tension. And his gaze became a fiery red ember of loathing as he watched the fog approach the child.

Yet, he didn't move a muscle as the grayish-black mist surrounded the crying infant. As it reached out to tighten its ghostly fingers around the newborn's neck...

Then just like that—the child was gone.

Valentine growled a low, angry snarl, his powerful frame trembling with rage, and then he simply turned away, lifted the remaining child high in the air, and smiled, a twisted grin exposing his perfect white teeth.

"You shall be named Derrian," he declared in a deep, resounding voice. "And now the Blood Curse shall never claim me. I am forever immortal." A wicked smirk crossed his face. "While Shelby Silivasi—*the beloved descendant of Jadon*—is forever dead."

He spat the words sarcastically, his laughter echoing all the way to the high cathedral ceilings.

"And this woman..." he gestured toward the stone where Dalia lay dead, her eyes still open wide in horror, "was truly a waste of a beautiful body, don't you think?"

He laughed again and held the newborn baby to his soul-less heart.

Waving a carefree hand over Dalia, he sent the tortured body

BLOOD DESTINY

up in flames, cremating her as he sauntered out of the chamber.
Softly singing a lullaby to his son.

three

Jocelyn raced frantically across the winding mountain path. She ran with all the speed she could muster, dirt and rocks kicking up behind her as her feet left the ground. The limbs of nearby trees reached out to scratch her skin when she got too close. Her heart pounded uncontrollably as images of the horror she had witnessed replayed in her mind.

She had waited in the dark cavern long after midnight, wanting to be sure the creature was gone before she attempted to make an escape. Taking only her identification from her backpack, she had placed her gun safely in its holster over her right shoulder and flung the half-full canteen of water over her left. Then, she had hastily thrown the heavy pack over one of the steep drops before sprinting wildly through the dark maze of tunnels in a frenzied effort to get out of the cave.

Jocelyn fell several times in her hasty escape, bruising and scraping her knees, but she barely felt any pain as her adrenaline carried her miles through the forest.

When she finally stopped to rest, her lungs labored for breath, even as her mind cried out for sanity. *It couldn't be!* What she had seen could not be real. What kind of creature was that?

And the poor, helpless woman…

How could anyone suffer such a heartless death?

Jocelyn bent over, panting heavily. Her hands were on her knees, and she fought to take in oxygen in the high, unforgiving altitude. She struggled to clear her usually organized mind.

Dalia.

The murdered woman.

Had she been one of the victims sold into slavery by the ring? Had that creature purchased her…*to breed?* To murder? Had he kept her for nine whole months? And if so, what in God's name had that poor woman endured?

BLOOD DESTINY

Most of the women involved in the ring she had been investigating were foreigners. Poor, unsuspecting immigrants forced to trust the wrong person in a desperate attempt to come to the United States. But Dalia had been American. At least she had looked American. And she had sounded American, too, when she had spoken the creature's name.

Valentine.

Jocelyn shuddered and blinked back a reservoir of pressing tears. The woman in the chamber had been beautiful. And she had suffered unbearably.

Jocelyn could not get far enough away…fast enough. She took a few more labored breaths, then forced herself to get moving again. She tried to keep up a steady jog even though her lungs felt like they were on fire. Her mind continued to piece the puzzle together as she ran…

What kind of a creature started fires with the wave of his hand? Who held down a struggling adult woman—pregnant or not—with only the tips of his fingers? *Whose children emerged from the body like alien beings as opposed to being born in the natural way?*

And the blood.

He drank blood.

Jocelyn tried to convince herself that he was just some sort of incredibly strong, psychopathic killer. Maybe a crazed addict pumped up on drugs, someone who had given himself so completely over to darkness that he no longer had a conscience. But she knew better. As impossible as it was, Jocelyn knew the truth: That thing was *undead*. Wholly evil. Dangerous beyond measure and definitely not human.

That thing was a *vampire*.

Even as the prospect settled in her mind, it was hard to accept it as true.

The narrow, uneven path beneath her feet was littered with branches, scattered with pine cones, and strewn with raised tree roots. The loose soil formed uneven divots beneath her feet, causing her to trip and fall far too often, having only a flashlight for a guide. The enormous gathering of shadowed, towering

20

pines, interspersed with quaking aspens, gave the forest a haunted appearance.

As if it were bursting with mystical beings. All of them lurking. Towering over and around her. Hiding just out of sight. Crouched and ready to pounce as she ran by.

Every shadow was a ghost. Every sound was the creature finding her. Every whisper was a vampire waiting to claim her.

Jocelyn put her hands over her ears. She could feel the desperate pounding in her head even as she tried to control her thoughts and keep her eyes focused on the path ahead of her.

One step at a time, she coaxed. *Just keep going one step at a time.*

A large, jutting tree root caught her ankle as she rounded a sharp curve in the path, just as a wolf howled from somewhere deep in the forest. The tree felt like two evil hands snatching her legs, and she was certain the howl was an insidious snarl, that the vampire had found her and was about to take her to his lair. She screamed a hair-raising shriek of terror as her knees struck the ground and her hands flew out in front of her to catch her fall. She clenched her eyes shut and trembled uncontrollably.

She was too afraid to open them.

Too afraid to move.

So gripped with terror she was paralyzed.

She huddled close to the ground, trying desperately to regain her composure.

As long as she lived, she would never get over what had happened in that chamber. No matter how tightly she held her hands over her ears, she couldn't shut out the echo of those anguished cries. Now, miles away from the bloody cavern, Jocelyn finally began to feel—not just to analyze or survive—but to deeply, intrinsically feel the full horror of what she had seen.

Like the rising tide of an ocean wave, the anguish swelled in her heart, and she began to sob. She gathered her knees to her chest, buried her face in her hands, and rocked back and forth while she wept.

Jocelyn Levi cried uncontrollably, maintaining a far too fragile hold on her sanity.

BLOOD DESTINY

Nathaniel had stood at Shelby's grave site deep into the night, so consumed by his grief that he'd lost track of time. It was only the harsh, desperate sound of a woman's cry, coming from deep within the forest, that brought him back to the present moment.

He lifted his head to scent the air, his mind becoming alert. The sound had come from the valley just beyond the Red Canyons. *The canyons once used by the Dark Ones to conduct their hideous rituals.* Was it possible that his shadow brothers had returned to the familiar chamber?

It had been many moons since a son of Jaegar had dared to sacrifice a human in the sinister ritual so close to the lands of his Lighter Brothers. The last Dark Vampire who had flaunted such arrogance had been Vladimir Lazaro, and he had paid a heavy price for his audacity when the sons of Jadon had punished him for his crime.

As was the only true way to destroy a vampire, a creature whose very life and power existed in the blood, Vladimir's had been drained from his body by the warriors. He had been dealt a lethal wound to enable his capture, and his blood had been siphoned from several major arteries to ensure a rapid loss of life-force.

Normally, his head would have been severed and destroyed along with his heart, but Vladimir's punishment had been much harsher. An example to the rest of his kind. He had been drained of *all but a few drops of blood*, leaving just enough essence to keep him weak but alive. The sons of Jadon had then staked him through the heart; anchored him to the ground; and surrounded him with their most powerful ancients, holding him there until the sun had risen the next morning.

Completely exposed, Vladimir's flesh had been incinerated beyond recognition, his unclean heart burned from his body in the most painful death a Dark One could endure. The Evil Ones continued to have children, to make human sacrifices, but like the cowards they were, they hid in the shadows and struck only when there was little chance of being caught. The Red Canyons, with all their hidden labyrinths and chambers, were far too close to the shared valley of Jadon's people. To use them was to commit certain suicide.

Nathaniel cloaked his presence and took to the skies, flying toward the canyons to investigate. He considered the world around him as he flew.

The night air was cool, but the skies were clear. The moon cast radiant shadows over the land. As Nathaniel basked in the glow, it occurred to him that the Rocky Mountains were not at all like the mountains of his ancestral homeland, a homeland he could only embrace through visits and genetically passed-on memories.

While the Transylvanian Mountains of Europe stretched from the mouth of the Vişeu and Golden Bistriţa rivers all the way to the great Hungarian Plain, the Rocky Mountains were located in western North America and stretched all the way from Canada to New Mexico. The eastern edge of the Rockies had been inhabited by the banished males of his ancestry, those who had been forced from the Transylvanian Alps many centuries earlier as part of the Blood Curse. Eventually, they had settled along the central Front Range, building a lasting society and a legacy of wealth.

Nathaniel had grown to love this "new" land, with its enormous, jutting mountain peaks, reaching impossibly high into the bluest of skies. He adored the endless valleys and forests, with their mild spring and summer weather, and he practically worshiped the purple and orange sunsets.

And he never grew tired of discovering the endless channels of water—rivers bursting with whitewater rapids, waterfalls pouring out of steep cliffs, and sparkling, crystal lakes hiding deep within secret meadows.

As he approached the Valley of Shadows, he surveyed the

land below. The descendants of King Sakarias had originally settled in the region some 2,800 years ago, separating the vast mountain ranges into two distinct regions: All the land to the west of the Red Canyons had been claimed by the Dark Ones, the descendants of Jaegar; while all the land to the east of the canyons had been inhabited by the descendants of Jadon.

The approaching valley below was a neutral zone that connected the two.

As Nathaniel slowed to make his descent, he could see the slender silhouette of a woman; she was rocking back and forth like a frightened child, kneeling on the ground.

Absently, he wondered how she had gotten so close to the Red Canyons. She should have been able to feel the dark hand of warning that safeguarded the region; it was set in place by the sons of Jadon to keep out humans who might wander too close.

Curious, Nathaniel landed out of view behind a small grouping of pine trees and watched the human female. She was clearly distressed, her narrow shoulders hunched over from the weight of her tears, but she did not appear to be in any immediate danger.

To be perfectly honest, Nathaniel was grateful for the momentary distraction from his grief, however slight.

Cautiously, he stepped out from behind the trees. His eyes immediately searched hers out to project a sense of calm.

"Hello," he called softly.

four

Jocelyn jolted and screamed in fright, the sudden appearance of the dangerous-looking man shocking her back into the moment. Although he immediately put up both hands—palms forward, in a timeless gesture of peace—she wasn't about to take any chances. She sprang to her feet, drew her gun, and cocked the trigger, all in one smooth motion. Holding it forward in a two-armed stance, she slowly backed away, her eyes glued to the stranger.

"Don't move!"

The tall, dark man raised his hands even higher, flashing a slow, easy smile that was loaded with heat. His perfect teeth gleamed in the night. "I'm sorry if I frightened you. I heard you scream and thought you might need help." His timbre was deep and alluring.

Jocelyn felt instantly drawn to him, like a paper clip to a magnet. His voice was pure poetry, a gentle caress to the soul, and it was edged with a faint, almost medieval accent.

Jocelyn had heard that accent before.

"I said don't move!" This time, she shouted the command, pointing the barrel of the gun directly between his eyes. "And don't come any closer."

"I'm not moving," he assured her. "I just came to see…are you okay?"

Jocelyn fought the subtle coercion in his voice. *"Quit talking!"*

His eyebrows shot up. "Interesting."

He muttered the word beneath his breath, and then he became deathly quiet as his eyes swept over her body, clearly searching for signs of injury.

Jocelyn took a small step back.

She could have sworn she caught him *sniffing* the air, using his sense of smell to scan for information. But what could he possibly hope to detect? Her sharp, detective mind began to analyze possibilities at a rapid pace, ferreting out the things one might pick up with an enhanced sense of smell.

Her blood for starters. It had to be laced with adrenaline, and that would betray a deep presence of fear, a heightened sense of survival. Her sweat glands were far too active for someone who had been sitting on the ground, so he would have to know that she had been running: obviously, *running away* from something.

Or someone.

And there might even be a faint odor of smoke in her hair, exposing the fact that she had recently been in the proximity of fire. Perhaps at a campfire.

But she was relatively unharmed.

Outside of a few scrapes and bruises on her knees, there were no other injuries to her body. Even as she thought it, his shrewd eyes drifted lower to her legs. He couldn't possibly smell such minor wounds, could he? There just wasn't enough—

Blood.

Jocelyn's heart skipped a beat.

And then his piercing gaze scanned her neck as if he were searching for something specific…

Bite marks.

Jocelyn had to resist the impulse to take one hand off of her gun and place it protectively over her throat, but then his scrutinizing gaze softened; he seemed satisfied with what he saw.

"I will ask you once again," he said, entirely undaunted by her order to quit talking. "Are you okay? Why were you screaming?"

Jocelyn couldn't believe the power of his voice: She felt compelled to answer the question. In fact, she *wanted* to answer it. She *needed* to tell this man exactly what she had seen, but something inside of her struggled to resist the impulse as she continued to make the connection between the man who stood in front of her and the creature she had seen in the chamber. She couldn't help but remember the horrific fate of the woman the creature had captured.

And there could be no doubt that they were the same species.

This man's voice was just too seductive and enchanting, exactly like the creature's had been. His height and body shape were almost identical, and he carried himself with far too much confidence, wearing a silent badge of authority on his sleeve. Power practically seeped through his pores as he stood there before her like some kind of mystical black panther, crouched in waiting.

And despite the fact that she was the one holding the gun, he was the one commanding the situation.

And then there was that hair: a perfect head of blue-black locks that fell just below his shoulders in glistening waves of perfection, accenting his chiseled features.

Everything about him gave him away.

The man wasn't just handsome: He was *flawless*.

No, there could be no doubt.

Jocelyn fought the overwhelming urge to answer his question. She knew precisely what he was. Not human. *Vampire.* She squared her stance, tightened her grip, and tried to come up with a plan.

The vampire frowned, his forehead creased with consternation. He seemed deeply surprised—and mildly annoyed—by her resistance. This time, he locked his eyes with hers in a steadfast gaze, staring straight through her, and then he pitched his voice an octave lower.

"You *will* answer me now: What are you afraid of?"

Jocelyn's legs went limp as the words flowed out like water through a sieve. "I don't want you to kill me."

She answered honestly.

She had no other choice.

He had demanded nothing less.

The man recoiled. "And why would I do that?"

This time, Jocelyn literally bit her tongue. She had to be strong. She knew enough to realize that he was controlling her with his voice. Just as she knew, without question, that she could not endure what she had witnessed in that chamber.

She had no idea whether or not a vampire could be destroyed with bullets, but she did know that she had only one chance to get it right. She could not be captured.

She would not be captured.

If she fired and missed—or worse, her bullets had no effect on the supernatural being—it would be too late. Her fate would be sealed.

Jocelyn swallowed a lump in her throat; she knew what she had to do. She had to take absolute control over the situation, create the one and only outcome she had complete authority over.

Jocelyn continued to resist the powerful coercion, her mind locked in fierce determination. She steadied her trembling arms and shifted the gun into her right hand. With iron resolve, she turned the nine-millimeter away from the vampire and brought it to her own temple.

In one smooth, determined motion, she pulled the trigger.

five

Nathaniel moved with all the supernatural speed and precision of his kind, wrenching the gun from the woman's hand even as she squeezed the trigger. As he turned it away from her head, the lethal bullet sailed into a nearby tree, striking with a loud thud as small fragments of bark exploded into the air. He was absolutely shocked by her reckless behavior.

"Are you insane?" he demanded, no longer bothering to be polite. "What were you thinking?"

The woman appeared stunned—like she was struggling to comprehend what had just taken place. She was supposed to be dead, yet Nathaniel had averted the gun before the bullet could leave the chamber. As the realization set in, her expression went from bewildered to defeated. Utterly dazed, the human tried to murmur an answer, but it just came out as a series of incomprehensible sounds. And then her hazel eyes began to fill with tears.

Nathaniel took a deep, calming breath and steadied his voice. Once again, he used a deliberate tone of coercion. "You will tell me right now—what is it that has you so deeply frightened that you would rather kill yourself than face me?"

"You," she whispered in a barely audible voice.

"Me?" Nathaniel frowned, surprised by her answer.

True, he had deeply startled the poor woman, but that was hardly a reason to commit suicide. "Why in the world would you be that frightened of *me*?"

The woman blinked back her tears, clearly irritated by her lack of control. "You are a…a vampire."

Nathaniel stepped back quietly. Now he was the one who was stunned.

"I see."

He said it matter-of-factly, not denying anything, and then he took a much closer look at the frightened woman standing before him.

She was modestly tall and fairly thin. Solid but shapely. And she held herself with a notable confidence, despite the situation. Her hair was a rich shade of brown that reminded him of creamy milk chocolate. It was gloriously long with soft waves of amber highlights cascading throughout the thick tresses.

Her eyes were positively enchanting, with an odd, shadowy mix of pale green and soft brown glowing in their depths, like the eyes of a tiger. Nathaniel thought they were stunning, as were the rest of her immaculate features. She was simply a striking woman.

And she was obviously frightened out of her wits.

A long moment of silence passed between them before she registered a response. "You aren't going to deny it?" Her skin turned pale, and she shook her head in disbelief. "Then you're admitting that you're a *vampire*? A mythical creature out of a horror movie?" Despite her attempt at courage, her voice faltered.

Nathaniel smiled, hoping to ease her fears. "I'm admitting no such thing," he quipped. "I am quite certain that I am neither a myth nor a creature from a horror movie. However, I will concede that *you* clearly believe that I am such a being. Although I can't imagine why you would think such a thing."

"You know exactly what you are," the human retorted. Her eyes met his, and she squared her shoulders.

Nathaniel rubbed his thumb against his chin and regarded her thoughtfully. The truth was he hadn't decided yet what he was going to do next. He had already crossed one line by forcing her previous answers. As it stood, he was going to have to remove her memories. While he didn't mind skimming her mind for further information, if necessary, he didn't want to probe too deeply without her permission.

Human beings had retained few divine qualities endowed upon them by their creator, but free will was one of them. And it was not to be toyed with lightly. There were too many potential repercussions, not the least of which could be a sense of hopelessness, and in the worst-case scenario, a lessening of the will to live—something this woman clearly had a problem with already.

Nathaniel sighed and softened his voice. "Tell me, beautiful woman with the eyes of a tiger, why is it that you think me to be Vampyr?"

He thought it was a reasonable enough question, but for some reason, the female went straight from upset to overload. Her eyes glazed over like she was on a mind-altering drug, and her mouth dropped open.

"Did you just call me *tiger-eyes?*" Her voice was sharp with disbelief. "And did you just pronounce the word *vampyr?* As if making it sound more...sexy...could possibly change what it means?"

He stifled a chuckle. This human's wit was adorable.

Hands on her hips, she huffed and regarded him defiantly. "Well, for starters, you seem to know the right pronunciation of the word." And then she laughed, insincerely, sounding more hysterical than amused.

And then she began to cry.

Nathaniel cringed. "You have a sense of humor, I see. More so, when you're not frightened to death, I imagine. *Please*...don't cry." He took a very slow step forward and placed a hand gently on her shoulder. "Would it help if I assured you that you have nothing to fear from me? I am not going to harm you—*no matter what kind of a creature I am.*"

The woman sniffled, wiped her eyes with the back of her hand, and crossed her arms in front of her, clearly thinking it over.

Nathaniel waited, their eyes locked for what seemed an eternity. The pretty woman was a welcome distraction from the day's events, but he didn't care to be out in the forest all night. And they were far too close to the lands of the Dark Ones for his comfort. Not to mention, there was an important mystery hidden behind those shadowy eyes: a fear so elemental that it shook him. What in the world had this woman seen?

"It might help," she finally said. "That is, if I thought I could believe you."

Nathaniel sighed. "Have I given you any reason not to trust me?"

The woman shrugged her slender shoulders.

Nathaniel's exasperation grew. "If I recall, you were the one who made a choice to harm yourself. I believe I was the one who stopped you."

She looked away. "That's true..."

It was a minor concession, but he would take it.

When her brow creased like she was deep in thought, the temptation was just too great for Nathaniel to resist. He dipped gently into her mind and was immediately taken aback by what he found: There was absolutely no question—the woman was positively scared to death of him. She unequivocally believed that he was *evil*, despite his continued attempts at kindness. She was convinced that he was determined to hurt her, and the more he tried to be polite, the more she saw his behavior as calculated. Nathaniel knew he wasn't going to win her over easily, not without using a healthy dose of his powers.

Maybe not at all.

The woman cleared her throat and stared down at the ground before looking back up to meet his gaze. "Do you intend to let me go?" She sounded like a condemned prisoner standing before a firing squad.

This time, Nathaniel was less than amused. "Of course, I do." He held up his hands in frustration. "I am not holding you here in any way, my dear lady. I truly only came because I heard you cry and was concerned for your safety." He glanced cautiously around the valley. "This is not a safe place for you." His voice sharpened. "But then, it would appear to me as if you already know that. And whatever you're running from, it isn't me. So perhaps you would be wise to accept my assistance."

The woman's eyebrows shot up in surprise, and for a brief moment, Nathaniel thought he saw the faint hint of a smile.

"I'm not an irrational person, *sir*," she insisted. She raised her chin, crossed her arms, and regarded him again. "And I'm willing to admit that you might have a point. *Might*."

"Well, thank you," he whispered as his tension eased. "*Ma'am*."

She sighed then and tucked her hair behind her ears, biting her lower lip, a gesture Nathaniel found curiously endearing.

Her eyes narrowed in concentration. "I want to believe you." She rested her forehead on the heels of her hands then, as if nursing a headache. "God knows…I *need* to believe you."

Nathaniel's heart immediately softened. "Tell me your name, *tiger-eyes*."

Maybe if the two of them became more familiar, she might begin to trust him a little.

"Jocelyn," she answered reluctantly. "My name is Jocelyn."

Nathaniel extended his hand. "It is nice to meet you, Jocelyn. I am Nathaniel Silivasi. My family owns and operates most of Dark Moon Vale, including the lodge and the ski resort just to the east of here. If you would be so kind as to allow me to escort you from this place, I give you my word that I will *let you go* once you are in a safer place."

"You actually *live* around here?" she asked, incredulous.

Nathaniel laughed. "Yes, I do. I actually live, work, *and play* around here. And I don't think it would bode well for me—or my business—if I went around harming the tourists. What do you think?"

Suddenly, a small light appeared in her eyes, and her posture relaxed a little. She cautiously reached out to take his hand. "Nice to meet you, Nathaniel."

"It is my privilege, Jocelyn."

She acknowledged him, a quick nod of her head, and then hastily let go of his hand, stepping a few paces away. Projecting what seemed to be a somewhat forced look of calm, she gestured toward the hiking trail and started walking.

Nathaniel fell effortlessly into step beside her. "I think you have made a good decision, *Jocelyn*. Much better than shooting oneself in the head, don't you think?"

This time, she looked up at him with wide eyes and just shook her head.

He chuckled beneath his breath.

"You really aren't going to hurt me?" she asked. Her voice was apprehensive.

Nathaniel stopped and placed both hands lightly on her shoulders, gently turning her to face him. "Jocelyn, look at me."

Impulsively, she obeyed.

"I am *really* not going to hurt you." He held her gaze, never once blinking.

Jocelyn let out her breath. "Okay." The response was a whisper. "I'm going to try to believe you." She tried to smile as they began walking again. "Just don't *do* anything. I mean, like don't make any more sudden moves or anything."

Nathaniel nodded and slowed his stride to a snail's pace. "I will move *very* slowly." He started to lag behind.

"Not that slow!" she snapped. "I am definitely ready to get out of here." This time, she smiled, a full, breathtaking grin.

Nathaniel loved the way her eyes sparkled when she smiled, lighting up the exquisite features of her face. She had a pleasant way about her when she was more at ease. He put his hands in the pockets of his waist-length jacket and fell easily into step with her again, hoping it was a good time to approach a more serious subject.

"You still have not told me what you were doing here in the first place. Why a beautiful woman would wander around a dark forest at night by herself."

Jocelyn frowned. "I wasn't wandering around. I don't *wander*. And I was actually here all day." She wrung her hands together. "Honestly, I'd really rather not talk about it right now, if you don't mind—not if you'd like me to stay sane." She paused then and whispered, "Please...don't make me."

"Make you?" He raised an eyebrow, meeting her gaze with concern.

"Yes," she replied. "*Make me*. You know, with your eyes—

and your voice. The way you *made me* answer your questions earlier."

Nathaniel was astonished. He caught his breath and turned to take a more serious look at the intelligent woman. She had incredible instincts. More than that, actually; she just seemed to know things she shouldn't have known. Humans were typically incapable of picking up on a vampire's mind control.

"I apologize." He said it respectfully. "I was concerned for you. With your...erratic behavior...and all. I was simply seeking answers. No, you do not have to tell me if you do not wish it."

Nathaniel really wanted to know what had happened— perhaps he even needed to know—but this human was unusually courageous, and he didn't want to violate her wishes unless he had to.

They walked for a time in silence, and then Jocelyn spoke in a hesitant voice. "I don't suppose it would be pushing my luck to ask for my gun back..."

Nathaniel eyed her warily. "Will you shoot yourself?"

She rolled her eyes. "Not as long as you don't make any sudden moves."

He laughed. "Will you shoot me?"

"Would it work?"

"No, it wouldn't."

As if swept away into an invisible vacuum, the humor left the air, even as the color left the woman's face. "What are you, Nathaniel?" she asked. "I mean the truth. What kind of a...being...are you?"

Nathaniel frowned. "You ask questions for which you already have the answers."

Jocelyn blanched.

He sighed then, wishing she didn't know so much. "I am someone who is going to give you your gun back and ask you, nicely, to please refrain from shooting me." He was teasing, hoping to set her mind back at ease. Then he carefully retrieved the gun from the rear waistband of his jeans and handed it back to her, the barrel facing away. "Once again, I apologize—I didn't mean to frighten you with my answer. Perhaps I should have lied."

Jocelyn shook her head adamantly. "No, that's the last thing I want. For you to lie to me." She bit her lower lip and gestured with her hands. "If you're telling me the truth about what you are, then maybe you're telling me the truth about letting me go...right?" Her long eyelashes fluttered up and down as she appeared, once again, to be fighting back tears.

"Right," he said softly.

"Nathaniel?"

"Right!"

Nathaniel still couldn't understand *why* this woman believed he was a vampire. He certainly had not approached her with bloodred eyes or fangs. And even if he had startled her by taking her gun away so easily, *vampire* was hardly the logical conclusion. Hell, superhero should have come before mythical creature of the night.

And he knew he had not given her any reason to fear him, personally, *because he honestly intended her no harm.* It was hard to pick up on something that wasn't there.

He frowned. It would be a relief to get her back to town and remove her memories. Perhaps relieve some of her suffering. And the sooner the better.

He still wished he knew what had scared her so badly, but he wasn't going to ask. And he wasn't going to take the information from her mind without her consent.

"I *am* telling you the truth, Jocelyn." He spoke with as much conviction as he could. "About everything."

Jocelyn wiped her lower lashes with the pads of her thumbs, looking a bit embarrassed. "You promise?"

He was silent then, cautiously reviewing all the words he had spoken so far, wanting to be sure that he had, indeed, been completely honest in all of his statements.

"Yes, I promise."

"And you're really not going to hurt me?"

"I'm really not going to hurt you."

"And you'll let me go?"

"I *will* let you go."

She nodded and shrugged her shoulders, her full lips accentuating a breathtaking smile. "Then I'm counting on it, just so you know."

"And you have every reason to count on it," he said. "Just so *you* know." He chose his next words carefully: "You do understand, however, that I cannot allow you to…keep…the thoughts you are thinking. About me. About what you believe I am."

"About what I *know* you are," she corrected, looking him straight in the eyes. She froze then, clearly waiting for a response. When he didn't speak, she asked, "What will you do?" Despite her casual voice, her eyes betrayed her fear.

He gently lifted her chin. "Relax. I am *not* going to hurt you. I have already made you that promise."

The human nodded and closed her eyes. "You still haven't answered my question."

"It is not complicated, brave one," he assured her. "I will simply remove your memories. You will not recall this conversation or anything else that happened between us this night." He paused, wishing he could offer a better explanation. "You are an extremely intelligent woman, Jocelyn. You know very well that I cannot allow you to retain such information. But please don't be afraid. I promise; it won't hurt."

"Does it involve drinking blood?" she asked. Her eyes were as wide as saucers.

Nathaniel laughed then—he couldn't help himself. "Why in the world would erasing one's memories involve taking their blood? You do have an active imagination, don't you?"

Jocelyn frowned. "I guess this is all very amusing to you, isn't it? Maybe you should try standing in my shoes."

Nathaniel's heart warmed at her words. "You are right, of course. And I apologize, *again*. I suppose it is not very funny from your point of view. No, my dear lady, I have no intention of taking your blood. In fact, I won't even need to touch you."

Jocelyn tilted her head to the side and studied him for an extended moment before slowly exhaling a clear sigh of relief. "I think I can live with that."

Nathaniel smiled. And then...very subtly...he checked her mind again, just to be sure that she was really starting to believe him. And there it was.

She expected him to let her go. He exhaled right along with her.

Although the human deeply disliked the idea of anyone messing around with her memories, she believed that his ability to do so was her saving grace: that if he had wanted to hurt her, he would have already done it. Now that she knew he could erase her memories, she realized that she posed no lasting threat. Like the first flicker of a candle igniting, a faint light began to gleam in her eyes. Trust was slowly awakening.

Without thinking, Nathaniel bent down and brushed a soft kiss on the top of her head, his touch as light as a butterfly's wing: a parent giving comfort to a frightened child.

"I am so glad to hear it." He sighed. "You must know by now that this world is a far better place with you in it. It is too bad we didn't meet each other under different circumstances. I believe we would have been friends."

The woman blushed, her high cheekbones turning a faint rosy red as she shook her head and rubbed her eyes. "I don't know how to respond to that," she whispered. "Thank you."

She looked up into his eyes—as if seeing him for the first time—and then quickly glanced away like a curious teenager who had been caught peeking.

Nathaniel smiled. He could hear the sudden increase in her heart rate, and a matching heat flushed over her skin. Only this time, her reaction wasn't motivated by fear. They walked in silence awhile longer before he cautiously made her an offer.

"You know, Jocelyn, whatever it is that frightened you earlier—whatever you saw before I showed up—I can remove that memory as well, if you like." He knew it was not entirely a selfless proposal.

Jocelyn stopped walking. "You would do that? For me?" There was a slight catch in her voice.

"Of course."

"Hmm." She studied his eyes.

Nathaniel's long black hair fell forward as he bent to look at her. She was standing perfectly still, studying his face. She followed the sharp lines of his jaw and the hard angles of his cheekbones until their eyes finally locked in the darkness. And then, Nathaniel sensed an icy shiver sweep down her spine, and he knew exactly what she was thinking about: the fact that he was a vampire.

Nathaniel stood motionless, allowing her to simply take it all in. The power and presence of such an unfamiliar being. A separate species. The fear and the awe. As he tracked the fluctuations in her pulse, he wondered what it must be like—for a human—to come face-to-face with a vampire, the living creature of superstition and legend.

When she was finally done examining him, she blinked her eyes several times as if coming out of a trance…and she had completely forgotten his question.

"So, is that a yes?" he asked.

Jocelyn raised her eyebrows. "Huh?"

"On erasing the bad memories?"

She sighed and shook her head as her recognition came back. "Man, you have no idea how badly I wish I could let you do that, but I can't." Her voice was strong with conviction, her mind clearly made up. "Unfortunately, those are some bad memories I have to keep."

Nathaniel pushed his hair back away from his face with a casual sweep of his hand and nodded, but he didn't respond. She had seen something in the shadow lands, and he really wanted to know what it was. He almost *needed* to know—for so many important reasons that had nothing to do with the human woman. But she was clear about her wishes. And he had given her his word.

Nathaniel could not bring himself to violate that trust or to lessen her strength by forcing her will. Moreover, he didn't believe that whatever she had seen posed any immediate danger to him or his brothers: to the descendants of Jadon. Her blood had clearly not been taken. And if one of the Dark Ones had found her, he would have forced her right then and there. She was far too beautiful to escape unharmed. She would have been used to breed, kept carefully locked up until the birthing, and tossed aside upon her death.

No, if this woman had met a Dark One, she wouldn't be standing in front of him now. She wouldn't be alive.

Nathaniel gently brushed his hand over her cheek. "Very well, then," he said as he continued to walk lazily beside her.

Without warning, the night air began to cool, the leaves in the trees began to rustle, and the sky darkened into a deep midnight blue. As dusty white clouds slowly evaporated from the heavens—leaving a blank slate in their wake—the sky grew darker still…until the muted canvas was completely transformed into a bottomless sea of black.

And then the moon began to change.

It turned from white to pink. From rose to wine. From wine to burgundy. Until it finally settled into a pure…*bloodred.*

And then, like the lighting of a thousand candles in a pitch-dark room, the sky began to illuminate as one bright star after another appeared, and Cassiopeia, the ancient Greek constellation, materialized as a brilliant beacon gleaming in the heavens.

Nathaniel stood in stunned silence. Motionless. Utterly astonished by the magic before him. He could hardly believe what he was seeing. His eyes swept over the beautiful woman with the strange eyes, and he viewed her with reverence.

It just couldn't be.

It had been less than six weeks since Shelby had seen Orion, his own birth constellation, appear beneath a bloodred moon. Less than six weeks since Dalia…

The omens never happened this close together.

Yet, even as he denied it, the animal within the man began to reach for control, a primal impulse raging for release. The vampire's blood came alive, practically singing in his veins, as a primordial reaction as old as time itself took over.

The ancient Blood Curse was ingrained in Nathaniel's memory: a prophecy that flowed like an endless river from one generation to the next, washing over all of the descendants of Prince Jadon at one time or another.

Cassiopeia.

Nathaniel's own birth constellation. Gleaming in the pitch-black sky.

Nathaniel's canine teeth began to elongate, and a low, feral growl escaped his throat. Like a male lion staking his claim, his territorial nature rose in response to the call.

Nathaniel's people may have once been human, but the slain ones had cursed them—as all the descendants of King Sakarias had been cursed—and they were now creatures of the night. More animal than human. The bloodred moon called to the beast within, offering a chance to live truly immortal. The opportunity to love in a lifetime of otherwise solitary existence. *Eternal solitary existence.* Promising the hope of a child of light to continue his species.

Nathaniel felt Jocelyn's unusual eyes staring up at him in horror. They were wide with fright, yet her growing fear only heightened his arousal. Inflamed his response. Like a wild tiger, Nathaniel spun around and crouched down into a fiercely protective stance, a creature with perfect stealth and grace. Power settled over him like a thick, inky fog rising up from the sea, and his cavernous eyes grew darker than the midnight sky above. Coming deftly alive.

He knew he appeared every inch the supernatural predator he was, but that was of little consequence now.

Nathaniel had thirty days—one full moon—to avoid the fatal errors made by Shelby. To honor the Spirit of Jadon. To be forever released from the curse that had haunted him like a shadow since the day he was born.

Suddenly, whatever had frightened Jocelyn in the forest was of grave importance. Her attempt to commit suicide was a threat beyond imagining. And whatever excuse he had made to avoid extracting her memories no longer mattered.

At all.

Forgetting to be gentle, Nathaniel reached out and grabbed her by the left arm. He turned it over in a viselike grip, pinning her wrist as he searched for the familiar markings.

They were all there.

The undeniable spheres. The irrefutable lines. The unmistakable evidence. Nathaniel's very own birth constellation: *Cassiopeia.*

This woman was his destiny.
She belonged to him.

six

Jocelyn was positively spellbound, unable to pull her eyes from the phenomenon appearing in the heavens above them. She had never seen anything so powerful or mysterious in all her life. How was it that they were viewing such an event without a telescope? How could any constellation appear so bright? And what in the world could cause the moon to turn the color of blood?

She slowly turned her head to look back at the creature standing beside her, and her heart began to pound in her chest.

The vampire stood motionless.

Transfixed by the magic before him.

He seemed to be lost in a daze; his eyes glazed over with wonder, and for the first time since she had met the self-assured male, he looked utterly...unsure of himself...completely caught off guard.

His eyes shot back and forth between the moon and her arm, until eventually, some primitive warning system began to go off inside her.

Something was wrong.

Really, really wrong.

Nathaniel was changing.

His eyes were narrowing, his posture stiffening, his countenance becoming all at once deathly serious. And then he caught at her wrist, flipping it over like a police officer about to slap on a pair of handcuffs, holding her captive in an iron grip.

Jocelyn cringed and tried to free her arm, but he only held on tighter.

Instinctively, she froze then, knowing he was no longer in full control of his actions. Curiously, her eyes followed his to the inside of her wrist, where the skin was beginning to burn and tingle. And then, like a microscope zooming in for a closer look, readjusting the lens to view something she couldn't have possibly seen correctly the first time, her gaze narrowed: The delicate skin on her inner arm was covered in cryptic markings. A strange series of discolorations taking the form of a brilliantly intricate tattoo.

This time, it was Jocelyn who looked back and forth between the sky and her arm as her mind began to connect the celestial dots. The exact position of the individual stars, the brilliant constellation in the sky, the very picture they were viewing in the heavens *was etched indelibly into her wrist.* And whatever the markings were—whatever they meant—Nathaniel was utterly captivated by them.

Jocelyn took a deep breath, trying to remain calm while she studied the obscure design. There was something important happening. Something magical that connected her and the man standing before her with that blood moon. It was both prophetic and foreboding. And although it felt odd—even frightening—it also felt strangely *familiar.*

She recognized a subtle stirring, almost like a faint awakening of…something…she couldn't name. And it was like being drawn into a dream, one she knew nothing about and wanted no part of.

She only knew that her once safe world had suddenly come to an end. And that the vampire who had been so kind, almost human, just moments before was something altogether different now. Dangerous and predatory.

What in the world had happened?

Had the sky somehow triggered the monster? Was it the color of the moon? *The color of blood?* Had Nathaniel become like the creature she had seen in the dark chamber?

As the enchantment wore off, a perilous cry of terror rose in her throat. In one desperate moment of clarity, she yanked back her wrist and drew for her gun.

Nathaniel was far too fast for her.

Using only his mind to disarm the threat, the vampire jerked the gun from her hand and sent it flying hundreds of yards into the forest, smoldering like a glowing red coal as it left her fingers. A fierce growl of warning rumbled in his throat, and his eyes pierced hers with a harsh, reprimanding glare.

Jocelyn cried out as the tips of her fingers were burned by the blazing iron. "Nathaniel!" she shrieked, her terror no longer contained. "You promised!" It was a desperate plea for compassion. "You swore you weren't going to hurt me." It was a pitiful cry for mercy.

Nathaniel reacted so quickly his motion was undetectable: He reached for her hand, swiftly turned it over, and blew freezing air like shards of ice over her fingertips, immediately healing the burns before they had a chance to blister. Instantly numbing the pain. "I am so sorry, Jocelyn," he soothed. "I did not intend to hurt you." Despite an obvious attempt to sound gentle, his words came out as a snarl.

Jocelyn struggled for breath and looked down at her hand, realizing that the burns were completely gone. The monster inside of him might be ruling his nature, but he was still reluctant to harm her. Slowly backing away, she tried to speak calmly.

"What is it, Nathaniel? What's happening to you?" She held out her left arm, palm facing up. "What are these markings on my wrist? And why are they here now—when they were never there before?"

She glanced back and forth between the odd designs and the dazzling work of art shining in the heavens, acknowledging a connection. "Does the moon have anything to do with it? That constellation?" Looking up into his smoldering eyes, she whispered, "Tell me why you're acting like this. You're scaring me now. I mean really, really scaring me."

Nathaniel didn't answer.

It was as if he couldn't speak.

He simply looked down into her terrified eyes like he somehow wanted to comfort her with his gaze, and then his eyes swept the surrounding area, veering off in the direction she had come from.

"We are far too close to the Red Canyons, my love, the

shadow lands of our dark brothers. I do not have time to explain right now. Not here. Just know that there are those who would harm you if they could."

He looked at her then—really looked at her—as if he had never seen her before. And his eyes held an absolute aura of possession in them. Complete, irrevocable ownership. His jaw held a hard line of resolve.

"You have no idea who you really are," he explained, "of the danger we are both now in. There are those who couldn't dream of harming one such as myself, but who can now achieve such a feat simply by taking you away from me."

Jocelyn shivered.

My love? Our dark brothers? Taking her away from him?

She started to protest, but he was already moving, his heavily muscled arms reaching out to...*claim her.*

Nathaniel caught her by the waist, his powerful body lifting hers from the ground as if she weighed no more than a feather.

And then he took to the sky as a vampire, the supernatural creature of myth and legend, flying with enormous speed, holding Jocelyn firmly in his commanding arms.

As a deep, primal growl rumbled in his throat, he locked her frame solidly to his and headed back toward Dark Moon Vale.

The place where he'd said that he lived.

An enormous man with broad shoulders and a knee-length black jacket was waiting for them on the top balcony of a sprawling log home when they arrived.

"You have her?" he asked. His voice was a harsh command.

Nathaniel released Jocelyn the moment their feet touched down on the deck. He carefully scanned the area like he was looking for danger, and it was apparent that the other man was doing the same.

"Yes, I have her!" he growled impatiently.

Tessa Dawn

Jocelyn steadied herself, trying to catch her balance after the dizzying experience of flying through the sky at warp speed in Nathaniel's arms. Her legs were shaking, her stomach turning over in waves of nausea. And then she caught her first real glimpse of the intimidating man standing so close to them on the terrace.

He was enormous, with powerful, rippling muscles and commanding, rock-hard shoulders. *Another vampire.* Like Nathaniel, he had long black hair and piercing dark eyes, only his eyes were beyond the color of the deepest sea—they were so black they appeared a bottomless, phantom blue.

Terrified of both beings, she muttered something incoherent and tried to back away.

"What is her name?" the fearsome one demanded, looking only briefly in her direction as if there were no need to address her directly.

"Her name is Jocelyn," Nathaniel replied. He spoke like a subordinate officer addressing a general. Clearly, he felt no need to involve her, either.

The second male was power personified, awesome in even the slightest of movements. "Jocelyn what?"

Nathaniel glanced over at Jocelyn, reaching effortlessly into her mind to retrieve her full name. "Jocelyn *Levi.*"

The fearsome one snorted and checked the skies again.

Jocelyn fell back against the deck in a mad scramble to get away. The long, circular patio formed an enclosure around the top floor of the estate, flanked on every side by towering aspen and pine trees. The apex of the structure stretched into a wide arc jutting just beyond the edge of a steep cliff, supported only by several wooden beams, which were anchored with iron bolts into the side of the mountain.

Jocelyn knew that she had to get away. She had to escape her fate.

Even if Nathaniel still possessed a few redeeming qualities, this new male was clearly without pity: absent of mercy or remorse. His blue-black eyes held a promise of swift retribution for anyone who crossed him.

Desperate to be free of the vampires, Jocelyn rushed to her feet and dashed toward the edge of the deck. Like an Olympic hurdler running the race of her life, she leapt over the railing in one smooth motion.

Nathaniel was there in an instant.

He caught her effortlessly by the arm—with only one hand—and placed her firmly back on the deck. "And she seems to have this thing about suicide," he remarked to the other male.

The powerful one moved swiftly toward her like a stalking panther. His glowing eyes, searing into hers, resembled two burning hot coals. "You will never, *ever* think to harm yourself in such a way again. Do I make myself clear?"

His voice reverberated like thunder as the command far surpassed a subtle attempt at mind control. It was an unyielding demand, and it pierced straight to her soul, removing even the possibility of resistance with its sheer force.

Jocelyn blinked and nodded. "I'm sorry."

She had whispered the words like a child, cowering beneath a harsh reprimand, reminiscent of her days growing up in so many foster homes. Her first instinct was to become angry, but then she noticed the haunting red embers glowing in the place where the male's pupils should have been. A scream of sheer terror arose in her throat, and she back-pedaled so quickly that she fell down...again. This time, her head landed hard against the deck, and a sharp pain shot through her skull. Her head began to throb.

The vampire bent over her trembling body and reached out his hand. She had no intention of taking it.

"Nathaniel! Help me!" Her cry was elemental, a frenzied plea for protection.

While she didn't trust either one of them, everything inside of her told her to get away from the menacing creature looming over her...*now*.

She kicked wildly, a trapped animal, aiming for the only part of his anatomy that she hoped he shared with human males. But just like Nathaniel, he was far too fast.

His hand movement was nothing more than a blur as he caught her flailing legs and held them in an iron grip of amazing strength. A menacing growl of warning escaped his throat, and his perfectly sculpted lips suddenly drew back. His canines threatened to lengthen along a row of brilliantly white teeth.

"Get up!"

Trembling, Jocelyn took his outstretched hand and obediently began to pull herself up. She shrieked in horror as her body shot weightlessly into the air and flew to the other end of the deck, landing with a heavy thud nearly fifteen feet away.

Nathaniel moved like an angry lion.

He roared his displeasure, and the skies answered his rage with a heavy clap of thunder followed by several loud strikes of blue lightning that lit up the heavens. He leapt the distance between them and crouched protectively between Jocelyn and the other male, his fangs fully extended into razor-sharp points. His muscles twitched with the need to strike, and his breathing appeared shallow, his body clearly pumped with adrenaline.

He was prepared to fight the other male on her behalf.

The vampire in the black jacket stepped back and eyed Nathaniel warily. His own powerful muscles rippled, and his broad, heavy shoulders rolled back as he met Nathaniel's seething gaze with one of his own. The blue streaks of lightning merged together in a deafening fusion as sizzling veins of white, red, and purple shot across the sky to meet them, exploding as they connected in a violent collision.

A slow, wicked snarl rumbled in the fearsome one's throat. "You think to fight me, Nathaniel?" He hissed the words, an unmistakable warning.

Nathaniel was not intimidated. He growled a deep, responding threat, never once averting his eyes.

Jocelyn shuddered and covered her ears.

The second vampire laughed then, softly but unrestrained. And instantly, the sky settled back into a calm sea of deep, radiant blue.

"This is good," he said with arrogant authority. "I was afraid you might be too soft where this female is concerned." His eyes darkened and the smile left his face. "That you might suppress the very nature you need to embrace at this time, Nathaniel."

Nathaniel stood upright, his eyes blazing with defiance. *"And so you threw my woman across the deck to provoke me?"*

The other vampire smiled elegantly and waved a dismissive hand. "Forgive me, *brother.*" He said the word with reverence. "I did not intend such a thing. I overestimated her resistance, and I underestimated my strength. I meant only to discourage her from kicking me in such an ill-advised way. Not to test you. And certainly not to toss her about the deck like a rag doll." He glanced over at Jocelyn. "I offer you my apology, Miss Levi. It was a substantial and inexcusable miscalculation."

Jocelyn blinked back tears of alarm and scooted even further away.

Apology not accepted.

The vampire looked as if he were actually considering coming over to help her up again, but then he clearly thought better of it and stayed where he was.

"I am Marquis Silivasi, Nathaniel's older brother. Please believe that I intend you no harm." His voice dropped an octave, so that it almost purred. "Know that I will not allow any other to harm you, either." And then his eyes narrowed into two almost imperceptible bands of warning. "But above all, know this: *I will not allow anything to happen to Nathaniel.*"

It was a clear, simple statement: There was no hint of menace buried in his tone, no overt threat warning her to behave. He didn't even growl or snarl. Yet, Jocelyn read it loud and clear: If she hurt Nathaniel, this one would kill her.

Nathaniel did not look pleased. "Why don't you ease up a little, Marquis!"

The male snarled. "The way I *eased up* with Shelby?"

Nathaniel frowned.

"Consider this, brother: We allowed Shelby to take matters into his own hands with tragic consequences, did we not? I will not make the same mistake twice. The same outcome will not befall you, *no matter what has to be done*. It is that simple."

Jocelyn stared from one vampire to the other, clearly reading the promise of enforcement in Marquis's eyes, but she didn't utter a single word of her own. She didn't dare.

The only thing more frightening to her than the male's dire vow of protection was Nathaniel's repeated claim of ownership where she was concerned. What did he mean, *So you threw my woman across the deck?* Surely, he didn't think she belonged to him—they hardly knew each other.

Jocelyn tucked her knees to her chest and wrapped her body in a tight little ball. With every moment that passed, she began to realize that she wasn't going to get out of this. She wasn't going to just walk away. And Nathaniel wasn't going to just let her go. The realization was surreal.

What were they planning to do to her?

She couldn't allow herself to think about the creature she had seen in the chamber, to think about the fate that had claimed the life of the poor suffering woman. Her sanity would not allow it. As it stood, she was barely holding on.

Marquis turned to face Nathaniel then and held both of his hands palms up in a gesture of peace. "So, are you done thinking you would like to fight me, brother?" he asked, smirking.

Nathaniel nodded. "I'm very relieved I won't have to."

Marquis chuckled. "You know I would never fight you, Nathaniel. I would choose to bind you to the deck first. Allow you to think for a bit. Cool down."

Nathaniel growled. "Don't be so sure you could, big brother. Perhaps you would be the one bound to the deck."

Marquis shrugged. "Perhaps, Nathaniel…perhaps."

He waved his hand as if to dismiss the silly conversation; then he suddenly became serious again. "Now, tell me what's happened. I saw the moon earlier…*Cassiopeia*…it is hard to believe…" His voice trailed off, and he shook his head, the red in his eyes receding back to the bluest black. He gestured at Jocelyn. "Tell me, how did you come to find this one?"

Jocelyn's eyes were as big as saucers. She made herself even smaller.

This one?

She was nothing to these creatures.

Nathaniel looked at her as if he had read her mind, as if he could not bear to see the fear and resignation in her eyes. He glided across the deck with the easy grace of a swan and gently lifted her to her feet, turning around briefly to glare at Marquis. Then he softly brushed his hand against her cheek and led her to two arched doors, the entrance to his dwelling.

"Jocelyn," he whispered, bending to her ear. "I know you are frightened and have many questions. I will answer them all soon. Please enter my home and wait for me while I talk with my brother alone. Marquis is a bit"—he paused, searching for the right words—"high strung at the moment."

Jocelyn didn't have to be asked twice.

She would gladly enter hell if it would just get her away from the fierce vampire. She immediately reached for the handle to the door, but before she could disappear into the temporary sanctuary of the home, Marquis appeared in front of her. His severe eyes locked unerringly with hers, and his pupils once again narrowed into two tiny slits of menace.

"Do not think to escape this place while we talk." His deep voice was stern and unwavering. "Do not even try." He paused, carefully considering his next words. "Such a thing would deeply upset me as it would place Nathaniel in great danger, and that is not something I would permit…from anyone."

His voice remained steady, smooth, pure as the driven snow. Yet, the crystal clear threat lingered perceptibly in the air, almost alive with electricity and promise.

Marquis shut the French door, with its stained glass and etched crystal panels, behind Jocelyn and turned to face his

Tessa Dawn

brother. "High strung?"

"Marquis," Nathaniel sighed with frustration, "I believe you were born high strung! And just for the record, would you please stop scaring the female senseless? Perhaps you should at least allow me to make a few inroads before you convince her that you are the devil reincarnated, and I am one of your evil minions—here to cast her into the fiery depths of hell. You are *not* helping me."

Marquis looked surprised...insulted. "I had no intention of frightening that woman," he said. "I only spoke the truth."

Nathaniel rolled his eyes in exasperation. He rubbed his forehead just above the bridge of his nose and took several deep breaths. "One man's truth is another woman's terror, Marquis. And this man's headache."

Marquis sniffed, indignant. "Vampires do not get headaches, Nathaniel. Is this some sort of metaphor? If so, just make your point."

Nathaniel shut his eyes and hung his head, shaking it back and forth...slowly. This particular conversation was pointless, but one thing was for certain: If he ever did get a human headache, Marquis was going to be the one who gave it to him.

He took a deep breath and regarded his brother with purpose. "We need to concentrate on the subject at hand—how I came across Jocelyn, and what we will need to do to protect her."

Marquis slowly exhaled with relief.

He stretched out lazily in the nearest lawn chair, folded his arms across his chest, and placed his feet up on the matching footstool.

"At last," he said, without smiling. "I'm listening."

seven

Jocelyn was hunkered over in the corner of a soft beige sofa, hugging her knees to her chest, when Nathaniel entered the living room. Her eyes were bloodshot from crying, and there was a vacant look on her face, as if she'd simply given up trying to reason or think.

"You look cold." Nathaniel sent a sharp bolt of sizzling blue electricity from the tips of his fingers into the fireplace. He focused the steady stream on a small pile of kindling until the logs caught fire and roared into a healthy blaze. He then picked up a green throw-blanket from the back of his favorite armchair and handed it to her.

Jocelyn didn't take it.

She didn't move or even look up. She simply stared blankly ahead into space, numb to the night's events, withdrawn from her fate.

Nathaniel unfolded the blanket and gently wrapped it around her narrow shoulders before kneeling down on one knee in front of her. "Jocelyn," he whispered.

There was no reply.

The crackling of the fire could be heard coming from several different directions at once as the acoustics in the vaulted great room bounced the sound from wall to wall, floor to ceiling, and back again.

The stunning hardwood floors were laid with large planks of knotted pine, and the floor-to-ceiling windows offered a breathtaking view of the northern mountain ranges as far as the eye could see. The bloodred moon had vanished, and the now soft-white moonlight illuminated the earth tones of the room, with its ancient pieces of art, like a celestial lantern burning in the night sky.

With another wave of his hand, Nathaniel lit several candles and turned on a large granite water fountain that sat adjacent to the stone fireplace.

Without even trying, the descendants of Jadon often arranged their homes to flow in harmony with the universe around them. They included the basic elements of earth, wind, and fire in the physical structures, and paid homage to the celestial gods by placing each piece of furniture in perfect synchronicity with the natural rotation of the planets.

They were the ancestors of Celestial Beings, the prodigy of humans who had once mated with gods, becoming a race of people ruled by the moon and stars, a culture that had walked in perfect accord with the world around them before they had been corrupted. Before the Blood Curse. And some things had remained instinctual.

"Jocelyn…" He tried again. "Won't you please speak to me?"

She squinted, her eyes narrowing as if gazing through a blanket of fog, and then she just shook her head. "You promised," she whispered. "*You promised.*"

Nathaniel looked away. "I know I did…" He sighed. "And there's absolutely nothing I can say to make up for breaking that promise." He looked back at her then. "But you have to believe me when I tell you; I had no idea this was going to happen."

Jocelyn shifted uncomfortably. "You had no idea *what* was going to happen, Nathaniel?" She spoke in a tentative voice, looking up at him from behind dark lashes.

"The Omen."

"You mean whatever happened with the moon and the stars?"

"Yes."

She looked down at her wrist and studied it absently, as if she knew it was of great importance but had no idea why.

"Angel…" He took her hand and held it gently in his own. "Look at me, please; do not just withdraw from the situation." He brought the back of her hand up to his mouth and brushed a soft kiss against her knuckles. This was his future—*his destiny*—

and she had much to learn.

She frowned and pulled back her hand.

"I know you're scared," he said, undaunted. "And I know you feel powerless. But I am willing to answer any questions you have...if you'll just ask."

She eyed him suspiciously. "Have you calmed down?"

He nodded. "You were never in danger, sweetheart. At least not from me."

"From the other one?" she asked.

"No." His tone was adamant. "My brother would *never* intentionally harm you."

Jocelyn shrugged and shook her head. "What difference does it make what I say or do, Nathaniel? You've already decided what's going to happen. Even your brother seems to have more control over me than I do." She sighed in despair. "So, tell me then, what do you need my opinion for? I'd honestly rather you didn't patronize me."

"*Jocelyn.*"

"*What?*" she huffed, this time sounding more exasperated than resigned. "Nathaniel, just tell me the truth for once: Will it make a difference? If I ask every question I can think of; say everything you want to hear; do everything you ask me to do, *will you let me go?*"

Ouch. Nathaniel stroked her cheek. His heart was heavy.

"It's not that simple, tiger-eyes." He forced himself to smile, his own gaze deliberately softening as he stared into hers.

Jocelyn frowned and turned away. "Of course not."

A moment of awkward silence passed between them before she spoke again. "And by the way, Nathaniel, I'm not your *tiger-eyes* or your *sweetheart.*" She sounded amazingly defiant, considering how helpless she looked. "And I'm not your *woman* either." She said the last statement in a somewhat softer tone, as if she suddenly feared that she might provoke him.

Nathaniel reached out and took her hand a second time, absently rubbing his fingers in slow, caressing circles just above her wrist. He knew she would continue to resist his touch. To resist him. But he also knew that he could impart far more warmth and reassurance through physical contact than with his eyes alone. He wanted her to begin to sense him, to begin to feel who he was, and he knew she had it within her to do so.

He wanted her to become aware of her own attraction—the preordained chemistry between them—to remember who *she* was.

Nathaniel deliberately made his touch light, like a cooling balm on a hot day, even as he braced himself against the images he was picking up in her mind: distressing pictures of his own eyes glowing in the forest, disturbing flashbacks of him appearing more predator than man, unsettling glimpses of him confronting his brother on the deck...*with fangs.*

"Don't look at me like that," she said.

"Like what, angel?"

"Like you're reading my mind. Like you know me. *Like I actually mean something to you.*"

Nathaniel shook his head. "I'm not trying to hide anything from you right now, Jocelyn. *Yes,* I am reading your mind—and your body language—and your emotions. And you mean far more to me than you realize." He continued to caress her hand. "But make no mistake; I know exactly who you are."

"Really?" she said sarcastically. "Who am I, then?"

"*You're mine.*"

Jocelyn winced and closed her eyes.

He found her listening to the trickling sounds of the waterfall in conjunction with the crackling of the fire, simply letting the ambient noise take her over for a time, while blocking out the overwhelming intensity of the moment, and he waited...

Nathaniel waited as she watched the flames dancing and dodging between the burning logs. As she tried to ignore the subtle heat she was beginning to feel in his touch. Her response to their contact was barely noticeable, but it was there just the same—magnetic, undeniable.

The attraction was evident in her scent: the faint smell of fear mixed with arousal, the subtle hint of anticipation behind her anxiety. She must have felt like her body was betraying her, as he sensed her mixed emotions.

Nathaniel purposefully turned up the heat between them.

After some time had passed, she lifted her head and met his steady gaze. "My emotions are not going to override my brain, Nathaniel, *no matter what you do.*"

Nathaniel didn't blink. "And I would never want such a thing."

Jocelyn sighed. "Fine…" She drew in a deep breath. "I suppose it doesn't do either of us any good for you to continue to talk in riddles—or for me to continue to remain in the dark."

He nodded, watching her intently.

"But I'll only talk to you on one condition—or there's really no point."

"What is that?"

He reached up and absently traced the arc of her eyebrow with the pad of his thumb. He tucked several loose tendrils of hair behind her ear and softly brushed her face from her jaw to her chin. And then he waited, while she leaned back and shut her eyes.

When she sat forward, her mouth was set in a stern line. "What is this continuous need of yours to touch me?" She sounded exasperated, yet the rosy flush of her cheeks betrayed something else.

Nathaniel held his ground without apology. He said nothing.

"It's unnerving," she whispered, even as she tilted her head slightly to the side, leaning in the direction of his hand.

Nathaniel caressed her again then, just beneath her ear…just above her vein. He was sending small bolts of electricity through her body each time he made contact, slowly letting her feel the power that existed between them. She couldn't possibly understand how strong their connection really was. At least not yet.

He knew she would continue to try and convince herself that it was all him. That he was somehow making her do things she wouldn't otherwise do.

BLOOD DESTINY

She had no idea that she was drawing him in as forcefully as he was drawing her.

A territorial male could not deny the needs of his female, not even if he wanted to. As long as she felt insecure, he would be compelled to touch her.

"Your condition, angel?"

She took a deep breath. "The condition is that you tell me the truth."

"Of course," he assured her.

"And don't avoid any of my questions."

"I'll do my best...." His words hung in the air like moisture on a rainy night.

She met his gaze for a moment, and the hazel green centers of her eyes immediately softened as she reacted to the waves of reassurance he was sending her.

"I don't even know where to begin," she told him honestly.

Nathaniel leaned in closer. "Start with something easy."

"Like?"

"Like what we are," he suggested.

"Vampires." She said it courageously.

"Yes."

She drew back, visibly shocked by his directness. He moved then, from the floor in front of her to the sofa beside her. He placed his hand on the nape of her neck and massaged it gently. It was not meant as an advance or to make her uncomfortable, but simply to make it clear that he intended to face this head-on with her. That he would not retreat from the truth of what he was...or what he wanted with her.

Her next question was surprisingly blunt. "Do you sleep in a coffin?"

He bit his lower lip, suppressing a smile. "No, I sleep in a comfortable king-size bed." He knew his eyes glittered with suggestion, so he briefly looked away.

She ignored the comment. "Can you be out during the day...in the sunlight?"

"Absolutely," he answered, "but we are nocturnal beings,

Jocelyn. I prefer to sleep in the day and work at night; although, often it is necessary to conduct business during normal hours."

Jocelyn slowly exhaled. She appeared to be gathering her courage. "Do you...drink blood?"

"Yes."

Her hand went instinctively to her throat. "Please tell me you don't intend to drink mine. *Please.*"

The room was silent. And so was he. Unsure of how to respond. He would never use her as prey—just to feed—but the idea of tasting her someday, if and when she was willing to freely offer, was more than just a little erotic. Staring at the soft shade of her caramel-colored skin, the graceful curve of her neck as it rose elegantly above her sternum, he could almost taste her essence now.

After several seconds—when he still didn't answer—she sat forward, shifted nervously in her seat, and asked him more directly, "Are you or are you not planning to drink my blood, Nathaniel?"

His smile was flirtatious. "Not without your permission, Jocelyn." He leaned guardedly into her, gently nuzzled her neck, inhaled her scent...and then groaned.

She jumped back and pushed him away. "What are you doing?"

"Just imagining..." He smiled, a crooked grin, like the proverbial cat that ate the canary.

She squirmed and sank deeper into the sofa. "Quit playing! I'm trying to ask you a serious question here. At least *I* think it's pretty damn serious."

He watched her with appreciation, intrigued by her anger. "I'm sorry. I was distracted. What was your question, love?"

She smirked. "Whether or not you plan to drink my blood, whether or not you *want* to drink my blood. Like right now, when you just...*smelled* me, did you feel some overwhelming urge to—"

"No. I was teasing you." He lightly traced the contour of her neck with his fingers. "You are so beautiful, Jocelyn, but I want your comfort *and your pleasure* as much as my own." His eyes swept over her face, and he reached out to twirl a few strands of her hair in his fingers. "In all honesty, you stir an altogether different kind of hunger in me."

She caught her breath and drew her hair behind her shoulder. "You are far too familiar with me, Nathaniel!" And then she brushed her hands over her arms trying to remove the goose bumps.

She cleared her throat. "So, when do you...*drink blood?*"

"My kind," he obliged, "we only need to *feed* every few weeks or so. Our lives and our power, our ability to regenerate, all of it is in our blood. We feed only to live."

She hesitated. "Do you kill people?"

"Not good people," he said. "I never hunt the innocent."

"So who do you *hunt* then?"

"Humans who prey on other humans for the sole purpose of deriving pleasure from their suffering."

His words seemed to surprise her.

"And you kill them? Like some kind of vigilante? Judge, jury, and executioner all in one?"

Nathaniel looked off to the side, contemplating her words. "I can read people's thoughts, Jocelyn. I can view their memories. It is not the same as the evidence used in your human trials, all the prejudice and fear that corrupt the truth. There is no question of guilt. And I don't drink blood because I am a vigilante; I drink it because I am a vampire."

Jocelyn shook her head slowly. "What if there are no...guilty...people around?"

He carefully took her hand and held it firmly in his own. "Then I can take blood from anyone, but I would not kill an innocent person in the process."

She was silent for a moment then.

"Do people hunt you? I mean with garlic and crosses, stakes...that kind of thing?"

"They would if they knew of our existence." His voice never wavered. "It has happened many times throughout the centuries."

Jocelyn blinked several times, plainly trying to process his words. *"Centuries?* Just how old are you, Nathaniel?"

"Can we skip that question?"

"No...*tell me.*"

"I am just over ten centuries old."

Jocelyn drew in a deep breath. *"You're over one thousand years old?"* She stammered the words, dumbfounded.

He patted her hand. "Yes, but you need not be concerned; I find you very mature for your age." His smile was once again crooked.

"How old is your brother?" she asked.

"I have *three* living brothers, but the one you met— Marquis—he's one of the oldest of our kind. He is fifteen hundred years old."

Jocelyn shook her head in disbelief, and then she became suddenly withdrawn, her light eyes turning a dark, misty hue, her skin becoming noticeably pale. She looked stuck. Like she didn't know how to ask her next question.

And instinctively, he knew...

"So, we are finally there, then?"

"Where?" she muttered, her voice barely audible.

"Back to what has been troubling you all along. Back to whatever occurred earlier in that forest. *Back to the fear that has caused you, twice now, to want to take your own life.*"

Jocelyn slowly exhaled and nodded, but she didn't speak.

It was as if she couldn't.

She closed her eyes, and her once steady hand began to tremble inside of his.

"What is it, angel?" he asked calmly. "What has you so troubled?"

She just shook her head.

"Can't you tell me?"

She sniffled. "I want to, but..."

"But what?"

"But, it's just...I'm just..." Her hands began to shake, and she rubbed them together, nervously. "I'm scared."

Nathaniel stilled her trembling hand. "Tell me then, what it is you're so afraid of—what do you think is going to happen if you tell me?"

She didn't answer.

"Are you afraid that I'll be angry—"

"No, that's not it," she murmured.

"Then what is it?" His eyes linked unerringly with hers, drawing her into him like a powerful magnet. "*Tell me*, Jocelyn. I know you have little reason to trust me, but just this once—"

"I know what you're planning to do to me, all right?" She rushed the words, as if it were the only way she could get them out. "And I'm telling you, I can't handle it. Do you understand what I'm saying to you? *I can't handle it!*"

"What do you think—"

"Why are you doing this?" Her voice was anguished. "Pushing me like this. At least right now, in this moment, I can pretend. Just a little longer, I can pretend like everything's okay. But once it's all out in the open..." Her eyes dimmed and she slowly looked away.

Nathaniel became uneasy then, although he tried to continue projecting confidence. "Jocelyn, I am not going to do anything to you without your permission."

"You're not hearing me, Nathaniel," she said, her voice growing desperate. "*I know.*"

Nathaniel sat back and drew in a deep breath.

Great Celestial Deities, what did this woman believe he was planning to do to her? There was no way—absolutely no way—she knew about the Blood Curse. And even if she did, he had no intention of forcing himself on this beautiful female. He had more faith in her than that. More faith in the providence of the gods. The rightness of their union.

"Okay..." He held up both hands, coaxing her like a frightened child. "Then we might as well face whatever it is you know together...right?"

She covered her face with her hands. "Please don't,

Nathaniel…just stop—"

Her voice broke off, and she dropped her head in her hands, her long hair falling forward so that it shielded her from his view.

She appeared so vulnerable that it made Nathaniel's chest ache, and he absently rubbed his hand over his sternum.

"You really can't tell me, can you?"

"No," she whispered. "I really can't."

Nathaniel gently pried her hands from around her eyes and massaged her temples. He lightly threaded his fingers through her silky hair, and then he raised her chin, forcing her to meet his gaze. "Look at me, Jocelyn."

She grimaced.

"*Look at me.*"

Her eyes met his.

"I'm going to ask your permission for something—"

"No—"

"Jocelyn, just listen."

She shook her head. "Please—"

"*Listen to me.*"

She sighed.

"I would like to go into your mind and view your memories for myself—"

"No!" Her eyes grew wide, and she audibly gasped.

Nathaniel didn't flinch.

"It will allow me to see whatever you saw firsthand. Do you understand what I'm saying? I can view the information myself, without you ever having to say a single word—but I am asking for your *permission.*"

Jocelyn looked pale…tired. "And if I don't give it to you?" Her voice faltered.

He sat back and regarded her squarely. "We have all night, angel. If you say no, then we'll wait." He sat forward then and grasped her by the shoulders. "But sooner or later, we *are* going to deal with this."

Jocelyn's eyes filled with tears, and the tiny drops began to roll one after another down her delicate cheekbones, leaving tracks of deep sorrow in their wake. Reluctantly, she nodded.

Nathaniel raised his eyebrows, surprised, and then he framed her face with his hands. "Yes, then?"

She clenched her eyes shut. "Yes," she whispered.

And then she visibly held her breath.

eight

For the first time since they'd met, Jocelyn appeared to be truly lost, spiraling like a piece of driftwood in a river, haphazard and out of control. Her intense fear was palpable, and Nathaniel sensed that she detested her own vulnerability.

He began to reach inside of her mind, to unravel her memories. Moving from the present backward, he started in his own living room—when she had first come inside from the patio.

He despised the way she thought of the house as a prison, almost as if she were an inmate on death row awaiting execution. He felt the unbidden horror she had experienced as a result of Marquis's behavior and the absolute *revulsion* she had experienced at the sight of his own animal nature, the changes in his body when he had confronted Marquis. He shifted uncomfortably on the sofa beside her, even as he forced himself to smile, sending her strong waves of reassurance in an effort to combat what he had just uncovered.

Moving further back into the forest, he recognized the trust she was beginning to feel as they were walking, and to his delight, he saw the strong physical attraction she had for him, despite her worst aversions.

He resisted smiling at the pleasing revelation: *Jocelyn found him incredibly sexy.* It was elemental. After all, she *had* been created for him, even if she didn't yet understand the connection.

And then he saw her terror.

He actually *felt* her distress as she ran from the canyon in a desperate attempt to get away from—*what?*—her mind a tormented cauldron of muddled thoughts and broken images. She was desperately seeking to draw rational conclusions to something that could not be rationalized, but since she had no internal frame of reference from which to begin, her mind just spun out of control in a free fall of disbelief and horror.

But what had caused such fragmentation?

Nathaniel followed her much further back now, going deep into the endless labyrinth of tunnels with their musty, damp hallways, until he finally arrived with her in the chamber.

The sacrificial chamber of the Dark Ones.

He almost jolted but immediately caught his reaction. The last thing he needed was to frighten her further. There was musty water, with the strong stench of sulfur, on her clothes—*in her hair*—and the freezing cave floor was hard beneath her belly as heavy, damp rocks loomed over her head. He felt her holding her breath, trembling, fighting back the impulse to scream. She wanted to run. Her muscles were primed to fight. Her stomach roiled.

And then Nathaniel saw the depraved son of Jaegar: *Valentine Nistor.* His heart turned hard as stone, his spirit colder than black ice on a winter road, as he watched it all unfold. The greedy hands of death claiming the firstborn infant, an infant with black- and red-striped hair like a human cobra. The hideous laughter of a depraved mind reveling in the pain of a tortured woman. And a beautiful, helpless female with flowing black hair and deep green eyes lying on—

Dalia!

Shelby's Dalia.

Nathaniel jerked back, breaking the telepathic connection at once. He withdrew his mind as absolute shock and revulsion crashed into him like a tidal wave against the shore. Devoid of reason, he sprang to his feet and turned away from Jocelyn. He could feel his fangs exploding in his mouth and struggled to maintain control.

She couldn't see him like this.

Not now. Not when he was supposed to be comforting *her.* Not when she was already so afraid. He shook uncontrollably.

Jocelyn appeared stunned by his reaction. She scampered to the other end of the sofa and stared up at his shaking form, her eyes wide with fright. Nathaniel shook his head. *Good Lord,* she had seen such an atrocity. No wonder she was terrified! But she couldn't possibly have known how personal the violation was...to him.

Nathaniel spared her a glance: She didn't speak a word. She didn't dare to even move.

He ran his fingers through his thick mane of hair, pacing restlessly back and forth across the hardwood floor in front of the fireplace. He distorted his image with a masking technique and waited for his fangs to recede, all the while, struggling to put the pieces of the puzzle together:

Ramsey Olaru, one of the three sentinels who guarded Dark Moon Vale, had reported directly to Napolean that Valentine had killed Dalia, that he had taken her from Shelby following a trip she had made into the nearby town of Silverton Park. The sentinels had found her body days later in a washed-up riverbed, thrown carelessly behind a group of thorny bushes at the edge of the creek. The corpse had been mutilated and drained of blood.

Napolean had immediately given the order to have Dalia cremated so that her soul would be released from the taint of the Dark One as it traveled to the next world. So that Shelby would never have a chance to see her bruised and battered body. As powerful as his little brother had been, Shelby could never have defeated one such as Valentine on his own, and Napolean knew that all the Silivasi brothers would have gone to his aid, setting off an all-out vampire war over a personal blood vengeance. Too many humans would have been caught in the fallout.

Nathaniel turned his attention to Jocelyn, who was still sitting in stunned silence on the far end of the sofa. She was watching him intently, and he didn't hesitate to read her mind. She was dissecting the situation like a computer, analyzing the obvious internal battle he was waging to remain in control, even as her own private fears threatened to consume her. She was frightened...and waiting for a response...and she had *no idea*, whatsoever, why he was so upset.

As far as the intelligent human was concerned, Nathaniel had to know the nature of *his own kind*; surely, he had seen such a thing before. That stone slab had far too much blood on it for the woman she saw to be the first. She thought he was angry because she had witnessed the perversion, like she had somehow ruined his plans...*for her.*

Oh, gods! Nathaniel cursed beneath his breath. This had to be what Jocelyn feared all along—that Nathaniel was going to do the same thing to her that Valentine had done to Dalia. His stomach rolled, and he had to fight to restrain his rage.

Although he couldn't fault her for her logic, he was furious with the conclusion. Staggered by the whole revelation. Dalia had been defiled by a Dark One, and now Jocelyn, his very own *destiny*, made no distinction between him and the evil son of Jaegar. *Made no distinction between him and Valentine Nistor.* And as if that weren't enough, she was terrified of experiencing the same fate at his hands.

Before Nathaniel could find the words to address her unfounded fear, Jocelyn jumped up from the couch. In his distress, he had momentarily released the barrier, forgotten to keep his image blurred, and she was seeing him exactly as he was. She was staring at the fire in his eyes, blanching at the involuntary contractions of his body, literally gawking at the points of his fangs...and her fear had finally gotten the best of her. She began to scan the room for an exit, prepared to fight to the death if necessary.

Nathaniel turned to face the terrified female and cursed in the ancient language.

"Jocelyn, don't!"

He made it a harsh command, taking momentary control over her body with his mind, effortlessly tossing her back onto the couch and holding her there. And then he held up his hand, his palm facing out. It was an apology. A universal request for patience.

"Please, just give me a moment."

He needed to collect his thoughts. To understand hers. To try and process the enormity of what he had just seen. The beast within him was far too aroused with fury to deal with a physical confrontation, and he was well aware of the fact that she was prepared to *physically* fight him if that's what it took.

"Be still," he warned. "Do not provoke me."

He released his hold and reconstructed the barrier, once again blurring his image. He was pacing even faster now as he analyzed more information:

Nathaniel knew Ramsey Olaru well. Ramsey would no more lie to Napolean than he would slit his own throat. Valentine must have staged everything. He had to have murdered some anonymous woman and drained her body of blood to stage the crime, knowing they would cremate the body.

He could have easily gotten away with creating a replica of Dalia using a single cell of her blood to interpret her DNA. From that one cell, he would then possess the genetic material needed to project an image of the whole, to create a holographic replica. Valentine was an ancient. Cloaking the woman's body to appear as Dalia would have been an easy feat to accomplish. He must have hidden her until the cremation and then taken her home...to breed.

Shelby's woman! Shelby's wife! Raped and mutilated. Tossed aside like garbage. Made to endure the unthinkable in order to produce Valentine a son, an abomination of evil who would take countless innocent lives in his lifetime. And they had allowed it to happen! They had failed to save her from such an agonizing fate. The anguish was overwhelming. The reality of it beyond comprehension.

Nathaniel clasped his hands over his eyes, desperate to get the picture out of his mind. He removed the barrier and turned to face Jocelyn. He spoke as calmly as he could: "The woman you saw in the chamber was my brother's wife." His voice trembled in spite of his effort.

Jocelyn looked up at him, stunned. "Marquis's wife?"

"No," he muttered, "my youngest brother's...Shelby's. He was killed last week as a result of losing her. His burial was this morning. I was at his grave site earlier when I heard you cry out."

Jocelyn blinked and her features softened. "Nathaniel...I'm sorry."

He continued to pace like a caged animal then, completely aware of the terrifying power he exuded but entirely unable to stop it. "I had no idea that he had her..." He was rambling. "She should not have died like that! Not that way!"

His voice thundered through the room, shaking the rafters above them. He tried to steady his breathing, but he just couldn't hold it together.

Nathaniel could not contain such grief.

He was hanging on by a thread as the rage continued to swell, threatening to explode at any moment. It was like trying to juggle a grenade with a loose pin in it; eventually, it was going to blow. And it could not be in front of Jocelyn.

He whirled around to face her. "Jocelyn, I have to go out for a while. I will call for Marquis to watch over you while I'm gone."

Jocelyn sprang to her feet then and threw up her hands. "No, Nathaniel! Please, don't leave me with him. Anyone but him!"

Nathaniel hissed. He did not have the patience to coddle her right now; he no longer possessed the self-control. He knew his eyes were a deep, feral red and his fists clenched almost convulsively. There was little he could do anymore to hide the rage that was overtaking him: Every muscle in his body was rippling in violent waves of fury...just itching for a fight. His top lip drew back into a snarl, and he lowered his head trying to avoid her piercing gaze.

Jocelyn sat back down. "Are you afraid you're going to hurt me, Nathaniel?"

"I'm not going to hurt you," Nathaniel snarled. His lips twitched as he tried, unsuccessfully, to pull them back down over his fangs.

Jocelyn looked like a frightened child, obediently still. "Your anger," she whispered, "is it at me? Are you mad because I saw what that vampire did?"

Tessa Dawn

Nathaniel shook his head; the room was spinning now. "No, Jocelyn. Never at you." He took a deep breath and closed his eyes. When he looked back up, he felt oddly disconnected. "What you saw in that chamber was an abomination." His voice was eerily steady. "What that woman suffered was unspeakable. *Evil.* Believe me, Jocelyn, when I tell you: *That is not your fate with me.*"

Nathaniel could see the relief wash over her face; she opened her mouth and tried to speak, but nothing came out.

He glided closer then, careful to keep his hands at his sides as he locked his gaze with hers. "You have seen me at my worst, Jocelyn…you know the creature that I am. Yet even in this moment, when my need to kill, *my thirst for blood,* is burning a hole through me, you must know that I am incapable of such an act as you saw in that chamber. I could never hurt you like that." His voice deepened. "*Never.*"

Jocelyn shuddered, clearly overwhelmed by his words.

Nathaniel felt the beast rising again, and he resumed his wild pacing.

In an effort to keep his claws from extending, he tore a gash in his fist with his razor-sharp fangs and absently sucked the blood from the wound. *Dear gods,* it tasted good.

And then the earth began to shake beneath them with powerful, violent tremors. Jocelyn clutched the corner of the couch and nervously eyed the room. She glanced up at the rafters as if she expected to see the high, spinning ceiling fan come crashing down at any moment.

"Nathaniel," she whispered, a clear urgency in her voice. "*Calm. Down.*"

nine

All at once, Nathaniel's great room lit up with soft, iridescent light, and a host of translucent colors danced through the air, narrowing into various distinctive forms, until a sparkling image of Marquis shimmered into view in the form of a hologram.

"Nathaniel, what is it?" Marquis asked. "Has something happened with Jocelyn?"

Nathaniel shut his eyes and slowed his breathing. He did not care to upset Jocelyn any further, but he definitely did not want to upset Marquis! "I cannot discuss it right now, brother, but I would ask a favor of you: Would you call the sentinels for me? I will need them to watch over Jocelyn while I step out."

"What could possibly make you want to leave your *destiny* so soon after the Omen?" Marquis snorted. "No, we will discuss it now—tell me what has happened, Nathaniel." As expected, Marquis made it an order.

Nathaniel sighed in frustration. Just as he feared, his brother would not be put off. Marquis had undoubtedly felt the quake, even from his own home ten miles away on the northeastern side of the gorge. But more than that, he had to have felt Nathaniel's rage: He had to know something was terribly, terribly wrong.

"Nathaniel?" Marquis persisted.

"Marquis, now is not the time."

"Do not force me to take the information from your mind, brother."

Nathaniel frowned. Like Marquis, he was also a Master Warrior and an Ancient. Taking information from another warrior's mind was never done among equals, and it was practically inconceivable between brothers: a show of profound disrespect.

But Marquis was on edge. He was angry…grieving…determined to protect his remaining brothers at any cost. Nathaniel didn't bother to argue. He knew Marquis would make good on his threat. Marquis didn't make idle threats.

"The body we cremated last week was not Dalia's," Nathaniel growled. "Valentine staged it to deceive us." He shifted uncomfortably as his blood began to boil again. "He kept her, Marquis! He bred his sons with her and sacrificed the firstborn earlier this night, before the Omen. Jocelyn was in the chamber when it happened. She witnessed all of it."

There was a moment of lingering silence as the holographic image began to project a dark, haunting aura around it. A thick, inky mist began to cluster around the image, yet Marquis's voice remained inexplicably steady. "So this is why she sought to kill herself rather than be taken..." Despite the calm tenor, his words settled in the air like a ghostly presence filling a cemetery. He paused to take a deep breath. "And now you seek to go where, Nathaniel?"

Nathaniel waved a dismissive hand and shook his head. "I will not discuss this any further."

"Nathaniel!" Marquis bellowed. There was an unyielding tone to his voice.

Nathaniel didn't answer.

"*Brother*, what do you intend to do? Do you think to hunt the skies tonight like a madman? Do you really believe you can draw Valentine from his lair? Valentine might have achieved the skills of a Master Warrior in his nine hundred years of depraved existence, but he is not foolish enough to fight you alone. You know this to be true."

A wicked smile curved along the edges of Nathaniel's mouth, exposing his dagger-like fangs. "Then I will pray that he has his worthless twin, Zarek, at his side to embolden him. *That I should be so lucky*. It is time to cleanse this earth of both of them anyway."

Though clearly displeased, Marquis nodded in agreement. "This may be true, Nathaniel, but not tonight. And not alone. Do you forget that where Valentine and Zarek go, Salvatore is rarely far behind? And he has lived long enough to be a full-fledged Ancient, who is well studied in the dark arts of his kind. You cannot take all three of them, brother, and Jocelyn need not deal with the aftermath of such a battle, even should you live. You know that I speak the truth."

Nathaniel clenched his fists. "He is mocking us, Marquis. He took her right from under our noses. *He murdered our brother and raped*—" His voice cut off. *"My mind is made up."* His powerful body was trembling with the need for retribution.

The figure in the hologram remained disturbingly calm, his eyes distant but focused. His next words were wrapped in black velvet. "Then this is how it shall be: I will send all three sentinels to watch over Jocelyn—should Valentine be waiting somewhere with his brothers, expecting you to do exactly as you're doing. You will go and *feed*, and you will not return to your female until your *blood lust* is entirely sated. I will search for Valentine myself, to see if I can draw him or his brothers out into the open—if they are indeed with him. You and I will speak again tomorrow before Nachari arrives."

Nathaniel was *not* in agreement. Shelby was his brother, too, and Valentine had placed a heavy burden of guilt on all of them. Revenge was the least of what they owed their little brother. "Marquis, I am sorry, but I cannot relinquish my right to hunt the Dark One this night."

There was a long moment of silence before Marquis pulled rank. *"I have spoken, Nathaniel."* His tone was one of absolute authority. There would be no more discussion, no further questions.

The descendants of King Sakarias lived by a powerful code of honor, just as their ancestors had done before them, long before the Blood Curse. There was nothing random about their hierarchy, as each member devoted centuries of their lives to learning the ancient arts, honing their supernatural powers, and perfecting their abilities.

Eventually, all males who sought the hard-earned title of *Master* were required to complete four centuries at the Romanian University, where they would ultimately become an expert in one of the Four Disciplines: Warrior, Healer, Wizard, or Justice. And even then, a Master had to live a thousand years before he earned the title of *Ancient*.

The fledglings obeyed the Masters; the Masters obeyed the Ancients; and all obeyed their Sovereign. In the case of Nathaniel and Marquis, where both brothers had achieved equal status as Ancient Master Warriors, the younger brother deferred to the elder. Much had been learned during Marquis's five hundred additional years on earth, and his decree was beyond reproach.

Knowing the declaration was final, Nathaniel suppressed his fury and respectfully bowed his head. It was a required gesture of deference and obedience. A gesture Marquis was owed in spite of Nathaniel's disagreement.

Marquis directly bowed in response. "Be well, my brother."

"Be well, Marquis."

The hologram shimmered out of view, and Nathaniel paused to collect himself before turning to face Jocelyn, who was now sitting on the sofa with her legs tucked beneath her, staring at him with both awe and apprehension on her face.

"You need not fear me," he said. "You are *my destiny*, Jocelyn, and I will fight to keep you safe as I should have fought for Dalia. Do not be frightened of the sentinels, either. They will gladly lay down their lives for you, and they will not enter my home unless you have need of their assistance. You will be safe until I return."

Jocelyn had a thousand questions, not the least of which was what would become of her if Nathaniel didn't return. It was strange, the mixed emotions he caused in her: On one hand, she feared him, as well as whatever he had planned for her future, probably more than she had ever feared anything in her life. But on the other hand, he made her feel safe, important, like maybe there *was* some hidden bond between them that he valued with his life. It was impossible to deny that there was *something* between them.

For a moment, she actually thought about asking him to stay. *She was afraid for his safety.* Of what might happen if he disobeyed his brother and went looking for the creature anyway, but she knew it was fruitless. She also knew that it was utterly insane to care.

As if he had read her thoughts, Nathaniel walked over to the couch and crouched down in front of her. He stroked her cheek. "I am truly sorry, angel." His voice was pure magic. "I know you have seen far too much this night. I will return before sunrise." Leaning over so that his mouth was directly at her ear, he added, "But Jocelyn, you must hear me when I tell you that as long as you do as I say, no harm will come to you; however, should you try to escape this place, you will have far more to fear than me." With a low growl of warning, he stressed, "*Obey me in this, tiger-eyes. Do not try to leave me.*"

Jocelyn felt a sudden flash of anger. "*Obey you?*" She spat the words before she could catch herself. "I don't even know you!" *Jocelyn had never obeyed anyone in her life.*

Nathaniel stood up then and took a small step back, clearly looking displeased.

Already committed, Jocelyn rose and faced him squarely. "If I were going to try and escape you, Nathaniel, do you think I would do it on a whim? Without a plan? And do you think I would be stupid enough to try and escape *your sentinels?*" Her voice was insistent. "I have absolutely no idea who these men...*males*...are, but if they're anything like you or your brother, I wouldn't stand a prayer anyhow." She didn't mention that she was more afraid of what was out there than what was in here. "No, Nathaniel. I will not attempt to escape you...*tonight.*" She crossed her arms and added, defiantly, "But it won't be out of *obedience.*"

Nathaniel regarded her thoughtfully but said nothing right away. He rubbed his chin with his hand, and then he took a step toward her.

Jocelyn stepped back.

"Jocelyn," he said in a gravelly voice, "trust me when I say I do not think you are stupid. You saw the monster in that chamber. You saw what he can do. In this particular matter, I am only thinking of your safety."

Jocelyn frowned and slowly averted her eyes. "I, uh…I know you're trying to protect me…it's just that…I don't like to be told what to do."

Nathaniel stared straight into her eyes, "You will learn in time, Jocelyn—obedience is not always a weakness."

Jocelyn watched as his eyes flashed a deep crimson red, and the hard angles of his jaw tightened. Once again, he was trying to suppress his rage at the situation…*for her.* And once again, she could see that the anguish remained too much. The truth was: As much as she feared him…as much as she knew she was right to fear him…*as much as she hated some of the things he said,* a part of her wanted to comfort him. He was carrying impossibly heavy burdens.

Without thinking, she stepped forward and gently took his hand. "You are hurt, Nathaniel," she whispered. "Let me look at your hand before you go."

Nathaniel stood in stunned silence. Unable to speak or move. Not wanting to say or do anything that might lessen Jocelyn's kindness.

He couldn't believe what he was seeing: This extraordinary woman whom he had plucked out of the forest like a wild flower was reaching out to him with concern. Despite his promise to let her go, he had taken her against her will. And they both knew that her life was about to change, forever…beyond her imagining. Under the circumstances, she had every right to be defiant, even angry, yet here she was acting like…*only his true destiny would.*

Nathaniel knew the wound on his hand would heal on its own, yet her concern moved him just the same. For a brief instant, the rage burning in his chest warred with the tenderness expanding in his heart. Without thinking, his warm mouth found the hollow of her throat, and he pressed a gentle kiss against her soft skin.

He wrapped his heavily muscled arms around her and held her to him, even as his soul continued to fume. His teeth scraped inadvertently back and forth over her pulse before he finally nuzzled his chin in the soft wealth of her coffee-colored hair and deeply inhaled her scent. And then he felt a curious mist forming in his eyes as affection, grief, and *fury* all danced together in some sort of primitive tango in his heart, as this breathtaking female stood so boldly beneath him.

When she didn't pull away, he held her even closer, this time pressing a soft kiss against her cheek before gently resting his forehead against hers. "Tiger-eyes, you move my soul," he murmured. His voice was husky and unfamiliar—even to his own ears.

And then the scent of her blood began to call to him, the soft echo of her pulse beating against him like a small, beckoning drum. His hunger stirred, and his rage threatened to come to the surface.

Jocelyn must have felt the shift in his countenance because she all at once became rigid, and then she slowly pulled away. "Nathaniel, what are you doing?" she whispered cautiously. "You don't want to hurt me." It was as if she were talking to a wild tiger, hoping to back her way out of his cage.

He frowned. "Come back to me, love." He hastily pulled her to him and held her in an iron grip, his powerful body pressed hard against hers. And then he quickly released her before he could frighten her any further…before she could provoke the beast dwelling so tenuously beneath the surface.

"I could never hurt you, my love. You belong to me. Hurting you would be like hurting myself."

BLOOD DESTINY

Jocelyn's eyes grew wide, but before she could protest, Nathaniel swept her up in his arms and carried her back to the sofa. He laid her down and covered her with the blanket. Holding his hand over his now protruding fangs, he spoke a single command: "*Sleep.*"

As her eyes fell closed, Nathaniel disappeared from the room and headed for the midnight sky.

How could he possibly explain? He may have looked like a man, but he was a predator first, an animal.

A male vampire.

And his anger had been stirred beyond the point of no return.

He had to have blood.

ten

Nathaniel's enormous, magnificent wings sprang forth from the small of his back to the blades of his shoulders, expanding more than six feet in width, like those of a mythical, primordial dragon or warrior angel. His silky blue-black feathers shimmered like dark crystals beneath the moonlight, a perfect match to the exact shade of his glorious hair, as he soared through the skies like a man possessed, scouring the landscape beneath him for fertile prey.

Although it was taboo for a vampire to hunt so close to home, his first instinct was to fly over the Dark Moon Casino. It was always full of tourists and travelers, many with dark secrets and hidden passions, not always so pure. But the more he replayed the vivid memories he had extracted from Jocelyn's mind, the more furious he became. There was simply no energy coming from the casino that was strong enough, vile enough, to satisfy the unquenchable thirst for blood Valentine had stirred in him.

Nathaniel dropped low to scan more closely.

There were petty thieves and alcoholics who beat their wives, professionals who scammed their clients, and even one young woman who had gotten away with poisoning her rich husband, but Nathaniel wanted more. He needed much, much more. Where were all the criminals tonight? Where were all the seriously sick, depraved minds who flourished on the misery of others? Nathaniel headed further and further away from Dark Moon Vale, putting on a preternatural burst of speed.

It would be necessary to find a major city.

He flew for over an hour in an endless haze of fury, aimlessly letting off steam. He passed through New Mexico and Arizona until he finally landed in California, where he thought to try Hollywood, but he only found runaways, drug addicts, and patrons of prostitution.

His next thought was to head into gang territory, but he immediately realized that would be an all-or-nothing proposition. Such weak-minded types rarely possessed the courage to stand alone. It would be either feast or famine. He'd catch an entire gang all at once or no one at all.

Feast. Where could he feast?

His blood was beginning to boil, and then all at once he made a sharp turn and began to descend.

The federal prison.

He easily dissolved the molecules in his body until he was only packets of quantum energy, rapidly firing waves of possibility, following no particular form. And then he moved right through the prison walls into the main cellblock and issued a powerful command to the guards to sleep. When he glanced up, he saw three rows of cells, all full of heinous, dangerous prisoners, just waiting for his attention. Predators of the human species.

Predators about to become prey.

He paced the walkways like a prowling lion searching for the perfect quarry, scenting their blood, reading their minds, until he finally came across a cell that interested him. A rapist and a child molester. Both had committed far more crimes than they had been arrested for, yet both still believed *they* were the victims— victims of a system that had the nerve to actually charge them with the crime they had been sentenced for.

He could read the telltale brain patterns of a sociopath: no remorse, completely self-absorbed, unable to see their victims as people...still reeling from the perceived injustice of their circumstances...and desperately missing the heady rush of their crimes. Sociopaths blamed everyone in the world for their circumstances except themselves.

Nathaniel slipped into the small, dingy cell, still invisible. Although the tiny cubicle was relatively clean, by the sterile standards of a large government institution, the heady stench of antiseptic cleanser and human waste was overwhelming. He immediately shut down his high-powered sense of smell.

It was late, and both inmates were sleeping on their narrow bunks, the guy on top, a heavyset man with enormous biceps all covered in menacing tattoos. He had a scraggly goatee with a pointed tip hanging down from his chin, and Nathaniel easily retrieved his name from his mind—Chris Taylor. Chris liked to beat and force himself on women. Particularly, very petite, young women who had little strength to fight him back and even less life experience to recognize the impending danger.

Nathaniel's pulse began to race, and his eyes narrowed into tiny slits of menace as he floated weightlessly to the ceiling and hovered above the vile man like a spider suspended from an invisible web, their bodies aligned face-to-face. It wasn't enough to take his blood or to rid the world of his stench; he wanted to see the fear in his eyes as he realized he was about to die. He wanted him to feel a mere pittance of what his victims had felt when he tormented them.

What Dalia had felt when Valentine tormented her.

Nathaniel pierced the veil of Chris's mind and gave him a strong mental command to awaken, even as he placed his bulging body in a state of paralysis.

Chris slowly opened his eyes, annoyed. It was late; why was he waking up?

Nathaniel snarled. The human had been enjoying a dream about a lonely woman he had been writing back and forth to for the past several months. He was looking forward to her first visit to the prison, looking even more forward to the money he knew she would start sending on a regular basis. She and the three others he had met through correspondence. And then the prisoner's eyes came into focus, and he saw the dark, looming shadow on the ceiling above him.

Nathaniel cherished seeing this particular image in the rapist's mind. His own reflection. A monster with gleaming red eyes and jagged, sharp teeth perched perilously above him like a stalking predator in waiting.

Chris's huge muscles contracted as he went to swing at the

creature, undoubtedly hoping to latch onto Nathaniel's throat and strangle the breath out of him as he often did his victims, but his arms wouldn't move. They just lay at his side like lead, a pair of heavy dumbbells with far too much weight on them.

Nathaniel met his gaze and burned a clear, vivid picture of his lethal intentions into the prisoner's mind, sending him detailed images of his own mangled throat. He almost lost the opportunity to kill the man as Chris's heart began to pound hysterically, beat irregularly, and seize with panic. The precursor to a heart attack.

Nathaniel was disappointed.

He would have to kill him far more quickly than he wanted.

In a frenzied attempt to call out to his cell mate, Chris struggled to open his mouth, but no sound came out.

"Do you mean to scream, Chris?" Nathaniel hissed, snapping his fangs at the terrified man, his mind a wild haze of rage and retribution. "I would think someone as strong as you would just take his death like a man. You do so enjoy a good cat-and-mouse game, do you not?"

Despite the heavy ropes of paralysis binding him to the paper-thin mattress, Chris shook uncontrollably from head to toe, sweat pouring from his pores like droplets of dirty water gushing out of a semi-clogged shower-head.

Nathaniel lunged so quickly that his movement was a blur. He tore a sizeable chunk of flesh out of the man's throat, shaking his head furiously from side to side like a rabid canine as he wrenched it free in order to inflict the most pain possible. Chris convulsed in agony as he watched the enraged creature spit a huge section of his own throat out on the floor.

It was then that Nathaniel noticed Martin, Chris's short, stocky cell mate, standing next to the bed with some sort of makeshift knife in his hand. The roommate lunged at the vampire, swinging wildly with tremendous force, certain he was about to score a victory.

Nathaniel stopped Martin's hand in midair. Using only his mind, he slowly turned the hand around, pointed the knife back toward Martin's face, and gave the prisoner a powerful command using the full force of his voice, a dark intonation of absolute power and seduction. "*Martin,* you will use that blade to gouge out your left eye now; but do keep your right one intact so that you don't miss Chris's farewell. I know how deeply you enjoy watching others suffer."

Martin's eyes grew wide with fright as he realized that he no longer controlled his own hand, and Chris's heart skipped several beats before it began to pound again like a heavy bass drum in a marching band, the sound so loud it could be heard across the room...a sharp, tightening vise seizing his chest.

Nathaniel shook his head with disgust. "You really have no heart at all, do you, Chris? I'm disappointed." He sighed. "Of course, you shouldn't mind at all when I remove it then, should you?" He held his hand in front of Chris's face and slowly allowed his nails to extend into claws, until five serrated talons were unsheathed right before the prisoner's terrified eyes.

Chris turned a ghostly shade of white, and his tear-filled eyes began to seize along with his heart, rolling back in his head with fright.

Ripping effortlessly through the outer layer of the orange jumpsuit, Nathaniel began to slowly carve a circle into the man's chest, just above the pitiful, failing organ. "This is for Ashley," he said as he sliced off his nipple and flicked it at Martin, who was now shaking in violent contortions of agony as he stabbed at his own eye relentlessly, dark blood pouring from the socket in shady pools of anguish, staining his already tortured face.

"And this is for Sheila," he continued. He slashed a deep vertical gash from Chris's chest to his stomach, and then he reached in and broke off a rib. It cracked like a flimsy chicken bone before Nathaniel flicked it across the room. "And this is for Lisa..."

He continued, name after name, rib after rib, until he tired of the game. Finally, his eyes glowing a feral shade of crimson red, spikes of rising menace flashing in his pupils, he reached in with all five claws and withdrew the useless heart. He held it up in

BLOOD DESTINY

front of Chris's face, and both inmates watched in horror as the dislodged organ continued to beat and sputter. "And this is for me." He hissed with satisfaction. And then he bent his dark head, long blue-black hair falling forward in cascading waves of darkness...

And he drank.

Nathaniel drank until there wasn't a drop of blood left in the body, and then he slowly turned his head to the side as a fiendish grin crept over his blood-drenched mouth. "How good of you to await my attention, Martin. I do apologize for keeping you. Now let's see that eye."

Nathaniel floated down from the top bunk, bending over the mutilated face to study Martin's work as he descended. "I suppose it will do," he sneered.

Landing upright, he walked casually back to the end of the cell, leaned against the wall, and crossed his arms in front of him. He released Martin's paralysis in order to allow him a few strangled whispers and groans: It really made no difference—the man was far too terrified to scream and in way too much agony to put up any worthwhile resistance.

Nathaniel waved his pointer finger back and forth in a scolding motion. "Now, Martin, you aren't really supposed to have that knife in here, are you?"

Martin shook his head, his one remaining eye glazed with fear.

"Then perhaps you should put it away."

Martin's one eye grew big. He shook uncontrollably and tried to back away from the vampire. Obediently, he bent toward the bottom bunk and began to slip the knife under the flimsy mattress.

"Not there," Nathaniel hissed.

Martin froze. Terrified. Not understanding.

"You are a child molester, are you not? You like young boys?"

Martin trembled and began to mouth the word *please* over and over again, begging for his life.

Tessa Dawn

Nathaniel sighed. "How shall I say this?" His dark eyes met Martin's. "Why don't you put it...where you so like to put things." He glared at the prisoner, then turned his head away, not wanting to see the vile act. Martin obediently shoved the jagged, bloody knife deep into his own back-end, and howled in agony.

"You find such torture enjoyable, yes?" Nathaniel winced. "I must admit, I don't get it, but then to each his own..."

Martin fell to the ground, writhing in pain, and sobbed like a baby.

Nathaniel waved his hand to silence him and rolled his eyes. "It is always the weakest of your species that prey on the vulnerable. *You disgust me.* I no longer wish to play." His face turned hard and cruel. "So crawl to me, then, like the animal you are." He hissed his next words with venom. "Crawl to me, Martin, and welcome your death."

The short, brawny man tried desperately to fight the command, but his body could not refuse the compulsion. He began to crawl slowly, blood flowing out from his body like a river of retribution as he continued to convulse in agony, until he was finally kneeling at the vampire's feet.

Nathaniel crooked his hand upward, encouraging Martin to stand. It was an excruciating exercise for the suffering man, but he had no choice.

"Very good," Nathaniel said, and then he tapped his own two fingers under Martin's chin, back side up, gesturing for Martin to raise his head and expose his throat. "Ear to shoulder, my good man, I would rather not have to touch you while I feed." Sniveling like a baby, Martin slowly complied; he gasped for breath and begged for his life even as he did so.

Inflicting as much pain as possible, Nathaniel viciously ripped out the man's throat and drained his body of blood. The vivid image of Shelby lying on the stone slab in the dark burial grounds of his people—the appalling vision of Dalia writhing in agony on the stone slab in the wicked cavern of the Dark Ones—each spurred him on like a tribal war cry.

BLOOD DESTINY

Demanding that he kill.

Again and again.

He went in and out of cellblocks, ripping out throats, gouging out hearts, drinking until there was no blood left in his victims. Until he finally dropped them to the floor like sacks of rotten potatoes.

Until there were seven bodies behind him.

As he entered the next unit, his mind completely immersed in a killing frenzy, he noticed that there was only one inmate in the room, and the young man had already awoken from the noise of the struggle in the cell beside him. He was crouched in a defensive posture at the back of the room, arms up, poised to strike. His fists were clenched into tight little balls, just waiting to see what rounded the corner.

As Nathaniel leapt the distance between them, landing in a predatory position in front of him, the man's mouth flew open in a moment of utter shock and horror. It was all the time Nathaniel needed. Before the inmate could react, Nathaniel sank his sharp fangs deep into his throat, anticipating the sweet taste of the thick, dark liquid.

All at once, as if he had been shocked by a cattle prod, Nathaniel jerked back and leapt away from the prisoner, stunned by what he had seen.

He had to battle to regain control of the beast inside of him, a beast that did not want to stop. The thin, blond-haired man standing before him, with tears welling up in his bluish gray eyes, was innocent, his troubled soul already weighed down with resignation and defeat. The prisoner had been framed for a double homicide he did not commit, and he and his family had suffered immensely.

Nathaniel took several slow, deep breaths, allowing the rage to settle into a manageable anger. He then walked directly toward the man, who was now shaking uncontrollably, and looked deep into his pleading eyes. "I can see your innocence: You are no longer in danger." The words were a whispered growl. "Let me attend to your wound so you do not bleed out."

Tessa Dawn

The blond kid stood frozen like a statue as Nathaniel bent once again to his neck. This time Nathaniel allowed his incisors to lengthen as opposed to his canines: The vampire's incisors were used differently than his canines in the same way a snake used its fangs to inject and disperse poison—except the vampire's venom held the ultimate power of healing and immortality.

It was sometimes used to create another vampire, transforming a human to the undead, but far more often it was used by their species to heal wounds and speed regeneration. Infused into a lesion or injected into a diseased organ, the affected part of the body would immediately begin to repair itself. Unfortunately for a human, receiving the slow injection was incredibly painful.

Sinking his piercing fangs only deep enough to allow an adequate infusion, Nathaniel released his own powerful essence into the innocent man, this time giving life instead of taking it. He was careful only to disperse a small amount of the poison, as he had no intention of attempting a full transformation, endangering the human's soul. As expected, the wounds instantly began to heal. The human male would have a powerful immune system from this point forward. More than likely, he would be resistant to most human diseases.

Nathaniel raised his dark head and floated back away from the man, who touched his neck and felt the smooth, flawless skin. Their eyes met for a prolonged moment of understanding, and then the vampire was gone. His killing rage over. His hunger fully sated.

Nathaniel ran rapidly through the cold, sterile prison, reawakening the guards. He glided just above the floor in the smooth, noiseless manner of his kind. And no one seemed to notice his presence, or the cold chill that accompanied him, when he stopped at the administrative offices to alter the automated computer system.

Reading the minds of the guards, he quickly ferreted out which program held the release-date information and how to generate pre-release orders. Touching his hand to the hard drive, he began to change the data to reflect months of pre-release preparations already completed.

Michael White.

First-degree murder.

Release date...*tomorrow.*

He sent the new data through the system, making sure there were no discrepancies, even as he effortlessly located the filing cabinet with Michael's back-up hard file in it and set it on fire.

The guards immediately jumped to put out the spontaneous blaze, but it was too late to recover any contradictory information. Satisfied, Nathaniel wiped the memories of the guards clean and whispered a soft command to a tall, brunette female on his way out of the office, reminding her to look into Michael White's release process immediately. She was already reaching for the computer as Nathaniel dissolved through the ceiling and shot out into the cool night air, his vast wings unfolding gloriously to embrace the deep blue sky.

His hunger had been sated.

He could now return to *his destiny*—to Jocelyn.

eleven

Marquis Silivasi scanned the shadow lands for hours, examining all of the deep, hidden caves and numerous rocky crevices concealed within the gorge. He scoured the valley floors, searched the hidden hollows, and soared to the top of the highest mountain peaks in hopes of finding any sign of Valentine and his brothers.

It was like trying to find a needle in a haystack, ferreting out a Dark One within the miles and miles of deep green forest, shrouded with its thick groves of pine, fir, and spruce trees; concealed by hearty vegetation which grew out of the hard soil and clung to the steep mountainsides, often adhering to solid rock.

It was late summer in the Rocky Mountains, and the nights were mostly cool, following a typical afternoon thunderstorm, which always left the night sky a brilliant midnight-blue. Today had been different. The afternoon had been sunny without even a hint of precipitation. And the Blood Moon had called to Nathaniel and Jocelyn, leaving a hazy mist in the sky, the now white moon casting a knowing shadow over the valley.

Marquis marveled at the beauty of the night, even as he remained so deeply disturbed by the day's happenings. There had been Shelby's burial, an overwhelming event that he could not bring himself to attend, and Valentine had sacrificed Dalia in order to spawn yet another evil descendant of Jaegar, a rightful son he had stolen from Shelby.

He could not comprehend how they had allowed it to happen.

How had the sentinels missed the evil one's presence in the Red Canyons? How had he and Nathaniel been so easily fooled by Valentine's deception? He should not have been able to pass off another woman's body—a human woman with no trace of

BLOOD DESTINY

Celestial DNA in her blood—as Dalia's. The sentinels had picked up on Valentine's scent in the riverbed; it was all over the mutilated corpse. Yet they had missed something as powerful as a birthing, *a blood sacrifice*, in their own backyard.

Marquis understood Nathaniel's rage. His need for vengeance. But he simply could not endure another loss such as the loss of Shelby. If hunting Valentine alone would help keep Nathaniel safe, then Marquis was more than ready to do so. Jocelyn had to be his brother's one and only priority right now.

Turning back toward the Red Canyons for the third time, Marquis left an obvious trail in his wake, should there be a Dark One present who was willing to confront him. He uprooted trees and turned over rocks, leaving strange weather patterns behind him. He formed several isolated rain clouds and created numerous miniature cyclones, sending each one to hover randomly in the air behind him. Any vampire within the vicinity would know that there was an Ancient in the area. And they would easily scent that he was alone.

It was of no use.

All of his effort.

Not a single Dark One was in sight.

Marquis decided to return home, but not before entering the Sacrificial Chamber to see the scene of the abomination himself. Perhaps Valentine had left some distinct energy pattern behind that would indicate his next move or provide a clue as to where he might be sleeping during the day while staying in the valley.

Unlike the descendants of Jadon, the Dark Ones could not tolerate the sun, not even for a moment, not even in the early hours of dawn or the late hours of twilight. Valentine would be sleeping deep within the confines of a crypt, albeit natural or manmade, during the day.

Marquis flowed effortlessly through the long labyrinth of tunnels that wound through the deep canyon, careful to avoid the low-hanging stalactites that hovered like forbidding daggers at the entrance to the actual chamber. Immediately, his blood came alive, coursing powerfully through his veins; his senses became heightened and aware. The smell of death was as thick inside the damp hall as a cloud of moisture on a humid day, clearly revealing the cruelty of the night as well as the identities of those who had been within its walls.

Despite the subtle smell of sulfur, and the not-so-subtle stench of burned flesh, Marquis recognized the lingering scent of Valentine's arousal, the noxious odor of Dalia's terror, and the faint aroma of Jocelyn's frantic escape, each remnant persisting like a visceral reminder of the hideous events. In terms of energy, Jocelyn's residual imprint rose strongest from the back of the cave, from a hollow just beyond a stagnant pool of musty water. Dalia's presence cried out loudest from the stone slab, and Valentine's abhorrent stench marked a path back and forth between the deathbed and the sacrificial altar like a heady trail of adrenaline laced with testosterone.

Marquis closed his eyes, allowing his already heightened senses to become even stronger. He was trying to detect whether or not anyone else had been in the chamber recently. There was no sign of another Dark One in the cavern. Nothing that gave a hint of Valentine's brothers, Salvatore or Zarek. Nothing that might reveal any other descendant of Jaegar in the close proximity. Clearly, Valentine had acted alone.

Without warning, the acrid stench Marquis had identified as Valentine's began to increase, all at once becoming stronger in the cavern. Marquis opened his eyes, wondering if he was receiving a psychic imprint from earlier. Something especially powerful. Perhaps an important clue that Valentine had left behind.

And then the scent grew stronger...unmistakable...a clear indication of something coming closer, until the entity emerged in the chamber and settled conspicuously near.

Marquis knew immediately that Valentine was there in the cavern with him, and the Dark One was hoping to remain undetected behind his poorly cloaked presence. He waved his hand across the shadowy cave, sending the many antique torches embedded in the sandstone walls into a fiery blaze of orange and red light; while at the same time, he used his mind to raise the room temperature to ninety-nine degrees Fahrenheit, two degrees higher than normal body temperature. Using infrared detection to identify any section of the air containing a hollow—a noticeable dip in temperature—Marquis scanned the interior for the anomaly.

The void was directly above him.

Marquis whirled around, leaping to the other end of the cave with preternatural speed just as Valentine materialized into view, raking his fully extended claws perilously close to Marquis's jugular. A high-pitched whistle buzzed through the air as the five seeking daggers swept past their target.

"How nice of you to join me," Marquis hissed, landing in a crouched, defensive stance. "But did you really think it would be that easy to sneak up on an Ancient?" He knew his enemy had hoped to score a quick, unexpected victory; he certainly had not shown up expecting to fight man-to-man.

Valentine roared his fury as he spun to face Marquis. "The night is still young," he purred. His raspy voice dripped with venom. Now that he was there, his pride would dictate that he finish what he started. He turned his bristling black eyes on Marquis, glaring straight through his soul with a murderous rage.

"That it is," Marquis drawled. "Yet all good things eventually come to an end, do they not, Dark One?"

Valentine sneered, "Shelby certainly did, *my brother of light.*"

Marquis's fangs exploded in his mouth as he snarled a promise of retribution, all the while rocking back and forth from his heels to the balls of his feet restlessly. He eyed the legendary vampire with contempt before finally settling into position, as silent as the night, his powerful muscles expanding and contracting in dangerous waves of readiness.

He could not believe his fortune.

Valentine Nistor.

Alone.

With him.

"Do not be so certain of your victory," Valentine spat.

"Arrogance does not become you, Marquis. And sunrise is a long ways away."

"Oh, I can assure you, my dark brother, this will not take long at all." Marquis's voice was a sultry caress of death as a raging fire of vengeance began to rise within him like the blistering lava of a volcano, ever ready to explode into a sweltering onslaught of retribution.

"If I recall, destroying Dalia did not take so long either," Valentine taunted. "Although, I hear your brother's death was an entirely different story: quite the drawn-out process, no?"

Marquis steadied himself. "Perhaps. But at least Shelby died with honor, and his soul now walks the Valley of Spirit and Light. You, on the other hand, will die like the wretched maggot you are and spend the rest of eternity in the Valley of Death and Shadows. We will see then what a long, drawn-out process really is…"

Valentine's eyes narrowed into angry slits of derision as each vampire continued to try and goad the other into a prideful state of fury, hoping to gain the upper hand. Emotions were an easily exploited weakness in mortal combat.

They circled each other like two stalking leopards. Pacing. Glowering. Waiting. Each one demonstrating his own physical prowess, promising the other a violent and painful death, until finally, a group of dagger-shaped stalactites broke free from the cave ceiling and crashed down around them, spurring the angry predators into action.

Valentine struck first, hurling a red-hot bolt of lightning directly at Marquis's heart. The chamber lit up with dazzling sparks of orange and blue electricity as the powerful bolt raced toward its target.

Marquis reacted so quickly the lightning never had a chance to connect. Holding both palms out in front of him, he intercepted the lethal missile and sent it sailing back at Valentine. He never once flinched as the bolt seared sweltering burns into his hands.

Valentine leapt adeptly to the side, laughing wickedly at the sight of Marquis's burning flesh.

Marquis stared down at the scorching fire blistering his palms and began to gather its energy. He could hear the wind picking up outside of the cavern, lashing wildly through the valley, howling its own rising fury, and he could feel the turbulence as it began to form rows of dark, skeletal funnel clouds, preparing to unleash the deadly result of the vampires' rage in the surrounding canyon. But he just didn't care.

Heat turned to fire. Fire turned to radiation. Radiation became two enormous balls of iridescent red flames, spinning and turning in Marquis's hands as the glowing conflagration pulsated out from their cores. And then, without warning, Marquis hurled both balls at preternatural speed, each in quick succession of the other. The first was aimed directly at Valentine, veering slightly off to the left. The second was thrust into the vacant space to his right, the exact spot Valentine would have to leap for in an effort to dodge the first ball.

The weapon struck its target.

Squarely in the chest.

Valentine howled with pain as his body became a hot blaze of fire and radiation. And then he leapt the entire distance of the cave in one smooth motion, grasping Marquis forcefully by the shoulders as he flew through the air.

Their powerful bodies came together like two large cannonballs colliding in the night, sending both of them spiraling backward into the murky pond of water behind them. Valentine rolled frantically in the shallow pool in an effort to extinguish the flames, and Marquis seized the opportunity to attack.

Slashing deep with his jagged claws, he pierced the wall of Valentine's chest and dug deep into the cavity. He wrenched at the muscle, trying to extract the heart, even as he struck at the vampire's throat with his other hand, slicing straight through the Dark One's jugular.

Valentine shouted in pain, and his fangs elongated. Harnessing all of his remaining strength, the son of Jaegar

lunged at Marquis in a desperate attempt to rip out his jugular—
to take his enemy into the next world with him.

But Marquis moved far too swiftly.

He jerked back, avoiding the enormous serrated teeth before
they could puncture his throat, and snatched Valentine up by the
shirt with two powerful fists. He launched him across the cavern
hard, sending him crashing into a solid wall of limestone. He
heard the vampire's bones splinter as his massive torso struck
forcefully upon impact.

And then Valentine's body slumped to the cave floor and
landed in a seated position.

Blood spewed forth from the Dark One's throat, his spine
too mangled to hold him upright. Choking on his own blood,
Valentine fought desperately to stay alive. Both vampires were
warriors. And with their shared centuries of discipline, as well as
lightning-quick reflexes, neither one was going out that easily.

The Dark One quickly constructed an invisible barrier
around his body, a pulsating force field of dense waves of
energy, in a fevered attempt to hold Marquis back long enough
to regenerate. He was losing blood far too quickly, which was
precisely what Marquis wanted…to drain his enemy of his vital
life force. To render him powerless to fight back. To dispatch
his head or remove his heart in order to prevent regeneration.
And to finally incinerate his body so that he could never rise
again.

Marquis watched as Valentine instinctively released his
incisors and sank the sharp fangs deep into his own hand,
rapidly filling it with venom until it began to swell up like a
blowfish. Using a sharp claw from his other hand, he tore a deep
gash into the swollen flesh, forcing the venom to seep out to the
surface, and then he held it up against his throat as a poultice,
smearing a large gob over the hole in his chest along the way.

"You will not kill me this night, Ancient One," Valentine
stuttered, choking on the words. He was still gurgling on his own
blood, yet he managed to growl a low, drawn-out snarl just the
same. His throat was beginning to repair itself, the blood loss

lessening.

Marquis tore wildly at the circular barrier then, like a madman unleashed in a rage, rapidly destroying each powerful layer, one at a time, until the entire obstruction finally came down.

With a fury so great the entire mountain shook, he went straight for the kill.

His hands became crimson-red blurs of light. His claws slashed wildly at the Dark One's arteries as he tore hundreds of lacerations into Valentine's flesh, long before the vampire could lift a weakened hand in defense.

Blood spurted out like geysers erupting from the earth, two powerful streams shooting straight from Valentine's upper arm and inner thigh. And then Marquis lunged at his enemy's throat, determined to reopen the carotid artery one last time.

Without warning, an enormous hand grasped at the mutilated body, snatching Valentine up by the arm just as the roof of the cavern began to cave in. Marquis covered his head reflexively, deflecting the falling rocks with his mind while whirling around to see what had happened.

When the rock slide stopped, Salvatore Nistor was kneeling over his injured brother in the middle of the cave as if he were a coiled cobra, frantically injecting Valentine's wounds with venom from his fangs. Salvatore was an ancient descendant of Jaegar, one who was well studied in black magic, and his venom was powerful.

His head snapped up, and he turned to glare at Marquis, a vicious snarl escaping his throat. Throwing back his wild mane of banded, black-and-red hair, he roared a deafening warning to the powerful descendant of Jadon, and then he leapt to his feet like an angry jungle cat about to pounce.

"Perhaps you should pick on someone your own size, son of Jadon!" His hard, angled jaw was set in a line of unyielding defiance and rage. "Come play with *me*, instead, Marquis!"

Standing with his arms out at his side, Salvatore began to build a fiery blaze of radiation. Only, instead of constructing two balls of fire to hurl at his enemy, he began to encase his own body in the burning arc of flames, until he was standing in the cavern glowing, a living pillar of fire.

Marquis recognized the arrogant display of power for what it was, a masterful attempt at intimidation, and he quickly built a matching arc around his own body; only, he didn't stop there. He absorbed the flames until they completely consumed his core, and the red-hot blazes shot out from his mouth, eyes, nose, and ears in a blistering display of sorcery. A much more difficult and deadly configuration.

Salvatore and Marquis leapt simultaneously into attack positions, two blazing predators dying to strike first. Marquis was about to lunge when he was stopped short by the sudden reappearance of Valentine, who was quickly regenerating with the help of Salvatore's ancient venom. The sadistic vampire leapt effortlessly to his feet at his brother's side, and then he jumped completely over Marquis, resembling a runner taking a hurdle, before crouching low on the opposite side of the cavern and growling with satisfaction.

They had him surrounded.

Marquis became deathly quiet. Listening. Anticipating. Waiting for the slightest vibration to indicate which of the two brothers intended to attack first. To his surprise, the first hint of movement did not come from either one of them. Rather, Nathaniel Silivasi, his own brother, silently materialized in the cavern, his eyes lethal and alert, his body swollen with power. He was perfectly poised and prepared for battle as he stood back-to-back with Marquis.

"Forgive my disobedience, brother," Nathaniel murmured, "but the opportunity was simply irresistible. Besides, I would hate to leave you at a couple's dance without a date."

Marquis smiled a wicked grin and glanced over his shoulder to assess his younger sibling. It was blatantly obvious that he had consumed an *enormous* amount of blood: His muscles rippled with raw power; his eyes were vivid with enhanced acuity; and his skin positively glistened with a fresh sheen of vitality.

BLOOD DESTINY

Nathaniel would be unstoppable.

"I can always ground you later," Marquis grumbled, a deep chuckle reverberating in his chest. He turned his gaze to Salvatore and Valentine and bowed slightly at the waist. "Shall we dance, boys?"

Before they could strike, a dark, malevolent laughter filled the chamber—as a fifth figure shimmered into view. The deep, resonant voice came from Zarek Nistor as he stood next to his twin, scanning his body to assess the extent of his remaining injuries. "I believe it is considered rude to start a party before all the guests have arrived," he snarled.

Marquis chuckled, more than happy to welcome the foolish vampire to the slaughter.

And then a sixth voice rang out, "I couldn't agree with you more." Kagen Silivasi stood leisurely at the entrance to the chamber, his powerful arms crossed idly over his chest. "Luckily, it would appear as if we are all accounted for."

Salvatore sneered, "All but Shelby, of course." He sighed. "Oh yes, Valentine, did you do something to...*discourage*...the youngest Silivasi from attending this night?" His laughter was evil. "Speaking of which, I must come and visit my new nephew soon; I understand his mother was simply *delicious*."

Nathaniel, Marquis, and Kagen all launched into the air at the same time, lunging with supernatural speed at their enemies. There was a hideous clash of flesh and bone. Claws and fangs. Blood and sweat. As hidden weapons were drawn and fury became a living, breathing entity within the cavern.

And then the walls of the cave simply buckled and exploded outward, hurtling all six vampires into the open valley, beneath a suddenly blackened, violent sky, where a war of untold proportions was about to take place.

A war that would give new meaning to the words *Blood Moon*.

Lightning sizzled and thunder roared.

And then the Great One spoke: "There will be no battle, tonight!" The voice rang out like a clash of cymbals as the Sovereign lord of the house of Jadon, *Napolean Mondragon*, descended from the sky, his feral red eyes ablaze with power, his face like a granite statue, etched with authority and resolve. Deep lines of age framed the Ancient's face as his striking silver-and-black hair whipped furiously in the wind, giving off a ghostly appearance of omniscience and immortality.

Napolean was the chosen monarch of the descendants of Jadon and an adversary far too powerful to oppose, to the descendants of Jaegar. His words were law among the Lighter Vampires, and his legendary prowess in war commanded unyielding respect from the Dark Ones. He remained deathly quiet, awaiting the reply of the eldest brothers.

Salvatore Nistor responded with a hiss. He looked up at Napolean and crossed his arms, before glancing off into the distance as if he were thinking it over.

Marquis figured the formidable enemy was assessing the situation from a strategic point of view, which only made sense. One did not live to be as old as Salvatore by being reckless.

"I am not afraid to fight you, Napolean," the Dark One scowled, his words ringing only partially true.

Then you are a fool, Marquis thought. *Anyone with half a brain would be afraid to fight Napolean.* But what the dark son of Jaegar clearly had no fear of...was death...which was good—because Marquis was more than prepared to give it to him.

"But to take on you, Marquis, Nathaniel, *and* Kagen..." Salvatore's voice trailed off.

Napolean remained quiet, awaiting the enemy's decision, while Marquis studied Salvatore's face. The ancient Dark One had to know they couldn't possibly win; the odds were stacked too heavily against them, with or without Napolean. And unlike Valentine, Salvatore wasn't one to take unnecessary risks. Still, Marquis could only hope. He had made a promise to avenge Shelby's death, and he had no intention of letting Valentine walk, not under the cover of his brothers or the protection of Napolean.

"We will agree to retreat," Salvatore finally conceded, his voice thick with contempt, "but only if you guarantee a safe exit."

Napolean turned to Marquis. "Warrior, what say you?"

"Never!" Marquis thundered. "As far as I'm concerned, Salvatore can burn in hell with his brother."

Salvatore hissed, his eyes glowing red, but he said nothing.

Just make one move, Marquis thought. *If it please the gods—just one move.*

Napolean regarded Marquis thoughtfully, and then he floated down until he stood at eye level with the enormous vampire, and the two engaged each other's eyes like powerful Vikings of old meeting on an ancient battlefield.

"Marquis…" The Sovereign lord spoke calmly but firmly, giving each word great consideration. "Under our laws, you have the right of vengeance on your side, but do you not see the sky?"

Marquis grumbled and reluctantly looked up.

There were terrible veins of purple and white lightning flashing in the heavens as far as the eye could see, angry whips of fire surging with violent intensity. The endless arcs spanned the sky from east to west and back again, even as the unforgiving bolts shot to the earth with fury, striking the land with such incredible force that the earth shook beneath the merciless assault. Fire and brimstone fell from the heavens, erupting into hot blazes all over the forest as thunder clapped and roared in its wake.

Napolean waved his hand out toward the valley. "Do you not see the land?"

The sheer enormity of the dense black clouds merging together in an awesome funnel of rage was enough to take one's breath away. Heat and moisture were being sucked into a violent swirl of power, wind, and wrath. It was as if every cloud for a hundred miles had joined together in a dark conspiracy to wage war upon the land and its inhabitants.

The wind was ferocious.

Ancient pine and fir trees bent to their breaking points, while gigantic birches and aspens snapped like twigs beneath the malevolent force.

And the funnel had not even touched down…yet.

"The tornado is headed toward the towns and the villages." Napolean's voice was steady and matter-of-fact.

Marquis cursed, and his fangs pierced his bottom lip in frustration. He briefly met Nathaniel's gaze before turning to look at Valentine, who was smiling like an arrogant child, a triumphant look of victory in his eyes. Disgusted, Marquis conceded: "We will retreat as well." And then his eyes turned cold, like two dark shards of ice. *"For now."*

He met Valentine's dark gaze one last time. "Know this, son of Jaegar; your days of walking this earth have come to an end. There is nowhere you can hide and no one who can protect you, so enjoy this reprieve: *for it is the last one you will ever receive.*" His eyes burned the pledge into the vile one's soul. The promise was absolute.

Valentine's lips drew back in a snarl, but Salvatore wisely placed a hand on his chest. "Words mean nothing, brother," he said, his voice ripe with arrogance. "Let us go." He turned to meet Marquis's glare. "We look forward to meeting again *soon.*"

Marquis hissed and narrowed his glare. "It cannot be soon enough, Dark One."

Napolean waved his hand. *"Enough."*

Like three evil spirits exorcised from a graveyard, the Nistor brothers departed from the night, and the earth began to settle.

The sky began to clear.

The lightning ceased.

And the tornado withdrew its wrath.

twelve

Marquis was still keyed up when he returned to his solitary home out on the northern edge of the Dark Moon forest, high up in the mountain ranges. Unlike Nathaniel's sprawling estate, Marquis's home was simple, elegant, and traditional. It was built like an old three-story farmhouse—complete with the wide wraparound porch and ornate railings; full of large, formal rooms with high ceilings, intricate moldings, and magnificent custom woodwork.

Every room had some type of fireplace in it, including the six upstairs bedrooms: There was a traditional, white brick chimney in the formal living room, an old wood-burning stove in the kitchen, and a hearth in the library made of large hand-picked stones from a river that ran through the property less than fifty yards behind the back porch.

In addition to its simplicity, everything about Marquis's home was constructed around nature: from the miles and miles of stunning views it boasted from the back terrace, to the intricate way it had been built around the existing lofty pines and aspens, weaving them into the natural architecture of the home as opposed to clearing them for construction.

The history adorning the mantels, walls, and stairwells was in the form of art, statues, photographs, and original oil paintings, and the display was as vast as his long life had been, containing something of great value from every era he had lived through, yet remaining simple and clean, the way he liked it.

As always, the silence that met him as he approached his home began to calm him down a little. Other than the trickling sound of running water snaking over rocks and fallen branches in the creek behind the house, the night was deathly quiet. Marquis stood outside for a moment taking in the fresh air before he headed up the old wooden steps to his front door.

All at once, he heard footsteps rounding the corner of the deck.

He spun around and crouched into a fighting stance, his movement as graceful as a gazelle's. His breath was still as the night. Had Valentine or Salvatore come so quickly to meet him? Perhaps all three brothers were waiting in ambush?

Instinctively, the hair on the back of his neck prickled, even as his canines grew into long, spiky points, and his knife-hard claws extended. And then he analyzed the scent. It was human.

Female.

Familiar.

Joelle Parker?

A shriek of surprise pierced the silence as his housekeeper rounded the corner and found him crouched down like an animal with extended fangs and talons, a threat of lethal intent emanating from his eyes. The housekeeper gasped and covered her mouth with both hands.

Although the human knew what he was, Marquis had *never* exposed himself like this before, and she was clearly shaken by his appearance. Her heart stuttered audibly, skipped a beat, and then stammered once more before returning to a normal rhythm.

"Joelle!" Marquis exclaimed, irritated. "What are you doing walking around out here like this? I could've killed you." He frowned. "Do you know how late it is? The sun will be up in a couple of hours."

Over the centuries, the Silivasis, like other descendants of Jadon, had formed a handful of close relationships with select human families. Often, they were humans who worked with them or helped to take care of their homes, businesses, and lives. Joelle Parker was the daughter of Marquis's trusted foreman, Kevin Parker, the one who ran the stables near the Dark Moon Lodge during the summer tourist months.

Marquis had known her father for almost fifty-five years, since the day he was born, just as Kevin knew Marquis—exactly who and what he was. The Parker family had been so well taken care of by the Silivasis that they had chosen to lay down their roots in the valley several centuries ago, passing the torch down from one generation to another, building their homes in the surrounding mountains and raising their families closely together, each fiercely protective of the other.

Joelle had grown up understanding the complex relationship between the two species, the special needs and challenges it posed, and the grave importance of keeping their knowledge of what the Silivasis were to themselves. She had first come to work for Marquis at the young age of seventeen, cleaning the house twice a week for the last six years. In payment, and probably due more to friendship and loyalty than anything else, Marquis had put Joelle through college and helped her to buy her first home. All in addition to the generous salary he paid her.

In truth, it wasn't as charitable as it seemed.

Living for centuries allowed one to amass an enormous amount of wealth. The increasing value of investments and commodities, items such as land and gold, art and artifacts, made it practically impossible not to become—and remain—wealthy. On top of that, Dark Moon Vale had been a gold mine for the descendants of Jadon.

Quite literally.

Among the many local enterprises that the vampires ran—the ski resort and lodge, the casino and restaurant, the stables and outdoor recreation tours, even the hot springs and hotel—their main industry was the mineral plant: a large factory used to design unique, handmade jewelry, harnessing the limitless resource of gemstones found deep in the local caves, abundant on their private property...gold included.

"I am sorry, Mr. Silivasi," Joelle murmured, gathering her sweater tight around her shoulders and rubbing her hands over her arms to warm up. The soft brown sweater was draped loosely over a white blouse, tucked neatly into a flowing, knee-length skirt, and the pale hues of the fabric matched perfectly with her soft brown eyes. Joelle brushed a strand of her honey blond hair out of her face and turned away, allowing Marquis a moment to regain his composure.

Once composed, Marquis simply stared awkwardly at his housekeeper, awaiting an explanation. It was easy enough to hand someone a check, to write out a large payment to a mortgage company, even to pay monthly college tuition bills, but outside of small talk and casual comments about his business, Marquis did not know Joelle that well. Of course, he'd scanned a few of her memories from time to time, whenever there might have been some concern for her safety, but that wasn't the same as *knowing her*. Marquis Silivasi did not hang out with humans.

When Joelle finally looked back up at him, Marquis was relaxed, standing casually on the porch. He leaned back against a tall, square post with his arms crossed over his chest and silently waited to hear her explanation.

Joelle squared her shoulders, as if she were trying to gather her courage. And then she took a long look into his dark eyes, swept her gaze lower to his lips, and winced, turning back away.

Marquis shifted his weight nervously and leaned on the opposite leg. He wondered if the tips of his fangs were still showing. "Is everything all right with your family, Joelle?"

"Yes," she answered in a hurried voice. "Yes, of course."

Marquis became once again silent and simply raised his eyebrows.

Still waiting.

Joelle closed her soft, almond-shaped eyes for several prolonged seconds, drew a deep breath into her lungs, and tried again to summon her courage.

When once again, nothing came out of her mouth, Marquis decided it was time to skim the surface of her thoughts. She was arguing with herself...

I can do this. I will do this. I have to do this!

The young, anxious human was absently waging an internal war, completely unaware that Marquis could "hear" every word.

If you don't do this now, Joelle, you're going to spend the rest of your life in complete misery, probably pining away your days like some kind of old maid, completely unable to sleep at night, miserable around the clock, until you eventually die of a broken heart. There is no other choice! You've tried everything under the sun to get over these—

Oh God, Marquis Silivasi! What is wrong with you?

He's a vampire!

He's your boss!

Joelle shook her head, looking utterly distraught.

Marquis cleared his throat to let her know he was still standing there.

She immediately opened her eyes, exhaled, and forced herself to blurt out her next words. "I, um…well…it's just that…I wanted to…talk to you." She sighed then, clearly in misery.

Marquis frowned. "Pardon me?" He was utterly confused and completely out of his element.

Joelle turned away for a moment and leaned against the railing as if the narrow boards could offer added support. When she turned back around, her cheeks were flushed the color of spring roses. "I have something I need to say to you." She pronounced each word separately. "Something I've needed to say for a long time. And if I don't do it right now, *tonight*, I'll never have the courage again."

Marquis's dark eyes narrowed into two focused slits of concentration, searing straight into her soul. He turned up both hands in question and continued to wait. Despite reading her scrambled thoughts, he had no idea where she was going with this, and half expected her to start asking him questions about being a vampire. But then, he knew her father had likely explained everything in great detail, as much of it became important over the years when two families lived in such close proximity.

"Okay," she began, her voice shaking with raw nerves, "so I know that all of you are bound by this…Blood Curse thing. And there's only one woman in the entire universe that you can be with once the signs and the stars…and all that…" She cleared her throat. "And I know that you could never love a human…and you're really, *really old*, but—" Her voice cut off, her eyes began to tear up, and she became short of breath.

"Joelle?" Marquis sounded as confused as he felt. What was she trying to ask him? And why the sudden interest in the Blood Curse? Did she have questions about what had happened to Shelby? Had her family already received news of Nathaniel and Jocelyn? And more important, *why was she insulting him?* What in the world did his *antiquity* have to do with anything?

Old was not a very polite word.

"Marquis," she huffed in exasperation as she stifled her tears, "are you really that blind?"

He may have grunted. He wasn't sure.

She sighed. "Can't you see that I am totally and hopelessly in love with you? That I have always been totally and hopelessly in love with you? That I can't eat, sleep, or breathe anymore for being so in love with you!" The tears began to flow down her delicate face, and she turned away, completely embarrassed, but evidently, still determined.

Marquis stared at her small, frail back in stunned silence. His ears heard her words, but his brain had not yet processed them. Over the many centuries of his life, he had become all too aware of the power their species had over human women, and it was one of the reasons he lived in such solitude—had very few passionate interludes—but this particular woman knew exactly what he was. In addition, Joelle Parker was very, *very young.*

And very, very human.

Marquis sighed. "Joelle, you are young. You do not yet know what you feel. You have not yet met the man who will sweep you off of your feet. In any case, you are not *my destiny.* You are correct in your understanding that there is only one, and I will go to her the moment I see the Omen. The most I could ever do is hurt you." He paused, reflecting. "I will look for another housekeeper. There is no need for you to continue in such an...uncomfortable situation. I'm sorry, I had no idea."

Joelle spun back around, clearly stunned. Heartbroken. Absolutely panic-stricken. "I'll admit, Marquis, I didn't expect you to confess some mutual undying love for me." Her voice raised at least an octave. "But I certainly didn't expect to be fired, either! Or to be told flatly that I'm not your *destiny*—you don't want me—and to just go away." She buried her face in her hands, almost hysterical.

"Those were not my precise—"

"Oh my God," she blurted out, "what have I done?" Her shoulders began to tremble, and then she started to sob uncontrollably, turning her back on him once more.

Marquis looked up at the sky, half expecting to see a red moon based on the sheer intensity of the female's emotion. He almost wished it were there. Anything. Just to stop the poor child's suffering, just to make her quit crying.

Placing a hand gently on her shoulder, he whispered, "Joelle, you must stop this at once. I will remove your memories of this night. If you'd like, I can remove your awareness of your feelings for me altogether. Perhaps plant something more appropriate in their place? Is there someone else you might—"

Joelle spun around and glared at him, this time even more visibly wounded than before. Without preamble, she struck him as hard as she could, directly in the chest, with an open hand.

Shocked, Marquis leapt back. Although he hardly felt the blow, a low, almost inaudible growl of warning instinctively escaped his throat.

"Oh, my God," she wailed. "Did you just growl at me? *You just growled at me!* You really don't have a heart, do you? You are like a caveman!" She slumped to the ground and buried her face in her arms. "You are, you know?" She sniffled. "Everyone knows that about you. You have no tact! You rarely show compassion! You're scary as hell most of the time: always glaring and snarling at everyone, ordering your brothers around like a tyrant, and just plain acting like the world's greatest menace...hoping everyone will stay away from you." She shook her head. "But I can't...because I love everything about you. Even those horrible...insensitive...obnoxious traits that everyone else fears." The tears ran like a river.

Marquis had seen and heard more than enough.

Reaching down, he scooped her up by the arm, turned her to face him, and began to speak in a silvery voice of pure enchantment. A clear hypnotic tone. "Look at me, Joelle. You will—"

"No!" she shouted, fighting his mind control. "Don't you dare!" She clenched her eyes closed and pointed a finger at his face. "Don't you dare mess with my memories! I mean it, Marquis! You stay out of my head, do you hear me? Please don't do such a thing...I'm begging you."

It was the first time she had ever directly asked him for anything, let alone begged. And it was also the precise moment when he realized just how serious she really was.

Completely at a loss for words, he delved deeper into her mind. Perhaps if he understood her better, had a stronger grasp on where she was coming from, he would know the right way to respond.

Marquis Silivasi was shocked by what he found.

All of the little comforts in his home, the precise way his treasured mementos were always carefully arranged, his favorite books alphabetized by author in the library, none of these things were random. They had all been small acts of kindness motivated by Joelle's deep affection for him.

She had an absolute awareness of everything he did, everywhere he went, and everyone he was with.

And it went back for...years.

Joelle had learned everything there was to know about the Blood Curse, about his past, and she had spent countless sleepless nights lying awake fantasizing about things she seemed far too young to fantasize about. This wasn't just some childish obsession. This woman had fallen in love with him without so much as the slightest hint of interest on his part. He had never even noticed her...*as a female*.

He stood quietly. Contemplating. And then he finally spoke in an even tone of voice. "We cannot have a relationship, Joelle. It is simply not possible. Tell me, then; if you are determined to continue working for me, and you are not willing to relinquish your memories, what is it that you want me to do?"

Joelle dropped her head, looking utterly humiliated. She hid her face in her hands and dropped her forehead against his chest. "I want you to give me a chance," she sobbed.

The young human looked up then, staring into his eyes; she appeared mesmerized by their depths as she forced herself to say what was really on her mind. "I've thought a lot about it—I really have. And here's the thing: You are always alone, Marquis. Whenever you aren't working or looking out for your brothers. And I know that you have a lot of responsibilities, but you're still a...male. You have to get lonely."

She rubbed her soft body closer against his, almost instinctively. It wasn't clear whether or not she was trying to comfort herself or seduce him. "I know I'm acting like a child, but I'm not. I'm a full-grown woman. And I understand perfectly well that you will leave me the moment you meet the woman who was meant for you." She stumbled over the words, her voice faltering at the mere mention of someone else being loved by Marquis. "But who's to say that it will happen in my lifetime? And what if it doesn't? It probably won't. Either way, you don't have to be alone right now."

Placing both of her hands cautiously on either side of his waist, Joelle looked up and held his dark eyes with her own soft, sultry gaze. "If I only have five years, or even just one, I would give my entire world away to be with you, Marquis." She reached up to touch his hair, as if she couldn't help herself. As if she had always wanted to do so and might never get another chance. "You could even change me if you wanted." It was a whisper. "To be like you." Her heart froze perfectly still in her chest, waiting for his response.

Marquis stared deep into Joelle's longing eyes, seeing her as if for the first time, taking her far more seriously than just moments before. She was a truly beautiful woman, with soft, sculpted features; full, pouty lips; and an enticing feminine body. Everything about her seemed delicate, like porcelain...and just as refined.

BLOOD DESTINY

He caught at her wrists and shackled them in front of him with powerful hands, forcing her body away from his while restraining her at the same time.

"I cannot make you as I am, Joelle, not even if I wanted to."

"How do you know?" she asked.

Marquis shook his head. "Joelle, the price of transformation...*the cost of immortality for a human is their soul.* Only those who are our chosen mates can be successfully changed without being damned. And even for them, the price is a firstborn son. I would never do such a thing to you. I would never allow you to do such a thing to yourself."

Joelle blinked back another onslaught of pressing tears. "Then let me be your lover," she whispered seductively...fearfully. Despite the iron grip he had on her wrists, she managed to press her body temptingly against his while placing a series of soft kisses in the hollow of his throat. She deeply inhaled his scent and nipped gently at his neck, just behind his ear...just below his chin...all the while pressing her lower body firmly against his in a blatant attempt to arouse him.

Marquis's hands tightened around her wrists in a viselike grip, and his body became as still as a statue. A deep, feral warning rose in his throat. "Do not move!" he warned. "Not. One. Muscle."

His fangs exploded in his mouth as the primal heat of a provoked predator rose in his blood. He could hear her pulse pounding in her neck, louder than he'd ever heard it before. He could smell the sweet nectar of her blood and almost feel the intense pleasure he would experience as he took her body with complete abandon, draining her, robbing her of reason, slowly...exquisitely...taking her life at the same time.

Outside of one's chosen *destiny*, it was not a natural mating, human and vampire. The call of the wild animal was far too hard to suppress when a male was that aroused, completely without inhibitions, devoid of all control.

Marquis's body stirred, becoming instantly thick and heavy at the groin, even as he fought the powerful red haze now invading

his mind. *She had nipped at his throat.*
Teased him.
Bit him.

Involuntarily, he scraped his teeth against her delicate skin, dragging them back and forth as a deep, guttural sound, somewhere between a snarl and a groan, rose up from his throat. He wanted to drink her blood. He *needed* to drink her blood.

Just one taste.

Marquis fought his primal nature, knowing that Joelle was in mortal danger. She had played with fire: a power far beyond her comprehension or control. She had not intended to provoke his predatory instincts; rather, she had only wanted to be with him...to be loved by him. To know him in every possible way.

Of one thing, Marquis was certain: She had not expected to die at his hands.

Joelle froze. Exactly as he instructed. Not willing to move a muscle. Not even daring to breathe.

Trembling, Marquis wrenched his teeth away, and then he hissed a long, slow warning like a coiled snake. "Do you have *any* idea what I am?"

His dark eyes were burning, undoubtedly glowing like fiery crimson coals, the phantom blue centers now absent of civility. Releasing her wrists, he shoved her back and leapt further away himself.

"Marquis, I'm so sorry!" she cried. Her small frame fell hard on the deck, and she slowly stood back up. "God, you must think I'm a terrible, selfish person."

Marquis lurked almost ten feet away, crouched down like a wild animal, behind the cover of a large fir tree. His head was dropped low to the ground, and wild mounds of thick black hair fell forward, concealing his panic-stricken face. He was fighting the beast within him with all of the strength he had.

The silly woman had absolutely no idea what he was capable of.

Either her father had failed to teach her, or he had not made his true nature clear enough. Either way, she needed to run.

And now.

Slowly, with grace and stealth, he raised his head like a hungry wolf. His lips drew back from his fangs, twitching with barely concealed menace, and his eyes turned cold and vacant.

Using the full power of his voice to control her mind, he gave her an order: "*Go!*"

Joelle Parker ran like a frightened deer off into the night.

She raced down the steep, unpaved road, flew to the end of the lane, slid across a patch of loose gravel, and finally crawled into her car—where she hastily locked the doors.

As if locks would help.

Shaking and crying, she fumbled wildly for her keys. Her dream was shattered. Her heart was breaking. Her world was no longer safe.

thirteen

Jocelyn awoke late the next morning to the smell of breakfast cooking and fresh coffee brewing in the large downstairs kitchen. Making her way from the sofa, where Nathaniel had left her the night before, to the first-floor dining area, she cautiously entered the adjacent room.

"You must be Jocelyn."

A tall, auburn-haired woman with light blue eyes stood over a large industrial stove, bordered by custom stone tiles. She was flipping pancakes and frying bacon, and her genuine smile lit up the room.

"I'm Colette," she said. "It's so nice to meet you."

Jocelyn eyed the unfamiliar woman warily. She looked human, but then how could one tell? "Where is Nathaniel?"

Colette flipped the last pancake onto a warming plate and turned off the gas burner. "Nathaniel was out late last night. He didn't want to wake you when he got in, so he asked if I would be willing to visit with you while he slept. Not to mention, his housekeeper is out running errands this morning, and Nathaniel is a horrible cook."

Jocelyn frowned. "You mean he asked you to *guard* me while he slept…"

Colette met Jocelyn's scrutinizing gaze head-on. "No, I wouldn't consider that statement accurate, really. It's not unusual for…males…like Nathaniel to sleep off and on throughout the day. They have far more energy at night. My sense was that Nathaniel didn't want you to wake up alone in a strange place." She placed two pancakes, a strip of bacon, and some scrambled eggs on a plate and set it on the granite bar behind her. "Here. Have a seat. Eat some breakfast."

Jocelyn reluctantly looked at the plate. She didn't want anything to do with Nathaniel or this new woman, but she had to admit she was starving. She hadn't had a bite to eat since hiking to the Red Canyons the day before.

Colette poured a glass of orange juice into a small ornate glass and set it beside the plate along with a fresh set of silverware, folded neatly in a linen napkin. "Would you care for some coffee as well?" She gestured toward the pot.

Jocelyn nodded and grudgingly took a seat at the bar while Colette poured the coffee and sat down beside her. "Nathaniel also asked me if I would be willing to talk with you." There was a long, drawn-out moment of silence before Colette continued. "He told me about what happened last night. What you saw in the canyon. He felt like you might be more comfortable speaking with a woman, maybe a little more likely to speak your mind."

Jocelyn stared at the confident, welcoming woman like she was a microbe under a microscope: dialing in on every little nuance in order to determine her species and origin. She wore a pair of faded Levi's and a blue cotton shirt. She walked with graceful ease and tactful confidence, like someone who had complete control of the world around her and knew it. She had kind eyes, and there was an obvious sincerity in her smile. Seemed normal enough.

"If you don't mind my asking, who are you anyway?" The words came out a bit harsher than Jocelyn intended, but then she wasn't accustomed to complete strangers speaking to her so intimately. To heck with it. She took a bite of her eggs and waited for an answer.

Colette flashed an apologetic smile. "I'm sorry—how rude of me. My mate, Kristos, grew up with Nathaniel. They attended the University in Europe together. We have been close friends for the last couple of years, ever since…well, let's just say that I was in the exact same position you're in now, not so long ago."

Now this caught Jocelyn's attention. "You're human?"

Colette's light blue eyes turned lighter still, softening beneath the dim, recessed lighting that hung above the bar. She smiled warmly. "I *was* human…like you."

Jocelyn shivered and continued to eat her breakfast. Despite her hesitation to be friendly, the food was delicious, and she was grateful that someone had taken the time to cook for her.

Colette continued speaking. "The truth is, while I don't know you personally, I do have my own understanding of what you're going through." She looked off into the distance. "And I still remember how afraid I was at the time, how many questions I had." She softened. "It's a lot to come to terms with all at once."

The woman had Jocelyn's full attention—how could she not? She sat up, tucked her hair behind her ear, and looked intently into Colette's eyes, studying her for signs of truth. "So, you're saying that you were just like me. You were completely unaware of...vampires...when suddenly, one appeared right out of the blue, scared the living daylights out of you, and then kept insisting that you *belonged* to him?"

She whispered the word *vampires* as if merely saying it out loud could get her locked up in a dungeon somewhere.

Colette nodded and leaned forward. "*Exactly like you.* And I have to tell you, I didn't take it nearly as well as you are right now. Not in the beginning, anyhow. And I already knew Kristos when everything happened."

Jocelyn finished her orange juice, sat back, and considered Colette's words. At least she had a law enforcement background and was no stranger to danger or frightening situations. Something like this must have been hell on someone as soft-natured as Colette. She leaned forward again. "Colette, what would *really* happen if I tried to escape?"

Colette didn't flinch. "You wouldn't be safe, Jocelyn." She lowered her voice. "There are fates far worse than whatever you fear with Nathaniel right now." She frowned and took Jocelyn's hand, rubbing it empathetically. "And the plain truth is—you probably wouldn't get very far. Between Nathaniel, Marquis, Kagen, and the sentinels, you would be back here faster than you could say your name three times." She sighed. "I know it's not what you want to hear, but it is the truth: Escaping is just not an option."

Jocelyn lowered her head and closed her eyes as the reality of her predicament began to sink in all over again.

It just couldn't be true.

This just couldn't be happening.

Only days before, she had been packing for a trip to the valley, safely unaware, at her home in San Diego. Although it wasn't much of one by some people's standards, she had established a comfortable, routine life.

She had her job. Her elderly next-door neighbor, Ida, whom she often looked after. And her beloved aquarium filled with rare, tropical fish…which had taken her years to acquire.

Oh God, she thought, *my fish are all going to die if I don't get back at the end of the week.*

It seemed an utterly crazy thing to think about, all other things considered, but the point was: She had been a normal person with a normal life, and now her entire world was about to change, and she was helpless to stop it. The sheer enormity of the situation threatened to overwhelm her.

"Jocelyn…" Colette's voice was compassionate.

Jocelyn looked up.

"Right now, this feels like your worst nightmare. Believe me…I know. But I wouldn't be surprised if you look back one day and see this as the best thing that ever happened to you." She patted her on the shoulder. "Here, let me get you another cup of coffee."

Colette rose from the sturdy knotted-pine bar stool, an exact match to the custom kitchen cabinets, and poured Jocelyn a second cup of coffee before returning to the breakfast bar, carrying a small tray with cream and sugar on it.

Jocelyn sighed and shook her head in frustration. "I don't think so, Colette." She frowned. "Look, I get that you love your husband. And you obviously think a lot of Nathaniel, or you wouldn't be doing this, but you don't know anything about me."

Colette ran her hand through her hair, the soft, medium-length tresses bouncing back and forth in response to the motion. "I don't have to know *you*, Jocelyn. I know the Omen, and I know what it means." She paused, as if searching for the right words. "Jocelyn, you are Nathaniel's *destiny*—just as he is yours. That means that fate decreed this long before you were born. And whether it happened now, a year from now, or ten years from now, your heart would've searched for his forever." There was deep conviction in her voice. "Vampire or not, his soul completes yours."

Jocelyn frowned and turned away. "How romantic," she smirked. Somehow, she just wasn't getting into the whole fairy-tale thing.

Colette was not deterred. "Now then," she said in an upbeat voice, "whether you agree or disagree with what I'm telling you, you should still take advantage of this chance to ask some questions, because you probably won't get another one before—" Her voice abruptly broke off.

"Before what?" Jocelyn asked.

Colette smiled warmly. "Before you and Nathaniel come together."

Jocelyn winced, feeling suddenly light-headed. She added a spoonful of sugar to her coffee, took a sip, and looked away as she collected her thoughts. She was a detective and a darn good one. Someone with reliable instincts and inborn intuition. Colette was absolutely right about one thing: The more information she had, the better.

She sighed and tried to distance herself from the situation. Setting her coffee mug down on the counter, she turned to face Colette squarely. "What *exactly* are these creatures?" she asked, sounding more courageous than she felt.

Colette smiled. "They are...*we are*...precisely what Nathaniel told you."

Jocelyn rested her elbows on the counter. "Then tell me more about *vampires*—because I'm still not sure if Nathaniel is a monster, a man, or something between. I just know that he has way too much power."

Colette folded her hands in her lap. "Not a monster—of that much, you can be certain. But not a man, either, at least not as you've come to know men. Nathaniel is a *male* who possesses both light *and* shadow. He's capable of amazing good, but..." She let out a deep breath. "He's also capable of dealing out harsh retribution and violence when necessary: The sons of Jadon are always trying to balance the two energies." She leaned forward. "In *my* opinion, the hearts of the Light Ones are good—very good—but their natures are wild."

"Light Ones?" Jocelyn asked. "Sons of Jadon?"

"Yes..." Colette's smile was infinitely patient. "There are two kinds of vampires, Jocelyn, and they both descended from a very powerful line of magical beings—human, but more. The Light Ones are the descendants of Jadon—" There was a sudden catch in her voice. "And I believe you had the misfortune of seeing one of the Dark Ones last night, a descendant of Jaegar."

Jocelyn shuddered. "The creature in the chamber. Nathaniel told you about that?"

Colette nodded. "He wanted us to speak freely." She absently brushed a few grains of sugar off the counter into her open palm and dumped them onto the tray. "The vampire you saw was Valentine Nistor." She cringed then. "Trust me, there's nothing good in one like him. He is definitely a monster."

Jocelyn nodded. There was no argument there. "What he did to that poor woman..." She held her hands over her stomach. "Why did that baby claw its way out of her body like that? She seemed so human."

Colette rubbed her arms like she was suddenly cold. "I've never actually seen the ritual of the Dark Ones. In fact, I think you're the first one who ever has...so maybe Nathaniel would be the better person to ask." She sighed. "But what I do know is this: The Dark Ones are more like reptiles than humans; they genetically reproduce their own offspring. In other words, they don't require women to *create* life; they just use them as *hosts* to support it."

"Hosts?" Jocelyn blanched. "You mean like an incubator?"

Colette nodded. "Exactly—just a warm place for the child to grow." She shifted restlessly in her seat. "From what I hear, they treat the host environment like a shell…they hatch…like out of an egg." She shuddered. "Blessed Mother, that must have been a horrific thing to witness."

Jocelyn didn't reply: There were no words, and Colette seemed to understand. A morbid silence hovered between them for what seemed like an eternity before Jocelyn finally spoke again. "So, tell me how you met Kristos." She needed to stay focused.

Colette sighed. "When I met Kristos, I was in Dark Moon Vale on a river rafting trip, and he was our guide." Her eyes lit up like sparklers. "I'm not gonna lie—I thought he was the sexiest thing I'd ever seen, and honestly, I still do." She looked away and blushed.

Jocelyn thought about Nathaniel then: his stunning features and his rock-hard body. "Yeah, they're definitely…gorgeous." The admission irritated her. "But then, that's hardly the point."

"True." Colette nodded, losing the nostalgia. She flashed a knowing smile and went back to her story. "On the last night of our trip, we stayed up late talking around the campfire. It was already a beautiful night, so you can imagine how stunned I was when I saw the sky change like that."

"Like last night?" Jocelyn asked.

"Exactly…the black sky, the blood moon…everything. Only Kristos's constellation is Lacerta."

Colette held out her wrist, and Jocelyn leaned forward to study the odd pattern of zigzag lines and mystical markings, all formed in the shape of a lizard. She looked down at her own wrist then, studying it closely for the first time. "What do the markings mean?"

Colette reached out and ran her finger over Jocelyn's arm. "They mean that out of hundreds of years and millions of people, *you* were the one chosen for Nathaniel." She leaned forward. "You know, the hardest thing for me was coming to understand that one simple point: the divinity of it all. Understanding that *Kristos* had not chosen my fate any more than I had chosen his. It just was. And since he didn't make it happen, he couldn't make it un-happen." She rested her elbows on the bar. "If I can give you one piece of advice, Jocelyn, something to make it easier, it would be this: Don't blame Nathaniel for what's happening to you. He didn't create the circumstances any more than you did. And the truth of the matter is, it's happening to him, too. And he's probably just as scared...although he would never show it."

Jocelyn sat back in her chair, carefully considering Colette's words. Somewhere deep inside of her, she felt the truth of them. Somewhere even deeper, she felt *Nathaniel* as if he were already a part of her. The power of those dark, sultry eyes, the fierceness of his passion when he looked at her, the flames that burned just beneath the surface of his touch. But it was all just...too much.

Overwhelming.

"What if I don't want it, Colette?" she whispered. "What if I don't want *him*?"

Colette shook her head reassuringly. "But you will, Jocelyn." She looked her deep in the eyes. "I know this sounds absurd to you now, but those marks on your wrist say more than I could ever say. Look, can you imagine a fish asking, *What if I don't like water?* Or a bird saying, *What if I don't want to fly?*"

Jocelyn frowned.

"You see my point, don't you?" Colette gently turned Jocelyn's wrist over and pointed to Cassiopeia. "You don't have to wonder...or try...to be *who you are*, Jocelyn. How could you possibly be anything else?"

Jocelyn took a deep breath. "Maybe, Colette—*maybe*—but I still need to know..." She forced herself to say the words: "What will happen to me?—what will happen to him?—*if I don't want it?* Tell me the truth, Colette; *what if I refuse?*"

Colette got up from her bar stool, stretched her legs, and motioned toward a small eating nook in the far corner of the kitchen. There were soft, earth-toned pillows propped up against the wall above an elegant cushioned bench, all tucked neatly beneath a large bay window. The views from the nook were of the eastern cliffs, and the breathtaking scenery spanned as far as the eye could see.

Jocelyn was glad to get up. She followed Colette to the large picturesque window and curled up in the corner, staring idly down at the steep drop below.

Once they had both settled in, Colette led with a question: "Did you ever study the ancient Aztec civilization?"

Jocelyn shrugged. "Yeah, I guess so. Why?"

Colette sighed. "Then you remember how obsessed their culture was with blood sacrifices, right?"

"Yes," Jocelyn answered. She wasn't sure she liked where this was going.

Colette took a deep, calming breath. "Well, a very long time ago, Kristos's and Nathaniel's ancestors did a very similar thing—they started sacrificing their females as an offering to the gods. I guess they wanted more power...more magic."

"More than they already had?" Jocelyn asked, incredulous.

"Apparently so," Colette replied. "At first, it started with the newborns, and then it progressed to the older girls—you know, the virgins—until after a while, there wasn't a single female left."

"Well, that was brilliant," Jocelyn quipped.

"Positively," Colette agreed.

Jocelyn sat forward then, encouraging Colette to continue.

Colette looked out the window and sighed. "Well, at the time, the ruler of their people had two twin sons, Jadon and Jaegar. The legend tells that Jadon tried to stop the sacrifices, but Jaegar had become mad with bloodlust, and he refused to give in to his brother's pleas. Eventually, both men were severely punished, cursed by the blood of the dead—"

"The...*blood*...of the dead?" Jocelyn raised an eyebrow.

Colette nodded. "That's how they became vampires—cursed with their own bloodlust—forced to feed on blood to survive."

Jocelyn sighed. "This is so not real." She forced herself to focus. "Go on…"

Colette patted her hand. "It was the Curse that stripped them of their ability to produce female children. And it was also the Curse that demanded a perpetual atonement for their sins: the repeated offering of a son as atonement for a daughter."

Jocelyn put her hand to her chest; she was beginning to feel queasy. Something deep in her gut told her to stop the woman from speaking, stop her before she went too far. Jocelyn knew that her own fate lay somewhere at the end of this road, and it was like racing forward at a hundred miles per hour through a dark tunnel—a horrible collision awaited at the end.

"Jocelyn?"

She heard Colette calling her name as if from a distance.

"Are you still with me?"

Jocelyn caught a sudden chill and looked back at Colette. "Yeah, I'm with you. So, how does the…sacrifice…work?" She almost choked on the word.

Colette didn't veer from the path. "A vampire's children are always born in sets of twins," she explained. "Two boys at a time. And out of the first set, one must be…handed over…to the ancient spirits. For the sons of Jaegar, it's the firstborn. For the sons of Jadon, it's the Dark One."

Jocelyn shook her head in disbelief and rubbed her temples. "I don't understand," she whispered.

Colette sighed and her eyebrows creased in concentration. "The Dark Ones…like Valentine," she began, "they're the descendants of Jaegar, and their twin sons are both born purely evil, everything you ever feared a vampire to be…and then some. But Kristos and Nathaniel are the descendants of Jadon, and parts of the curse were lifted for them. They also have twins, just like the Dark Ones, but only one of the infants is cursed…evil. The other is of the light."

Jocelyn rested her forehead in her hands; they were racing through the tunnel at warp speed now, and the collision was approaching fast. Bracing herself, she chose to get it over with: "What exactly are you saying, Colette? Please, just cut to the chase."

Colette remained steady as always. She looked Jocelyn directly in the eyes, refusing to blink. "The Blood Moon signals the beginning of the Omen, Jocelyn—the start of the required sacrifice. It only happens when one of the descendants of Jadon has found *his destiny*, the woman he's meant to fulfill the Curse with. Before the Blood Moon has passed, she will give him twin sons, one born of light, the other of darkness. And the Dark One must be sacrificed."

And there it was—a five-car pileup—shrapnel flying everywhere.

Jocelyn recoiled, too repulsed to speak. It took a moment for Colette's words to fully sink in, but once they did, she had heard more than enough.

She leapt from her seat, beads of sweat beginning to form in the alcove between her breasts, her shoulders and arms visibly shaking, as something between disbelief and panic began to take her over.

"Then it is the same!" she yelled. "You lied to me! And so did he!"

Colette looked shocked.

"He wants me to *breed* him a sacrifice. Just like that...thing...in the cave! Exactly like that monster!" She was hysterical now, her voice betraying her panic.

Colette shook her head adamantly. She jumped up, braced Jocelyn by the shoulders, and shook her gently. "Calm down, Jocelyn. If you don't stop screaming, you're going to wake Nathaniel, and then you'll be having this conversation with him instead of me. Is that what you want?"

The look in the woman's eyes told Jocelyn that Colette was far more afraid of having to face Nathaniel herself than having Jocelyn awaken him.

Colette lowered her voice and loosened her grip on Jocelyn's shoulders. "You are so wrong, Jocelyn. I did not explain this very well, and that's my fault. I apologize. But trust me; Nathaniel doesn't want you...*to breed*. He wants you because he's already lived an eternity alone. He wants you because in all of his centuries of walking the earth, he's never had anything or anyone to call his own. He wants you because you are *his destiny*...his partner...the other half of his soul. And yes, you can give him what no one else in the universe ever can or will: a son to *love*, a family to cherish, and a future worth living. He wants you to *love*. *And he needs you to live.*" Colette's voice was thick with conviction.

Jocelyn gulped. "What do you mean, *he needs you to live?*"

Colette sighed, looking suddenly morose. "Jocelyn, Nathaniel has thirty days from the night he saw the Blood Moon to hand over the dark child, or he'll be destroyed and no one can stop it or save him. *And believe me; his death will make what Dalia went through look like a walk in the park.* It's the Blood Curse. Their legacy. *Our legacy.* It can't be changed."

Jocelyn's chest constricted and her heart ached. All of a sudden, she couldn't catch her breath. "Is that what happened to Nathaniel's brother?" she asked, her mind beginning to connect the dots. "He said he was burying his brother yesterday...and that woman in the chamber...she was his brother's wife..." Understanding dawned in her heart like the sun rising over the horizon. "Oh, God."

She sank back down into the seat cushion, the weight on her chest unbearable. "*Oh, God.*"

"Jocelyn? Are you okay?" Colette asked.

Jocelyn's head was spinning. And she was certain she was going to faint: a rare, if not completely unheard of, occurrence for her. It was simply all too much to take in at once. She was expected to have a child with a man she didn't know. *A vampire.* No, two children! And to *sacrifice* one of them, just turn him over to be taken by that evil...mist...she had seen in the cavern. That aberration. And what was all this business about thirty days?

"Thirtydays!" she exclaimed, as the words finally reached her brain. "That's impossible! Even if I were crazy enough to...no one can have a child in thirty days."

Colette bit her bottom lip; this time, she remained silent.

"What now?" Jocelyn demanded.

Colette shook her head.

"Don't you dare!" Jocelyn shrieked. "You've already told me this much, now tell me the rest!"

"It would be better if Nathaniel—"

"Nathaniel's not a woman!" Jocelyn shouted. She was beginning to lose control, her voice ripe with anger. "*Nathaniel* doesn't have to give birth to anything! Colette, what aren't you telling me?"

Colette grabbed Jocelyn by her forearms this time, pleading with her eyes. "Please calm down, Jocelyn." She looked around nervously. "Nathaniel's going to be *so* angry with me."

"To hell with him!"

"Jocelyn." Colette spoke with a deliberately soothing voice, the kind one might use to comfort a cornered animal. "*Calm down.* You're worrying about the wrong things. Trust me; you don't have to *give birth* to anything. In fact, of all the things you need to come to grips with, that isn't one of them. That part is easy."

"*Easy?*" Jocelyn was incredulous.

Colette sighed. "When you decide...*if you decide*...to have children *with* Nathaniel, the entire process will only take forty-eight hours."

Jocelyn was beyond dazed now; she was positively stupefied. And she fully expected someone to wake her up any moment from the bizarre, fantastical dream she was having. She covered her stomach in an unconscious gesture of protection. "How is that possible?" She stammered the words, terror beginning to take a real grip on her mind.

"Sit down, Jocelyn," Colette ordered, her own face visibly pale.

Jocelyn sat.

"First of all, *yes*, from the time you decide to have the children, the entire process takes forty-eight hours, but it is *not* a scary or painful event. Nathaniel will put you in a dreamlike state, almost as if you're sleeping, so you won't feel any of the rapid changes in your body. You will not be frightened or overwhelmed—"

BLOOD DESTINY

Jocelyn held up her hand in a *stop* gesture.

That was enough.

She could hear no more.

All at once, Colette became stern and persistent. "In terms of giving birth, *you won't*. It's that simple." Her voice was firm. "You have seen his power, Jocelyn. You know what he can do—what his kind can do. Among other things, they can dissolve their physical forms, walk through walls, pass through solid objects—that kind of thing. When the time comes, Nathaniel will *call* your children from you. You won't give birth to your sons, Jocelyn; they will simply dematerialize and pass through the womb when they're summoned by their father. You won't even feel it."

Jocelyn stared up at her like a wide-eyed child listening to an adult weave a fanciful tale about magical creatures and things that go bump in the night. She turned her head to the side and just let the words wash over her like a river of absurdity, gently flowing in one ear…and right back out the other…as they made their way back into the ever expanding land of make-believe, taking all common sense and adult reasoning with them.

She looked around the room, waiting for someone in a sterile white uniform to enter through a back door and haul her off, but not before giving her a heavy injection of some kind of sedative. She pinched herself to make sure she was actually awake: Yes, she was still conscious—she could definitely use a sedative.

"Jocelyn…" Colette whispered, her eyes soft with compassion.

Jocelyn blinked as if all at once re-emerging in the room. "I'm *human*, Colette: a different species. How can I have a child with…one of them?"

Colette gently shook her head. "That's enough for one day, Jocelyn. I think—"

"That's right," Jocelyn went on, "you're not human anymore, are you?"

Colette looked away.

"Are you?"

"No."

"Did you...change...before or after you had Kristos's children?"

Colette closed her eyes. "Before." The word was a mere whisper.

Jocelyn sank back in the seat. "Nathaniel has to make me like he is, then?"

"It's the only way," Colette confirmed.

Jocelyn laughed then, almost hysterically. "Oh my God, he's going to turn me into a vampire." She wiped a tear from her eye and gripped her sides, trying to contain her sudden amusement. "Okay, let's see if I have this straight: By the end of the bloody moon, I'm going to dream my way through a two-day pregnancy, and then Nathaniel's going to call our unborn children... How? On the cell phone?" She cackled like a hyena. "Hey—I know—maybe he could just text them with a BlackBerry." Her voice was rising along with her hysterical laughter. "And all of this so we can pay back a bunch of dead, pissed-off women before we fly off into the sunset as unholy, blood-sucking creatures of the night—complete with fangs and a bushel of undead children. Have I got that right, Colette?" She slumped over on the bench, clasped her hands over her stomach, and laughed until her sides hurt.

Colette frowned. "Not a bushel of undead children, Jocelyn. Beautiful, perfect, wonderful children, if you want them. Children who won't ever get sick or die. Children who will love and honor you probably more than your human children would have...certainly longer...since you will also be immortal. And yes, you will have to go through a short pregnancy and a completely painless childbirth.

"And when it's all said and done, you will have *saved the life* of an incredible male, one who would willingly die for you. One who will never lie to you or cheat on you. One who will love your children with all of his heart, live for your happiness, and probably save you right back. Yeah, I'd say that's pretty hysterical."

Jocelyn watched as Colette sat back down on the bench beside her. She appeared more frustrated than angry as they both stared out the window in silence. After some time had passed, she spoke again: "Tell me, Jocelyn…do I look like an unholy, blood-sucking creature of the night to you?"

Jocelyn froze then. Uncertain. And a little ashamed.

Colette turned away and walked over to a small built-in row of shelves just outside of a compact butler's pantry. She picked up a delicate, beautifully framed oil on panel painting and brought it back to the nook.

"This is Keitaro and Serena Silivasi with their five children," she said, handing the painting to Jocelyn. "Nathaniel's parents…his family. It was done almost four hundred and eighty years ago." She pointed to a tall, handsome young man with a brilliant smile and eyes that lit up the canvas; he was standing on the far left side of the painting. "And this is Shelby Silivasi, Nathaniel's youngest brother. The one who was buried yesterday." She took a deep, steadying breath. "Shelby was the kindest person I've ever met—human or vampire. He taught snowboarding at the ski resort, and during his time off, he gave private lessons to kids with disabilities. I don't think I ever saw Shelby without a smile on his face or a kind word on his tongue." She sighed then. "And he had all of eternity ahead of him…." She paused. "Just hold onto this, Jocelyn. Look at it for a while. Decide for yourself if these people are monsters."

Jocelyn sat up straight, feeling horrible for losing it like she had. "Colette, I'm sorry; I never meant to imply that—"

Colette waved her hand and reached to smooth a loose strand of Jocelyn's hair before resting her palm on her trembling shoulder. "Jocelyn, it's okay to be afraid. And angry. And a whole bunch of other things. Just know that this is not a game to Nathaniel…or his family. And you are definitely not just some object to breed with."

Jocelyn felt the full weight of Colette's words as she looked down, once again, at the picture. "They all look the same age."

Colette smiled. "Immortality has a way of doing that. The two on the right are Keitaro and Serena."

The couple was stunning. The man had a thick head of black hair just like Nathaniel's, and the beautiful woman had elegant features and graceful arms and legs. Jocelyn tapped the painting. "I recognize Marquis and Nathaniel…and now Shelby…but who are these other two?"

Colette looked over her shoulder and pointed as she spoke. "This one, right next to Shelby, is Nachari. He and Shelby are twins. And the man standing to the left of Nathaniel is his twin, Kagen."

Jocelyn studied the painting in great detail. "Why doesn't Marquis have a twin?"

Colette's eyes softened. "Shelby and Nachari are the youngest, born last. And Nathaniel and Kagen were born in the middle. But Marquis was one of the first born."

Jocelyn still didn't understand. "I don't get it."

"Marquis's twin was the…Dark One…the one they had to let go."

Jocelyn looked up and grimaced. "Oh." She wondered if Marquis might be darker than the other brothers as a result of having such a twin. "And it's this way with all the families?" she asked. "All the vampires?"

"All the lighter ones," Colette answered. "The descendants of Jadon," she clarified.

"How many children do you and Kristos have?" Jocelyn asked, trying to be polite: Regardless of what she thought about Nathaniel and her own situation, Colette didn't owe her anything. And she had made a genuine effort to answer all of her questions…as honestly as possible.

"Just the one," Colette answered. "He's at the academy now."

Jocelyn didn't ask.

She had taken in more than enough information for one day, and her mind was on overload. She could think about all of it later—worry, analyze, and process things another time.

BLOOD DESTINY

She knew her choices were not going to be as cut and dried as she had first thought. She had never held another person's life in her hands before, at least not like this. It was one thing to stare down a criminal at the other end of a gun, when his or her own actions ultimately controlled the outcome. But this was completely different, the kind of thing that would make for great debate in a college ethics class.

And Colette was right.

There was something elemental between her and Nathaniel. She could already feel it. Sense it. And it terrified her to think she was going to have to confront it at some point.

"Colette?" She had one more question.

As always, Colette sounded infinitely patient. "Yes?"

"If I don't choose to be with Nathaniel, if…when it's all said and done, I just can't…will Nathaniel *force* me?"

Colette hesitated, clearly giving the question thought. "I don't know what Nathaniel is or is not prepared to do, Jocelyn. Just as I don't know what influence Marquis or Napolean…or any number of others might have on him, assuming it comes down to that. But I do know that he would never hurt you in the way that you're thinking. Whether or not he would use coercion, or mind control…or some other form of seduction, I really don't know. It's hard to say what one will do when their life is on the line. Hopefully, for both of your sakes, it won't come to that."

Jocelyn wasn't sure whether or not that was the answer she was looking for, but like everything else Colette said, it was honest.

She ran her fingers reverently along the edges of the oil painting. It was almost as if she already knew the people captured so beautifully within its borders. Of one thing she was quite certain: The face of the young man with the gleaming smile—Shelby Silivasi—was going to haunt her long after Colette was gone.

Despite all of her mounting fear, her revulsion and desperation, she could hardly bear the thought of what happened to Shelby happening to Nathaniel. The mere possibility turned her stomach.

When Nathaniel entered the kitchen, Jocelyn was still sitting in the breakfast nook, her knees tucked tightly against her chest, her arms wrapped firmly around her legs, her eyes fixed on the panoramic view from the window.

"You okay?" Nathaniel asked, stopping in the doorway. His large frame took up the entire space.

Jocelyn looked over her shoulder and spared him a glance. "What do you think?"

Nathaniel sighed. "What can I do?"

Jocelyn chuckled, although there wasn't any joy in her laughter. "I don't suppose you could just let me go—maybe call me in twenty years?"

Nathaniel smiled and took a tentative step forward. "You know I cannot."

Jocelyn frowned and leaned toward the window.

"Do you really think any of this would be easier in twenty years?" he asked.

Jocelyn tightened the grip around her legs and shrugged. "Probably not, but at least I wouldn't have to deal with it now."

Nathaniel knew better than to respond. After all, what could he possibly say? The woman had been thrown abruptly into a foreign world, and what was being asked of her was more than most beings, human or vampire, could absorb in such a short time. *Gods, he wanted to go to her and hold her.* Show her who he was. Make her see that their destiny together was nothing to fear. But how could he convince her when he wasn't sure himself?

"What does it feel like?" she asked out of the blue.

"Excuse me?" Nathaniel leaned back against the wall and crossed his arms in front of him; he was careful to remain a safe distance from the table, not wanting to come too close.

She turned to look at him then, her beautiful eyes unbearably sad. "Being you. How does it feel to have that much power over another human being?" She laughed again, that same insincere sound. "I mean, you're faster than me, stronger than me, and from what I can tell, completely capable of controlling me if you want to. So, I was just wondering how it felt...to be you?"

Nathaniel frowned and rubbed his jaw, trying not to let her words upset him. "I may be all of those things, love, yet it is you who holds my life in your hands. It is you who will determine whether or not I ever have a family...live the life I've only dreamed of. It is you I have waited on for a thousand years." His voice trailed off as the reality of his words sunk in. "From where I stand, *draga mea*, you are holding all the cards."

Jocelyn turned around to face him squarely; she seemed surprised by his words. "*Draga mea?*"

"My darling."

"Oh," she said, making fleeting eye contact. She rubbed her hands together nervously and started to say something else—a protest, perhaps—but then, apparently, she thought better of it. Her eyes swept over the small oil-on-panel painting lying on the table beside her. "I really am sorry about your brother," she said sincerely. "Losing family must be hard."

Nathaniel nodded. "Thank you. It is...*very hard*. You've never lost anyone?"

Jocelyn studied her hands. "Nope. Never had anyone to lose."

Nathaniel shut his eyes. *Gods, if she would only let him go to her. Hold her. Touch her.* His groin hardened, and he felt like a beast for reacting so primitively. He sighed. "You do now, Jocelyn. Have someone, that is."

Her look was one of both trepidation and confusion—fear and uncertainty. "You know as well as I do that it's not that simple. You can't just waltz into my life...or my heart...regardless of some ancient curse. And you can't possibly pretend to care for me when we've only just met."

Nathaniel could no longer stay away.

Moving silently, he glided to the nook, knelt down in front of her, and reached out to take her hands in his. She started to pull away but hesitated—as if she knew it was futile. And, of course, it was. Bringing her slim fingers softly to his mouth, he kissed the back of her hands, each one in turn. "You might not believe this, Jocelyn, but I do care…more than you know. And if I could take this burden from you, I would."

Her eyes met his with skepticism. "If you could let me go, you would?"

Nathaniel shook his head. "You misunderstand me." He caressed the center of her palms with his thumbs. "If I could take away your fear, your uncertainty, the difficulty of this situation, I would. But you are my *destiny*, whether you know it or not; how could I ever let you go?"

Jocelyn just stared at him then, her beautiful hazel eyes softening despite her discomfort. "God, you almost sound like you mean that."

He released her hand and softly traced the line of her jaw with his fingers before lightly cupping her cheek. She was so incredibly beautiful—and stronger than he could have ever imagined—this woman warrior so perfectly made just for him. Though his heart ached to see her discomfort, he couldn't help but thank the goddess for finally bringing her home. "Do you know what I want more than anything, angel?"

Her lips began to tremble ever so slightly, and he removed his hand from her face. "What?"

"To make you unbearably happy one day: to take all the sadness from your eyes and spend the rest of my life earning your trust."

Jocelyn's eyes grew wide, and she quickly turned away, staring once again out at the endless canyons.

Nathaniel slid into the booth behind her then and carefully slipped his arms around her waist. He braced himself for her rigid response, half expecting her to physically push him away, but when she simply froze, like an uncertain deer, he poured as much warmth and reassurance into his touch as he could. And then gently—oh so carefully—he rested his chin against her silky hair and simply stared out the window with her, allowing the silence to embrace them both.

After a pregnant moment, her tension began to ease, and to his surprise, she leaned back against him. It was hardly a full embrace, a far cry from a glowing endorsement, but he would take it.

When her hand came up to absently rest on his forearm, Nathaniel shut his eyes and held his breath.

He didn't dare challenge the moment with words.

fourteen

Jocelyn sat dutifully on the sleek, modern-lined black sofa in the formal downstairs living room, Nathaniel leaning into her possessively, while he, Marquis, and Kagen waited anxiously to get their first look at Nachari. Alejandra, Nathaniel's housekeeper, had just gone to the door to greet him.

Jocelyn smoothed out the material on her swirly sage-green skirt, watching as the cotton voile ruffles tumbled playfully down her legs. The matching, exotic V-neck top, with its three-quarter bell sleeves and soft, flowing lines, hugged her feminine curves as if it had been tailor-made just for her. It was one of a dozen outfits Nathaniel had purchased in the trendy, high-end catalogue Alejandra had dropped off for him earlier that morning, requesting special, same-day delivery so that Jocelyn would have a variety of her own clothes to wear.

The morning had passed in a companionable silence despite the intensity of the situation, the overwhelming repercussions of what was happening between them, what the "celestial gods" had decreed.

Knowing she had already checked out of the local bed-and-breakfast the morning she hiked to the canyons, Nathaniel had simply made a few calls, had her rental car returned, and *strongly encouraged her*—in his not-so-subtle way—to alert her boss that she would be staying for an extended time in Dark Moon Vale. Just like that, she had become his captive. Locked away in a hidden valley deep within the Rocky Mountains, with a man whose desire to hold her grew stronger by the hour.

She had given him her word that she would not try to escape. That there would be no attempts at suicide. And that she would remain at his side as he welcomed Shelby's twin, his youngest brother, Nachari, into his home. Nathaniel had explained that Nachari was back from the Ancient Romanian

University of his people. Originally held in the very castle King Sakarias had lived in, the huge house of learning had become a secret campus in the Transylvanian Alps of Europe, an historic monument where the descendants of Jadon spent their second through fifth centuries learning the ancient arts, histories, and laws of their people.

It was at the University that they perfected their skills with weapons, honed their psychic powers, and learned how to manipulate the physical laws of nature, ultimately choosing to master one of the Four Disciplines in their senior year. Both Nathaniel and Marquis had chosen the most common path of mastery—that of the Warrior—while Kagen had gone the path of Healer, but Nachari's choice to become a Master Wizard had surprised them all. And they had no idea what to expect when they saw him again.

Nachari strode into the spacious receiving room, boasting its modern pieces of furniture, original works of art, and high, vaulted ceilings made of massive log beams and arched alcoves, with all the power and stealth of a jaguar—his overwhelming confidence, if not subtle arrogance, immediately apparent. There was a regal quality to Nachari Silivasi, an air of dignity and purpose that clung to him like a cloud of mist in a rain forest. He walked like a prince, with his broad shoulders pulled back and his head held high. And there was something else, too. Something radiating in his unfathomably beautiful eyes, deep forest green with golden irises, an awareness of dark mysteries, a promise of hidden secrets, a quiet but complete command of the world around him.

Nachari swept his perfectly manicured raven-black hair out of his face and turned to greet his brothers, the eldest first. "It is with great respect that I greet a fellow descendant of Jadon, an Ancient Master Warrior, my eldest and most honored brother, Marquis." He placed both hands on Marquis's broad shoulders and stared respectfully into his eyes.

Jocelyn was certain that this was the first time she had ever seen Marquis truly smile with abandon, and his face lit up the room, his smile beguiling enough to stop a woman's heart. "I greet you, my brother, fellow descendant of Jadon and Master Wizard." The words almost caught in his throat, his pride so apparent. He gripped Nachari's shoulders, and the two stared at each other for a long time before they embraced fully.

Jocelyn was surprised by the obvious warmth between them.

He greeted Nathaniel next with the same formality, using all of his titles and expressing his admiration. Nathaniel responded in kind and waited patiently while Nachari and Kagen completed the same ritual of welcome. Once all of the greetings were exchanged, Nathaniel gestured toward Jocelyn.

"Nachari, I would like you to meet *my destiny*." He reached for her arm and gently turned over her wrist, revealing the odd conglomeration of spheres and lines that marked her as his. "A daughter of Cassiopeia, Jocelyn Levi."

Nachari looked suddenly surprised—as if he hadn't heard the news, but then he flashed the most breathtaking smile Jocelyn had ever seen. "Greetings, sister." He said it humbly. "It is an honor to meet you."

Jocelyn was spellbound. She tried to return the smile and say her own hello, but her words came out as no more than a series of muttered sounds. Embarrassed, she looked away.

Nathaniel snapped his head to the side, glanced down, and eyed her suspiciously, snarling a soft, almost inaudible growl of warning.

She looked up at him, amazed: Nathaniel was a breathing reincarnation of an ancient Greek god. Only taller, darker, and *far* more handsome. Surely, he wasn't jealous of his little brother. To her surprise, the thought made her smile.

Nathaniel sat back down, took her hand possessively in his own, and leaned back against the thick cushions of the sofa, while Nachari casually sank into a large black armchair directly across from the two of them, his feet going instinctively up onto the matching ottoman.

Nathaniel's eyes lit up. "So tell us, Nachari, how long will you be staying?"

Nachari leaned forward, his green eyes suddenly becoming a rich, dark emerald. "I think that will depend on what is happening." He paused, scrutinizing Jocelyn as if wondering how much he could say in front of her. Apparently, deciding that she was family, he spoke candidly. "I talked with Kagen this morning; he informed me of your little...family reunion with the Nistor brothers last night." He cleared his throat, uncomfortably. "Of what happened with Dalia."

His eyebrows creased and his mouth curved down in a deep frown. The golden irises of his enchanting eyes suddenly flashed a feral red before returning back to their haunting jade, like waves in a pond becoming still again after a subtle disturbance. His anger was so peacefully contained, yet so clearly intense, that it took Jocelyn's breath away, sending a stark, uneasy feeling deep into her gut.

"I intend to pay my respects to my twin—" His voice broke off, and he had to take a moment to collect himself before continuing. "To visit the burial grounds and speak with our Sovereign before I return to the University, but I will stay as long as I'm needed." He eyed each of his brothers carefully. "I can tell you this much; I will not leave Dark Moon Vale until Valentine Nistor no longer walks this earth."

Marquis stirred in his seat and brought his hands together, fingertips touching in the shape of a temple, as he contemplated Nachari's words. "I, too, have made a choice that these crimes will not remain unpunished. Perhaps we can speak with Napolean together."

Kagen nodded in agreement and then turned to Marquis. "With or without Napolean's permission, it is our right to seek vengeance. I do not intend to wait around while the Nistors head south for the winter with the birds."

Kagen Silivasi was the only one of the handsome brothers whose luxurious hair was clearly a deep, dark brown as opposed to raven black. His eyes were also a stunning, rich, dark chocolate, and they sparkled with a reflection of silver light like the surface of a crystal lake beneath the moonlight.

Tessa Dawn

Nathaniel tightened his hold on Jocelyn's hand. "Then we're all in agreement."

The brothers all nodded, but before they could begin to talk in earnest, a loud clanging noise resounded from the front entrance, and a strange rustling sound reverberated in the doorway.

Marquis sprang to his feet, but Nachari held out his hand and motioned for him to sit back down. Shaking his head slowly from side to side, Nachari closed his eyes, took a deep breath, and sighed—"Oh yeah, there's someone I want you guys to meet." He rolled his stunning eyes.

All heads, including Jocelyn's, were turned toward the entryway hall, awaiting the newcomer to round the corner. It seemed to take forever for the guest to walk a mere ten feet, as a series of loud thumping noises, followed by an immediate swishing sound and then another loud thump, announced his impending presence.

It wasn't clear whether Marquis actually gasped or snarled when the young visitor finally turned the corner, but the room fell silent as everyone stared, dumbfounded, at the spectacle before them.

The young boy appeared to be about fourteen or fifteen years old, and he was dressed like a character from an old Count Dracula movie: complete with the long, flowing cape, the high, stiffened collar, and a silky white shirt tucked neatly into a pair of soft black trousers. Only, it wasn't entirely clear if he was actually trying to dress the role of vampire or magician…perhaps a confused medieval gentleman who had lost his top hat.

As if the clothes themselves were not enough to draw unnecessary attention to the kid, his beautiful tan skin was painted a ghastly white with some kind of makeup, and his eyes were tinted to appear bloodshot and demonic. His right arm was normal, appearing like the limb of a human, but on his left side, there was a contorted black wing, like that of a vampire bat, dragging heavily behind him. Thump. He took a step with his foot. Swish. He dragged the heavy wing behind him. Thump. He took another step…

Exasperated, the young man dropped his duffle bag and stepped…dragged…stepped himself into the living room. "What's up!" he said, smiling at everyone, while offering an especially pained look of apology to Nachari.

Kagen grunted, unsure how to respond.

Nathaniel simply stared, his eyes open wide in disbelief.

Nachari grimaced, looking down at the ground.

And Jocelyn, despite all of her uneasiness with the situation, had to fight to stifle a laugh.

It was Marquis who finally spoke…in disgust. *"What the hell is that?* And why in the world would you bring it home with you?"* His gaze shifted immediately to Nachari, his lips turned down in a frown.

Nachari smiled ruefully and gestured toward the young boy. "Jocelyn, brothers, I'd like you to meet Braden Bratianu, the son of Dario and Lily Bratianu."

No one said hello, so Braden waved his one good arm enthusiastically. "Hey, everyone. How's it goin'?"

Marquis snarled a low, drawn-out growl and then all at once snapped at the boy. His teeth came together in a sharp clash of menace, a feral hiss lingering in the air, even as his blue-black eyes began to shift toward red.

Braden jumped back, so startled that he stumbled over his wing and had to use the wall to catch his balance.

"Marquis!" Nachari chastised, giving his brother a harsh, reprimanding stare. Then he turned to look at Braden. "Braden, what has happened to your left arm?"

Braden looked down at the ground and frowned before shrugging his shoulders. "I got stuck." And then he lifted his chin with pride as he exclaimed, "I was shape-shifting into the form of the bat."

Marquis looked irritated. "What is the matter with you, boy? Do you have some kind of disability?"

"Marquis!" Kagen swung his gaze to Marquis's impassive face, narrowing his eyes in warning.

Tessa Dawn

Nathaniel could not restrain his laughter as he scrutinized the half-boy, half-bat in his living room. He turned to look at Nachari and smiled. "Apparently, *he got stuck*, Nachari." He raised both eyebrows in a high arc, awaiting Nachari's response.

Nachari grunted, ignoring his older brother. "Why were you trying such a thing?" His voice was reasoned...paternal. "You are far too young, and do not yet possess the knowledge or discipline to shape-shift." It was a simple statement of fact.

Braden shrugged again, wincing. "I dunno. I thought it might be cool to fly in, instead of walk, ya know? Since your family has so many ancient warriors and all." He looked down, clearly dejected.

Jocelyn's heart softened in response to the poor, clearly confused boy.

Kagen stirred. He didn't speak at first; he simply leaned back in his chair with a crooked smile on his face. After a minute or two had passed, he finally asked, "Can't you change back?" His tone was genuine. Curious.

"I've tried," Braden sighed, looking as upset as he was determined. He yanked at the wing several times, clearly trying to get it to fold into a normal resting position so that he could begin the mental process of rearranging the molecules back to fully human form. But the uncooperative limb just kept jerking, flapping wildly, then falling back down awkwardly at his side. The harder he tried to fix it, the more unruly the wing became, until it finally began to jerk and flutter about wildly as if it had a life of its own.

Seeing the boy worked up into an utter frenzy, Marquis lost his patience. "Stop, already!" It was an imperious command, and his voice resounded through the large, open room like a clap of thunder. "I have never witnessed such affliction in all my centuries of living!"

Braden looked mortified...absolutely humiliated.

Clearly desperate to save face, he decided to snarl back at the Ancient Master Warrior. Curling back his lips, he hissed his fiercest growl at Marquis, forced his canines to sharpen, and glared with such intensity that the centers of his eyes actually glowed a slight red…well, maybe more like a dusty rose, but they at least changed color.

When his left canine elongated to about one-half inch, leaving the right one at about two centimeters—and still curved—Marquis flicked a hand in extreme annoyance at what he undoubtedly saw as an audacious, disrespectful boy and sent a single crackling bolt of lightning from the tips of his fingers right to the tip of Braden's nose. Stopping it only a hair's length before scorching him.

Braden jerked back in terror, shrieked like a little girl, and fell over onto the floor, his teeth now as stuck in their awkward *mis*-configuration as his arm.

"Marquis!" Nathaniel glared at the ancient bully with a look of complete disbelief on his face, and then he shot him a sharp look of disdain. "Do you wish to burn down my house, warrior?" Turning to his youngest brother, he pleaded, "Nachari, do something for the child…please."

Braden looked like someone caught in an awful nightmare as the word *child* registered on his stricken face…as it undoubtedly sank in that a powerful ancient vampire had just called *him* a child.

Nachari waved his hand, and Braden simply disappeared, floating as a hazy cluster of molecules, rapidly firing translucent waves of quantum energy, suspended in the air. Speaking a series of Latin words, while weaving a strange pattern with his hands, Nachari made Braden instantly reappear as a fully formed bat with perfectly elongated teeth and two normal wings: The bat gracefully receded then as he fluidly shifted back into the form of a poorly dressed boy.

Nathaniel did a double-take at his younger brother. "Wizardry, huh?" He grunted, sounding impressed. "Okay, I'll bite—how'd you do that?"

Nachari just smiled.

Braden looked down at the ground, his eyes glossing over with moisture. He was already insulted, and now, he also appeared jealous—as if he had hoped to be the one to impress the Silivasi brothers, not Nachari—as if some well-rehearsed plan had gone terribly wrong.

Jocelyn didn't know whether or not Braden had ever met a true ancient vampire before, but it was painfully obvious that he wanted Kagen, Marquis, and Nathaniel's approval more than life itself in that moment. Huffing his hurt feelings, he flipped his cape behind him in true melodramatic fashion and waltzed in long, ridiculous strides across the living room to the only remaining open chair. He spun in a half-circle then, his cape flapping so hard it whirled all the way around and smacked him back in the face, and then he sat down, almost missing the seat.

Kagen bit his lip, struggling to keep from laughing. "So what's the story?" he asked Nachari.

Marquis shook his head in disgust. "Yes...do tell."

Nachari cracked his knuckles. "Well, as you guys know, I finally finished my senior studies, and in the *school of wizardry* one has to demonstrate exceptional patience by completing an assigned task before they're accepted into the *fellowship of wizards*, even though they're already considered a Master Wizard by our people." He rolled his eyes and shook his head. "Jankiel Luzanski was given charge over a virtual harem of beautiful women with the task of not allowing his eyes to leave the path directly in front of him...*for three months.*" He smirked. "We all know what his weakness is. And Niko Durciak was actually sent out into the Transylvanian Mountains to find one of the lost tablets of Sakarias; he won't be allowed into the fellowship until he returns with it. All very brave, worthy deeds."

He looked over at Braden and sighed. "But me? No...I was given the task of mentoring young Braden over there for one full moon. His parents came to Romania to vacation for a few months and decided to stay in the guest wing of the castle. They were trying to find something for Braden to do when it suddenly occurred to the elders that the young man might be able to...assist me...in my evolution. Apparently, they felt I needed a bit more humility." He rubbed his forehead in consternation.

"So here we are…"

Kagen chuckled. "Now, why in the world would they think that, Nachari?"

"I can't imagine," Nathaniel added, his voice full of amusement.

Both brothers laughed, but Marquis only snorted. "Okay, so that's *your* story. What's *his* story?" He eyed the young boy disdainfully.

Braden puffed out his chest and raised his chin in defiance, but when a single tear escaped his eye, he couldn't hide his unmistakable hurt.

Marquis paled and leaned over in his chair, as far as he could, to make sure he was actually seeing what he thought he was seeing. "Dear God!" He sounded mortified. "Are you *crying?*" He looked utterly appalled.

"Marquis!" This time, it was Jocelyn who chastised him…angrily.

Marquis immediately snapped his head to the side in order to meet her scolding gaze; his eyes were glowing with heat, and he looked shocked at the tone of her voice.

Jocelyn didn't back down. "Quit being such a Neanderthal!" She barked the words bravely…maternally. And then she immediately ducked behind Nathaniel, allowing his broad shoulders to act as a barrier between herself and the dark-haired tyrant, just in case there was another bolt of lightning coming her way.

Kagen and Nachari laughed out loud, even as Nathaniel shifted his powerful frame to shelter her beside him, possessively placing a strong arm securely around her shoulders.

Jocelyn allowed the shelter of his arm, needing the reassurance she was beginning to feel as a result of his constant vigilance. When she finally gathered the courage to peek at Marquis from around Nathaniel's chest, she was surprised to find a faint, amused smile on his chiseled face, his blue-black eyes glowing with warmth as he stared back at her.

"Braden's story?" Kagen reminded Nachari.

Nachari shifted into a more comfortable position and cleared his throat. "You guys remember Dario Bratianu, right? He used to run one of our tropical vacation resorts in Hawaii?"

Kagen nodded.

Marquis grunted.

"Tropical vacation resorts?" Jocelyn whispered to Nathaniel, the words slipping out before she could censor them.

Nathaniel turned to face her. "Dark Moon Vale is our primary home, and a lot of our businesses are run right here, but we do hold various time shares and vacation properties all over the United States, in Europe, and South America. They're mostly run by property management groups, but every now and then one of our males will get tired of doing the same thing, so he'll go work one of the other properties for a while."

Just when Jocelyn thought that nothing else could surprise her about these almost human—but ferociously not—creatures, something did. She nodded, and turned back toward Nachari. "Sorry for interrupting."

Nachari waved a dismissive hand. "Not at all." He shifted again in his seat. "So, Dario met Braden's mother in Hawaii at the resort—apparently, she already had Braden at the time, from a former marriage." He looked at Braden. "I think he was about five then."

Braden nodded.

"Anyhow, it turned out that Lily was Dario's true *destiny*." Nachari looked over at Jocelyn then. "Lily had the markings of Pegasus on her wrist, and the Blood Moon was revealed to them one night. So when they finally came together...when she gave him his sons...they had to figure out what to do with Braden."

"What to *do* with him?" Jocelyn asked, appalled. Her body stiffened beneath Nathaniel's arm as the reminder of her *purpose* was, once again, made so glaringly apparent. It was humiliating.

"Not like that," Nachari corrected. "How they were going to...build a life together...with a human son."

Nathaniel tightened his grip around Jocelyn's shoulder and pulled her close under the shelter of his arm, clearly sensing her growing fear. "It's okay, angel," he whispered, his words both soft and tender. "You are so much more to me than that...far more than you realize."

Jocelyn stared straight ahead at Nachari, but she felt Nathaniel's warm breath against her ear like a glowing ray of heat, subtly caressing her skin.

"So when Dario consulted Napolean," Nachari continued, "Napolean told him that there was a good chance that Braden could be transformed—"

"Transformed?" Jocelyn asked, unable to stop interrupting.

"Yes," Nachari answered, patiently. "*Sired*...converted?...changed from human to our species."

Jocelyn shifted nervously. There it was again, the constant reminder of what she was facing. She turned to study Braden, to try and read his expression, knowing he had already gone through this *transformation*.

Braden was listening with interest, seeming to enjoy the fact that he was finally the center of attention: Everyone was thinking about him, yet no one was growling or throwing bolts of lightning in his face. He didn't look at all disturbed by the memory of being *sired*.

Nachari looked at Jocelyn, waiting for another question. When she remained silent, he continued with his story. "As I was saying, since Lily was Braden's biological mother, the two of them share the same Celestial blood. And since Lily was also Dario's *true destiny*, it was possible to convert Braden under the protection of Pegasus...without any danger of him losing his soul."

"Pegasus?" Jocelyn asked.

"My step-dad's constellation," Braden supplied. "Mine is Monoceros, the unicorn." He raised his head proudly.

"You sure it's not Jake the jackass?" Marquis mumbled.

Braden stuck out his tongue and rolled his heavily painted eyes.

Marquis chuckled then and leaned forward, largely ignoring the insolent gesture. "I have never heard of such a thing. Have you, Kagen?"

Kagen shook his head and brushed his dark brown hair out
of his eyes with his fingers. "No, I haven't. Every story I've ever
heard of someone trying to convert a human other than their
blood destiny had to do with the Dark Ones, and it never turned
out very well…" His voice trailed off as he caught Jocelyn's
frightened gaze. She was beginning to feel like a frail deer caught
in Nathaniel's headlights.

Nathaniel's hand slid gently up and down her arm in a
reassuring caress. "So, it can be done, then?" he asked, eyeing
Braden curiously.

Marquis looked at the child with suspicion. "Apparently not.
At least not successfully."

The words were said without emotion, yet Braden almost
crumbled at the insult. He put his head down in his arms.

"Marquis," Nachari whispered, softening his censure this
time, as if a gentler approach might have more effect. "Braden
was successfully converted. There's no question about that. But
he was raised as a human, and for them, the first five years are
very formative, kind of like our first one hundred. His body
contains all the instincts of our kind, but his brain fights against
it, insisting on using old neuro-pathways and other no longer
useful…yet still automatic…brain patterns. It's a constant fight
for him to do what comes natural for us."

Nachari gave Braden a comforting smile then. "And like
most humans, Braden is impatient. He doesn't understand that
these things take a great deal of time and practice…but, he'll get
there."

Braden's face lit up.

Jocelyn frowned, confused. "I don't understand. How could
Braden's mother…transform…without any problem, while
Braden has had such difficulty? I mean, they *both* spent their
formative years as a human, right?"

She obviously wasn't asking about Lily. The bottom line was,
she had spent her entire life as a human, too, and needed to hear
that a vampire's *destiny* always transformed successfully. *Always.*

Nachari looked at Nathaniel as if to ask permission to speak.

Marquis didn't bother. "Because Braden's blood was only part Celestial—half Lily's. The other part was human—half his biological father's."

Jocelyn raised an eyebrow, still not understanding.

"Lily's blood was never the exact same as other humans' to begin with. She was created for Dario, so she was born...compatible," Marquis explained.

Jocelyn turned the enormous male's words over in her head. "What are you saying? How could our blood be different? I'm human. My blood is *human*." For the first time, she forced herself to hold eye contact with the fierce vampire's intimidating glare.

"It means that while you might find much to question about our species, you're already closer to it than you think," he said bluntly.

Jocelyn blanched, appalled at the idea, which obviously irritated Marquis.

"You are not as fully human as you believe you are, Jocelyn! *That is all.*" Marquis's voice was strong and unwavering.

"Marquis!" This time, Nachari, Nathaniel, and Kagen all said it in unison.

Nathaniel brushed his hand softly through Jocelyn's hair, twirling a small handful of tresses in his fingers. "Celestial blood means sacred blood, Jocelyn. Chosen by the Ancient Ones. It means that you were born different...special...destined. *That is all.*"

Jocelyn sighed and turned her attention back to Marquis, who turned his attention back to Braden. "Well, I still think something went wrong. I've never seen anyone actually want to be a vampire so badly, or be so ghastly awful at it!"

At that, Braden stood up, his feet shoulder's length apart, folded his arms over his chest, and closed his eyes. To everyone's amazement, a small, intact vampire bat appeared. Flying over to the corner of the room, he turned upside down and just hung there, his back turned to all of them.

Marquis looked afraid to ask, but he obviously couldn't help himself. "What the hell is he doing now?"

Nachari just sighed. "He's pouting."

I'm in the bat cave! Braden argued, broadcasting the thought loudly.

With Nathaniel's hand resting firmly on her arm, Jocelyn was able to hear the telepathic words as clearly as everyone else in the room. She shook her head, just watching the drama unfold.

"The bat cave?" Kagen spoke aloud.

Yes, you know: a bat plus a man equals a bat man! Like Batman and Robin!

Marquis had clearly had his fill of the strange child. He rose and glided directly over to the hanging bat. "Batman and Robin were not vampires, Braden!"

With a graceful flow of hand motions, he placed an impenetrable barrier around the little hanging rodent, locking him into his chosen corner like a prisoner in a cell…blocking all transmission of sound or thought along with him. And just to avoid having to see the nuisance for a while, he cloaked him in a shield of invisibility, rendering him completely inconsequential.

Nachari started to get up—to go to the young boy's aid—when suddenly he stumbled back as if he had been struck in the chest by an invisible hand, his rear-end landing right back in his seat. When he looked up, Marquis was glaring at him with cold, vacant eyes, a fierce, guttural growl of warning emanating from deep within his throat.

"I am through being chastised by a child," he growled. "The boy is silly, disrespectful, and horribly undisciplined. And if he wants to hang out with real vampires, he had better learn his place."

It was abundantly clear that Braden would remain in the corner until Marquis released him.

Nachari took one good look at Marquis's face and folded his arms, sinking deep into the chair.

No one else dared to say a word.

fifteen

It was late in the evening when the stranger arrived. Although they had moved outside to the upper deck in order to enjoy the crisp night air, the four brothers were still talking, catching up on one another's lives, and reminiscing about old times. Young Braden had fallen asleep in his...bat cave...where they had safely left him, still hanging upside down, while Marquis, Kagen, and Nachari lounged comfortably in lawn chairs, and Jocelyn leaned against the railing. Nathaniel stood slightly to the side of her, his powerful frame locking her in, just in case she got any more wild ideas about trying to leap over the banister.

"Excuse me, Señor Silivasi?" The hurried voice of Nathaniel's housekeeper drew his attention from Jocelyn.

"What is it, Alejandra?"

"The county sheriff and another gentleman are here to see you." Her keen eyes flashed with worry as she gestured toward the two men standing slightly behind her.

Before Alejandra could move out of the way, both gentlemen strolled onto the deck. They brushed against her as they passed by, stopping a few feet in front of Nathaniel and Jocelyn. The housekeeper huffed, rolled her eyes, and muttered something in Spanish as she turned and went back to her work.

Marquis, Nachari, and Kagen instantly stood up, but it was Jocelyn who spoke first: "Tristan! What on earth are you doing here?"

Nathaniel quickly spun around and placed his body squarely between his *destiny* and the tall, husky man who stood like a tower next to the local sheriff. There was a sinister air of authority swirling around him, a tainted aura of power.

"You know this man?" Nathaniel asked, his eyes carefully assessing Jocelyn.

She nodded, her mouth falling open, her face suddenly growing pale.

"I'm really sorry to bother you at home like this, Nathaniel," Sheriff Thompson said, "but I'm afraid we're going to have to ask your lady friend some questions."

Nathaniel had known Jack Thompson for many years, and unless it was a matter of great importance, the sheriff always gave him and the rest of the Silivasis free reign over the valley. "What is this about?"

"Oh, just a question or two about her visit." He glanced at Jocelyn and then nodded at Marquis. "Good to see you, Marquis."

Marquis inclined his head toward the sheriff but said nothing.

"And you, Kagen."

Kagen followed suit.

The sheriff sighed, obviously aware of the mounting tension between the Silivasi brothers, the startled-looking woman, and the tall blond stranger. "It's good to see you home, Nachari." He averted his eyes. "I was sorry to hear about your loss."

Nachari nodded, showing no emotion. "Thank you, Jack." *Nathaniel,* he said telepathically, *break your connection with Jocelyn.*

Nathaniel immediately shifted his body, breaking contact with his *destiny.* The situation was about to become explosive, and the brothers needed an open line of communication without having to worry about Jocelyn overhearing their conversation.

As soon as Nathaniel had shifted, Nachari finished his thought. *The golden-hair is a hunter!*

Nathaniel nodded, almost imperceptibly. *I am well aware of this fact, Nachari.*

A low growl rumbled from the far end of the deck. *He's lycan, all right! I can smell him from here.* Marquis was already moving into a combat-ready position.

Nathaniel held up his hand, cautioning his brothers to stand down. "You two know each other?" he asked Jocelyn, eyeing the tall blond male with a clear, unmistakable warning in his eyes.

Tessa Dawn

The hunter smiled, seemingly unconcerned. He was wearing a pair of faded blue jeans; scuffed, tan cowboy boots; and a plain black button-down shirt. His hair was a wild mane of blond curls hanging halfway down his back, with gold and auburn streaks scattered throughout like the crown of a lion. His eyes were a strange, haunting hazel, and they shifted between piercing yellow and deep amber, even as his gaze swept far too possessively over Jocelyn.

Jocelyn continued to stare at the large male with stunned recognition as if she were afraid to answer the question. "We…we…work together. Tristan is my partner back in San Diego."

Nathaniel and Marquis exchanged inquisitive glances. *Why does this hunter know your woman?* Marquis asked telepathically.

Good question. "Tristan?" Nathaniel repeated the name, waiting for an introduction.

It was the sheriff who took the liberty: "Nathaniel, this is Tristan Hart. Tristan, Nathaniel Silivasi."

The hunter smiled a sly, wolfish grin. "Pleasure to meet you…Silivasi." His voice was a low growl, and he folded his arms across his chest as opposed to extending a hand.

"Likewise, I'm sure," Nathaniel hissed. His back and shoulder muscles rippled in a series of involuntary contractions, his lips twitching in an effort to hold back his fangs.

The sheriff eyed both men apprehensively, drawing in a deep breath. His short brown hair began to dampen around his forehead just below his brimmed hat as he clearly realized there was going to be trouble. "Tristan here was concerned about—"

"Jocelyn," Nathaniel supplied. He was well aware that Jack Thompson was no fool; the sheriff had to know he had just walked into a powder keg.

"Jocelyn…" the sheriff repeated, flashing a tentative smile in her direction. He brushed his chin with the back of his hand and regarded all four brothers with his dull brown eyes, clearly trying to take inventory of each man's level of agitation. Then he cleared his throat and tapped the toe of his standard-issue, hard black boot against the deck, patiently watching to see how Nathaniel was going to react.

Nathaniel relaxed his body on purpose. "How long have the two of you worked together?" He spoke directly to Jocelyn.

Jocelyn blinked as if coming out of a trance. "Almost three years now." Her voice was barely audible.

Once again, Tristan smiled with far too much satisfaction. "Long enough to know my partner wouldn't run off to some mountain resort and take up house with a total stranger." His eyes swept to Jocelyn. "Joss, I came with the sheriff to escort you out of here."

Nathaniel felt his stomach muscles clench. He stilled his mind and regulated his breathing, when what he really wanted to do was rip the arrogant male's larynx from his throat.

Jocelyn paled, her eyes immediately meeting Nathaniel's.

Marquis pressed forward then and stood next to his brother. Nachari flanked him on the opposite side, and Kagen glided noiselessly to stand in the door frame, his powerful, muscular body blocking the only exit.

The sheriff's eyes darted nervously from one male to another as he silently released the leather strap at the top of his gun holster. "All right now, men...let's just...everyone calm down."

Tristan smiled, threw back his wild mane, and coughed in what could only be described as a cross between a deep, feral growl and a territorial grunt. Immediately, the surrounding forest lit up with an eerie sound: There was a series of long, plaintive howls as an answering chorus of wolves echoed Tristan's call from one end of the canyon to the other.

He has filled our valley with hunters! Marquis scowled.

The people are not prepared for an attack like this, Nachari warned.

Nathaniel glared at Tristan and bared a lightning quick flash of savage fangs. "My lady needs no such escort. So why don't you just turn around and see yourself out." He was offering him an exit...just one exit. He turned to the sheriff. "Jack, I would expect you to know better."

Jack Thompson sighed. "Nathaniel, if a citizen makes a

160

report, I have to follow it up." The uneasiness in his voice was apparent.

"What kind of report?" Kagen hissed.

"Uh...missing persons," Jack answered reluctantly, his voice faltering with embarrassment.

"Well, as you can clearly see, no one is missing." Nachari's tone was low, steady, and dripping with venom.

Jocelyn pushed her hair behind her ear and looked down at her feet nervously, her shoulders visibly shaking. Nathaniel gently brushed the pads of his fingers over her cheek and frowned when her body stiffened in response to his touch.

Tristan followed the subtle interaction with his eyes and glowered at Nathaniel. "I think the lady can speak for herself."

Nathaniel growled a warning.

Jack looked down at the ground before regarding Nathaniel squarely. "Nathaniel, you won't mind if I speak to...Jocelyn...directly, will you?" His eyes were practically pleading. "The sooner we get this over with, the sooner I can leave you fellas alone."

Nathaniel slowly tilted his head from side to side, popping his spine as he stretched his neck. He was struggling to calm the rising beast within him, wanting to remain objective. He could not discern the age of the lycan, but a male his size would be a formidable enemy. Depending on how quickly the male could shape-shift, protecting Jocelyn might be impossible...should Tristan choose to strike her first in order to weaken Nathaniel. Even with his brothers so near, the male was far too close to his woman. Partner or not, Tristan was a hunter, and he would do whatever was necessary to take down his prey. On top of that, a dead or injured sheriff was not the kind of thing they needed in the valley, and there would be no time to consider the human if Jocelyn's life was in jeopardy.

Nathaniel shared his thoughts with his brothers: *If this lycan is Jocelyn's partner, then he must have smelled her Celestial blood the moment he met her and attached himself in hopes of being led to one of our kind.*

Nachari made eye contact with Nathaniel. *It has been nearly a century since the last pack of lycans made their way into our valley.*

The vampire race was always extremely careful to keep their existence hidden from their natural enemies—human societies and werewolves. And the Silivasi brothers all had terrible, vivid memories of the last time their valley was overcome. Nathaniel forced himself to keep his attention in the present.

From the sound of the answering call in the forest, Nachari continued, *I would estimate at least twenty males. Tristan is obviously their Alpha, and he has placed soldiers strategically throughout the valley in order to insure his safe retreat with Jocelyn. For what reason, I'm not sure: she's done her duty, led the hunter to his prey—why take the woman now?*

Perhaps he has no intention of starting a war, Marquis offered. *Perhaps he came only to assassinate Nathaniel. If he can take Jocelyn and…dispose of her…he'll take down Nathaniel with her. Perhaps that is enough for him. The death of one Ancient Master Warrior would be a great feat. And a high honor within the Lycan Society.*

That is my thought as well, Kagen agreed. *The lycans do not wish a war with us any more than our Dark Brothers wish a war with us; the beta males are no match for our warriors. In fact, it would take half his soldiers to bring down Nathaniel, alone. No, even a skilled lycan hunter attacks with strategy first. This one seeks to pick off one Ancient Warrior in the easiest way possible…by taking his female.*

The unspoken implication lingered in the air.

Shelby.

Nathaniel looked squarely at Jack Thompson. "Ask whatever you like, Sheriff."

Jack Thompson cleared his throat. "I'm sorry to bother you, Miss…Jocelyn…but your friend here seems to think you're being held without your consent."

Jocelyn swallowed hard, obviously contemplating her options; her worried eyes darted back and forth between Tristan and Nathaniel as if she were trying to calculate potential outcomes. And Nathaniel could smell her fear as she took a step back. "No, Officer. I'm fine." Her voice was shaky and unconvincing.

"Are you sure?" the sheriff asked, catching her hesitation.

Jocelyn nodded, her eyes focused downward. "Yes, of course."

Tristan moved forward then, and all of the brothers almost sprang at him. Sheriff Thompson drew his gun from his holster. "Step back, Tristan: The lady says she's fine."

Tristan ignored the sheriff's warning, stopping just short of touching Jocelyn on the shoulder as he looked into her eyes. His own golden pupils narrowed with intensity. "Jocelyn, listen to me very carefully: You *can* walk out of here safely. I know *exactly* what you fear, and I am telling you, on my life, that you will not be stopped. You do not need to fear for my safety." He looked directly at Nathaniel, then over at Marquis, Nachari, and finally Kagen, before turning back to Jocelyn. "My blood will not be shed here tonight, and neither will yours. *Trust me.*"

Nathaniel bared the full length of his fangs and snarled a low, guttural hiss, uncaring of the stunned look on Sheriff Thompson's face: He would wipe the human's memory later.

The sheriff yelped and jumped back, palming his gun with a sweaty hand. His eyes shot frantically around the deck, eyeing each of the Silivasi brothers in turn. *"What the hell!"* he shouted.

Okay...maybe *now* was in order: Nathaniel waved his hand and erased the sheriff's memory, taking him back to Tristan's question.

"Come with me, Joss," Tristan repeated.

Jocelyn hesitated, and for the first time, Nathaniel saw the indecision in her eyes. She was wringing her hands together, clearly trying to weigh the enormity of the past forty-eight hours in a matter of a few seconds, her growing bond with Nathaniel warring with her powerful sense of self-preservation.

Marquis's eyes flashed red, and he shifted his heavily muscled body. "Don't be so sure of yourself, *hunter.*" He was wound as tight as a coiled snake and just as likely to strike.

The sheriff lowered his gun in an obvious effort to diffuse the situation. "Hunter?" he repeated, not understanding the true meaning of the word. "You came here for hunting season?" His voice was low, calm, and unbelievably steady, a clear effort to calm the men.

Tristan smiled elegantly, his voice heavy with arrogance. "Absolutely, Sheriff. I am an *avid* hunter." He met Marquis's menacing glare with one of defiance.

The corner of Marquis's mouth curled up in a wicked grin, and a low hiss, like that of a rattlesnake, escaped his lips. He was positively itching for the lycan to make a move.

"Well," the sheriff countered, "then you know you have to have a tag if you're planning to hunt first season; we don't take too kindly to poachers around here." It was a pitiful attempt at lightening the subject.

"Of course," Tristan replied. "So many rules and restrictions to keep up with...it would seem as if only the bears and the *wolves* get to hunt freely these days." His eyes met Nathaniel's in a narrowed gaze of warning.

Nathaniel raised his eyebrows. "I understand that many breeds of wolves are endangered species...*these days*."

"Perhaps it's because they are so easily tracked—and killed—themselves," Marquis snarled.

Tristan shrugged. "Could be...but that's the beauty of running in packs." He leaned back for a moment and rubbed his chin with his thumb as if deep in thought, stopping to look around the valley. "Wouldn't it be interesting if wolves hunted people, instead? I think if I were to lead a pack of wolves, I would place one male in the doorway of every innocent woman and child's home within a hundred miles...just to keep my enemy in line."

Sheriff Jack Thompson bit his bottom lip and frowned with frustration. "What the hell are you guys talking about?" The question was clearly rhetorical. He turned to face Tristan. "We don't hunt wolves in these mountains, and our wolves don't hunt people, so if you're really serious about hunting first season, you better have a doe or a buck tag."

Tristan gave the sheriff a mock salute. "I would never break the law, sir."

Nathaniel linked his mind with Napolean Mondragon's and

immediately sent him the information. The powerful leader's presence was instantly felt as a gentle but alert energy settled in the air around them: The Sovereign was perched like a seasoned general in the back of Nathaniel's mind, waiting patiently to see how the scene played out.

The sheriff turned back toward Jocelyn. "Miss, would you like to leave here with us?"

She will leave over my dead body, Marquis snarled, letting his brothers know exactly what was about to happen should Jocelyn make the wrong decision.

Jocelyn looked briefly at Nathaniel, her beautiful hazel eyes cloudy with distress, and then she turned back toward Tristan. "How did you find me here? The only person who knew where I'd be was my informant."

Tristan shrugged. "I know. And Captain's gonna have your ass when you get back for pulling such a dumb move, but luckily for you, I know who your informant is. I've always known."

Jocelyn looked surprised by her partner's words and genuinely torn by the entire situation. Once again, Nathaniel placed his hand gently on her shoulder. "Jocelyn, this man is not who you think he is."

Jocelyn looked overwhelmed then.

Confused.

And more than a little scared.

She cleared her throat and forced herself to look up at Nathaniel. "I have known Tristan for three years now, Nathaniel." She paused as if trying to draw strength from a waning well of courage. "I haven't even known you for three days…" She shook her head back and forth as if trying to clear the cobwebs and then turned to face him more directly, her back turned to Tristan. "Nathaniel, maybe the best thing I can do right now is to get away for a little while. By myself. Where I have a chance to think and make some sense of things without any outside…influences." She looked down, clearly ashamed.

Nathaniel felt as if all the air had left his body. His eyes were burning, and he knew they were turning a feral red. He thought he was prepared for her to make such a decision, especially given the fact that they had shared so little time together, but hearing the words come out of her mouth was an altogether different experience.

He stared at her thick brown hair, with its impossibly soft, silky tresses...at the pale green clouds that dotted her otherwise brown eyes...at the beautiful slope of her neck, the soft, gentle curve of her chin, and the almost regal lines of her raised, angled cheeks. This woman was *his*. The *destiny* he had waited on for hundreds of years, the only thing standing between him, this world, and the afterlife. Yet, she had chosen to send him to his death that easily....

In front of his brothers.

In front of his mortal enemy.

Never had any warrior, hunter, or son of Jaegar wounded him so deeply.

Nathaniel didn't move a muscle; he didn't even blink. "Do what you must." He dropped his hand from her shoulder and turned away.

She's not going anywhere, Marquis snapped, his fury barely contained.

Marquis, you heard the hunter, Nachari implored. *He has his males positioned at the homes of our people, ready to strike the women and children if he is in any way threatened. We have to think this through.*

And what of your own *flesh and blood? Your brother!* Marquis demanded.

My own flesh and blood, Marquis? Nachari fumed. *Right now, even as we consider Nathaniel, the flesh of my flesh, the blood of my blood, and the twin of my soul lies deep within the cold, barren ground, and I am certain all that was good, light, or worthy within me lies there with him...so do not remind me of* my brother, *Marquis. I know full well what is at stake here.*

The decision must be mine, Nathaniel pointed out to the Ancient Master Warrior. *Nachari and Kagen are both fierce fighters, but Nachari has been trained as a wizard, not a warrior, and Kagen is our healer. Should our males engage in battle this night...should I or Jocelyn be injured...he must be somewhere safe, far from the fighting. I cannot risk the lives of our people for my own.*

Jocelyn looked as if she had been physically struck by Nathaniel's words. "Nathaniel, I...I honestly don't know what to do."

"You know how to put one foot in front of the other," Tristan insisted. "Take my hand, Jocelyn, and let me escort you back to the world you belong in. Do not be intimidated."

The sheriff looked stunned. Astonished by the fact that she was actually thinking of leaving. He studied Nathaniel...then Tristan...and finally Jocelyn, again, before stumbling over his next words. "Ma'am, do you—" He cleared his throat. "Would you like to...file charges?"

"Charges!" Marquis thundered, finally losing his cool. "For what? I assure you, Jack, you do not want this family for an enemy."

Nathaniel put his hand on Marquis's arm while Jack Thompson cringed and stepped back; his knees were practically knocking together as he waited for Jocelyn's answer.

"No! No...absolutely not," Jocelyn said, her eyes misting over with tears. "Tristan, let's just go." The words were a mere whisper as she reached out for the hunter's hand.

This time, it was Marquis and Nachari who placed their hands on Nathaniel's arms in a gesture of restraint.

Nathaniel? The voice belonged to Napolean Mondragon, their supreme ruler. *I have alerted the sentinels and called for a council of the Master Warriors. The women and children are already being moved to the safety of the lodge, and Julien Lacusta, our very best tracker, is on his way to your home...to retrieve Jocelyn.*

He intends to kill her, Nathaniel said coldly, fully aware the decision he was making was one of sacrifice: trading both his life and Jocelyn's for the life of his people.

His, he could bear.

Hers, he could not.

There was a slight pause. *No, I don't think so*, Kagen muttered. *In fact, I'm sure he won't—at least not right away.*

BLOOD DESTINY

And you know this, how? Marquis demanded.

Kagen sighed. *His scent. It's not just the scent of a wolf, but of an Alpha male marking his territory. He is sending a message to his betas, letting them know she* belongs *to him. Because I can smell his arousal. He wants her...first.*

Nathaniel sprang forward and caught the lycan by the jugular before Tristan could shift, before his brothers could restrain him, shoving his thumb deep into the male's throat. He pressed his face so close to the hunter's that their noses almost touched, and his body shook with the effort to remain in control. The forest instantly came alive with the angry howls of the wolves, and Napolean flooded Nathaniel's mind with a warm, calming influence, even as Nachari began to weave a spell to capture his brother's rage.

"You touch one hair on her head, and I will rip you limb from limb, hunter. With God as my witness, I will tear the skin from your body one strip at a time and remove your heart through your throat. Do we understand each other?"

Sheriff Thompson looked bewildered. "Good Lord, Nathaniel! *Let him go.*" He started to raise his weapon, but Marquis moved so quickly that the sheriff never saw him coming. He wrenched the gun from the sheriff's hand, removed the clip, and tossed it to Kagen before Jack even knew it was gone.

"Do not get involved," Marquis growled. "The woman is leaving." He pried Nathaniel's hand from Tristan's throat and moved his brother back.

Nathaniel shook himself out of his rage and lowered his eyes to glance at Jocelyn one last time. His jaw was set in a hard, unmovable line, his lips pulled taut against his expanding teeth. "If that is all, Sheriff?"

Jack Thompson looked like a man who had just stepped off a roller-coaster ride and had yet to catch his balance. He looked around the deck for his gun and visibly blanched when he saw Kagen extend it to him. *"What-the-hell..."* The words were mumbled beneath his breath. He scurried over to retrieve the

168

weapon, and then he just stood in stunned silence gawking at all four Silivasi brothers like he'd never seen them before.

"*If that is all, Sheriff,*" Nathaniel repeated.

Jack Thompson gestured toward the door and quickly ushered Jocelyn and Tristan in front of him. The crooked smile on Tristan's face glowed amber in his eyes.

Unable to help herself, Jocelyn glanced back at Nathaniel one last time. When their eyes met, she looked as if she had just seen a ghost...as if she were in mourning...the horror of what was occurring etched deeply in her face.

As she slowly turned away, she pressed a firm hand against her stomach and caught at a falling tear.

The silver SUV had barely pulled out of the drive when Nachari's panicked voice rang out from the first-floor receiving room. "Marquis! Did you release Braden?"

Nathaniel and Marquis entered the room at the same time. "No, I was just about to come get him," Marquis responded. "Why?"

Nachari's heart skipped a beat, but his voice held steady. "He's not here."

"What do you mean he's not here?" Marquis flared, rapidly working to undo his own *restraining cell*.

Nachari sighed his frustration. "I'm a wizard, Marquis. I know how to take apart a cell. *He's not here!*"

Marquis stepped back, visibly shocked as he viewed the empty space with his own eyes. The cell had already been disassembled. The enclosure was open. And the bat was gone. "Kagen!" he called.

"No," Kagen answered, entering the room quickly, "I didn't release him, either."

Nachari's stomach sank into his boots. "We have to find him!"

All four males began to scour the house, rapidly moving from room to room, calling out to the youngster as they searched the most unlikely of places.

After several minutes had passed, they met back in the foyer and Nachari bent down to retrieve Braden's red duffle. There was a folded piece of paper stuffed just inside the zipper: *I'm not a dummy! And I'll be back when you can all respect me.*

Nachari crumpled up the paper and tossed it across the foyer. He made his way to the window. "Where the hell is that tracker?" he spat. He didn't even try to conceal his worry as he dropped his head into his hands: Blessed Moon, the child had been placed in *his* care.

His voice was heavy with concern as he met Nathaniel's knowing gaze. "*Holy Celestial Beings,* Nathaniel..."

Jocelyn and Braden were gone.

And the forest was full of hunters.

sixteen

The old, secluded cabin sat like a weathered remnant of times gone by. Nestled serenely within the remote pristine valley, its rustic boards, modest appearance, and untouched surroundings blended effortlessly into the Dark Moon Forest.

The textured, square lines were a sharp contrast to the smooth, rocky face of the jutting cliffs that flanked its rear. Just as the simple welcoming porch seemed a soft extension of the crystal blue river meandering along its front.

Jocelyn wrapped a heavy wool parka around her shoulders and sipped the hot cup of tea Tristan had made for her. She took a seat on the sturdy oak bench that leaned against the battered wall of the remote cabin's front porch and warmed her hands against the mug while Tristan set out to gather firewood.

She watched curiously as the tall blond man who used to be her partner walked into the woods, nervously checking over his shoulder—right, then left, then right again—like a skittish animal waiting for an attack.

Tristan had been acting out of character, to put it mildly, ever since they arrived at the cabin. Anxiously pacing back and forth across the wooden deck, making several secretive phone calls from his satellite phone, and repeatedly rubbing his hands together…clenching and unclenching his fists…as if preparing for a fight.

Jocelyn had no idea what to make of him now that the revelation of who he was, and what he really did, had been made to her.

A modern-day vampire hunter.

Knowing full well what Nathaniel and his brothers were capable of, Tristan had gone to great lengths to cover their trail: They had switched vehicles at least three times after leaving Nathaniel's home, prior to heading out on foot. They had hiked deep into the rugged terrain of the eastern forest, boarded a raft at the end of the gorge, and taken the last leg of the journey along an endless, snaking waterway, a channel far too narrow to be followed on foot.

The snow had begun to fall heavily only moments after they left, and the unexpected storm was blowing in fast and furious now. A sudden torrent of crystalline flakes, each one heavily weighted with dense moisture, barreled down in a haphazard spiraling pattern. It was the kind of blizzard that chilled the bone and stuck to the ground, creating heavy drifts, impassible roads, and white-out conditions in a very short period of time. Any tracks they may have left would have been covered by now, easily concealed by the mounting snow. Any scent blown away by the heavy gusts of wind.

Tristan had hired a private helicopter pilot to come in the morning and airlift them out of the gorge, explaining that it would be the safest way to get out of Dark Moon Vale before the money, power, or influence of the Silivasi family could cause them problems. But from the looks of the worsening storm, any helicopter transport might have to be postponed.

Jocelyn sipped the warm tea, laced with honey and lemon, and tried to gather her thoughts. Her head was still spinning from the events of the evening, her stomach tied in knots as the realization of what she had done set in more and more.

She had left Nathaniel.

And she had left him to die.

To suffer the same horrific fate as the handsome young man in the painting: his brother, Shelby. While she knew it wasn't her responsibility to take care of a man she had never met—and absolutely no one had the right to snatch a person from their life and force them into a personal relationship—a part of her heart was breaking from the choice she had made.

And the look on Nathaniel's face.

The memory of those dark, haunted eyes staring at her with such…hurt…in them chilled her to the bone; she had walked away without mercy, leaving him to his fate, when he believed there was something special, if not divine, between them.

Jocelyn drew in a deep breath, taking the chilled mountain air into her lungs. The icy snowflakes swirled around her, stinging warm skin as the wind slapped aimlessly at her exposed cheeks and neck. She pulled her parka closer and turned just in time to see Tristan return with an armful of chopped wood.

"What are you still doing out here?" he asked, looking up at the sky. "It's freezing. You should go inside."

Jocelyn nodded and followed him into the tiny three-room cabin, stopping in front of the fireplace to warm herself while Tristan placed several new logs on the fire. "Tristan," she said, rubbing her hands together, "I've been thinking about our partnership...all these years working together. Were you ever there for the job? For me? Or was it always about finding...vampires?"

Tristan rearranged the newly placed logs using the long iron poker and leaned his heavily muscled frame against the mantel, resting the bulk of his weight on one arm. "Jocelyn, I don't know what you want me to say. The truth of the matter is, I'm a vampire hunter. I always have been. Being your partner back in San Diego was just a front to help me find this valley."

Jocelyn already knew what his answer would be, but now that he had spoken the words out loud, the betrayal stung all over again. She had trusted Tristan with a lot of her secrets over the years. With her life. She had relied on him to always have her back, and in the process, they had formed a bond that no longer seemed real. She shook her head trying to force the reality of what he was telling her to sink in.

"All these years, Tristan...I trusted you."

Tristan sighed. "I'm sorry, Jocelyn."

"Yeah, I guess." Her voice was regretful. "Tell me something else, would you? Did our *partnership* mean anything to you? *Our friendship?* Or was it all just part of the plan?"

Tristan ran his large hands through his wild mane of hair, trying to push it away from his face. "Of course our partnership meant something to me, Jocelyn. Lying to you was the hardest part of this whole thing. And you have to know that once I realized Nathaniel had you..." He looked at her then, his eyes full of possession, a territorial hint of...something...she had never seen in him before. Something that made her uneasy. "All I could think of was getting to you. Rescuing you. Taking you as far away from that monster as I could. I had to see you safe before I could even consider hunting him."

Jocelyn took a step back as his words began to register.

Tristan seemed to sense her uneasiness. "Are we really so different, Joss? I mean, think about it: How many friendships have you made with informants? How many times have you gone undercover or built a relationship with someone you were cozying up to in order to get to a suspect? I'm a hunter. You're a law enforcement agent. We do what we have to do."

Jocelyn shook her head. "Is that what it was, Tristan? Cozying up? It's not the same and you know it! *We were partners.*"

All at once, Tristan stepped forward and cupped her face in his huge hands. He brushed the bones of her cheeks with the pads of his thumbs as he leaned in to kiss her: The kiss was soft, tender, and totally unexpected. "And we still can be." His voice was a low, husky whisper.

Jocelyn gasped, her eyes growing wide. "Tristan! What are you doing?"

He smiled. "Something I've wanted to do since the day I met you." There was no apology in his voice.

Jocelyn rubbed her temples, trying to focus on the situation at hand. Dealing with this new romantic revelation would have to come later. As it was, she was already overwhelmed. *All I could think of was getting to you. Rescuing you. Taking you as far away from that monster as I could...before I could even consider hunting him.* She replayed Tristan's words in her head:

Hunting him.

Hunting Nathaniel!

Her stomach lurched and her heart skipped a beat. "Wait a minute! When you say you needed to rescue me before hunting Nathaniel, what exactly do you mean by *hunting*? Are you talking about trying to…kill him?"

Tristan sighed and looked her directly in the eyes, his deep golden irises growing dark with intent. "Nathaniel is a *vampire*, Jocelyn—far more dangerous than you realize. Yes, of course. And not *trying to kill him*. Killing him."

Jocelyn staggered back as if he had physically struck her, and fear began to take hold where only confusion had stood before…as the gravity of what Tristan was really doing in the valley finally sunk in. This man she believed to be her partner had come to Dark Moon Vale for one purpose—and one purpose only—to take a strong, intelligent creature with hauntingly beautiful eyes, fearsome power, and unexpected gentleness…and kill him. The flesh on her inner wrist began to burn even as her heart began to ache.

"You can't be serious, Tristan. He may be a vampire, but he isn't evil. You can't just *kill* him."

Tristan looked at her then with a hint of derision in his eyes. There was something dark, barely discernible, just below the surface: jealousy, maybe? Anger or contempt? The look of a boss who had been challenged by a subordinate? It wasn't clear exactly what he was feeling, but his determination to finish his job, *to kill Nathaniel*, was unwavering.

"He *is* evil, Jocelyn, and tomorrow morning, after I fly you out of here, I *am* going to do what I came here to do." He caught at her wrist with his hand, held her in a viselike grip, and stared directly into her eyes with absolute authority. "And then I will return to you, and we will have the *partnership* we were always meant to have."

Jocelyn caught her breath and let out a shrill, high-pitched sound. She yanked at her wrist, but it didn't budge. "Tristan, let me go!" She made it an order…when it was really a plea.

Tristan slowly released her wrist, but he continued to hold her in a steady, unyielding gaze. "Don't look at me like that, Jocelyn. Your sympathy for this vampire is beginning to wear thin. Did you know he killed *seven* inmates in a California prison the other night?"

BLOOD DESTINY

Jocelyn frowned and shook her head. "Impossible...when?"

"Sunday. Around four o'clock in the morning."

Jocelyn looked down at the blazing fire, watching as the glowing orange flames sent sizzling sparks across the hearth, shimmering upward as they disappeared into the chimney. Her own life, and everything she had known to be true up until that moment, was just like the fire, vanishing before her eyes. Melting. Disintegrating. Simply going up in flames as reality continued to do a tailspin in her mind.

She closed her eyes as she tried to remember: *Saturday night...and four a.m. Sunday.* What had happened that night? Ah, yes...Nathaniel had discovered her memories of Valentine and Dalia, and he had become so enraged that Marquis had needed to calm him. In fact, Marquis had ordered him to go out and...*feed.*

Tears welled up in her eyes, burning her retinas, even as she tried to deny the conclusion. It was true then. Nathaniel could have easily killed a dozen people that night with his devastating rage. And he would not have shown any mercy to a gang of criminals, especially if they had committed crimes against women, innocent victims like Dalia. Yet she still couldn't accept Tristan's verdict; she still couldn't believe he was evil.

Jocelyn had seen the face of evil, and that wasn't it.

"Tristan," she said cautiously, trying to appeal to his better nature, "I'm asking you...*as your partner*—" The words caught in her throat because she knew it wasn't true anymore. Still, maybe their past would appeal to him on some elemental level. "As your *friend*...don't do this. Don't go after Nathaniel. Come with me when I go tomorrow and leave Nathaniel and his family alone."

Tristan stepped forward, his body so close to hers that he towered over her. His once familiar eyes glowed a pale yellow, and the lines of his face hardened with disapproval. "I would've expected more from you, Jocelyn. After all these years, chasing and taking down bad guys, I would've thought you would despise a killer...of any species. And now, you offer to trade your company for his safety?"

Jocelyn shook her head, indignant. "What do you mean, *trade my company?*"

He bent his head and nuzzled his mouth against her ear, his long, wild hair spilling forward. "You only ask me to leave with you because you're afraid for Nathaniel. If I had any thought to spare his life, you can believe it's gone now. Know this: I will take his head and remove his heart before I return him to the world of the dead."

He slowly traced the front of her body with the pad of his index finger, drawing a straight line from her chin to her navel, stopping just short of the waistline of her skirt. "And I will have you, *his celestial bride*, for myself." He nipped at her throat like an animal and purred against her jaw.

Jocelyn jolted and stumbled back, both stunned and confused; she was completely disoriented from the continuously changing events. As her heart froze in her chest, she began to think of ways to escape, *ways to get away from a man she had thought to be one of her closest friends for the past three years.* She put her hands to his chest and gently shoved him back, trying to push him away. She needed distance, but she didn't want to set him off. What in the world was going on with this man? *Oh...no,* she thought, *is Tristan even a man?*

After all, what kind of a man knew about and hunted vampires? And why did his eyes darken when his mood changed? Where had that throaty growl come from? And why in the world did he care about her *celestial blood?*

All at once a knock came at the cabin door.

Tristan stepped back, unfastened the front of his long, wool coat—opening it just enough to show her the heel of his gun—and pointed to the old brown sofa beside the fireplace in a gesture that told her to sit down.

Once she was seated, he gave her a harsh look of caution, and then he held his finger to his lips as he approached the front door.

The knock came again. "Tristan, let me in! I just locked up

the shed. It's cold as hell out here!" The voice belonged to Willie Jackson, Jocelyn's longtime informant.

"That's Willie!" Jocelyn exclaimed. "What is he doing here? How the heck did he find this cabin?"

When Tristan turned around to regard her, she saw the answer in his carefree shrug and tentative smile.

"Another hunter?" she asked, already knowing the answer. "The two of you work together?"

Tristan didn't respond. He didn't have to.

Jocelyn shook her head in disbelief. She didn't know what emotion she felt the strongest—betrayal, fear for herself, or fear for Nathaniel. How in the world was she going to get out of this? Her head was beginning to spin.

"What's in the shed?" she asked.

Tristan frowned. "The truth?"

"I see no reason for you to lie to me now." Her voice betrayed her hurt.

"An arsenal," he quipped. "And a dangerous one at that: you stay away from that shed, Joss."

"*Jocelyn.*"

"What?" He sounded annoyed.

"*My name*: it's *Jocelyn.*"

Jocelyn sat further back on the sofa, suddenly feeling even more trapped than before, all at once realizing she had been far safer with Nathaniel. What was it he had told her? *This man is not who you think he is.*

Nathaniel knew!

He knew Tristan was a hunter.

And if that was the case, then he would come after her. She was sure of it. After all, his life depended on it, and maybe hers did too, now.

Tristan studied her intently, as if he were trying to read her mind, and then he frowned, not bothering to address her last comment. He opened the door and stood back as Willie rushed in out of the cold. A thick blanket of white powder blew in after him, creating a miniature whirlwind of snow in the doorway before Tristan shut the heavy wooden door behind him.

Willie shivered. He was headed toward the fire when he noticed Jocelyn on the sofa and smiled. "Hey, cop." There was a telltale note of satisfaction in his voice.

Jocelyn smirked.

Willie looked at Tristan, over at Jocelyn, and then back at Tristan again. He removed the hood of his jacket from his shiny, rapidly balding head and smoothed a calloused hand over his unkempt goatee. "Oh c'mon now. Don't be pissed, Levi. You thought you were playin' me and you got played. All the same game, though, right?"

Jocelyn glared at him, her fuse running short. "This isn't a game, Willie." She turned to stare angrily at her *partner*. "I've been…hunting…human traffickers all this time, while the two of you have been hunting…vampires! And using me as bait! What if I had gotten killed out here?"

Willie took a step closer to the fire and rubbed his hands up and down his arms. The flames reflected back in his muddy brown eyes. "And what if I'd gotten killed givin' up info on the traffickers? I don't remember you gettin' all worried about me, cop."

Jocelyn shook her head, clearly disgusted. "You're wrong, Willie. I have always protected my sources."

Willie smiled a sly, mischievous grin. "Well, you don't look any worse for the wear, Levi." His eyes met Tristan's. "You two good? Or did I walk in on somethin'?"

Tristan smiled and looked Jocelyn up and down. "No, we're good. *We're real good.*"

Jocelyn sneered. "What about the trafficking ring, Tristan? The women…the dead bodies…the suspect we've been investigating for the last several months? Was I way out in left field with that whole thing as well?"

"Actually, no," Tristan answered, matter-of-factly. "In fact, you were dead on with that whole investigation: Luca Giovanni *was* running a human trafficking organization. And he was selling the women for slaughter…but just not to some sick human psychopath. He was selling them to vampires without even knowing what they were. Luca knew some of the girls were being murdered, but he had no idea his clients were—"

"A bunch of blood-sucking ghouls." Willie spit into the fire, then wiped his mouth with the back of his hand. He looked up toward the front window. "This storm is lookin' real bad, Tristan. We're gonna need to hold up a night or two before we do any serious hunting."

Tristan's eyes narrowed as he frowned at his cohort. "I think we'll manage to stay warm *somehow*." His voice was heavy with sarcasm, and his eyes held a hint of menace.

Jocelyn winced. "You guys aren't going anywhere *tonight*, are you?"

A heavy wind picked up outside the cabin and began to howl so fiercely that it muted Tristan's voice as eddies of icy snow whipped against the windowpane like small handfuls of pebbles being thrown against the glass. Jocelyn only heard the last three words... "We hunt tonight." But the tone of Tristan's voice was absolute.

She swallowed her anger and tried to maintain her calm. Nathaniel and his brothers would not be easily defeated by the likes of Tristan Hart and Willie Jackson—that was for sure. She needed to keep her wits about her and find a way out of her own predicament. And the fact that they were going *hunting* was probably to her advantage: It might be her only opportunity to escape. Even as her mind thought it, her heart had a hard time believing it. Tristan. Her partner. Now her greatest threat.

Jocelyn shook her head. She needed a moment alone. Some space. An opportunity to think. "Does the water run in this place?"

"Sure," Tristan answered. "Why?"

"Because I'd like to go take a shower." She hesitated then, waiting to see how Tristan would react. Waiting to see just how strict her confinement was.

When he didn't respond, she pressed on. "I'm freezing, Tristan. I need to warm up."

Tristan nodded and walked over to a tall birch armoire that stood at the entrance to the hall. He pulled a large bath towel and a travel bag of toiletries out of the upper cabinet and tossed them to Jocelyn. "First door on the left. You have to let the water run for a few minutes to flush the pipes."

Jocelyn nodded and tried to fake a smile of appreciation. The more room Tristan allowed her, the better. Resisting his authority would only get her tied up or handcuffed to a chair somewhere. She was better off playing on their old partnership as long as she could.

"Thank you, Tristan," she said. Her voice was flat, but at least she managed to get the words out.

Tristan shrugged, and then he moved his hard, muscular body to the center of the hallway and blocked her path. As she stopped in front of him, he looked her straight in the eye, refusing to blink. "*Joss*, understand this: *You are with me now.* Nathaniel isn't coming to get you. Not tonight. Not ever. And as much as you might resent me for all of this…one day you're going to thank me. So don't try anything, *partner*—we can do this the easy way or the hard way—and you know me well enough to understand what that means."

Jocelyn shoved at his chest, ducked under his arm, and quickly walked by, careful to hide her mounting fear. "I understand, Tristan."

She knew exactly what he meant.

"We'll figure it out later. Right now, I'm going to take a shower. And you have my word: I won't try anything."

seventeen

Joelle Parker had just snuggled under the warm goose-down comforter at the Dark Moon Lodge when she heard a heavy knock at the door. She sat up quietly and listened, her senses fully alert.

The women in the Parker family had been rounded up and ushered to the lodge along with all the women and children of the lighter vampires, the round-up taking place less than an hour ago, right before an early, freak winter storm had begun to blow into the valley.

Being human, Joelle had not been given so much as a cursory explanation as to what was going on, but it had only taken one glance at the sentinels—the three fearsome Olaru brothers, who stood like splendid Greek statues at the base of the stairway just outside the lodge entrance—to let her know that whatever was going on…it was serious. And she needed to follow orders. The lobby had been full of warriors.

Joelle sighed and held her breath, hoping whoever was at the door would just go away. Ever since the night Marquis had frightened her half to death, the night he had rejected her, the last thing she wanted to see was a lodge full of female *destinies* and their children: mated women who were loved and cherished by males like Marquis.

Women who had not only been wanted but *chosen*.

It was like having a knife thrust into her heart over and over, every time she saw a wife smile or heard a husband say good-bye, but her family was one of the few that had established a long, loyal partnership with the descendants of Jadon—and she could not have refused the order to take shelter at the lodge even if she had wanted to.

The knock came again, louder this time, and then she heard a deep, melodious voice: "Joelle? Joelle…are you in there?"

Joelle's heart stopped beating in her chest and the air left her body. Her stomach did a funny flip as she turned her head to the side and closed her eyes, listening attentively, trying to identify the voice.

It couldn't be...

One more loud, insistent knock: "Joelle, can I come in?"

There was no mistaking that voice—Marquis Silivasi.

Joelle slid deep beneath the comforter, knowing that Marquis could materialize through the wall at any moment. She wasn't sure whether or not she wanted to see him, whether or not she could withstand any further humiliation, but then, he had to have come for a reason. Was he concerned about her welfare? She didn't dare hope.

Joelle adjusted the straps on the pale satin nightgown she was wearing and quickly ran her fingers through her hair. Oh hell, it was dark as midnight in the room. It wasn't like he could see her anyhow.

"Marquis?" she called, knowing he could hear her no matter how faint her voice. "Is that you?"

"Yes," he answered.

Her heart skipped another beat. This just wasn't happening. "What do you want?"

She heard him knock again, lightly this time. "Open the door, Joelle. I need to see you."

Joelle swallowed hard, her heart pounding so loud she was afraid he would hear it. "Okay...just hold on." Her voice was shaky.

Marquis knocked again. "Joelle, I need you to invite me in."

Joelle paused for a moment then, confused. Why didn't he just materialize through the wall? "You can come in without me answering the door, can't you?" She didn't want to leave the safety of the covers, however false the sense of security. What if he hadn't come out of concern? What if he had decided to fire her, after all?

"Not this time, sweetheart," he answered. His voice was a soft caress. "I need you to *invite* me in."

Joelle's eyes opened wide. *Sweetheart*. Had Marquis Silivasi just called her *sweetheart?*

She slowly pulled back the covers, her hands shaking. She checked her posture in the small oval mirror mounted just inside the doorway and peeked through the peephole. His image was blurred, but she would know those strong shoulders and that wild mane of raven black hair anywhere. Trembling, she unlatched the lock and pulled open the door.

Marquis leaned back in the door frame...looking sexy as silk...as he stared at her with something she had never seen before in his eyes. "So, are you going to invite me in or not?" he drawled. The statement was deliberately provocative. Sinful. Dangerous.

Joelle gestured toward the room, but he didn't budge. Nervously, she cleared her throat. "Will you please come in?"

She gave him the formal invitation he seemed so insistent upon having.

With that, he smiled a wicked grin and sauntered into the room.

Joelle noticed that there was nothing soft or impersonal in the way he moved: His demeanor with her had changed.

"I needed to see for myself that you were safe," he told her.

Joelle swallowed hard. "You did?"

"Of course, I did," he purred. His eyes softened to a dark, misty hue, illuminating the hard lines of his cheekbones, and then, to her utter amazement, he brushed the tops of his fingers along the underside of her jaw and simply stared into her eyes. The corners of his mouth turned up in a sinful smile.

Joelle felt butterflies in her stomach, and her knees weakened beneath her. "M...Mar...quis," she stuttered, "wh...what...are you doing here?"

Marquis strode further into the room and removed his snow-dusted jacket, laying it carelessly over the back of a chair. There was just enough moonlight to cast an enchanting shadow over the large, king-size mattress, a celestial spotlight beckoning to lovers.

"Did you mean what you said the other night?" he asked.

Joelle stared like a schoolgirl, utterly transfixed by his masculine beauty. "Yes...every word."

He reached out and clutched the small of her waist, his strong hands pulling her body beneath the hard frame of his own. "And you would let me...love you...even knowing it couldn't last forever?"

Joelle felt her spine soften like warm butter as he held her tight against the solid perfection of his chest. She was acutely aware of the feel of her breasts against him, satin pressed to steel.

"Yes," she whispered, unable to look him in the eye for fear he might vanish, for fear it wouldn't be real.

He nuzzled his head into the small of her neck, deeply inhaling her scent. She could feel his fangs lengthening as he scraped them...oh so gently...across her throat.

Her stomach clenched, and she felt an answering ache deep inside her core. She exhaled then, allowing herself to take in the fullness of the moment, the miracle of a dream come true.

"You like that, don't you?" he whispered, his voice pure seduction.

Joelle's heart did a strange pitter-patter as excitement, fear, and desire began to coalesce into a warm heat that radiated at the juncture between her legs. Her breasts started to feel heavy, to ache, and her nipples became erect as a sure hand swept greedily beneath the straps of her gown, cupping and massaging her soft flesh.

Marquis swept the pads of his thumbs across the hard peaks, caressing them in lazy, gentle circles. "And being lovers is enough for you?" he whispered.

Joelle nodded, breathless, her eyes glazing over with tears. "However we can be together, Marquis." Of course, she wanted more. *Everything*. All of him. But she would take whatever she could get, and she didn't care how pathetic that sounded.

All at once, he put her away from him, his hands gripping her shoulders in a strong, unyielding grasp, as he met her stare head-on: "Be sure, Joelle." His eyes were dark with lust, his pupils burning like red-hot embers. "Because there is no turning back."

He glanced down at her breasts and let out a long, aching sigh. "Once I start, I won't be able to stop."

Joelle took Marquis's words into her heart like a sponge absorbing water...and simply held them there, treasuring the moment. "I would never ask you to."

An erotic growl escaped his throat. "I am not a gentle man, Joelle. I am not...as you are."

Joelle reached up and stroked his handsome, angular jaw, melting at the sight of his unbelievably edible...perfect lips. "I know precisely who you are, Marquis." She smiled, but she knew her anxiety showed.

Marquis stepped back then and gestured toward the bed. "Then lie down for me, Joelle." The command was implicit, leaving no room for refusal.

Joelle was surprised...aroused...afraid.

Experiencing all three emotions at once.

Hesitantly, she crawled onto the bed and turned to face him, kneeling with the silk of her gown bunched up in a satin pool around her knees.

The air in his lungs rushed out in a deep, throaty moan. "Let me see you," he commanded, his eyes slowly scanning her body from head to toe. "*Now*."

Joelle shivered as she complied, slowly taking down the straps of her nightgown to reveal soft, trembling shoulders. She continued to lower the lacy material until her breasts were completely bared and exposed to his hungry gaze.

The growl that escaped his throat was guttural and harsh. He licked his bottom lip. "More."

His eyes moved lower, focused like a laser over the juncture between her legs. When he finally looked back up, his smile was positively sinful.

Joelle shivered, becoming increasingly unsure of herself. Did Marquis expect her to kneel before him fully naked while he just stood there...watching...like a hungry wolf ready to devour his prey?

"I don't expect you to kneel before me naked, Joelle," he said, easily reading her thoughts. "I expect you to lie before me naked."

Joelle swallowed her fear and cautiously complied, her eyes never leaving his starving gaze. By the time her thin panties fell to the side, her sense of vulnerability had reached an all-time high. Uneasiness began to overwhelm her, and she reached for the comforter in an effort to cover her exposed body.

Marquis moved like a silent predatory animal then, gliding to the side of the bed. He swiftly caught at her wrist before she could cover herself. "Lie back."

It was a stern command.

Joelle averted her eyes, betraying her nervousness. She knew she had tried to seduce him on his front porch: she had portrayed herself as far more experienced than she really was, but the truth remained...she was still a virgin...all this time saving herself for him.

Joelle was inexperienced.

And completely unprepared for the demands Marquis was making of her.

She couldn't hope to comply with such erotic requests—not without the patient tutelage she had expected him to provide.

"Marquis," she whispered. Her voice sounded tentative.

"I said lie back." He pushed her down against the bed.

Joelle lay there, uncertain, staring up at the male she had worshipped and loved for as long as she could remember. Despite the undeniable feeling of satisfaction—Marquis Silivasi was standing over her bed, and he wanted to make love to *her*—she was afraid.

She wanted to submit.

She wanted so much to please him, to be all she had pretended to be, to be everything he could ever want or need. But the sight of his thick arousal straining at the front of his pants gave her pause.

Tessa Dawn

He was enormous.

And she was…inexperienced.

Her eyes narrowed, drawn to his groin like a moth to a flame, as he slowly unzipped his jeans and pushed them down over his hips, as he carelessly allowed the thick, heavy erection to come free from his pants.

Joelle tried to hide her shock—and her rising fear—but she knew that she had failed. Marquis leaned over her delicate body, his broad, well-defined shoulders and flat, muscular stomach creating a wall of power that boxed her in. He pinned her against the mattress, helpless, as his enormous body descended to blanket hers.

"Are you afraid of me, Joelle?" he asked, his deep, melodic voice harsh with a raspy growl. He reached down to flick at a nipple. Groaning, he lowered his head and took her into the hot cavern of his mouth, where he tasted, suckled…and nipped…until she felt like she might die from the sensuous torture.

"I'm…I'm—" She tried to tell him, but the words were reduced to a whimper as his hand found its way between her thighs.

His touch was strong and aggressive, his fingers sinking deep with one probing thrust.

Reflexively, she clamped her legs shut and clutched at his wrist. "Marquis…*wait.*"

She didn't know exactly what she wanted—she knew that she wanted him, desperately—it was just that…it was all moving way too fast.

Marquis freed his wrist from her grasp in an easy twist, catching a cluster of her thick blond hair in his fist. He planted his free hand on the inside of her thigh, and thrust her legs back open with a hard tug. "Relax, baby," he purred.

"Marquis," she cried, sounding increasingly desperate, "can we…slow down?"

Marquis frowned and pulled away. His dark eyes met hers in a scrutinizing gaze. "Do you or do you not want me, Joelle?"

Instantly, the rising passion and heady warmth she had been feeling left her, and her heart became heavy. Tears stung her soft brown eyes as she registered the unmistakable tone of disapproval in his voice. She was failing him. Disappointing the man of her dreams. She was blowing the only chance she might ever have to be with him: *to make him love her.* Marquis had always made her feel so safe and protected in his presence, but now, she simply felt inadequate.

"Yes," she whispered in a barely audible voice, "I want you, Marquis."

He claimed her mouth with an unforgiving kiss, his perfect lips coaxing hers to open for his possession. His tongue swept roughly as he traced the contours of her mouth, nipped at her bottom lip, and moaned when their tongues tangled together.

And then he knelt in front of her, staring down with insatiable, hungry eyes, clearly more animal than man. He leaned over, clutched her by her thin waist, and lifted her from the mattress as if she weighed nothing, placing her further back on the bed. He caught her legs by the ankles as he did so, pulling them effortlessly apart, opening her to his view, restraining her for his invasion.

Joelle gasped at the vulnerability of the position. She looked up at the powerful man looming over her as he held her open and knelt between her legs. She watched, holding her breath, as he reached down to adjust the enormous staff of masculine flesh in his hand. His gaze held something far beyond passion in it. Possession perhaps? Conquest?

Extreme satisfaction.

He lined up the thick, rounded head at her entrance and pushed it firmly against her, a groan of pleasure escaping his throat as their bodies met.

Much to her distress, Joelle felt her body clench and tighten, becoming rigid instead of wet, in anticipation of his invasion. Her hands seized the comforter, balling it up into two tight fists as she braced herself...knowing she wasn't ready.

And worse, she was afraid.

Her body was doing the exact opposite of what she needed it to do: There was no way she could accommodate such a massive arousal in such a frigid state. Her anxiety rose to alarm; her alarm escalated to panic. Instinctively, she reached out, placed both palms against his powerful chest, and shoved at him hard...in an age-old gesture of *stop*.

"Marquis, I'm sorry..." Her voice weakened with sobs as she twisted, trying to crawl out from underneath him.

But Marquis only tightened his hold.

He firmly caught at her knees and held them back apart.

"Marquis!" she shrieked, her voice now a shrill cry of fear, her heart caught in her throat.

When his eyes finally locked with hers, she knew...when he'd said he wouldn't be able to stop...that was precisely what he meant.

The man above her—the vampire—was utterly carnal, his once blue-black eyes turning deep amber. The tips of his fangs were extended and his breath came in heavy gasps. Joelle saw the determined set of his jaw, felt his heavy breathing as it racked his chest, and observed the heavy-lidded lust that framed his eyes. And she knew...

"What, baby?" he asked, his voice sounding foreign.

"I'm a virgin," she whimpered. It was a mere squeak of a sound, a timid confession: a plea for understanding.

Marquis groaned...low...feral...even more aroused. It was almost as if her heartfelt admission had thrown him over the edge of control, taken his excitement to a whole new level. All at once, he thrust his hips forward, his enormous shaft driving into her like a heavy steel blade.

Joelle cried out—it felt like he was slicing her right down the middle.

The searing pain shot through her core, catching her completely off guard, and she struggled to catch her breath as the sensation radiated throughout her body. She twisted. She turned. She kicked. She tried desperately to get him out. *Now.*

But it was like being held in a vise: the power of his muscular thighs keeping hers apart, the weight of his heavy frame pinning her to the bed, the rhythm of his violent possession...thrusting over and over...piercing deep into her core.

Beneath the wild vampire, Joelle struggled to remain calm, to withstand the horrible tearing sensations. She couldn't cry out or ask him to stop. It was all she could do to maintain awareness as he stretched her impossibly, plunging deeper and deeper until she thought her body might literally come apart, until she was certain she had been nearly torn in half.

Joelle held her breath. She grimaced. She bit her lower lip and whimpered. She clutched at the covers with her fists and choked back her tears. She tried so hard...*for him*. Her beloved Marquis. While he gave himself up to the sheer gratification of her body, taking his own pleasure with wild abandon and brute force. Seemingly unconcerned—if not completely unaware—of her pain and her struggles.

And just when she thought it might never end, that she might actually pass out from the brutal possession, she felt an even greater agony: the piercing bite of his fangs.

Like two steel daggers, they sliced into her artery, sinking deep, as he pulled...and drank...like a starving beast. And then she heard a primal shout of release as he exploded deep inside of her, still taking from her vein as wave after wave of his seed poured into her...and he finally collapsed in exhaustion.

At last.

Blessedly.

It was over.

Joelle lay perfectly still beneath her beloved—torn, bleeding, and full with his seed. She was frightened and confused as she struggled to catch her breath, pushing at his heavy weight.

He slowly removed his fangs from her throat, released two small drops of venom to seal the wounds, and exhaled deeply. Then, he lay his head against her chest for an extended moment before leisurely rolling onto his back.

Joelle fought to hold back her tears. She was relieved that it was finally over...yet deeply confused by the reality of the act as

Tessa Dawn

opposed to the fantasy she had always imagined. And God help her—she still didn't want to lose him.

Lying there so quietly beside him, she listened to the steady beat of his heart and tried desperately to remember all of the things she had loved about him. She tried to take solace in the fact that he was her lover now, that he had taken *her* blood for sustenance.

Joelle desperately wanted Marquis to wrap his strong arms around her and comfort her. To give her some excuse, any excuse, as to why he had lost control. She wanted him to tell her he was sorry, and he would never hurt her again.

She wanted Marquis to make everything right.

And she craved the simplicity of his friendship, a reminder of his tenderness, more than she had ever craved anything in her life.

She knew she should never have presented herself as someone experienced: not to a male such as Marquis. Not to a vampire...a wild being. But it was far too late to change that now. Joelle knew her body would heal; it was her heart that needed reassurance.

When Marquis sat up and began to search the floor for his clothing, she almost cried out with despair. "Where are you going?"

She could hardly hold back her tears when he rose languidly from the bed and began to dress. "I have to get back to my brothers, my love." His tone left no room for argument.

Like a sailor tossed from a ship into a turbulent sea, Joelle clutched at the only life jacket she had. She seized those two little words and held on for dear life: *my love*. Marquis had called her *my love*. And she would hold onto that knowledge...because she had to hold onto it.

For if ever someone was drowning, it was Joelle Parker in that barren, heartbroken moment.

BLOOD DESTINY

Valentine Nistor flew across the sky like an ancient bird of prey, gloating in the power of his black magic, reveling in the invigorating feeling of conquest. Very few vampires had the knowledge or the skill to cloak their own presence for an extended period of time, let alone to take on the voice, mannerisms, and physical appearance of another.

But he had done just that.

And he had brutally taken Joelle Parker's innocence while pretending to be Marquis Silivasi. Not only did he best the cocky Ancient Warrior, but he insured himself two more offspring in the process: sons who would never have to be sacrificed. That debt had already been paid...by Dalia.

Valentine could hardly believe his good fortune: his decision to follow Marquis home the night they had sparred in the sacrificial chamber. He had hoped to catch the ancient one off guard, but what he'd stumbled upon was so much more valuable. Marquis had sensed his presence then, but the young, lovesick female had distracted him.

The pathetic female had been such easy prey, so willing, so gullible. So enjoyable.

He dipped low and sailed through a cloud, invigorated by the fresh human blood flowing through his veins. It had been so hard to stop. To keep from draining the last ounce of life out of the human. To keep from watching as her hot, supple body went limp beneath his...lifeless at his hands.

Such awesome power over another being. Such decadent pleasure.

Valentine thought about the fate of their species—*the house of Jadon* and *the house of Jaegar*—how such a simple, but profound, circumstance as birth could so dramatically alter one's fate. The light vampires were so arrogant and proud: walking in the sun, keeping their souls, being loved and cherished by women like Joelle. It was disgusting.

He scoffed at their weakness. They were hardly a step above humans, always having to suppress their true power. They would never understand the rush of the kill, the gratification of taking one's pleasure from a helpless woman…the supremacy of black magic.

Valentine turned in jubilant circles as he plunged toward the ground. Maybe it was time to consider siring a human. With three sons to raise, he would need a nanny who could stick around for a while. In the past, such a thing was impossible. The thrill of the kill, the insatiable draw of bloodlust, was always too hard to resist.

The nannies never lasted.

They never lived long enough to provide proper care.

Valentine sighed. Perhaps it was time to find a dark mate, a human woman hungry enough to relinquish her soul for the promise of immortality. A woman he could convert *and keep*. A woman he could control. A woman he could force and brutalize, and take his pleasure from at will.

His heart beat strong in his chest. What did it matter? Whether he sired a human woman or went through fifty nannies? His son Derrian was thriving, and soon, in just forty-eight hours, he would have two more offspring.

Life was good.

The ancient one, Jaegar, would have been pleased.

eighteen

Tristan and Willie had been gone for at least an hour by the time Jocelyn found the keys to the shed. The storm had become so violent, the temperature so cold, and the snow so heavy, there had been no need to restrain her. As it was, they were already facing white-out conditions: a situation where one could get lost within ten feet of their own home and never make it back.

Tristan was smart enough to know that any attempt at escape would mean certain death at the hands of the elements. Without a satellite phone or two-way radio, Jocelyn posed no threat. And she clearly stood no chance of escape. The only remaining chance she had was to get to the arsenal in the shed, but Tristan and Willie had been careful to make sure it was securely locked before they headed out...to hunt.

To find...*and kill*...Nathaniel.

Fortunately for Jocelyn, she had known Tristan for three years, and she knew how he operated. Tristan always had a backup plan. And Jocelyn was certain he wouldn't have taken the only set of keys to the shed with him: It was just a matter of finding the spare set. After a great deal of searching—and more than a little thinking—Jocelyn was able to locate Tristan's hiding place by figuring out the most unlikely place she could think of: the one spot no one would ever dare look unless they absolutely had to. The keys were attached to the underside of the septic tank, neatly taped to the lid in a small plastic bag.

Wincing from the bitter sting of the frigid air, Jocelyn jiggled the last of three keys inside the keyhole of the small, dilapidated outbuilding, less than twenty yards from where the Snake Creek River met the base of a steep, rising cliff. The key turned and the latch gave way so that it only took one shove to force the heavy wooden door open. The odor that rushed out from the shed's interior almost took her breath away, and she struggled to keep her balance in the face of the assault. In an effort to breathe, she covered her nose with her hands.

What was that stench? A dead animal? Rotting meat? Had the shed been used as a butcher house?

Jocelyn pulled her heavy wool scarf up from her neck to shield her face, wrapping it tightly around her nose. She needed her hands free while she explored the shed but knew she wouldn't make it far unless she could control that awful smell.

The wide arc of her flashlight cast shadows throughout the dingy building as she slowly crept forward. She needed to find a good weapon. Maybe even some materials she could use to rig a booby trap before the men returned. She didn't dare hope to find a radio, but she was determined to search every square inch of the rundown shed anyway, just to make sure.

As her eyes adjusted to the dim light of the interior, she began to take in its contents: A waist-high, dilapidated wooden bench stood on the right-hand side of the shed with a myriad of rusted tools and assorted items laid out on top. There were several boxes of bullets, one large box of matches, three or four different rolls of tape, and a small carton of flares laid out haphazardly over the surface. All materials that had potential.

There were several pieces of old, rusted farm equipment spread out along the floor throughout the front of the building, and various tools hung from the ceiling along with several sealed boxes, most likely containing outdated supplies. There were two small tires piled on top of a dented red wheelbarrow with a broken handle; and two doors stood at the back of the shed, erected side by side, each one hinged in the opposite direction of the other, opening to adjacent rooms.

Jocelyn carefully made her way to the first door on the left, hoping to find what she was looking for on her first try. When she swung the heavy door open, her heart slammed into her chest with a heavy thud, and a shriek of absolute horror escaped her throat as her eyes fixed on the horrific scene in front of her: It was Braden Bratianu. Nachari's young charge. Hanging lifeless and bloodied against a thick wooden cross.

His body was savagely torn and badly bruised, his hands pierced all the way through the palms with heavy iron spikes. His chest wall was impaled by a large wooden stake, and he looked more fragile than any victim she had ever seen. Jocelyn's heart shattered into a thousand pieces as she thought about what the poor young man must have endured.

Had Tristan done this? The thought was as sickening as it was hard to believe. And if so, why? Why would anyone take pleasure in inflicting so much suffering on a helpless boy? Even if Tristan were a vampire hunter, what reason could he possibly have to brutalize a helpless child?

And Braden of all people.

His heart was as pure as gold.

The reverberation of Jocelyn's scream must have roused the child because he slowly inclined his head and turned his tear-stained eyes in her direction, struggling to bring her into focus.

Jocelyn gasped, shocked that he could still be alive. It seemed impossible.

"Braden!"

She ran to the heavy cross, trying desperately to prop him up, to lift the heavy weight of his body off the piercing stakes that were tugging at his skin, continuously using his own mass to cause him further agony. But Braden was far too heavy to lift. His entire body was dead weight.

As Jocelyn tried once more to move him, a strangled cry ripped from his throat. It hovered in the air like the echoing howl of a wounded animal, a young bear caught in a trap. Braden's tears began to flow uncontrollably, his pleading eyes suddenly matching his ghastly makeup.

"Jocelyn?" His voice was a mere whisper.

He blinked several times in an effort to remove the blood that was trickling down his forehead from a deep gash in his scalp. Some of it had already dried and clotted in his hair, yet much of it still ran in small rivers of anguish down his face.

Jocelyn had to fight to restrain her own tears. "It's me, Braden," she crooned. She stroked his cheek as gently as possible. "Do you remember me? Jocelyn, Nathaniel's…wife?"

She couldn't think of any other way to explain who she was. To make it clear that she was a friend, not an enemy. Now was not the time for pride or propriety. Now was the time for making Braden's world as simple as she could.

"Help me," he whimpered. "Please get me down before they come back." His voice was heavy with desperation, and the sound fell like a heavy weight on her heart.

"I'm trying, Braden. I'm trying."

Jocelyn surveyed the entire scene, her mind racing frantically in a whirlwind of thoughts. Feelings of helplessness, desperation, and rage churned in her gut. All the while, her stomach fought the impulse to heave. How in the world was she going to help him? She couldn't lift him. And she couldn't leave him.

A harsh moan escaped Braden's throat, and he sniffled, fighting back more tears.

Jocelyn studied one of the heavy metal spikes in his hands: If the stake had pierced him all the way through, a mallet would only pound it halfway back. Maybe there was some way she could pull the stake out. She knew the pain would be unbearable if she tried, but the alternative seemed far worse.

Leaving him for Tristan and Willie to finish the job.

To complete their sick, depraved torture.

Jocelyn could not allow that to happen. *She would not allow that to happen.*

Taking a deep breath, she whispered, "Hold on, Braden." And then she reached up to test the heavy pin, needing to get a measure of its strength, trying to figure out what kind of tool she might need to remove it. She was hoping against hope that the wood was rotten, or the nail was bent, that it would somehow give way against the strain.

"Stop!" Braden cried, his agony halting her dead in her tracks. His voice was hoarse with misery. "Please…*please*…stop." His chest heaved with sobs. "Don't touch the spikes. You'll never get them out. Please, just go get Nachari. *Please…*" He coughed between words.

"I can't, Braden." Jocelyn shook her head apologetically. She closed her eyes and placed her hands over her face. "I'm a prisoner here, too." She glanced through the open door of the back room toward the front of the shed, her heart beating rapidly. "I don't know how much time we have before they come back, but I promise—I'll get you out of here…somehow. Unfortunately, it's probably going to hurt."

Braden managed to lift his head and look around the shed, as if trying to come up with a solution for her. Every movement brought more unbearable pain. "You can't undo these pins, Jocelyn." It was a statement of fact…of defeat. "I'm gonna die here."

Her heart was breaking. "No! No, you're not, Braden! We just have to think."

The longer she considered his wounds and his predicament, the more she feared he was right. It would take superhuman strength to get him down from that cross, and those pins were not going to budge. Jocelyn rubbed her forehead at the bridge of her nose. *Think. Think!* Maybe she could get him down without removing the pins. What if she sawed through the boards around the stakes, leaving his limbs attached to the wood, but freeing him from the bulk of the cross?

"I'll be right back."

"Don't leave me!"

"I'm not going to leave you, Braden. I have to go look for a tool." She frantically searched the shed for a chainsaw, but the only thing she found was an old tarnished hacksaw. "Damnit!" She clenched her fists in frustration and struck out at the wall. It would take a month of sawing to get through that thick wood with such a rudimentary tool.

She found a straight razor and an ice pick in a small red toolbox and groaned, considering the alternatives. What if she could cut him free? Enlarge his wounds so that his hands could slide over the spikes? She peered into the back room and cursed beneath her breath. *Great idea, Joss! And just how is that supposed to work?* What was she planning to do after she carved out the center of his hands? Cut into his chest to remove the thick wooden stake as well?

Jocelyn shook her head. She wasn't thinking rationally anymore: Cutting up the poor boy's body in an attempt to get him off of a cross was hardly a reasonable alternative.

"Jocelyn... Jocelyn? Jocelyn!"

Braden was calling out to her now, a new surge of panic beginning to set in. Tears welled up in her eyes as his groans and his suffering, his endless pleas for help, increased.

Stop this right now, Jocelyn! she said to herself. *Concentrate. Just slow down and think! Use your brain. What can Braden do to help you?* Jocelyn went back to Braden's side, calmer now: determined to find a solution.

"Braden, I need you to pay attention for a minute. I'm going to ask you some questions. Try and figure out a way to help you. I need to know about your powers. The things you can do. The other night at Nathaniel's house, Nathaniel was in trouble and Marquis came to him in the form of a hologram. Can you do anything like that? Could you go to Nachari like that?"

"I can't do holograms yet." His voice was growing weaker, and he sounded so defeated.

Jocelyn sighed. "Nathaniel can also read other people's thoughts. What about that? Can you send a thought to Nachari? Or maybe shape-shift? Colette said vampires could dissolve in order to pass through walls and solid objects. Can you do anything like that with your body, Braden?"

Braden shook his head, slowly, looking unbelievably sad. "I don't have the skills to shape-shift. You already know that. You saw me earlier. And especially not in this much pain." He choked out the words.

Jocelyn frowned. "You know what I saw earlier?" she asked defiantly. "I saw a very strong, courageous young man—that's what I saw. I saw you challenge Marquis when he pushed you too far, something I would never have the courage to do. And I saw you turn yourself into a perfect little vampire bat and storm out of the room. So, don't tell me you don't have any special powers when I know full well that you do!"

She hated speaking to him so sternly when he was suffering so badly, but she had to give him hope. She had to push him to try.

A faint light appeared in his eyes. "I…I might be able to link our minds…mine and Nachari's. If I could reach him, *he* could help me shape-shift, even from a long ways away. Maybe he could use his spells to help us. He knows a lot of magic."

Jocelyn's heart skipped a beat. She didn't dare hope.

And then the light suddenly faded from his eyes. "But I'm telling you, I'm too weak to do it now." He turned his head and gestured to indicate the inside of his arm, the brachial artery. "They took too much of my blood."

Jocelyn looked at the torn, blood-soaked shirt hanging from Braden's thin frame. Why hadn't she seen that before? The young man had lost a tremendous amount of blood. She stepped back and covered her face in her hands to hide her dismay. And then she began to cry, unable to remain strong for him any longer.

Braden slowly raised his head and looked at her. He steadied his gaze like a predator studying potential prey. Intent on survival. "Unless—"

"Unless what?" Jocelyn asked. "Braden, do you have an idea?"

Braden shook his head and then let it drop again. "No, I don't have any ideas."

He was lying. Why?

Jocelyn gently cupped his face in her hands. His beautiful burnt-sienna eyes were dark with anguish, his pale, painted white skin streaked with blood and tears. "Tell me, Braden. What were you thinking?"

Braden swallowed hard. "Blood." The word was a mere whisper.

"What?" she asked.

"If I could take your blood, it might make me strong enough to reach Nachari. Maybe even long enough for him to help me.

Or at least to figure out where we are."

Shamefully, Jocelyn stepped back from the cross, her eyes open wide with alarm.

So much for strength and courage.

Not that, she thought. *Anything but that!*

She swallowed hard and summoned her bravery. "What exactly do you mean, Braden? If I...gave you my blood...what exactly could you do?"

Braden sniffled. "I'm not sure exactly. But I know I would be strong enough to call out to Nachari for help. At least for a minute. Maybe I could even hold a mind-merge long enough for him to use his power to get me down from here. Remember? When I got stuck? How he turned me into a bat and then back into my own body? When I couldn't do it myself?"

Jocelyn nodded. "I remember."

Braden dropped his head. "But I won't have very long, maybe only like thirty seconds or something." All at once, the golden irises of his eyes lit up as a spark of hope appeared in their depths. "Jocelyn, did Nathaniel convert you yet? Did he ever take your blood?"

Jocelyn's hand went instinctively to her throat. "No, never." Her denial was adamant.

The light in his eyes extinguished.

"Why?"

Braden shook his head slowly. "Because, if he had converted you, the two of you could talk telepathically. You could talk to any of them. And if your blood was inside of him, he could find you anywhere. Anytime he wanted. It's kind of like radar: GPS for vampires. Without it, there's no way he can find you."

Jocelyn closed her eyes. Nathaniel had avoided both converting her and taking her blood, even though his life depended upon her safety, her staying with him. He had not acted selfishly, and now they might all die because of it.

Jocelyn ran her hand softly along Braden's cheek, bracing herself against his constant shivering and the agonized grimace of pain that accompanied his every spoken word. This young boy was innocent. The son of a woman who had been claimed by a vampire. A human. Just like her. Someone taken and converted. Braden had been brought into this dangerous world without any choice in the matter, so how could she possibly leave him to die such an agonizing death? And God forbid, what if he didn't die?

They had kept him alive this long for a reason: What were they planning to do with him when they returned?

Jocelyn's stomach turned over. She couldn't afford to be afraid right now. She couldn't possibly be that selfish.

When she thought about her informant, she knew Willie had been the one in the shed with Braden. And God help her, but she wanted nothing more than to put a bullet through his head right now. To call Nachari, Nathaniel, Kagen, and Marquis to Braden's aid—not just to save him *but to avenge him*. If the cost of that vengeance was her own blood, then so be it.

Steeling her resolve, she looked Braden straight in the eyes. "What do I need to do, Braden? How do I give you my blood?"

Braden winced. "To be honest, I'm not so sure I'm strong enough to take it: My dad…and Nachari…they still mostly feed me." He looked away like he was embarrassed, as if he hated having to tell her that secret. "I tried a couple times, but I wasn't very…smooth at it. You know what I mean?"

Jocelyn shook her head.

"I mean that it's probably…" He sighed, his frustration growing. "It's probably gonna hurt…for you…if I try."

Jocelyn placed a hand over her stomach.

He could have kept that information to himself.

"Don't talk like that, Braden," she admonished. "Trust me; you're not helping your case. Let's just both keep focused on what we need to do here. There's no way I'm going to leave you in this shed, so this thing we're going to do, it's not optional."

A crimson tear escaped his eye, and Braden turned away.

Jocelyn stroked his cheek. "Oh man, Braden. We're in quite a mess, aren't we?"

Braden nodded, and then he blinked back his tears, equally

determined. "I could try your wrist, but the vein's not as good. Not as much blood flow. A lot slower, too. Your neck would be easier...for me."

Jocelyn all at once felt her legs begin to give out from underneath her. She reached up and clutched at the cross in an effort to steady herself...only to end up rattling Braden, who immediately cried out from the pain of the unexpected movement.

"Oh, shit! *I'm sorry.* I'm sorry, Braden..."

Man, they needed to get this show on the road.

Braden sniffled and tried to nod.

Jocelyn took another deep breath. "Okay...since we both know we're going to do this, and you're going to be just fine at it, let's make sure we're on the same page before we start."

She wanted to make sure Braden would use his time with Nachari wisely. And even more than that, she wanted to be sure they would not have to attempt it more than once.

"The moment you connect with Nachari, I want you to tell him the extent of your injuries—make sure he understands that you're pinned to this cross. You need to let him know that you're with me, and there's no way I can get you down. Tell him he has to be the one to help you, and he has to do it *fast* since you only have a few seconds to maintain contact. If you have any extra time after that, try to describe the contents of the shed, what kind of tools we have access to; maybe he can come up with an idea that I can't. Can you remember all of that, Braden?"

Braden looked overwhelmed.

And if Jocelyn was being perfectly honest with herself, she had to admit it was a tall order.

She had seen the young man at Nathaniel's house, trying as hard as he could to utilize his abilities, and the truth was, the kid just didn't have a lot of...aptitude. But if there was one thing she knew for sure, it was that necessity truly was the mother of invention, and matters of life and death had a way of inspiring all kinds of newfound talent in people.

Hopefully, vampires were included in that theory.

"I'll try," he muttered.

Jocelyn felt her knees knock together and knew she needed to act quickly, before her courage left her. "Okay, then: the neck it is. Where do you need me?"

Braden looked down at her. "Can you pull your hair out of the way? And get up on your tippy toes. Bring your neck up to my mouth."

Despite the gravity of the situation, the young man sounded a little shy...as if he felt embarrassed saying those things to a female. Jocelyn paused for a moment, hoping there was no sexual association with the act of feeding for a male vampire. But when the thought became just a little too creepy, she pushed it out of her mind. There were plenty of other things to worry about right now; she would keep that concern to herself.

"You ready?" she asked.

Braden let his head fall to the side for a moment, as if he were resting, trying to gather his strength. When he was finally ready, he lifted his head and turned to face her again.

"I'm ready."

Jocelyn started to approach the young vampire, and then all of a sudden, she stumbled back: Young, shy little Braden looked positively alarming. His beautiful sienna eyes had dimmed into harsh shadows, darker than the night, and his normally golden pupils had narrowed into small little slits, glowing like those of a predatory animal, the centers a deep, feral red. His soft, pouty lips were drawn back in a snarl, and they twitched in some sort of automatic response. The boy was practically salivating with anticipation.

This was *not* the shy, unsure child she had met at the house, the human who didn't know how to be a vampire. This was the real deal. And he was gearing up to sink those jagged fangs deep into her neck.

Jocelyn sent up a silent prayer and pressed her body as close to the cross as possible.

Don't flinch. Don't faint. Don't pull away.

She repeated the words like a mantra.

BLOOD DESTINY

Don't flinch. Don't faint. Don't pull away.

And then she rose up on her toes, swept her hair to the side, and pressed her face, cheek to cheek, against Braden's.

Despite her resolve, her body shook with fear.

She could feel his warm breath against her neck, a strong contrast to the bitter cold of the night, as his head slowly turned to the side. He nuzzled her neck, gently sweeping his mouth back and forth several times as if trying to find the best angle, and oddly, the sensation had a calming effect on her body. And then, all of a sudden, when she had finally relaxed, a guttural hiss escaped his throat and he struck with unbelievable speed and accuracy.

Braden's head snapped down, his mouth latched onto her throat, and his sharp fangs sank deep into her artery with a ferocity she hadn't expected. The powerful bite almost dropped her in an involuntary reaction as a piercing pain shot through her neck, radiated through her shoulders, and traveled down the length of her spine.

Her legs shook. Her body convulsed. The reaction lasted almost thirty seconds before she finally surrendered to the power of the vampire's hold, before she finally went limp against him, relaxing into a growing web of enthrallment.

Her blood felt cold flowing out of her vein, and she could feel the powerful tug as he sucked, his mouth drawing deep gulps of the life-giving fluid out of her body and into his. And then just like that, she was there: merged with Braden— connected to Nachari.

She could feel the distinct presence of Nathaniel, Marquis, and Kagen as well, each of them projecting their individual essence as clearly as they presented their own personalities in person. Braden relayed the information exactly as Jocelyn had instructed...forgetting nothing.

Life and death, Jocelyn thought.

Nachari responded with quick, decisive action: *You will drink until I tell you to release her, and then you will give your mind completely over to me so I can free you before we lose our connection.*

Tessa Dawn

Braden grunted an affirmative.

Jocelyn? The voice was Nathaniel's. *Listen carefully, my love.*

Jocelyn didn't know whether or not Nathaniel could hear her reply, and frankly, she was far too paralyzed with pain to respond even if he could, but the sound of his voice bathed her heart in warmth and hope. She hadn't realized until that moment how deeply she missed him, how strong their connection truly was.

Nachari has fed Braden before, but he has never taken his blood...so we cannot track you through that bond. We were able to follow your trail as far as the Snake Creek River, but the river forks in three directions and the storm has taken all other signs away. As soon as Braden is free, I need you to get to the flares and release as many as you can. Do not worry about the storm. Even if we can't see them, we will be able to smell the phosphorus. Just keep releasing flares. I promise: We will come to you immediately.

Jocelyn blinked her eyes, unable to move her head, hoping Nathaniel could sense her understanding. Hoping he knew how truly sorry she was for walking away the way she had.

And Jocelyn? It was Nathaniel's voice again. *You need to know that Tristan is not alone. He has several soldiers with him, and they are not human, sweetheart. They are lycan—werewolves. They can only be destroyed through extreme trauma or with a silver bullet through the heart. So do not try and fight them. Get to the flares, tiger-eyes.*

Jocelyn was almost grateful that she was being held up by a massive set of fangs, by some kind of vampire enthrallment, that Braden had complete control of her body at that moment—because, otherwise, she was going to lose it.

Werewolves?

Enough was enough.

And then a powerful male voice resounded in their minds: *Braden, it's Marquis.*

Braden became very still, listening intently.

How are you holding up, son?

Jocelyn heard Braden's heart skip a beat. Marquis had called him *son,* and he was practically holding his breath, straining to hear the fearsome warrior's next words.

I need you to do something for me: I need you to take care of Jocelyn...to do whatever it takes to keep the two of you safe until we can follow the flares. I know how difficult this is right now. I know that you are hurting, but this is what warriors do. And I believe that under all that silliness, you are a true warrior. Can you do that for me, son?

Despite his enormous suffering, his inability to speak, Braden's response could be felt clearly. His intention was almost audible: He would succeed in meeting the Ancient Master Warrior's request, or he would die trying.

Kagen spoke next. *Do not forget to use your venom, Braden. It will help to stabilize your wounds until I can attend to your injuries. We will be there shortly, so hold on; know that you only have to endure a little while longer.*

Nachari came back then, his voice soft, melodic, and unwavering with authority. *That is enough blood, Braden. Release Jocelyn and seal the wound. When I take control of your mind, it will not be gentle, as I have to move quickly, so do not resist my total control.*

At Nachari's command, Braden began to withdraw his fangs. As his canines receded, his incisors lengthened, leaking minute drops of venom onto Jocelyn's neck. The puncture wounds were instantly healed.

Jocelyn dropped to the floor of the shed. She grasped her neck, trying to massage the pain away as she gasped for air. She lay there, dizzy, looking up at the cross, watching as Braden's solid form began to shimmer into a translucent outline, and the wounds in his hands and chest began to radiate a pulsating orange glow as his body released itself from the piercing spikes. Like air flowing through space, Braden gently floated to the ground.

And just like that, he was free of the cross.

The moment Braden's feet touched down, Jocelyn heard voices coming from around the corner.

Angry voices.

Cursing. Guttural.

Tristan and Willie.

They were back from the hunt and clearly in a foul mood, obviously unable to prevail in the violent storm. They sounded frustrated but determined...desperate to make at least one kill. And who better to go after in the bleak, limiting conditions than helpless, dying Braden?

Jocelyn was as disgusted as she was afraid, but as luck would have it, Nachari was still merged with his young protégé. And he had picked up on Braden's observations.

As Jocelyn and Braden frantically scampered for cover, Nachari quickly built the illusion of Braden still hanging on the cross, staked to the wood, bleeding, and almost dead. They dashed into the adjacent room, just to the right of the one Braden had been tortured in, and they hid.

Holding their breath, they took cover in the back of the shed.

nineteen

The moment Jocelyn and Braden entered the musty back room, they both hit the floor, silently shutting the door behind them. Braden scampered to the far left corner, ducking behind a large wooden crate, while Jocelyn dashed to her right, hunkering down beneath a strange, looming object.

As soon as she was settled, her eyes began to adjust to the pitch black of the room, and the massive object in front of her began to take shape. Jocelyn clasped her hands over her mouth in an effort to stifle a scream—it just couldn't be.

The large wooden device stood like a glowering phantom, a living remnant of evil transported from a dark, revolting past. It was a statue of history carved out of torture and pain, molded by the shadowed hands of inhumanity.

The ancient guillotine stood almost five feet tall, with a heavy iron blade poised at the top of two adjacent square posts, its sides welded into vertical grooves. The massive blade was held back by a long, rusted pin, and beneath the sharp edge was a hard platform…a horizontal wooden bed.

The bed stretched out perpendicular to the blade so that its occupant's head would hang off the end, dangling helplessly beneath the looming steel, facing up or down, depending upon the executioner's desire.

Jocelyn strained to adjust her eyes. Once. Twice. Another time. And then, in absolute horror, she scurried back from the contraption, kicking up dust in her frenzied effort as her heels dug into the ground. Her eyes remained transfixed on the helpless male lying in front of her, manacled to the wooden platform.

Nathaniel had called the thick head of hair *the crown of the King Cobra*, but whatever its name, it was unmistakable: red-and-black bands of wild, wavy tresses, the signature coronet of the Dark

Ones—long, silky locks of midnight and crimson, intermixed in a glorious and terrifying mane.

The vampire's eyes flashed open, glowing like two red embers of fire surrounded by blackened coals, as they smoldered in the back of the darkened room. To Jocelyn's horror, he continued to stare at her as she sat trapped by the wall, no less than two feet away from his protruding fangs. Jocelyn pressed as tightly against the wall as she could, praying she would disappear from the creature's view. But his gaze remained steadily locked with hers.

His body was battered and bleeding with what had to be hundreds of flesh wounds, deliberate, shallow cuts made for the sole purpose of bleeding him out...slowly, draining his blood. His arms and legs were shackled with four heavy manacles, two at the ankles and two at the wrists. And a coordinated lock system held the manacles in place, sustained by another large pin, situated just below his right shoulder.

The creature yanked at the heavy manacles, and he growled a harsh, guttural warning as he thrashed around wildly trying to free his tortured body. His cold eyes pierced hers. And then he flashed a look so demonic that Jocelyn froze in place, certain he was about to rip her throat out all the way from the platform, shackled or not.

Jocelyn scanned the room for a weapon: a pipe, a hammer— anything—just so long as it gave her some defense against the wrathful being in front of her. Although the platform looked secure, and the creature looked weakened, there wasn't a doubt in her mind he was searching for a way to break free. And she was his target.

His newfound inspiration.

All at once, the door to the shed flew open and Tristan's deep voice could be heard reverberating across the distance, roaring with anger. "Jocelyn! Where are you? What the hell have you done?"

He obviously knew she had found the keys. Holding her breath, she followed the sound of his footsteps as he stomped around the shed, furiously tossing things out of his way.

He cursed like a sailor as he smashed objects against the walls, all the while shining the bright oval of his flashlight in a crisscross pattern, over the floor, up to the ceiling, then back down again to the corners of the shed.

"The boy is still here," Willie said, "so she couldn't have gotten far."

Jocelyn shut her eyes. *Thank God.* At least they didn't know Braden was free. Even as she thought it, Braden made his way quietly along the floor to the front of the blackened room, where he perched in waiting behind the heavy door.

Tristan grunted. "She's not strong enough to free him, or believe me, she would have. Jocelyn!" His voice thickened in anger.

Jocelyn held her breath and waited for what felt like an eternity as Tristan's footsteps slowly moved closer, coming toward the back of the shed. As the snarl of his grunts and the hiss of his curses grew louder and louder. Her heart skipped a beat when she heard the door to the adjacent room open…and then close…signaling that the two men were now headed toward the room they were in.

When Braden crouched low behind the door in a predatory stance, Jocelyn cringed: The boy was no match for Tristan or Willie, not if they were the creatures Nathaniel had named them. Her eyes grew wide with fright even as her heart pounded out a beat of fearful anticipation. *Werewolves.* Such creatures did not exist. They could not exist. But then, neither did vampires until a few days ago.

Jocelyn's arms and legs began to tremble uncontrollably as the heavy wooden door creaked open and death stood in the doorway. Who was she kidding? She was a detective. She had great self-defense skills, but she was in no way prepared to battle the kind of creatures that were now only seconds away.

And Braden?

He was a terrified boy with a huge heart and a whole lot of guts…who was about to die a gruesome, unjust death. A human turned vampire who couldn't even shape-shift into a bat without assistance.

As Tristan's footsteps finally entered the room, Jocelyn resigned herself to the inevitable conclusion: They were doomed. She only hoped it would be quick and painless.

And then, in her resignation, her eyes swept down to the guillotine, to the creature laid out so heinously before her...the one who would be joining them in death.

And her heart skipped another beat.

What had she learned in all her years as a detective about the nature of a species? *Any species.* Self-preservation was instinctual...primal...fight or flight. It didn't matter if they were thieves committing burglary, guards watching over inmates, or cops attacked by criminals; in the heat of battle, the actual moment of sink or swim, self-preservation *always* took over.

Despite the best intentions, one instinct—and only one instinct—ruled supreme: the instinct to survive. That deep, primal voice inside that screamed, *Stay alive!*

Jocelyn hugged her arms to her chest, trying to gather her courage. It was true—wolves had been known to chew off their own legs to survive a hunter's trap, and humans had been known to eat their dead in the perils of winter. Whatever the threat was, no matter the obstacle that stood between a living being and their life, pressed far enough, they would go after it.

Jocelyn swallowed hard and forced herself to look at the dark creature before her. The sheer loathing on his face made her wince, but she continued to stare into his hate-filled eyes. She was not his enemy. Not right now.

Praying he was capable of telepathy, she reached out a trembling hand and placed it cautiously on his head. He jerked. A feral hiss escaped his throat, and daggers shot from his blackened eyes.

Unless you are set free, you will die tonight, she said, her voice quivering even in her mind. *I may be your enemy, and you might want me dead, but we both know that I am no threat to you. Not here. Not now. Not tonight. And neither is the child. He is a victim like you.* She drew in a deep, steadying breath, her hand trembling against his hair.

She couldn't help but think of the monster Valentine in the chamber: recall his blackened soul, remember the evil, *recognize that she was bargaining with the devil*. She pushed the thoughts from her mind and pressed on.

The werewolves have come to hunt the descendants of Jadon and the descendants of Jaegar alike—to destroy your kind without distinction. If we fight each other, we all die here tonight, but if we fight them, we may survive.

The creature stirred and hissed, clearly unimpressed with her soliloquy, his bared fangs resting against his lower lips as his breath came in raspy pants and growls. His eyes narrowed even further until they were nothing but two identical slits of fury.

Jocelyn studied his face, refusing to look away. *The enemy of my enemy is my friend*. She whispered the words, almost as a mantra. *The enemy of my enemy is my friend…*

The enemy of my enemy is my friend!

She knew she was trying to convince herself more than the seething creature laid out before her, the battered male waiting helplessly to resume his torture and eventual death. And she also knew the ugly truth: that this vampire knew nothing of friendship. Or loyalty. Or teamwork with the likes of her. But he was a living, breathing being. And that meant he had an instinct to survive. They shared a common enemy, and it was clearly *that* enemy which posed the greatest threat to his life…not her.

Her argument was cut short as Tristan howled and a horrific roar of fury shook the entire outbuilding. The hunter threw a ferocious punch right at the face of the crouching vampire who was waiting behind the door, and Braden ducked with incredible speed. He easily dodged the heavily muscled rocket, but he was completely outmatched in every other way.

His fangs exploded.

His eyes glowed.

He lunged at the lycan's throat, jagged teeth tearing wildly into flesh as a guttural hiss echoed in the night.

Jocelyn froze…terrified.

She watched the scene unfold like a grisly horror film she

couldn't turn away from. As if the entire thing were being played in slow motion.

Braden's arms thrashed wildly. His claws slashed and stabbed. He wrenched his head from side to side, snarling like a rabid dog as he pulled, twisted, and tore at Tristan's flesh, trying desperately to dislodge the man's jugular. And then what Jocelyn saw next etched terror into every living cell of her body.

Tristan, her partner of three years, the man she had known, worked with, and trusted, threw back his wild mane of hair and let out a twisted, unnatural cry—a demonic howl of fury that rocked the foundations of the small decaying shed so hard the building nearly caved in. All at once, his bones began to lengthen. His joints cracked, and his muscles stretched impossibly. Fur began to ripple along the pores of his skin— wiry, thick, blondish-brown fur—and his jaw jutted forward to reveal a mouthful of daggers, tucked neatly beside a vicious set of canines.

The wolf was positively enormous, standing at least ten feet tall. His muscles rippled in angry waves, and his eyes glowed a fiendish yellow. With one strong hand, he grabbed Braden around the throat and wrenched the boy's teeth from his neck, slamming him straight through the shed wall. Braden's neck snapped back as his head took the brunt of the blow, opening up and spilling blood like a geyser shooting from a pressured well. And then Tristan sunk his fearsome canines into Braden's shoulder, just above his heart, and tore him open like a wild animal…a lion bringing down a gazelle.

Braden shouted his pain, and Jocelyn impulsively jumped up to go to his aid when all of a sudden, his cries fell silent, and the sight of an enormous gray wolf moving stealthily in her direction tore her attention away from the atrocity occurring behind the door.

Willie!

He was fully transformed and fevered in his rage, his hungry yellow eyes glaring at Jocelyn. He slowly swept around the corner of the room, stalking her in a wide arc, with his teeth drawn back in a snarl so distorted—he appeared to be smiling.

Jocelyn's heart stopped.

Surely, Braden was dead.

And now, so was she.

Her end had come in the dark corner of a blackened shed, in the middle of the forest…at the hands of a loathsome creature. In the midst of her fear, as a part of her soul withdrew in acceptance of her fate, a calm determination suddenly took hold of her, and she glanced downward. Once again, the thought came…unbidden: *The enemy of my enemy is my friend.*

She said the words aloud—as there was absolutely nothing left to lose. Death at the hands of the vampire would surely be less violent than the rabid wolf.

Without thinking or pausing, Jocelyn reached down and pulled at the heavy pin attached to the locking mechanism: the only safeguard holding the manacles in place.

With a burst of preternatural speed, the creature launched himself from the wooden platform like a ferocious rocket, hurtling into space at the lycan. Willie and the Dark One met in midair, their bodies tangled in a desperate struggle for life, and the ensuing carnage that rained down upon the werewolf was like a cloud of volcanic ash hailing from the sky. The vampire's claws and fangs mangled Willie's throat in an explosion of violence and rage.

Flesh tore. Blood spattered. And bones cracked…as Willie's agonized screams pierced the air.

Jocelyn didn't stick around to watch the show.

She was desperate to help Braden, but she knew his only hope, *their only hope*, lay with Nathaniel and his brothers. She practically hurdled the guillotine on her way out the door, dodging just outside of Tristan's reach as she raced frantically for the bench where she had seen the flares.

She was still in full stride as she grabbed a handful of the fiery sticks and a small box of matches, careful not to miss a step as she sprinted out the front door into the frigid night. The cold wind knocked the air out of her body, and she could hear Tristan closing the distance behind her, growling like a wild animal, yet she kept her focus on the flares...as her trembling hands caught at a match.

He was close. Too close.

"Damnit!" She was trembling. Her fingers refused to work. The first two matches failed to light, and she dropped them in the snow.

Tristan, the golden wolf, was bounding across the snow now in full stride. A primal scream of terror pierced the night as Jocelyn saw his fangs and turned back once again to the flares.

"Light! *Light!*" she pleaded, striking the match again. Once...twice...three times. A small flame flickered delicately in the wind, and she held it under a trembling hand, willing it to stay lit, praying the snow would not extinguish her only hope.

The match held, and she lit the end of the fuse, even as she felt Tristan's warm breath on her neck, searing her skin.

Panting, he caught her arm in his muzzle. As huge teeth sank deep into her flesh, he tried to wrench the flare free, but Jocelyn refused to let go. She knew how to operate under pressure. She had been trained to stay calm under duress, and she poured every ounce of her willpower into shutting out the pain and getting off that flare. Deftly, she switched the flare into her other hand, trying to hold back the powerful bout of nausea that was threatening to make her pass out.

As Tristan released her empty arm and lunged at her other hand, Jocelyn quickly turned her back to him and took the full brunt of the blow between her shoulder blades. Her body flew forward, flying facedown into the snow. Still, she held the hand with the flare in it up and over her head, like a circus acrobat trying feverishly to prevent a glass of water from spilling...while walking on a tight wire.

Tristan was shape-shifting behind her now, the wolf giving way to the man. His powerful arm reached out to overtake hers, but not before the flare shot free, soaring up into the sky like a shooting star. Red and orange flames exploded like fireworks, snow mixing with phosphorus, as the glowing embers rained back down on their heads.

Tristan was enraged. Mindless from the fury of her disobedience and the pain Braden had inflicted upon him. He grabbed her by the back of her jacket and lifted her off the ground with one hand. And then he flipped her over like a rag doll, brutally slamming her back into the hard white ground, her face staring up into his wild eyes.

"He won't make it in time," he snarled. "Your boyfriend. And when he does, he won't want you anymore." He laughed, his guttural bark an evil, twisted sound. "Vampires are like that. Territorial bastards."

Jocelyn cried out as he straddled her body, his muscles contracting, one knee on either side of her waist. He ripped at her clothes, and the material came apart like paper, shredding easily into rags as he tossed it aside, glaring hungrily at her exposed flesh.

"Tristan, please…stop!"

She tried to struggle but it was no use. Her head was spinning, and her mangled arm was on fire. And Tristan seemed a man possessed. An animal without conscience or mercy.

He grabbed her by the throat and pressed down, strangling the air out of her with one powerful hand while he ripped away her remaining clothes with the other. Only when she was close to passing out did he release her throat, and then, only long enough to pry open her legs.

Already naked from the transformation—man to wolf and back again—there was nothing to block his enraged arousal from swift, easy penetration.

Jocelyn's eyes teared up as the freezing wet snow clung to her hair, the frigid cold numbing her brain. She could feel Tristan's breath on her face, the head of his shaft pressing against her entry. In a last-ditch effort to escape the full impact of the assault, she shut herself off from her emotions and glanced up at the sky. The soft, swirling flakes glittered like a thousand diamonds beneath the midnight canvas, the faint hue of red and orange still glistening in the storm like a fiery rainbow.

She sniffed the air, smelling the wet, the cold, the hot burning metal, and tried to look for a star. A constellation. Maybe her and Nathaniel's *Cassiopeia*. Yeah, that would be good. She would search for Cassiopeia. Anything to remove her from where she was.

But Tristan wasn't about to let her get away with being somewhere else. Feeling anything else but him.

In a pitiless act of domination, he reached for her hair and pulled her head forward. "Look at me when I take you!" he ordered.

His eyes were wild with lust.

His mouth twisted in anger.

He snarled like the beast he was. And then he thrust his hips forward.

twenty

Nathaniel Silivasi descended from the sky like the angel of death, his eyes ablaze with wrath and fury. With a haunting silence, he perched behind the crazed hunter as the monster knelt above Jocelyn.

And then he struck with preternatural speed.

Fueled by rage and vengeance, he unsheathed his claws, drew back his arm, and plunged his hand forward between the hind legs of the creature, seizing his shaft and scrotum with an iron fist of fury.

Nathaniel wrenched back at the same exact moment as the lycan thrust forward, dislodging his flesh in one fluid motion. When he was through, all that remained of Tristan's manhood was a bloody heap of tissue dripping from the enraged vampire's hand.

Tristan never saw it coming.

The assault occurred so swiftly, his apparatus detached so deftly, that there was a pregnant pause between the completion of the attack and his dawning awareness of what had just happened.

Time stood still.

And then the humongous male let out a cry so anguished it shook the ground beneath them. Still in shock, he tried to spring to his feet, to turn and fight, but his body was too weak, gushing rivers of blood. He sank to his knees at the glowering vampire's feet.

Jocelyn screamed at the horror of what she had just witnessed—the all-consuming rage that burned like an Olympic torch of victory in Nathaniel's eyes—as the vampire stood there watching the bleeding hunter, his dagger-like fangs fully extended, his mouth turned down in merciless contempt. He took a casual step back as if waiting for the brunt of the pain to take hold.

Tristan bent his head forward then and surveyed his private parts. The air rushed out of his lungs, and his face went gaunt. Stunned and disoriented, he raised his head and met Nathaniel's penetrating gaze. He opened his mouth...but no sound came out.

Nathaniel bent his head. "Not quite the party you planned on, is it?"

His voice was like ice: harsh, cold, and unforgiving. He brought his face closer to the lycan's. "I told you if you laid one hand on my woman, I would rip the skin from your body." He held up the contents of his hand and frowned in disgust. "I suppose this will have to do."

And then he reached down, wrenched Tristan's head back by his thick mane of hair, and plunged a fist like a spiraling rocket into the lycan's gaping mouth. He drove down through his throat, plunging deep into the cavity of his chest, while muscle and tendons ripped, bones and joints exploded, and blood shot out in fountains. And then Nathaniel retracted his arm, pulling at the heart with such brute force that the organ gave way as if it were no more than a yo-yo on a string.

Nathaniel's final words dripped with venom. "And I also promised to remove your heart through your throat."

Tristan's eyes blinked two or three times as he choked on his own blood and slowly slumped forward, finally landing in a heap of mutilated flesh on the ground. The last sight he saw was that of his own beating heart—and what was left of his manhood—dangling in Nathaniel Silivasi's hands.

Jocelyn gasped and tried to cover herself. Despite her relief at being saved, her first reaction was to try and crawl away: Nathaniel was fearsome, and the sight of him engulfed in so much power, absorbed in such primitive rage, sent terror through her body. He stood over her like a tower of menace: Tristan's dead body slumped at his feet, blood dripping down his arms, his wild black hair whipping in the wind...a long black coat wrapped around his powerful frame like the pelt of a panther. The male was all stealth and power, grace and purpose. *He was hell and fury.* Awesome in his rage. Frightening beyond anything she had ever seen.

"Jocelyn." Nathaniel spoke her name with reverence. "Do not be afraid, my love. I could never harm you."

He bent to wash the blood from his hands in the snow before scooping her up in his arms. And then, in one smooth motion, he leapt the distance between where they stood and the front porch of the cabin, landing silently on the balls of his feet. He kicked the door open and carried her inside.

Nathaniel glanced around the front room, locating a heavy wool blanket to cover her with even as he laid her gently on the couch. His hands cupped her face, tenderly lifting her head to meet his gaze. "Sweet gods...I have never been so afraid," he whispered. "Were you injured?" The red in his eyes retreated to obsidian.

Jocelyn lifted her left arm, the arm Tristan had attacked when he had tried to wrench the flare free; it looked bad. Not only were there numerous puncture wounds, but the flesh was torn off to the bone, and there were several obvious fractures along her radius. She had been so caught up in Tristan's attack—and Nathaniel's vengeance—that she had forgotten the pain until that moment.

"Tristan..." She winced.

Nathaniel snarled a low, angry growl. "I'm so sorry, Jocelyn." He took the arm and gently turned it, studying the wounds carefully.

Jocelyn fought not to cry out. "You have nothing to be sorry for. I'm the one who left you." She averted her eyes.

Even now, she had a hard time facing how easily she had turned her back on him. It was obvious he held no hard feelings, and there was nothing he wouldn't have done to get her back safely...yet knowing that only made it worse.

Nathaniel reached out and gently brushed his fingers over her cheek; his touch was like a warm breeze, soft and inviting. "*Don't,* my love: You did what anyone in your position would do. And you trusted him."

Jocelyn nodded, her eyes glossing over. And then all at once, like a dam breaking free, the last couple of days came to a head—the fear of what she'd witnessed in the chamber with Valentine, the reality of Nathaniel's possession and what it meant for her future, the betrayal of her friend and partner, the attempted rape, and the piercing pain in her arm. She wanted to be strong; she hated her vulnerability...especially in front of Nathaniel. But the weight of it all was just too much.

Tears began to flow like a river, her chest heaving beneath the weight of such heartfelt sobs. Her body shook and she buried her head in her hands, unable to lift her mangled arm.

Nathaniel grasped Jocelyn's hands and gently pulled them away from her face. Wrapping two strong arms around her, he gathered her close to his heart, careful to keep her injured limb tucked in at her side. His grip was firm and unyielding; his chin nestled lovingly in her thick hair. All at once, a warm pulse of electricity traveled over her arm, and the pain melted away...as if he had simply taken it from her.

"Iubita mea..." The words were a mere whisper of the old country. *"My beloved*, you are safe now."

He kissed her forehead and then her cheeks, her temples, and her eyelids. He caught her tears with his lips, and then he gently lifted her chin, his heated gaze sending rays of warmth so strong she thought she might melt beneath his tenderness.

Jocelyn stared into his impossibly beautiful eyes, noticing how his pupils shined like a glittering midnight sky. There was a deep, haunting power resting in their depths, and the shape and perfection of his mouth took her breath away: such perfectly sculpted lips—firm...inviting...flawless.

He brushed away her tears with the pads of his thumbs and bent to her mouth. She shivered with anticipation as the sinfully handsome male caressed her as if she were his world, worshipping her with his eyes.

And then his lips met hers and the earth shifted beneath her.

His mouth took ownership—teasing and tasting—even as

his tongue began a slow, torturous exploration. It was both a kiss and a claim. It was a promise of heated nights to come...

It was the stamp of his soul burning into hers, and she knew from that moment forward that he had her...completely...irrevocably. He had been right all along: She had always *belonged* to him.

When Nathaniel pulled away, Jocelyn was breathless. He had touched her so deeply, and it was only a kiss. What in the world would happen if they ever made love?

Nathaniel pulled her close and just held her. "*If* we ever make love?" His voice was a husky murmur, the soft timbre of a cello playing a concerto in her heart, as he whispered the tantalizing words directly in her ear: "When, my angel. *When* we make love."

Jocelyn ducked her head beneath his arm and grimaced. "You were reading my mind?" The question was rhetorical.

His answering laughter was low, amused, and completely unapologetic. He exhaled, as if taking in the moment...as if wanting to hold on to their first intimate connection as long as he could before abruptly becoming serious again. "Kagen will be here soon: I know your arm looks bad, but it will heal swiftly with his assistance. And I do not believe there will be any scars."

He stood then and turned to look out the front window. There was frost building up along the sides of the pane, and the snow seemed to be coming down even heavier now—if that was even possible. He turned to face her. "You know this is not over. Tristan did not come here alone. Soon, there will be dozens of lycans surrounding the cabin."

Jocelyn cleared her throat, uneasy. "Nathaniel? Did you know all along...what Tristan was?"

"Of course," Nathaniel answered. "But there was little I could do without putting many of our people at risk."

Jocelyn frowned and shook her head. "I didn't pick up on anything." She felt so ashamed.

Nathaniel shrugged. His eyes were warm, his voice soft with compassion. "I don't think it would have mattered, Jocelyn...if you had known. In fact, things may have been far worse for all of us if you had resisted." He returned to the sofa, absently lifting the blanket to cover an exposed part of her shoulder, and then he took her hand in his own. "I want you to stay inside...*no matter what.*"

Jocelyn tried not to look as afraid as she felt; two werewolves were already two more than she ever hoped to see in a lifetime. She wanted to ask about Braden, *but she already knew...*

She had seen it with her own eyes before she escaped the shed: The young vampire's head had been split open and his neck broken. And that was before Tristan began to rip apart his sternum, no doubt in an effort to get at his heart.

It was one of those strange tricks the mind played on its host, an irrational but necessary means of coping, a way to delay the inevitable: If she didn't ask, if she wasn't told, then up until the moment she was forced to acknowledge it, it didn't have to be real. Somewhere in the recesses of her mind, she could still believe...she could still hope...she could still keep Braden alive in her psyche.

At least until that dreadful moment when the truth took her hope away: when she had to face his unwavering bravery...and her own miserable failure.

"Do you have reinforcements?" she asked, forcing her thoughts back to the subject at hand, true to her detective nature.

Nathaniel smiled, clearly attempting to reassure her. "I have my brothers and they're all the reinforcement I need."

Jocelyn's eyes grew big. Her heart began to pound in her chest. "Just you, Marquis, Nachari, and Kagen? Against *dozens* of those things?"

Nathaniel walked back to the side of the sofa, knelt down, and brought her hand to his mouth. He kissed the back of her knuckles and nibbled softly on the tips of her fingers as his eyes lingered on her face. "Baby, we'll be fine."

Jocelyn lay her head on his chest.

He paused then. "After you left, the lodge was attacked by

several of Tristan's soldiers; our warriors and sentries were needed to protect the valley. We simply could not justify sending more than three warriors out to retrieve two people. I'm sorry it took us so long to find you."

Jocelyn nodded, and Nathaniel looked off into the distance. His eyes turned dark and a deep sorrow seemed to weigh down on his shoulders. "I'm sorry we did not arrive in time to save Braden." It was as if he had read her thoughts and was trying to give her the only comfort he knew how.

As if responding on cue, the door to the cabin swung open and Nachari rushed in holding Braden's limp body tenderly in his arms. Jocelyn cried out at the sight of Braden's twisted, broken neck, and a bitter gust of wind swirled around the two males, biting at their skin as Nachari ducked in out of the cold.

Marquis was right on his heels. "Damn, that wind is really picking up," he barked, slamming the door behind them.

Nathaniel went immediately to Nachari's side and looked down at Braden. "He was brave, this young one. Is he…"

His voice trailed off as he looked back at Jocelyn.

Tears ran down her face as she pulled the blanket closer around her, acutely aware that she was wearing nothing but a few torn strips of clothing underneath the heavy wool blanket. She immediately got up from the sofa to make room for Braden's lifeless body, clutching the blanket and her tattered arm at her side.

"We found him just outside of the shed," Nachari replied. "It looks like Tristan got to him, too." He eyed Jocelyn's arm and looked away. "And there was another lycan…a hunter…lying dead in the doorway; his body was shredded beyond recognition."

"Willie," Jocelyn offered. "Tristan's partner."

Marquis frowned. "Braden fought Tristan *and* another lycan?" The disbelief was apparent in his voice.

"No," Jocelyn answered, "there was another vampire: one with red and black hair. He was being tortured in the shed. He fought with Willie."

Marquis and Nathaniel gave each other an uneasy glance. "Did you see this male?" Marquis asked.

"No, I didn't," Nathaniel answered. "Nachari?"

Nachari shook his head and laid Braden down gently on the sofa, cradling his head in his hands like delicate porcelain, placing his body in the most comfortable position possible. The stunning male vampire had tears in his deep, numinous eyes, their typical forest-green hue deepening to a cloudy emerald.

Jocelyn steadied herself for the inevitable before she revisited Nathaniel's question. "Is he...dead?"

Nachari shook his head. "He's lost a tremendous amount of blood, he has a skull fracture, and his neck is broken...but his heart is still beating."

Jocelyn caught her breath, tears streaming down her face. She went to Braden's side. "I'm so sorry I couldn't help him...there was just no way. He saved me." She brushed the tears from her eyes, trying to regain control over her emotions. "If it weren't for Braden, I would've never gotten to the flares; you should've seen how he went after Tristan." She turned to face Nathaniel, and her voice trembled. "I did this, didn't I?"

If she had only refused to walk away with Tristan to begin with...

Nathaniel caught her by her uninjured arm and pulled her to him. "No, Jocelyn: *Tristan did this.* Kagen may still be able to save Braden—you have to have faith."

I am still a couple of minutes out, but I will be there shortly. I got sidelined by one of Tristan's soldiers when I went back for my supplies. The voice was Kagen's, and once again, the clear telepathic message was transferred to Jocelyn through Nathaniel's touch.

Nathaniel, Marquis, Nachari: you need to be ready. I passed at least fifteen hunters on my way in; they are no more than five minutes away from the cabin. They are breaking apart in small teams to mount a circular attack.

Marquis, you can't afford to wait for my arrival. Give Braden as much of your blood as you can afford to lose without weakening yourself for the battle.

Tessa Dawn

Marquis went immediately to Braden's side and opened his long leather jacket. He withdrew a sharp stiletto from one of the many internal compartments and sliced it deep across his wrist in one smooth, vertical motion.

Jocelyn cringed as she watched him kneel beside the unresponsive body, force Braden's mouth open, and pour the rich, dark liquid into his mouth. He never even winced.

Nachari began to stroke the muscles of Braden's throat with his hand, clearly using the additional aid of his mind to coax the unconscious child to drink.

"Why did Kagen ask Marquis for blood…instead of Nachari?" she whispered to Nathaniel.

Nathaniel watched as his brother gave the essence of life in an attempt to save the young male. "Marquis is the most ancient—and the most powerful—among us; his blood will heal him quicker than the rest of ours."

Nathaniel turned to face her then, holding both of her shoulders in his hands. "I'm going to give you something, and I want you to use it if you have to. But remember what I told you, *stay inside!*" His eyes held hers in a stern, commanding gaze, and then he reached into the flap of his jacket and withdrew a nine-millimeter semiautomatic weapon.

Jocelyn's mouth gaped open in disbelief when he unwrapped the flap of his coat to search for an extra clip of bullets: The inside lining of the leather trench coat looked like a military arsenal—there was so much hardware concealed inside, tucked into various straps, holsters, and compartments, that she couldn't even begin to make out what each item was.

There were razor-sharpened stilettos, all with handcrafted grips and polished silver blades; a monstrous forty-one magnum single-shot revolver with a polished pearl handgrip; and a sawed-off double-barrel shotgun that looked like something he'd brought back with him from the wild west.

He had a military grade AK-47, with several extra stripper clips, and an awe-inspiring M4 carbine with a thirty-round magazine, tucked into some kind of makeshift hip holsters running down the length of his rock-hard thighs. Jocelyn couldn't be positive, but she could have sworn she also saw a couple of semiautomatic revolvers tucked into two ankle holsters, just beneath his heavy leather boots.

Beyond the NRA billboard, there were several ancient weapons she couldn't identify, an old-world arsenal of treacherous-looking monstrosities, things she had read about but never seen, all cast in solid silver. A curved sickle, some sort of spiked iron bolas hanging from the end of a chain, and a double-edged battle-axe.

Nathaniel handed Jocelyn an extra clip for her Beretta. "It's loaded with silver bullets, so aim for the heart. It's the only way to kill them."

With military precision, he began locking and loading the weapons, including the AK-47 and the semiautomatics strapped to his shins just below his jeans. From the opposite side of his jacket, he pulled out some sort of leather holster, which had several pockets tailor made for holding munitions, and draped it around his shoulder.

He tucked a twelve-inch blade, with an ornately carved handle that looked like something one might find in the Ming Dynasty, into the back of his belt; donned a spiked leather cestus on his left hand; gripped the M4 carbine in his right; and turned to face his brothers.

In her wide-eyed fascination of Nathaniel, Jocelyn hadn't noticed Marquis and Nachari doing the same thing, and she definitely didn't remember seeing Kagen enter the cabin. But he was there, already kneeling beside Braden, checking the young male's injuries. He reached into a soft leather bag and pulled out a circular container, with a flexible, sealed lid on top.

"Fill it," he commanded, tossing it to Marquis.

Jocelyn stared in abject wonder as Marquis drew his lips back in a relaxed snarl and struck the top of the container like a coiled snake. His long incisors sank deep, releasing a steady stream of venom into the container. When it was finally full, his lips twitched back, his incisors retreated, and he tossed the container back to Kagen.

Then all at once, his eyes began to glow a hollow red and his fangs came back: Only this time, the jagged daggers were canines, twice as long, and the hair on the back of his neck was visibly standing up. All three of them looked like otherworldly demons...positively possessed. They were Vikings from another era whose only purpose for existence was to bring death to their enemies...to leave carnage in their wake.

Nathaniel's head snapped to the side in a serpentine-like movement, more animal than man. "Stay close to Kagen." The command was a low hiss, and it was delivered with absolute authority.

He led the way out the front door, Nachari close on his heels. As Marquis took the rear, he turned to look back at his brother, then Braden, and finally Jocelyn. His eyes were alive with anticipation...and fever...like a dog salivating over a bone. The awesome sight took her breath away, and she involuntarily backpedaled and gulped.

Marquis growled a low, indistinct rumble in his throat. The corner of his lip turned up in what appeared to be the hint of a smile, and as he left the cabin, *he winked at her.*

Jocelyn's heart skipped a beat—

Nathaniel was fighting for his life...for the lives of those he loved. He was fighting for her. Nachari was steady...and arrogant...and sure as always: a soldier doing his duty. But Marquis? He was a kid in a candy store. He lived for the adrenaline and approached the upcoming battle as a sport.

Jocelyn's heart rested a little easier: These warriors would not go down easily. Not against an entire lycan army.

She double-bolted the front door and took a place on the floor next to Kagen, the heavy wool blanket still wrapped securely around her shoulders, the nine-millimeter Beretta packed with silver bullets...and nestled snugly in her hand.

BLOOD DESTINY

The cabin was deathly quiet and eerily dark, the only remaining light the soft dancing yellow of flames flickering in the fire and the subtle reflection they cast as shadows against the adjacent wall.

Kagen had carefully cleaned Jocelyn's wounds and wrapped her arm in a soft cast using a poultice made from Marquis's venom. She had managed to find an old pair of sweat pants and a long-sleeve shirt, probably belonging to Tristan, in one of the back rooms, and she was already feeling better, the sharp pain in her arm subsiding.

Braden was finally awake and at least resting peacefully. His skull fracture and chest wounds were healing rapidly, and Kagen was working tirelessly to reset and fuse the broken vertebrae in his neck, once again, injecting Marquis's venom into the surrounding tissue, providing repeated infusions into the bone. Kagen splinted the neck in an effort to keep it still, using two straight pieces of wood torn from the fireplace mantel to hold it in place.

The sound of the ferocious battle taking place outside was more than unsettling: Savage howls of rage cut through chilling stints of silence, and horrifying shrieks of pain sporadically pierced the night as rapid waves of gunfire went off in short bursts amidst the intermittent sounds of blades clashing, claws tearing, and bones cracking.

And then there was the unmistakable sound of *death*.

Anguished cries of defeat—as immortal beings were repeatedly forced to embrace the irony of mortality.

The sound of thunder roared through the heavens, even in the midst of the heavy snowstorm. It was an awe-inspiring phenomenon to behold: an amazing paradox of nature.

It was as if the universe was caught in a war of juxtaposition: flaunting wrath and peace at the same time, hurtling intense heat and severe cold all at once, whispering and screaming with one voice.

Jocelyn clutched at her stomach as another wave of thunder shook the sky with a deafening roar, and the answering lightning once again rocked the earth beneath them with a fury so powerful, she caught at the arm of the sofa, afraid the earth might just open up beneath them.

All the while, the snow continued to fall in heavy blankets, swirling noiselessly around the cabin, as shimmering crystals of white ice were occasionally upstaged by an orange and red encore.

The temptation was just too strong. Jocelyn could no longer bear the suspense or the endless waiting. Moving slowly in order not to draw attention to the cabin, she got up from her position next to Kagen and approached the window.

She had to see.

She had to know that Nathaniel was still alive.

Wiping her hand against the glass to clear the fog, she peered out into the night, straining to catch a glimpse of the battle firsthand...

And what she saw stole her breath away: Blood. Everywhere.

The snow was crimson, the trees painted red. There were scarlet puddles running into snowy rivers, snaking along the ground. There were parts of bodies strewn haphazardly like morbid statues randomly erected in the snow. Heads, limbs, and claws were scattered about like garbage, and spent gun shells littered the ground.

Jocelyn watched in wonder as the vampires moved in and out of the stalking lycans. It was obvious the wolves had enormous physical strength on their side. Their powerful jaws were lethal, and they continuously launched attacks relying upon the strength of their upper bodies, their strapping arms, and their treacherous teeth to bring them victory. But the vampires were far too fast, and they had the added power of invisibility on their side—the ability to cloak their appearance at will.

Jocelyn watched as two lycans approached Nachari, one from the front and one from behind. Nachari whirled around with dizzying speed, keeping his eyes fixed on both. He never even blinked, tracking their every move effortlessly, no matter how cunning. The wolves leapt in unison, counting on the fact that he couldn't defend two sides at once, but Nachari simply disappeared, dissolved in midair, and the heavy, lunging animals crashed into each other with perilous force, like two freight trains colliding on a misguided track.

As if he were a spider dangling from a web, Nachari reappeared above the dazed animals, spraying silver bullets in a fountain of lead. The lycans slumped to the ground.

On the far side of the gorge, about fifty yards in front of the cabin, Jocelyn watched in horror as Marquis was taken down, tossed onto his back, and thrown to the ground. As a blanket of snow-matted fur descended upon him. There were so many wolves; the odds seemed impossible.

Cringing, she covered her mouth and turned to glance at Kagen. He seemed completely unaffected by whatever she was witnessing; his attention focused solely on healing Braden's neck. His faith in his brothers' abilities was absolute.

Marquis's movements were undetectable: a blur of preternatural speed.

Did he use daggers or claws? There was no way to tell. The blurred image looked like an invisible blender, a storm of sharp blades engulfing the wolves, the snow, and the very air around them. He was a whirl of silver—spinning and turning in every direction—slicing the lycans into dozens of pieces...even as they twisted and turned this way and that trying to get a stranglehold on the vampire's constantly shifting neck.

Although the cuts didn't kill them, they left the wolves incapacitated; they were unable to leap, turn, or lunge—their great, muscular frames carved into mere remnants of the powerful creatures they once were. Covered in scattered and bloodied body parts, Marquis sprang to his feet; he went from flat on his back to vertical in the blink of an eye like some kind of ninja. He was positively graceful, his movement fluid and effortless.

He turned up his palms and spun a pair of daggers, one in each hand, and then he began to carve out the hearts of his enemies...one after the other. A fourth lycan leapt at the vampire, undetected and closing in from his blindside, just as Marquis was thrusting a dagger into the third lycan's heart.

Marquis was hit in midair by the awesome force of the hunter, only to spin around, draw back his arm, and throw a fierce uppercut with a spiked fist…a fist cloaked in an ancient cestus. And then there was a hail of silver bullets, a strike of deadly precision, as the lycan hit the ground, already dead.

Nathaniel: from all the way across the yard.

He sat perched like a bird of prey on a high branch of a snow-covered birch tree, surveying the scene from above, covering his brother's back like a sniper. He was orchestrating the battle like a general as he reached into his coat to retrieve a fresh clip and reload.

Jocelyn drew in a sharp breath; he looked like a wild thing. Part warrior. Part animal. No part human. The vampire took her breath away. She could hardly believe he was real.

One after another, the lycans approached the tree, trying to gain Nathaniel's ground. They leapt up at his perch, using powerful hind legs as spring-boards. She even saw one huge male shape-shift back into the form of a human in order to climb an adjacent tree. He took out an automatic weapon and tried for a straight shot at Nathaniel.

The lycan fired, getting off a clean round of shots, but once again, Nathaniel simply moved faster than the bullets. He sped out of the line of fire and threw off the trajectory using the force of his motion…the vacuum created by his velocity. It was as if he had a built-in radar system: as if he controlled the laws of physics.

In one effortless leap, he cleared the distance between him and the hunter, landing in the adjacent tree, a sickle extended from his arm like a silver extension of his own hand. With one smooth flick of his wrist, he started to whirl the weapon around, creating a high-pitched humming sound like the buzz of a helicopter blade.

Jocelyn never saw the weapon connect.

She never saw any interaction at all between the two mortal

enemies. She simply saw a suspended moment in time where both creatures stood still, perched in the same tree, their feral eyes locked together like two savage animals; and then the hunter's head rolled off of his body and tumbled to the ground.

Jocelyn slowly exhaled as the reality of what she was witnessing struck her. Even with all she had seen, all she had learned about Nathaniel in the last couple of days, she still had no idea whatsoever of the power the vampire possessed: the lethal potential he wielded. The sons of Jadon were simply—for all intents and purposes—invincible.

And they knew it.

No wonder Marquis had left the cabin with a wink and a smile. This was child's play for them.

And then, without warning, Jocelyn saw movement coming from the edge of the forest, the unmistakable image of lycans tangling with…vampires.

Her eyes shot back and forth, trying to understand what she was seeing, stretching to account for all the combatants. Nachari stood only yards from the cabin, taking inventory of the dead bodies surrounding him, searching vigilantly for any remaining enemies.

Marquis had moved away from the shed and was heading toward Nachari, reloading the double-barreled shotgun in his hand as he moved on the balls of his feet, his senses flaring out in all directions.

And Nathaniel had come down from his perch in the tree.

So who was fighting at the edge of the forest?

Jocelyn's heart began to race and she swallowed hard. There were red and black bands of hair, wild manes the color of a king cobra, blowing in the snow-gusted wind, as several Dark Ones warred with their werewolf enemies.

Jocelyn watched, spellbound, wanting to cry out, to say something to Kagen—she needed to alert him—but she was too paralyzed by her own fear to get out the sound. She was catapulted back into the cave with Dalia and Valentine; she was still in the shed staring into a crazed creature's eyes as he lay strapped to a guillotine; she was still witnessing the quick, easy work the Dark One had made of Willie the moment she had released him.

And she was frozen with the knowledge of who—and what—they were.

These creatures had the same speed, the same capacity to become invisible, the same weapons as Nathaniel and his brothers. These were enemies of equal ability.

In a very short time, the world had grown silent, and the land in front of the cabin was still. There were no more lycans. Only blood. And bodies.

The forest had ceased its own violent show as the last of the hunters had fallen, and Nathaniel and his brothers were now walking toward the cabin, each nursing various injuries, none of which seemed life-threatening, at least not from a distance. And then all at once the brothers spun around facing the forest, their backs turned to the cabin.

They spread out in a wide semicircle, facing their new enemy as the Dark Ones approached like powerful jungle cats: pacing...turning...slowly creeping closer and closer.

"Kagen!" Jocelyn finally managed to croak out his name, but not before her own body unwittingly sprang into action.

Whether out of instinct born of too many years in the field, or just a primal reaction to the threat to Nathaniel, Jocelyn forgot the pain in her arm. She forgot that she was human, and she forgot that Nathaniel had ordered her to stay inside...no matter what occurred.

She only knew that there were four of *the Dark Ones*, warriors from the house of Jaegar, slowly approaching the cabin, and only three of the Silivasi brothers to meet them.

Why she didn't wait on Kagen, she would never know.

twenty-one

Fingering her Beretta with all of the comfort and expertise of years of training, Jocelyn headed out the front door and ran toward Nathaniel.

Nathaniel spun around with a look of pure menace on his face, anger flaring deep red in his eyes as he watched her approach. The fearsome look caught her by surprise and almost stopped her in her tracks.

"Get back to the cabin," he hissed, slowly turning his body to shield hers, placing his broad, powerful frame between Jocelyn and the dark vampires.

Jocelyn stood frozen for a moment, uncertain what to do: She did not want to incur Nathaniel's wrath, not after what she had just witnessed with the lycans—and Nathaniel's eyes looked absolutely furious—but she was there now. And she was not some helpless maiden in constant need of being rescued.

She was *his destiny*.

His other half, right?

It was time for her to start acting like more than just a scared victim. Like more than just a captive. If this was going to be her new world, then she might as well enter it with a bang.

Jocelyn squared her chin. "No."

Somehow, it sounded a lot more confident in her head. She took a step forward, attempting to join their line.

Nathaniel moved like the wind then, completely cutting her off. His hand caught her wrist in an iron grasp, twisting with such force that she thought her bones might crumble, even as Kagen closed in on her flank. And then Nathaniel shoved her behind him, trapping her between his own body and his twin's.

Jocelyn grimaced, but she refused to cry out in pain: to even acknowledge that it hurt. And then with a courage she didn't really possess, she pushed her way next to Nathaniel and turned her head to face the Dark Ones in a show of solidarity.

This was her family too now, and she would fight with them.

As all four of the undead slowly turned their heads to measure the defiant female, glaring directly at her with four pair of hate-filled eyes, Jocelyn's knees began to buckle and her stomach turned to jelly.

The piercing glares seemed to burn right through her, and then a depraved smile curved along the lips of the tallest male. He was standing closest to the front and took an almost imperceptible step forward as his eyes measured her up and down, stopping momentarily to sneer at the nine-millimeter in her hand.

Oh hell, Jocelyn thought, as common sense finally began to replace valor, and the desire to survive finally began to trump her previous fanatical impulse to…do what?

She was standing in front of four supernatural beings: *vampires*. Each one baring lion-sharp fangs. Each one possessing the ability to move so swiftly that she would be dead before she ever saw them coming. Not one of them was capable of being shot, and all of them were more than capable of becoming invisible. Yet there she stood: holding a weapon loaded with *silver bullets*, a method that only worked on *werewolves*.

As if the tall Dark One could read her mind—and truth be known, he probably could—a low, wicked laugh rumbled in his throat. Their evil gazes turned back to the males, but she was certain her stupidity was now the main element of Nathaniel's strategy. She had placed him in a much more vulnerable position than he had been in before, and the growing awareness made her sick to her stomach.

As if the battle with the lycans had not been enough for him, Marquis's hand began to twitch, and his eyes lit up…turning from red to yellow then red again. He fingered a dagger just inside of his coat sleeve, allowing the silver blade to slide noiselessly into his hand.

"Ready to play when you are," he hissed, his mouth turned up in a smile.

Tessa Dawn

The tall one turned ever so slightly to regard Marquis, and then a sudden, unexpected movement startled him from behind, a strong hand placed on the leader's chest in a gesture of...*restraint.* The confusion was palpable. The tension unbelievable. As they all stood...waiting...to see what the male was going to do.

Jocelyn recoiled, immediately calling unwanted attention to herself, but she couldn't help it. She'd know those familiar eyes anywhere.

Until the day she died, the enraged look of those pupils, the deep lines of desperation etched into the male's brow, the feel of that tangled mass of hair beneath the pads of her fingers would be scorched into her memory. In the throes of life and death, she had stared at that face and taken in every nuance.

She had memorized every detail. She had been terrified by his overwhelming desire to kill. She had been drawn in by his desperate yearning to survive.

It was the vampire from the shed, the one who had been manacled to the guillotine. As he stepped beside the leader, he looked her over thoughtfully, his face still reflecting the unmistakable malevolence so characteristic of his kind. Yet there was something else reflected in his features as well: a recognition in his eyes, a reasoning that went beyond instinctual.

Nathaniel looked from the Dark One to Jocelyn...and then back to the Dark One again...immediately picking up on the unspoken connection between them.

He saw it. And he didn't like it.

A low growl of warning rose in his throat as he subtly shifted his posture; his sinewy muscles expanded and contracted with the promise of lethal attack. His focused glare burned like a laser straight into the Dark One's eyes, and his face held the swift assurance of death.

The Dark One hissed in response, but his eyes never left Jocelyn's. And then he exhaled and inclined his head in a faint nod. "And you are?"

The Dark One waited, his eyes fixed on hers.

Jocelyn cleared her throat, trying to find her voice: "Jocelyn." The sound was hardly a whisper.

Nathaniel's head spun around and he glared at her with unadulterated scorn. She felt a strange constriction in her throat—a numbing, like paralysis—and she knew Nathaniel had taken control over her voice: She could no longer speak.

Jocelyn would not utter another sound—not even if she wanted to.

The Dark One seemed wholly unaffected by Nathaniel's blatant show of authority. "I am Saber Alexiares." He introduced himself... *to Jocelyn.*

Marquis, Nachari, and Kagen all caught their breath at the same time, stunned by the Dark One's audacity, his blatant provocation to battle.

"You wish to decree your own death sentence, Dark One?" Nathaniel asked, his voice as hard as stone. "Do not be a fool! Such arrogance will not go unpunished."

The Dark One quickly turned his gaze to meet Nathaniel's and nodded with deference, a clear understanding that Jocelyn belonged to him. "The female is yours. I meant no disrespect."

The tall vampire standing in the front snapped his head around and hissed at Saber, clearly incensed, but the male continued. "We have one wounded in the forest, and a dead child who was taken yesterday behind the shed." He gestured toward the cabin. "You have an injured child as well."

This time when his eyes scanned Jocelyn, it was not a direct connection with her as much as an indication to Nathaniel. "For this night only, let us gather our dead and our wounded and return to our homes; we can kill each other tomorrow."

Marquis grunted, then snarled, "You are already dead, foolish one."

Saber hissed, his muscles twitching in a clear effort to maintain control. He obviously wanted to fight as much as Marquis did, and the insult didn't sit well with him. But he looked once more at Jocelyn...and took another deep breath.

"Perhaps." His eyes remained focused on Nathaniel.

The sons of Jaegar standing beside him were visibly staggered. They looked completely appalled, as if his words were a direct affront to their pride, and they weren't sure how to handle the unexpected situation.

"We do not need permission from *ones such as these*, Saber, to gather our dead and our injured. What the hell are you doing?" It was the prominent one who spoke.

Saber shook his head. "Rest assured, I am not *asking permission* of anyone." He turned to regard the one who spoke as their leader and indistinctly bared his fangs. Then he gestured toward the shed and the forest and began to walk away. When the others reluctantly followed, it became blatantly clear who their leader really was.

Jocelyn exhaled as relief washed over her. Nathaniel would not have to fight anymore tonight; she might actually get to live until tomorrow, and hopefully, he would not grow any angrier than he already was. She had escaped her own foolishness…this time.

As she watched the dark vampires walk away, she couldn't help but take one more look at Saber Alexiares. Had her actions in the shed had anything to do with his decision?

As if he was reading her thoughts, he turned to look over his shoulder, and the faint corner of his cruel mouth turned up just a fraction. "If only for this night," he snarled, the truth of what he was evident in the evil hiss of his voice, "the enemy of my enemy…" His voice trailed off.

Jocelyn looked down at the ground, not wanting to incur any more of Nathaniel's wrath.

"What does that mean?" he hissed.

Jocelyn put her hand to her throat; it was a gesture asking him to release her voice. As she felt her vocal cords relax, she cleared her throat. "The enemy of my enemy is my friend. In the shed…earlier…I saved his life. And he saved mine."

Nathaniel looked up toward the forest, staring at the son of Jaegar incredulously. "Dark One," he called, "is this true?" He looked every bit as stunned as the other vampires had been only

245

moments earlier. Kagen, Nachari, and Marquis looked equally astonished.

Saber shrugged his shoulders and stopped to face the brothers. "Don't worry, sons of Jadon: I would've killed her if you hadn't shown up." He ran his hands through his thick black-and red-banded hair. "The lycan was just a more *immediate* concern." He inclined his head. "But she was wise to reason the outcome and brave to take the chance. And that is the only reason we do not wage war here tonight." He winked at Marquis. "Tomorrow, warrior; there's always tomorrow." And then he disappeared behind the thick wall of the forest.

Jocelyn covered her throat with her hands, realizing just how close she had come to dying earlier that night. "I had no other choice," she whispered. "I was already dead." And then she immediately turned to walk toward the cabin.

She was shocked when her head hit the hard resistance of what felt like a cement wall, and she immediately realized she had never been in any danger at all: Nathaniel had placed her in an invisible fortress much like Marquis had done to Braden earlier. He had constructed a barrier that was next to impossible to penetrate for the ensuing battle. She felt embarrassed. Humiliated. Yet she waited without a word to be released.

"Never...*ever*...for any reason," Nathaniel thundered, "believe that one of the Dark Ones is your friend! He *will* be back to kill you...if for no other reason than because he let you go tonight. And I thought I told you to remain in the cabin!"

Nathaniel was too angry to speak another word. Too enraged to release her. He stared at her for a long moment, disapproval heavy in his eyes, and then he simply turned his back and walked away.

Kagen looked into the makeshift prison and shrugged his shoulders apologetically. He was smart enough not to pull a tiger by its tail, and followed Nathaniel to the cabin.

Marquis approached the barrier then, and Jocelyn slowly stepped back until she bumped into the other side. He was uncharacteristically calm. Too calm, in fact. Much too reserved.

"Every time you place yourself in danger, you jeopardize Nathaniel's life. Know this, little sister: If you risk my brother's life again, you will lose more than your vocal cords. I will take over your actions and your thoughts until the blood moon has completely passed and Nathaniel is no longer at risk. You will be a walking puppet on my string, and no one will know the difference…not even Nathaniel. Is there anything unclear about what I am saying to you?"

Jocelyn swallowed and looked down. She didn't dare answer.

"You will not get another warning."

Like Nathaniel, Marquis simply turned his back and walked away.

Nachari sighed and approached the barrier. "I guess that leaves me, then, huh?" He flashed a soothing smile of understanding, breathtakingly handsome as always. "It's been a long night."

Jocelyn looked down, hating that her eyes were filling with tears, not wanting Nachari to see how badly Nathaniel and Marquis's reprimands had hurt her…just how lost and overwhelmed she was feeling. It was humiliating to be a grown woman treated like a child: even more humiliating to be a grown woman acting—and taking unnecessary risks with other people's lives—like a child.

Nathaniel had turned his back on her. She would never belong in this life.

It didn't matter who Nathaniel believed she was. She wasn't anyone's *true destiny*, and she would never be a true member of their family. She would always be some…lesser species…that simply served a vampire's purpose.

Nachari shook his head as if he knew everything she was feeling, and then he began to carefully take apart the barrier, one layer at a time. "When I was just a fledgling, about one hundred and fifty years old, I made a decision that I would no longer feed…I would no longer take human blood to live. I thought I would have a deeper connection with nature—you know, with the animals—if I took their blood instead." He shrugged his shoulders, smiling.

"When Marquis found out, he absolutely forbade it. So, being stubborn as I am, I pretended to continue to feed from humans while refusing any blood at all. Well, my twin, Shelby…" He stumbled over the word, his voice growing hoarse. There was an uncomfortable pause while he struggled to collect himself before continuing. "*Shelby* knew what I was doing, and I was getting weaker by the day. So finally, he went to Marquis and told on me."

Jocelyn's eyes grew big. She could only imagine where this was going.

Nachari shook his head in disgust as another layer of the barrier came down. "You want to talk about being made into a puppet?" He laughed. "Marquis took control of my physical body, something I was too young and inexperienced to prevent back then. He sat me on the stoop of his back porch and began calling animals from the forest, one after another…all day long."

Nachari raised an eyebrow. "And we're not talking about nice, friendly, normal animals. I mean porcupines, skunks, rats, snakes, badgers, the kind of animals that bite you back. He lined them up one after the other like an endless buffet, forced me to sink my teeth into them, and made me drink until I puked. Then, he refused to let me wipe my mouth, and brought on the next animal."

Jocelyn was appalled.

Nachari shook his head as the barrier finally came down, and he reached out to take her hand. "To this day, I haul ass when I see a porcupine."

Jocelyn couldn't help but laugh a little.

Nachari smiled. "I'm not saying any of this to frighten you, but just to make a point: If Marquis didn't care, if he didn't already accept you as family, he wouldn't bother. The male is my brother—and I love him dearly—but Marquis is an…intense…individual. He's had a really hard life. Harder than the rest of us. And honestly, I think he grows weary of living after so many centuries alone. We are all he has, all he lives for.

You can never take it personally."

Nachari paused then, appearing to consider his next words carefully. "And as for Nathaniel, you can only imagine what a difficult time this is for him. He has his own fears, and rightfully so, not the least of which is your safety."

They stepped up onto the front porch. "By the way, I wanted to thank you for Braden. He wouldn't be alive if it weren't for you." The sincerity was strong in his voice, his deep forest-green eyes growing soft with appreciation. He released her hand with a reassuring squeeze.

Jocelyn smiled. "Braden didn't deserve what was done to him in that shed." She grimaced at the memory. "It was so awful."

"I know," Nachari agreed.

The door opened, and Nathaniel stepped aside to allow Nachari entry, while blocking the way for Jocelyn. He had obviously been watching the entire time, knowing all along Nachari would release her. He closed the door behind him, shutting the two of them out on the porch.

Jocelyn averted her eyes. "Are you as mad at me as I think you are? Do you hate me now?" Despite her best efforts, the words came out choked up.

Nathaniel grunted. "I don't know whether to hug you or to take you over my knee, Jocelyn. I could kiss you...then kill you."

Jocelyn raised her eyebrows. "Don't even think about the knee thing. I've been humiliated enough for one day." Despite her best effort, there wasn't even a hint of humor in her voice.

Nathaniel managed a faint smile. "Oh, baby, I didn't mean to humiliate you. Maybe just scare some sense into you." He gently lifted her head by her chin. "I'll tell you what: How about no more suicide attempts; no more walking off with strangers; no more trying to fight vampires with silly, human weapons—silver bullets only work on werewolves, Jocelyn—*and no more holding Nachari's hand.* And we'll be just fine."

Jocelyn started to protest at the first three items on his list, wanting to remind him of her very good reasons for all three, but she was stopped short by the last request. She managed a faint smile. "You're kidding, right?"

Nathaniel looked at her, but he didn't smile.

"Nathaniel, you *are* kidding…right?"

"I don't see any humor in the way you look at my little brother, and I don't think you should be touching anyone but me. Besides, what is all this forest green, emerald green stuff? His eyes are green, Jocelyn. Just plain green. Rather boring in my opinion." His voice never wavered.

Jocelyn frowned, perplexed. "You're crazy." It was all she could think of to say.

Nathaniel reached down and grasped her by both sides of her waist, pulling her tightly against him. "Vampires are extremely territorial by nature, Jocelyn. We're predators first— instinctive animals—never forget that."

Jocelyn looked up at him, surprised, still trying to grasp whether or not he was completely serious.

"You might not like it," he said, "but you are *mine*." He growled then. "I thought I might have to carve out that Dark One's heart, put it on a rotisserie, and serve it up on a platter for you. You still eat food, right? At least until your conversion." He smiled.

Jocelyn rolled her eyes. "Oh, Nathaniel…you're pathetic."

He laughed and cupped her face in his hands, declined his head, and nuzzled her hair, allowing his fangs to elongate just enough to show her he meant business. He bit down on her neck, gentle enough to show her he cared, forceful enough to cause her some pain. It was a soft reprimand, a clear warning, and a gesture of affection…all in one.

His hands followed the contours of her body, clearly dominant in the familiar way he touched her, almost as if he really did believe he owned her. And why not? Jocelyn knew without a doubt that he did. And God help her, but at that moment, she wanted him to.

He ran his fingers down the long arc of her neck, across her slender shoulders, and slowly along her waist, possessively outlining the sides of her breasts. His thumbs lingered selfishly over the two hard peaks at the center, caressing her nipples in a slow, rhythmic circle, until they finally came to rest on her hips.

"This is all mine." His voice sounded husky. Sure of himself. "Your heart...your mind...your body. Mine to touch. Mine to love. Mine to worship. All my territory. *You belong to me.* Do you understand?" He lifted her chin to force her gaze. "I want to smell no other scent on you than my own."

Jocelyn inhaled sharply, somewhat surprised by his statements. Her body was on fire from his touch, and she realized that he meant every word. He was marking her, rubbing his scent on her, establishing his dominance over her.

And then he *bit her.*

And heaven help her, she almost went to her knees...wanting more.

Jocelyn had always been a strong woman: a fiercely independent, powerful personality in her own right. And she probably always would be, but she knew somewhere deep inside, this man could make her want things...do things...*obey things* she would mock other women for even thinking about. She wanted his complete possession.

Gazing up into his mesmerizing eyes, she blinked, trying to keep him in focus. He was positively sinful, brutally handsome, and absolutely primitive. And then he bent to claim her mouth fiercely with his own. The deep kiss was that of an expert— strong yet gentle, demanding yet coaxing, erotic yet loving— leaving her breathless and wanting in its wake.

She felt provoked and aroused. And more than a little hungry in places she hadn't thought of in a long, long time.

"It is time for me to bring you fully into my world, Jocelyn. I don't think I can live through another night like tonight."

Jocelyn simply stared at him.

And then she blinked...

Like some nerdy, lovesick teenager who had somehow stumbled upon a date with the star quarterback.

Dignity was becoming a rare commodity around this man,

and she wasn't sure she was going to get it back any time soon. But hell, when he looked at her like that, she lost all rational thought, gave up all logic and reason.

The truth was…she was ready to be his.

She was hungry to be brought into his world.

twenty-two

Jocelyn woke up late Monday evening, realizing she had slept the day away and the sun had already set. She stretched her arms and looked around the room. She was back at Nathaniel's sprawling log retreat, an architectural wonder of modern convenience, rustic décor, and soft, earthy palettes. She had never seen the master bedroom before, and the room was a sight to behold.

The entrance to the bed chamber was a twelve-foot, double-arched doorway, encased in wide hand planks of oak with subtle, mystical designs snaking throughout the natural grains. The ceiling was high and came to a peak with several heavy beams running horizontally from one end to the other.

Like the rest of the house, the room was decorated in soft earth tones of rust, amber, gold, and deep brown, giving it the appearance of an orchard of trees in the height of autumn. The furniture was made of natural wood and clearly hand carved with the same design found in the moldings that surrounded the floors, ceilings, and windows.

The lines were neat and clean, drawing the eye to the focus of the room—a large inset fireplace flanked by floor-to-ceiling windows, which displayed a breathtaking view of the forest valley as far as the eye could see.

Jocelyn pulled back the Egyptian cotton sheets and took a closer look at the four-poster bed she was lying in. It was made of knotted pine and looked as if it weighed a ton. It had two thick, rounded columns at the base and an intricately carved headboard rising at least five feet from the top of the mattress at the head. The jutting crown was more like a work of art than a bed frame; it was expertly engraved with detailed carvings of forest predators: a grizzly bear, a mountain lion, and a pair of wolves, all surrounded by beautiful aspens and pines as if the animals had been captured in their natural habitat.

Jocelyn noticed a beige robe lying at the end of the bed and leisurely put it on. As she slid her left arm into the soft material, it occurred to her that the cast Kagen had made for her was gone, and her wounds were perfectly healed.

She brought her arm up to her face to study it more carefully, searching for scars or markings, any evidence at all that the terrible injuries had once been there: There were none. As she headed in the direction of the bathroom, a shadow moving in the corner caught her eye and she jumped, momentarily startled.

Nathaniel was sitting languidly in a comfortable-looking chair, his legs crossed in front of him, propped up on a matching ottoman. And he was staring directly at her...a dark look of hunger in his eyes.

He blended into the background like a jungle cat watching its prey: perfectly motionless...silent. His eyes were focused and alert, and a small smile curved around the corners of his mouth when he saw her take notice.

"Good evening, beautiful." His voice positively purred.

Jocelyn inhaled sharply as a bolt of electricity shot up her spine, causing her to shiver. That voice—that raspy, sultry, mesmerizing voice—she would never get used to the sound of it.

"Good evening," she called in return. "How long have you been sitting there?"

He shifted restlessly in the chair. "Not long." A low hiss escaped his mouth as he slowly exhaled. "You are so incredibly beautiful when you sleep."

Jocelyn blushed and turned away. "Did I sleep all day?"

He smiled. "We both did."

Jocelyn looked at the bed. She didn't remember getting into it, and she certainly didn't remember Nathaniel lying beside her. That would not be something a woman would easily forget. She clutched her robe. "How is it that you're dressed and showered, and I'm not?"

The moment it left her lips, she regretted the question; it

sounded like a come-on when she had only meant it as a casual observation.

Nathaniel smirked like he was reading her mind. "You took a shower late last night. I, on the other hand, just collapsed in exhaustion." His pupils widened with that strange shifting she was beginning to find so characteristic of a vampire.

She frowned. "I don't remember taking a shower."

Nathaniel leaned forward. "Kagen gave you some pretty strong medicine for the pain in your arm since I couldn't continue to block it in my sleep. There are probably many things you do not remember."

Jocelyn's eyes grew big, but she didn't dare ask.

Surely not…

Nathaniel laughed. "No, my love; I assure you…*that* you would remember."

All at once he stood up and started walking toward her, his movement the confident glide of a predator.

Reflexively, Jocelyn took a step back. It wasn't that she was afraid of him; well, at least no more than usual. It was just the *way* that he moved. It sent chills down her spine and flirted with her every *fight or flight* instinct. She was a human, after all, and he…was not. It would take some getting used to.

Nathaniel's eyes narrowed with decadent purpose, a predator inching his way gracefully toward his prey. "You back away from me?" His faint laugh vibrated through the room, heavy with masculine amusement, and for a moment, he appeared every bit as much a lion as a man.

Jocelyn clutched her robe, watching, as her fear and excitement grew with every step he took in her direction.

He appeared to relish the increasing beat of her heart, to enjoy the subtle look of panic she knew was in her eyes, and to savor the blatant, carnal reaction he no doubt could pick up from her scent. The room felt suddenly hot…very hot…and her body felt…uncomfortable.

A deep, delicious growl rumbled in his throat as he finally closed the distance between them and reached down to take her hand in his. He slowly brought it to his lips, kissing the inside of her palm and then her wrist, before taking a finger gently into his wickedly perfect mouth.

"You are not still afraid of me, are you?" His voice was a slow drawl, positively dripping with sin.

Jocelyn shivered. She opened her mouth to answer, but no sound came out. Nathaniel responded immediately to the invitation: dipping his head to taste her lips, lightly sweeping a tongue inside the irresistible offering. He traced the curve of her mouth with the tip of his tongue.

"Mmm," he purred.

He cupped her face in his hands then. "Jocelyn Levi, do you have any idea how *delicious* you are?"

Jocelyn shook her head, blushing.

He stared into her eyes. "And your eyes are amazing. You truly do have the eyes of a tiger…otherworldly…the most stunning mixture of green and brown I have ever seen." He kissed her temples and then each eyelid, one at a time. "And the colors blend together in shadows…like maybe they're trying to hide something." He leaned over and whispered in her ear, "Secrets, perhaps? Are you keeping secrets from me, Jocelyn?"

He dropped his fingers to the front of her robe and gently brushed against her breasts, cupping the soft mounds in his hands. He took his time, exploring each breast languidly, first one and then the other, massaging with intimate authority.

"I would like to know your secrets, tiger-eyes. Will you share them with me?"

Jocelyn's head fell back, and she moaned softly.

He pushed the robe off of her shoulders and drew in a sharp breath as the gentle curves of her skin were exposed to his hungry gaze.

"Will you?" he repeated, his voice growing deep and demanding.

"Wh…what would you like to know?" Her voice came out husky and slow, like that of a temptress, surprising even to her own ears. She didn't know where the sound had come from, but

Tessa Dawn

Nathaniel's response was instantaneous, his thick erection rising in his jeans, pressing against her stomach.

Nathaniel noticed her noticing him, and he made no effort to conceal his arousal, grinding his hips in a slow circle, pressing firmly against her.

She was wearing a midnight blue silk nightgown with a low, dipped back and thin spaghetti straps, one of the many garments Nathaniel had purchased for her on her first day in his home, and he wasted no time at all, lowering the straps from her shoulders, pushing them aside with his thumbs. The nightgown fell to her waist, caught beneath the loosely tied robe, both her shoulders and breasts exposed.

He groaned when her nipples came out of the silk, bending his head to blow hot air over the erect peaks, gently circling one then the other with his tongue. "I have been dying to know what you taste like, my love."

Jocelyn arched into him, reveling in the sensations. She couldn't help herself…and she didn't want to. Her breasts felt incredibly heavy, the tips beginning to tingle—the mounds beginning to ache. She moaned when he tugged at a nipple with his teeth, flicked the sensitive bud with his tongue, and then took the entire tip vigorously into his mouth. The sensual heat engulfed her like a fire as his hands cupped, his fingers massaged, and his mouth suckled.

Jocelyn clutched a fistful of beautiful blue-black hair, bringing Nathaniel even closer. His mouth was creating an inferno between her legs, jolts of electricity sizzling through her body…cresting at the apex between her thighs. He was turning her core into liquid heat as he feasted on her breasts like a ravenous, glorious animal.

"Nathaniel…" She whispered his name in a hoarse plea for…something…a soft moan of pleasure escaping her lips.

His mouth tightened, even as his hands began to venture lower, slowly tracing her stomach and caressing her hips before reaching lower still…to lightly brush over the heat between her legs.

257

"And I would like to know what you feel like, angel." He cupped her feminine mound, pressed the heel of his hand tightly against her sex, and rubbed her in harsh, arousing circles. "Deep inside," he moaned.

She gasped, which only aroused him further. "I want to crawl so deep inside of you, Jocelyn," he growled, "that I touch your soul." His lips fastened over hers, his tongue probing her mouth as he tasted...commanded...explored. "Will you let me, Jocelyn? Will you take me inside of you?"

Jocelyn was too caught up to speak. She felt a powerful surge of moisture flood her core, and a painful ache began to radiate inside of her womb as the rising waves of desire grew stronger with every sure stroke of his hand. Every soft pull of his lips. Every sensual swipe of his tongue.

She pushed against him: tempting him...needing him. She was drenched with wanting him, desperate to feel his total possession.

Nathaniel reached down to loosen the tie on her robe, and she shivered as a sudden drift of cool air caressed her skin. And then she pulled back and looked up into his hauntingly beautiful eyes. His thick crown of hair was falling forward in gentle waves, framing the masculine perfection of his face, and his shadowed pupils were shining with the reflection of moonlight. And there was something else in his gaze, something stark and primitive and wild being unleashed: *a fierce animal hunger.*

Jocelyn knew all of his gentleness, his soft caresses and lazy explorations, were for her. The lust in his eyes was impossible to ignore, the stark nature of his hunger, undeniable.

If it were simply up to him, he would take her with abandon. Brand her. Mark her. Claim her...with complete authority. The unyielding dominance of his species would demand absolute control.

Yet he lingered.

He held back. He reveled in the responses she gave him...the slow building of a raging fire.

When he finally met her gaze, his full lips were turned up in a smile, revealing perfect, glistening teeth, and his flawless skin positively glowed beneath the light in his eyes as he began to purr even louder, pressing his hard sex shamelessly against her.

And then she felt it: the gentle scraping of his fangs against her neck, the soft graze of two sharp edges moving lightly over her artery. He nibbled once, bit at her skin, and then he quickly pulled away...even as she relaxed into him.

"Another time, *draga mea,*" he sighed, his voice sounding strained.

Jocelyn nuzzled his chin, feeling deserted by the momentary lack of contact. She found herself kissing the hollow of his throat, her hands reaching up to unbutton his shirt. Her hips began to circle and grind into the hard length of him—the thick, throbbing erection pressed so tantalizingly against her.

"Draga mea?" she asked, groaning the words.

He shrugged out of his shirt, exposing a rock-hard chest with astonishing definition, and as her eyes dropped lower, her breath caught in her throat: the male had a sinfully gorgeous six-pack, row after row of flawless abdominal muscles rippling beneath baby-smooth skin on a hairless, flat stomach.

Jocelyn sighed as he slowly began to unbutton his jeans...unable to hide her satisfaction: The man was a gladiator. *Her gladiator.*

"My darling," he whispered, interpreting the phrase in her ear. And then he held her gaze for a fraction of a second...although it felt like an eternity. When he next took her mouth with his, she could taste the lust, the increasing intensity of his need.

His shaft jerked against her stomach. His hands reached down to cup her bottom. And he pulled her tightly against him.

Jocelyn melted into his hard frame, lifting her leg to wrap it around his powerful thigh. She offered up her body. She strained and arched into him. She rubbed the uncomfortable heat between her legs over his hamstring, shamelessly riding his thigh as he stroked and explored her body.

His breath grew heavy then, coming in short gasps as his

heart began to pound against his chest, and a lusty groan of pleasure escaped his throat. He lifted his leg, pressing the heavy weight of it back against her core, rotating in leisurely, circular motions, encouraging her slow ride.

He kissed her with far more demand, while nipping at her bottom lip and swirling his tongue around hers. He tasted every part of her mouth with a growing, insistent hunger…a harsh, commanding lust.

With one hand still grasping her waist, he reached down to remove his jeans, freeing the rigid length from his pants.

Jocelyn caught her breath at the sight of his enormous arousal, now standing at full attention. He was pressed painfully against her belly, his sex, positively magnificent…smooth as silk yet hard as steel…an erotic promise of ecstasy just waiting to be thrust into her welcoming body.

Nathaniel removed her open robe and tugged at the silk of her nightgown. "Take these off." His voice was husky with need.

Jocelyn wiggled out of the gown and stood before him clad in nothing more than a pair of thin silk panties. His lustful gaze revealed his appreciation, the growl that followed causing her sex to throb with rising need.

"You are so…incredible, Jocelyn."

He went to his knees then, his hands tracing her slender waist, following the supple curves of her hips, outlining her flat stomach, until finally, he hooked his thumbs over the thin strings of her panties and gently tugged at the insignificant piece of cloth. His head dropped forward, and he let out a deep, hungry sigh, his shoulders slightly trembling…

And then he clutched her bottom, pulled her hips forward, spread her legs with his hands…and drank. With both reverence and abandon, he devoured her core as she stood helplessly above him.

Jocelyn cried out with pleasure as his tongue explored her warmth: licking, tasting, stabbing deep inside of her. Her legs grew weak and her body began to shudder. She held onto his thick mane of hair as an anchor, struggling not to shatter into a million pieces as she called out his name. Every nerve ending came alive in response to the urgency of his mouth, the expert exploration of his tongue, the deep, throaty growls he released as he swallowed her essence. Her head thrashed from side to side and she tried to push him away. "Nathaniel, I can't take it! It's too much." Her voice was a husky plea, replete with pleasure and desire.

Nathaniel didn't budge.

His mouth pressed even harder into her core, his tongue working in a frenzied tutorial of urgency. He teased her, took possession of her, drove her wild with a fevered passion, all the while his hands continuing to gently massage her bottom.

"Your taste…" He groaned. "Dear gods…you taste so…good. I could never get enough."

The groan that escaped his lips was ravenous…hoarse…and dripping with passion. And each time he moaned, her body responded by giving him more of what he loved—with a powerful rush of liquid heat that he then lapped up like a starving animal.

"You're killing me," she whimpered.

His hands felt like hot flames licking across her skin, filling her core with fire, until she was utterly helpless with need. She tried to twist out of his grip, to backpedal toward the bed, to pull his head away with her hands, but he only clutched her tighter, holding her helpless against his invasion as his tongue dove deeper.

Jocelyn arched her back and cried out in desperation as her body clenched like a drum, winding tighter and tighter with pleasure until it threatened to explode. Her head fell back as she continued to squirm and writhe beneath his merciless assault, unable to hold on much longer.

She caught at his shoulders, pulling him upward…needing him inside of her so desperately she thought she might die if he didn't take her now.

"I want you," she pleaded, "please…stop…I can't take it."

His tongue dipped and swirled, lapping up the center of her

heat, circling the hard bud at the tip until her body trembled with ecstasy. "Of course you can take it," he purred, "as long as I wish to give it to you." The sound of his voice, the sexy blend of power, lust, and masculinity instantly threatened to throw her over the edge.

"Stop," she pleaded once again. "It's too much…"

"Come for me, Jocelyn," he urged, his voice thick with male satisfaction. "I want to watch you lose control. Let go for me, and I'll give you what you need."

Jocelyn didn't know why she was fighting so hard.

Maybe it was the desire to hold onto her last vestige of control—in a life that had been so completely turned upside down in only a matter of days. Or maybe it was the need to feel like she still had the power to resist him—at least in the bedroom—but whatever it was, he was as determined to break it as she was to keep it: He wanted her total submission, and he would accept nothing less.

To her utter shock and amazement, she began to sob with the pleasure and intensity of what he was doing to her, tears of ecstasy streaming out of her eyes.

"Oh God," she whimpered, "you're making me cry. Please, Nathaniel…*I need you.*"

"Tell me what you need, baby." It was a sultry command.

"You," she uttered helplessly, "inside of me…"

Her hips were bucking wildly now against him, her body threatening to shatter completely out of control.

"That's it, baby," he purred. "Let go…give yourself to me, tiger-eyes. Come for me. Let yourself go, so I can take you the way you need me to."

He inserted a finger then, deep into her hot, wet sheath, and began to gently knead the tight, soft folds, drawing liquid heat from her like a sieve.

"Mmm…baby…you are so wet for me."

A soft moan escaped her lips as she felt him insert a second finger, and then a third: stretching her, caressing her, stabbing deep in an erotic effort to push her over the edge.

Jocelyn couldn't take another second.

She fractured into a thousand pieces, her body trembling in violent waves of pleasure as the powerful orgasm shook her. She cried out, fisting her hands in his hair, tears streaming down her face at the voracity of her release. She felt utterly and completely exposed...vulnerable...entirely open to his command. And she knew that was what he had wanted all along.

"My God, you are sexy when you come, baby."

He stood up then. He lifted her as if she weighed nothing and laid her back on the bed. He grasped her thighs with his strong, firm hands and knelt between her legs, gently easing them apart. And then he took the length of his rigid, engorged sex into his hand and pressed the head against her core.

His erection felt enormous against her entrance—so much so that she wondered if she would be able to take all of him inside her. But she wanted him. All of him. Every hard, throbbing inch.

"Is this what you need, baby?" he groaned, his voice rough with desire.

Jocelyn didn't answer. She couldn't.

A low, throaty hiss escaped his lips as he thrust forward into her tight, hot sheath, stretching her impossibly with the heavy width of his sex.

She started to moan as her body stretched to accommodate his size, her hands pushing against the muscular wall of his chest in an automatic response to the slight burning sensation of his dominant entry.

Nathaniel took her hands from his chest and held them down above her head, pinning both arms gently in one strong hand. "Relax. Isn't this what you wanted, baby?"

Jocelyn groaned. "Yes..." The word was a throaty whisper.

"I want you to take all of me," he growled.

He bent to taste her breasts again, easing up on the pressure while her body adjusted to his size. "That's it, angel: you were made for me...you can take more."

He groaned in sheer ecstasy when her body finally accepted

the full length of his, and her answering groan told him all she couldn't say.

Together, they slowly began to move in unison: a sultry, languid ride, her hips rising to meet his every thrust, his hard, flat pelvis lingering and rotating against her cleft to heighten her pleasure.

"You are so pretty, my love," he whispered, his eyelids half closed. "You feel so…damn…*good*."

Jocelyn reached up to cup his face and the rhythm picked up.

Nathaniel continued to bury himself deep inside of her, pulling back almost to the point of withdrawal only to thrust forward again and again, until the passion grew so intense between them he could no longer restrain his need.

He began to plunge harder…faster…each stroke more urgent, more possessive than the last.

Jocelyn clutched at his shoulders, dug her fingernails into his back. She cried out in ecstasy, raising her hips to meet his, writhing beneath him. She took all he could give her and wanted even more…always wanted more.

They were so right together: *so perfect.*

Their bodies fit like a hand and glove; their souls matched each other's passion for passion. He seemed to know her every desire and need, not just physically, but emotionally.

Spiritually.

And she was only too eager to meet his every dark command—her body no longer belonged to her. She had given it completely to him, the lust for his sex insatiable, the trust in his care absolute.

Jocelyn pulled back her legs and wrapped them around his powerful waist, completely letting go as he rode her, harder and harder…pistoning deeper and deeper until his breath was coming in short, ragged gasps, coarse hisses of ecstasy coming closer and closer together.

She felt her own release approaching as the pressure mounted once again to a fevered pitch, an imminent peak from which the fall would take her soaring into a whole new universe.

Her voice sounded foreign and far away as she heard herself calling out his name, her body responding with a new blast of liquid heat each time he moaned. The soft, feral hiss he made when his shaft jerked was not at all human, yet more erotic than anything she had ever heard.

The pace was almost frantic now as Nathaniel drove into her with a wild, animal abandon: plunging, stretching, demanding, claiming. Marking her for all time like the powerful creature he was. His pupils had narrowed into tiny slits of crimson heat. His fangs were fully extended and beautiful in the moonlight, his thick, wavy hair shining like the midnight sky, wild and spilling out all around her.

His perfect face was stamped with pleasure and lust.

And then she fractured again, her body bucking and trembling beneath his.

Nathaniel threw back his head and cried out, a harsh, guttural shout of pleasure, as his body shuddered beneath the violent force of his release. His back arched and his muscles clenched as he spilled stream after stream of his seed deep inside of her, filling her with his essence until his body collapsed over hers...raw...spent...

And totally sated.

twenty-three

Jocelyn sighed and lay her head on Nathaniel's shoulder, reveling in the feel of his strong arms around her. She still could not believe the amount of pleasure he had given her, the powerful way her body had responded to his.

He kissed her on the top of her head and nuzzled his chin into her thick wealth of hair, sighing with contentment.

"You are truly a miracle," he whispered.

Jocelyn smiled and snuggled even closer, tilting her head to look up into his mesmerizing eyes. "You're not exactly everyday, ordinary material yourself."

She found herself giggling like a schoolgirl.

Nathaniel laughed. "You may end up being very good for my ego, Miss Levi." He paused and then lowered his voice to a soft, husky tone. "*Mrs. Silivasi.*"

Jocelyn blinked several times. Her eyes grew wide in mock surprise. "Do you mean to tell me that *this* was our wedding ceremony? I mean, don't get me wrong; it was wonderful, but a girl needs a few bells and whistles now and then."

Nathaniel turned on his side, intrigued. "*This* was just the two of us getting better acquainted: Our union will not be…complete…until your conversion. And trust me, sweetheart, you can have all the bells and whistles you want."

He lowered his head to meet her gaze. "Would that please you? A wedding?"

Jocelyn shrugged. "I don't know. Actually, I never really gave it much thought. To be completely honest, I never saw myself settling down."

Nathaniel looked surprised. "As beautiful and intelligent as you are? I find that hard to believe. You must have received a dozen proposals."

Jocelyn started to respond but was cut off by a deep,

rumbling growl emanating from his throat.

"On second thought," he said, "I don't want to know."

Jocelyn laughed and shook her head, kissing him beneath his jaw before settling back against the warmth of his chest. "You really are a jealous one, aren't you?"

Nathaniel brushed the pads of his fingers lazily along her soft, narrow shoulders, dipping low to caress her breast as if he couldn't help himself. "I don't know that I understand the human concept of jealousy. I'm not afraid of any other male taking you from me, because no man who ever tried such a thing would live. But yes, I hold what is mine close to me."

Jocelyn sighed. She was growing accustomed to his primitive nature, beginning to see it...and accept it...in a different light.

"Nathaniel?" she whispered, her voice all at once becoming serious. "Can I ask you something?"

"Anything," he answered, propping himself up on his side to hold her tightly beneath him, staring adoringly into her eyes.

Jocelyn took a deep breath. She knew what was coming. Well, sort of. She knew about the curse and what was ultimately *required* of her, but she hadn't had the courage to face it until now. It had taken the terrifying events of the previous night, the horror of what had been done to Braden, to move the last several days from the realm of fantasy into the world of reality. It had taken her horrible encounter with Tristan to realize how far Nathaniel would go to protect her, how much safety, kindness, and love he had to offer her.

No one had ever really looked out for her before, and certainly, no one had wanted to *possess* her—to please her—the way Nathaniel did. When he looked at her, it was as if she were the only thing in his world, as if she could hang the moon and the stars.

Colette was right: There were far worse fates than ending up with a man such as Nathaniel. And now that she knew what kind of lover he could be, she had no intentions of ever letting him go.

Jocelyn's hand slid down over her belly, and she braced

herself, forcing her eyes to maintain contact with his. "So then...am I...pregnant?"

She almost choked over the word, but having managed to get it out, she now held her breath, waiting for his reply.

Nathaniel studied her face, brushing her cheek softly with his hand. "Ah, *iubita mea*," he sighed, "there is so much I have asked of you in such a short time. It will not always be this way."

He kissed her forehead, her cheeks, the tip of her nose, and then he planted a long, languorous kiss on her mouth, his lips equally soft and firm, his passion equally ardent and gentle.

His manhood stirred but he made no attempt to arouse her further. "I intend to make you happy, my love." An intriguing smile lit up his face. "In fact, I've been studying your memories, and I hope you don't mind because I already have a few ideas..."

Jocelyn couldn't resist, her curiosity getting the best of her. "Like?"

He sighed. "Like having an aquarium built here in the house." He brushed his fingers lightly along the length of her arm and took her hand in his. "If you like, we can keep it simple and just have the...*pets*...you have in San Diego transported here: *very carefully*, I might add." He lifted her hand to his mouth and gently kissed her knuckles. "I have no intentions of allowing even one of your beloved fish to die." He chuckled. "Or, if you're up for the adventure, we could expand on your collection."

Jocelyn smiled. "How so?"

"I have always wanted an atrium: a large, tropical rain forest of my own, complete with mist, exotic birds, and waterfalls. And what better place to build an aquarium, maybe something panoramic, something naturally occurring, than in the midst of a tropical paradise. We could bring in the rarest fish from all over the world." He kissed her mouth then, tugging on her bottom lip with his teeth before releasing her. "Would that please you?"

Jocelyn knew her face was flushed because she could feel the warmth, the joy bubbling over. "Yes!" she exclaimed. "Oh my

God, I was so worried about what was going to happen to my fish." She laughed at the absurdity of the statement, all other things considered.

Nathaniel laughed too. "Do you really think that little of me, Jocelyn?" He was playfully sarcastic. "I have already made arrangements for their care in San Diego until we can have them transported."

Jocelyn kissed his cheek and brushed her hand across his sexy chest, smiling as she gazed up into his eyes. "Thank you, Nathaniel."

His eyes lit up with satisfaction. "You're most welcome. And speaking of care, there is the matter of your next-door neighbor: Ida, is it?"

Jocelyn sat up, staring into his eyes like a child full of anticipation, waiting. "Mmm hmm."

"Of course, it's hard to say what she will or will not let us do. When a human lives to such an age, they are usually quite set in their ways, but I know she has no other family and her care is extremely important to you. If necessary, we can hire someone to continue her care in San Diego."

Jocelyn's eyes grew wide with excitement.

"And I don't just mean someone to carry out the day-to-day functions of looking after her, but someone kind, someone willing to provide companionship. However, if she is willing to move, then I would have no objection to providing for her here, setting her up in a comfortable place of her own, surrounded with all of her favorite things, so you could continue to see her as often as you like."

Jocelyn felt a warm tear escape her eye. Nathaniel caught it with his mouth as it made its way along her cheek. "No tears, my love," he whispered. "Never tears. Does this make you sad?"

"No..." She shook her head. "It makes me unbelievably happy." She looked away then. "You know, I never really had a family of my own; I never even knew my birth parents. And after growing up in so many different foster homes, I eventually learned how to get by without really...connecting...with anyone.

Tessa Dawn

They were all just caretakers—people to whom I owed a certain amount of time and courtesy—people I had to learn to get along with until I could finally move out on my own and become self-reliant. Ida was different because I chose her. I wanted her in my life. And she chose me."

Nathaniel sat up and held her then, pressing her tight to his chest, his strong arms enveloping her in warmth and security. "I know this, baby; I have seen so many of your memories. Believe me, you have a family now, wanted or not."

"Marquis," she responded, matter-of-factly.

"Marquis," he agreed, grinning. "Don't worry; he grows on you."

Jocelyn sighed. "Yeah, I suppose. And who knows, maybe if I ever get past the urge to take off running every time I see him, I might just find something I like about him."

Nathaniel laughed. "Don't hold your breath on that one. I still get the urge to take off running every time I see him, and he's my brother." There was a playful note in his voice.

"Well, I guess there's one great advantage to Marquis."

"What's that?"

"Security. I will certainly never be afraid of anything again with him around."

Nathaniel sat up straight—rigid—the lines of his face becoming harsh. He snarled a low, feral hiss. "*Marquis* is the one who makes you feel safe?" Despite his valiant attempt at humor, there was a subtle but clear warning in his tone.

Jocelyn nuzzled her head in his chest, loving the fresh, masculine scent of his skin, the warmth and strength of his arms, the protective way he held her. "You are so silly, Nathaniel. *Marquis* was not the one who came to me that first night in the forest—even before the blood moon." She twirled her fingers in his thick mane of hair. "And Marquis was not the one who...rearranged...Tristan's anatomy. I think you keep me safe enough."

Nathaniel's eyes turned cold, his pupils like two hard stones of granite. "I exercised *enormous* restraint with Tristan...you have no idea. I did not want to frighten you, or his death would have been far more…painful…and much, *much* slower."

Jocelyn shuddered, studying his face for the slightest hint of an exaggeration. There was none. She didn't answer. What could have possibly been more painful than removing his manhood? More gruesome than ripping his heart out through his throat? She honestly didn't want to know. One thing was for certain, however—she might need to rethink her assessment of the Silivasi brothers as a whole: Marquis might not be the most dangerous, after all.

All at once Nathaniel relaxed again. He reached out for her hand and held it to his heart. "Now then, to answer your original question, my love. No, angel, you are not pregnant…yet."

Jocelyn let out a deep, animated sigh, unsure if she was relieved or disappointed. Her hand went absently to her belly and she covered it protectively. "It takes several tries?" she asked, blushing. Then all at once, a very real sense of dread began to overtake her. "Nathaniel, what if it doesn't happen? What would happen to you if I can't become—"

"Shh, angel of mine." Nathaniel pressed a finger to her mouth and placed his own hand over her abdomen. "There is little to fear: You are my *true destiny*. There is no question that it will happen. In a sense, it has already happened."

Jocelyn shook her head. "I don't understand."

Nathaniel smiled a mischievous-looking grin. "Now that we have already…come to know each other so intimately…it is simply a matter of *speaking it into being*. Anytime within the next seventy-two hours, I can command your body to conceive, and it will be so."

Jocelyn abruptly sat up, turned to face him squarely, and gulped, her eyes wide with surprise. "You have that kind of power…over me? Over my body? With just your words?" The thought was more than a little unsettling.

"Jocelyn," he admonished, "you have the power of *life and death* over me right now, too. We each have tremendous power over each other—it is as it should be."

Jocelyn slowly nodded and lay back down, her head finding a pillow in the comfortable nook between his chest and arm. "I guess that makes sense." She looked up at him, her eyes soft with compassion, her heart emboldened with as much courage as she could muster. "Nathaniel, after what happened the other night...after what I did...walking away with Tristan..." She looked away, still feeling ashamed. "I really couldn't bear for something to happen to you—and especially not because of me and my fears. I might not understand exactly what you are, or how all of this came to be, but I know in my heart that it's right. And I know that I want to be with you. So I guess I'm ready. And honestly, the sooner the better."

Nathaniel stroked her cheek, his eyes wide with wonder. "As much as I detest the Blood Curse, I always marvel at the wisdom of the ancients, how the souls of *our destinies* are so perfectly suited to our own. You are a miracle to me, Jocelyn Levi; you will never know just how much of a miracle...how long I have waited for you...how I have dreamed of you, imagined you, longed for you. And now that I have you here in my arms, you are more amazing to me than any dream could have ever been."

He closed his eyes for a moment, and when he reopened them they were absolutely beaming with affection. Yet, there was also something else hidden in their remarkable depths, something Jocelyn had never seen there before—

Fear.

"Nathaniel, what is it?"

He took both of her hands in his and brought them to his forehead. He bowed his head as if praying. When he opened his eyes, they were gravely serious. "You cannot conceive my child—or go through the pregnancy—as you are...as a human. You have already seen the results of such a thing."

He nestled his chin in her hair. "I have to convert you first, my love, make you as I am." He closed his eyes and lowered his head. "As soon as the conversion is complete, I will command your conception."

Jocelyn shrugged warily. "Okay, so what's the problem?"

Nathaniel frowned. "The change is *very difficult,* Jocelyn; it can be quite painful. I wish I could spare you from the worst of the transition, but I'm afraid it cannot be done. Fortunately, it does not last that long."

"How long?" she asked, certain her fear was reflected in her eyes.

"It depends on the individual. For some, no more than forty-five minutes to an hour—for others, as long as five or six...but rarely more than that."

Jocelyn let out her breath, unaware she had been holding it until then. "I can do that, Nathaniel. I'm stronger than you think."

Nathaniel smiled then, brushing her cheek with a soft kiss. "Of course you are, but I need you to be truly prepared. Truly ready. There is no stopping the transition once it begins, no going back. To do so would risk your life, and I will not do that...no matter what occurs."

Jocelyn winced as the weight of his words sank in. He wasn't kidding: This *transition* had to be bad—really, really bad. Because she had never seen anything give Nathaniel pause before.

"It's necessary, though, isn't it?" she asked. "For you to live? For us to be together?"

Nathaniel nodded solemnly. "Yes, it is."

"Then I want to do it. And not just for you, Nathaniel. Not just to save your life from that horrible...curse. But because I really want to be with you." She looked down. "Sometimes you don't even know what's missing in your life until you find it." Her voice was soft.

But powerful.

Nathaniel cupped her face in his hands and kissed her long, hard, and thoroughly. He sat up against the headboard of the bed and raised one knee, completely unashamed of the enormous, jutting erection standing up against his thigh like an iron statue in response to the kiss. "Why don't you go take a shower, then? Wash your hair, relax for a moment, have a cup of tea, and come back. When you return to me, I will have you sit

in front of me, lean back into my arms where I can hold you…"
He gently swept the pad of his finger down her neck, from just
beneath the lobe of her ear to her collarbone. "Where I will have
the easiest access to your—"

"I get the picture." Jocelyn pulled back but tried to smile.

Nathaniel reached forward to take her hand and gave it a
firm, reassuring squeeze. "When you are comfortable and safe in
my arms, I will convert you. We will do it tonight then, yes?"

Jocelyn nodded—unconvincingly.

"Yes?" he repeated.

She looked into his dark, enchanting eyes, the love and
kindness he felt toward her so brilliantly glowing in the centers.
"Yes," she said with authority. She leaned over and kissed his
beautiful lips. "Yes, Nathaniel."

Nathaniel smiled, staring at her like she was an angel,
something he could hardly comprehend. "Go then, my love.
And when you are ready, come back to me."

Jocelyn crawled slowly off the bed, retrieved her bathrobe
from the floor, and began to make her way to the bathroom. Her
eyes took in her surroundings: the view from the glorious
windows; the tall, rustic beams on the ceiling; the gorgeous,
powerful being gazing at her from the bed. It was all hers now.
This life. This home. The beauty all around her. *A family*.

He was hers now.

As she left the room, her eyes caught the glory of the
luminous white moon shining down upon them from a tranquil
night sky, and it occurred to her that it was the last sky she
would ever see as a human being.

By this time tomorrow night, she would be like Nathaniel.
And there would be no turning back from him. Or her new life.

Vampires were immortal beings.

And even if they weren't, she knew one thing for certain:
Nathaniel Silivasi—that gorgeous, powerful, primitive male, with
all of his strength, tenderness, and cunning—would
never…*ever*…let her go.

Good thing she didn't want him to.

BLOOD DESTINY

Jocelyn sauntered into the bathroom, determined not to look back.

twenty-four

Marquis was sitting on the back porch relaxing, simply taking in the soothing sounds of nature and the soft, rustling melody of water trickling in the shallow, meandering river behind his house, when he heard a frantic knock at his front door.

He sighed. *What now?*

The last several days had been nothing but action.

And anxiety.

And he just wanted to unwind in the serenity of his home. Although he had to admit, at least one weight had been lifted from his shoulders; he had brushed Nathaniel's mind several times earlier that evening, a habit of checking in on his younger brothers that he hadn't been able to break in centuries—so he no longer tried, only to find that Nathaniel was planning on converting Jocelyn later that night.

Marquis didn't envy his little brother the trauma of conversion—or Jocelyn either for that matter. She'd had so much to absorb in such a little amount of time. But the woman was a female warrior as far as he was concerned, even if she did take occasional reckless chances without always thinking. Marquis chuckled, remembering the look on her face when he had told her he would turn her into a human puppet if he had to. It was certainly no laughing matter, but the woman was a spitfire.

Marquis sighed as he walked around the side deck toward the front door. He knew Nathaniel and Jocelyn would get through the conversion okay: His brother was too strong to accept any other outcome. And then, *finally*, Nathaniel would be one step away from freeing himself from that damnable blood curse—the blight of their kind that weighed like a heavy burden from the moment a male was born until the moment he finally secured *his destiny*. It was an ever present cloud that followed them like a shadow, blocking out the full warmth of...existence...the ability to fully embrace one's immortality up until that fateful moment finally came.

For better or for worse.

When Marquis rounded the corner, his eyes caught a wealth of medium-length honey-blond hair and the delicate frame of a woman, her back turned to his. She was weeping uncontrollably, utterly frantic; in fact, her slight fists pounded anxiously on the front door as she repeatedly called his name.

Marquis quickly scanned the area and scented the air. He closed his eyes, putting out feelers, trying to detect any hidden source of danger, to identify whatever it was that had so deeply shaken the woman at the front door.

"Joelle?"

"Marquis!" His housekeeper spun around and struggled for breath, frightened by his sudden appearance.

Marquis took a step back then, absolutely stunned by what he saw—his mind whirling around in a fog of confusion as his brain tried to process what his eyes were telling him. It was like trying to put together an obvious, yet elusive jigsaw puzzle: a riddle with such a horrifying conclusion that it hid in plain sight, taunting his sanity with the hideous truth—

Because if what Marquis was seeing was true, then he was staring at the face of...death.

"My God!" he exclaimed. "What the—"

There were no words.

Joelle leaned over, clasping her hands protectively around her protruding stomach, her eyes wide with fright. "Help me," she uttered.

Joelle Parker looked no less than five months pregnant. And Marquis could smell the fear emanating from her pores as the rapid process unfolded in her body. The exact phase of gestation, the precise stage of fetal development, was easy to pinpoint using the natural ability given to all males of his species: Joelle was twenty-four hours into a forty-eight-hour cycle, a cycle that was going to end with the birth of those babies.

Tessa Dawn

Marquis scanned the inside of her wrists, looking for something he knew wasn't there—the raised, telltale markings of a constellation—proof that somehow, in the last twenty-four hours, she had been revealed as the *blood destiny* of one of their males.

Proof that her babies were conceived—and consequently going to be born—naturally.

He knew better...even as he examined her arms.

The blood moon, heralding the revelation of a male's *destiny*, was a rare but unforgettable event. The brilliant celestial canopy was breathtaking. The sky was hypnotic. The Omen was unmistakable...impossible to ignore.

With the exception of the female who bore the actual markings, humans never saw the celestial revelations: Their eyesight was too limited to register the distant constellation, their telescopes unable to pick up a phenomenon meant solely for another species. But the sons of Jadon, even the sons of Jaegar—those who were forever lost and had no hope or *destiny* of their own—never missed it. It was a compulsion implanted by *the Blood Curse* as a safeguard for the males: No matter where they were, no matter what they were doing, they were inexplicably drawn to the blood moon sky. It was how Marquis had known about Jocelyn the moment it happened.

Joelle staggered as her stomach rolled in visible waves, her body jolted by the rapidly progressing pregnancy, the evidence of two small beings developing at record speed inside of her womb.

Marquis glided smoothly to catch her. "Joelle—"

He was still at a loss for words.

She looked up into his anxious face, her soft blue eyes dilated with terror, her face soaked with tears from hours of crying. "I don't understand what's happening to me." Her words were a choked whimper. "I got pregnant...and I couldn't find you."

Marquis shook his head, hoping to clear the cobwebs. "Tell me what happened." He made it a command.

Joelle's eyes opened wide. "What do you mean, *what happened?*" She sounded horrified. "What do you think happened? You were there! *You* got me pregnant." She looked down at her bulging belly as it continued to twist and turn beneath her. "And now…I think I'm dying."

Marquis took a step back, her words striking him like the sting of a scorpion: *You got me pregnant?* He immediately pierced the veil of her mind in order to extract her memories. He needed a firsthand account, and he needed it now.

All at once, he dropped her arm. "Dear gods…" he uttered.

And then her frail body hit the deck. She landed on her knees, practically doubling over, before he caught her up with a strong arm.

His mind was racing, spinning wildly out of control.

Marquis was known for his calm in battle, his seasoned ability to become still, remain alert, and process information at amazing speed when faced with a crisis. His ability to remain unruffled was legendary in the house of Jadon, but now, he was at a total loss. Disbelief and rage swirled like bands of inky darkness through his head, seeping deep into his soul and piercing his heart, as he slowly came to the full understanding…

And the inevitable conclusion: Valentine Nistor.

Again.

Joelle Parker was going to die a horrific, unthinkable death, and there was nothing he or anyone else could do to stop it.

Marquis wrapped his arms around the frail, trembling woman, his heart absolutely breaking for her. He had been the one Valentine had used to trick her, to steal her innocence, to handle her so brutally; and his soul ached with the knowledge that, even now, she looked up at him with eyes of love…*after all that she'd been through.*

What was the point in telling her the truth?

She was going to die. And it couldn't be stopped.

Did she also need to know she had been deceived…used…violated? Would it ease her suffering to know she had lain with a Dark One, that the demon had brutally taken her life even as he had viciously debased her body? The woman was absolutely terrified—she was suffering—and the only thing he could possibly give her before her death was a moment's peace.

Marquis wrapped his strong arms around her, pulled her tightly to his chest, and began to breathe with her.

To breathe for her.

"Relax, love." His voice was a delicate whisper, a lullaby. "It's going to be okay."

Joelle hiccupped her sobs and tried to stop crying. She stared helplessly into his eyes, searching for repose.

Marquis forced a smile, sending a tender wave of reassurance into her mind. "You are not the first woman to be with child, Joelle. *It's going to be okay.*"

He lied.

Joelle sniffled and wiped her nose. A faint light illuminated her sad eyes, and then she clutched tightly at her stomach as the ever expanding belly constricted once again. The babies were growing at an alarming rate.

Marquis sensed a series of Braxton Hicks contractions as they tightened her womb: standard second trimester stuff—only it was happening far too swiftly for comfort. He scooped her up in his arms and took her inside to the front room, where he laid her down gently on a pale green chaise and knelt on the floor in front of her.

"The first thing we must do is stop this pain, my love." He bent to her neck and carefully, as gently as possible, took a small amount of her blood. And then he injected a minute amount of his venom into her bloodstream.

She cried out at the unexpected pain of the injection, but it was short lasting.

"I'm sorry," he whispered, "but without the exchange, I cannot block your pain for you."

Joelle nodded and stared at him with wide, trusting eyes. She was like a child awaiting his assistance, believing with absolute faith he would take care of her.

BLOOD DESTINY

Marquis did as he promised.

He sent a positive electrical charge from his own body into hers, slowly intercepting the negative pain impulses as they traveled through her body, effortlessly blocking the connections before they could reach the appropriate receptor sites in her brain. He then absorbed the energy...so that Joelle's pain became his.

Until she no longer felt a thing.

"Are you comfortable now?" he asked. His voice was uncharacteristically soft with compassion.

Joelle sighed, visibly relieved. She rested a delicate hand on her stomach and her eyes closed. "I can't feel anything anymore." She sounded comforted. Grateful.

"Good," he said. "There will be no more pain, sweetheart."

Joelle reached out tentatively for his hand and seemed surprised when he gave it to her so willingly.

Caressing her wrist with his thumb, he linked his fingers in hers and bowed his head. "Joelle?" His voice was a mere whisper. "I need to apologize for the other night. It was your first time, and you deserved so much more. My treatment of you was...selfish...and cruel...and shameful. And I want you to know that you have my word as a warrior, it will never happen again. Please forgive me."

Joelle's eyes shot open in surprise, and there was something else shining in their soft brown depths as well: tenderness...love. "Of course, I forgive you." She sighed with relief. "I thought it was me, my inexperience. I thought you were disappointed, and that was why you left so quickly."

Marquis winced and shook his head. He wanted to scream— *to rage*—to cry out at the heavens and break something. *Someone.* But that wasn't going to help Joelle right now.

"Never, love," he reassured her. "How could you even think such a thing? You are an amazing woman, Joelle." He lightly stroked her cheek. "How could any man be disappointed with you?"

Her smile at that moment would have rivaled the sun, and it

made Marquis loathe himself for lying.

Marquis was not a man to apologize often, and especially not for an act someone else had committed, a reprehensible act he was virtually incapable of committing. But being inside of her mind as he was, he could sense her overwhelming anxiety: Joelle believed she was going to be the mother of his children. That they were going to have a future after all. And her one remaining fear was that Marquis would hurt her again. That the powerful vampire would continue to humiliate and brutalize her for his own selfish pleasure.

Marquis knew Joelle could never fully embrace peace as long as she believed she was going to spend the rest of her life with a male who would use her so callously, regardless of how much she loved him.

Her fear was a real, living thing.

And if removing that fear, that lone worry, could make her feel special and give her the one thing in the world she wanted more than anything else, to believe Marquis loved her, then he could do nothing less. And maybe, just maybe, she might even experience a moment of joy, the slightest hint of the pleasure...and peace...that had eluded her for so long.

"Are you going to stay with me now?" she whispered.

Marquis smiled, his eyes holding hers in a steady, unwavering gaze. "Of course, I am." He tightened his hand around hers. "Absolutely."

"Forever?" she asked sheepishly.

Marquis swallowed hard. The deception seemed so unjust. "Forever."

Joelle started to say something else, but Marquis gently lifted a finger to her lips. "Shh, don't talk, baby. Be still. Rest for me. Just let me hold you."

Joelle seemed utterly content and at peace as Marquis moved onto the chaise, gathered her into his arms, and held her tightly against his chest, his heart beating beneath her ear. He bent to nuzzle her hair, noticing that it smelled like fresh cut roses in the spring. Funny, he had never noticed that about her before.

BLOOD DESTINY

The night crept on.

Moving painfully slow.

Marquis held Joelle Parker in his arms, all the while hiding his rage, burying his sorrow, concealing his regret. He stroked her hair, spoke words of love and mystery in her ear, gently kissed her cheek, and rubbed her stomach—as if she carried his own precious unborn children in her womb.

Marquis gave the performance of his life.

When at last she had fallen into a peaceful sleep, he lifted her soft body up to his shoulders and nuzzled his mouth against her neck. He took a long, deep breath, and then he threw back his head and raged silently at the heavens, cursed the gods for their bitter indifference, made a promise of swift and terrible vengeance.

And then he released his fangs, allowing his canines to grow to a lethal point. Harnessing all of his remaining energy in one final effort to block her pain—and prevent her awareness—he sank his teeth deep into her carotid artery…

And sucked with lethal efficiency.

He extracted her life's blood—without emotion, without clemency—drinking until not one drop remained in her lifeless body. And her dead weight collapsed in his arms.

There would be no more heirs for Valentine Nistor: no more agonizing births to watch; no more demon spawn ripping the life out of another beautiful, innocent woman. Joelle Parker would go into the Valley of Spirit and Light peacefully—and with dignity—believing she was loved.

Laying her lifeless body carefully against the chaise, Marquis slowly stepped out from underneath her. How was he going to explain this to her family? What in the world was he going to tell her father? A man he had known all his life—a man who had trusted Marquis enough to allow his beloved daughter to come and work for him at such a young age.

Kevin Parker would die a thousand deaths when he saw his precious little girl—lifeless, pale, and heavy with child. He would lose all faith and friendship at the knowledge that Marquis had

284

failed to protect her. *Marquis had failed to protect…*

Shelby.

Dalia.

And now Joelle.

Marquis's chest heaved with the weight of the burden, shook with the rage of it all: *Nachari, I require your direct attention.*

Marquis called out telepathically to his youngest living brother—the brother whose twin he had also failed.

What is it, Marquis? Nachari's concern was immediately evident. *What causes you such sorrow?*

Marquis couldn't bear to repeat all of the details, so he sent the information as a series of visual images straight to Nachari's mind—starting from the night Joelle had met him on the front porch to the last few moments when he had ended her young life.

Nachari was deathly quiet. Jarringly still. For what seemed an eternity. *My brother,* he finally sighed.

Another long, protracted silence.

Tell me what I can do for you, Marquis. Name anything…and it will be done.

Marquis ran his hands through his thick wealth of raven black hair and rested his elbows on his knees as he sat in a chair across from the chaise lounge, across from Joelle.

Have you ever heard of a Dark One possessing that much power before? he asked. *Enough to hold another's persona for that length of time? To be that convincing?*

Nachari sighed again; this time his frustration showed. *I had heard rumors that Valentine's older brother, Salvatore, might be capable of such a feat, but he is well studied in the black magics. I had no idea Valentine had become that powerful.*

We underestimated our enemy, Marquis growled. *I underestimated our enemy. Again.*

Nachari didn't respond.

Is there any of our kind who can match such a feat? You are a wizard now; can you do such a thing?

Nachari paused, as if thinking it over. As if he wanted to be absolutely certain before he answered.

I can.

Marquis sat back in the heavy armchair, his large body taking up the entire frame. He was tired. So very tired.

Then I accept your offer...for assistance...and this is what I ask of you: Together, we will bring justice to this insufferable son of Jaegar.

For Joelle.

For Dalia.

We will exact our revenge for Shelby.

And there will be no more delay.

First thing tomorrow night, immediately upon his rising, Valentine will come to claim his children...

And we will be waiting.

twenty-five

Jocelyn lingered in the shower, washing and conditioning her hair, using the special lavender perfumed body wash Nathaniel had purchased for her, applying a moisturizer made of aloe and jasmine to her skin, before she dressed in another silk nightgown. This one was a soft pale rose color with a low-cut back that came together in a downward V at the apex of her hips. It revealed a high, sexy slit along the left thigh and a soft, flowing hem that fell all the way to the floor.

She drank a hot cup of chamomile and mint tea, sweetened perfectly with honey, and then she wandered around the first floor, looking at all of the beautiful artwork—the handmade pottery and crafts, treasures collected over centuries of living—before making her way back up to the third-floor master bedroom, *her new master bedroom.*

As if he understood her need for privacy, Nathaniel had given her all the time she wanted. He had left her, respectfully, alone, not once checking on her whereabouts or invading her space. Although Jocelyn had sensed his presence in her mind on several occasions, his light touch and genuine concern, he had never once intruded.

When she was finally ready, she entered the master bedroom to find him lying back on the bed, patiently waiting, with a look of absolute peace and confidence on his face.

There were several soft, glowing candles lit. And the enchanting sound of trickling water echoed from a polished stone waterfall, an accessory Nathaniel seemed to have in every room, as a faint Celtic instrumental played in the background. It was like walking into another world, entering another time and place.

Jocelyn wondered if this wasn't how his ancestors, the Celestial Beings, had lived: embracing the sights, sounds, and textures of nature in everything they did.

The curtains were still drawn back from the windows, and the night sky was radiant with stars, the luminescent moon peaceful as if it were smiling down upon them. The atmosphere could not have been more perfect. The man could not have been more handsome. The night could not have seemed more surreal.

Yet, somehow she knew…

What she was about to embark upon would be in grave contrast to their peaceful surroundings. An emergence into light? Yes. But only after a slow and painful journey through darkness.

Drawing in a deep breath, Jocelyn approached the bed and sat on the edge, looking up into Nathaniel's spectacular eyes. He held out his hand as an offering and she took it.

"Come here, my love," he whispered, his voice steady and reassuring.

Jocelyn nodded. Was one ever truly ready for something of this magnitude?

Nathaniel propped up several large down pillows against the headboard, the blue satin slips crisply laundered and brusquely fluffed behind him. As he leaned back against the comfortable piling, he opened his arms, smiled a heart-stopping smile, and gestured for her to join him.

Hesitantly, Jocelyn crawled onto the bed; she stopped to bury herself in the warmth of his arms, burrowing in for a long, languorous hug before she turned around. He didn't say a word. He simply held her as long and as close as she needed…until she finally pulled away, ready to take the next step.

As she leaned back against him, sinking deep into the comfort of his chest, she could hear his heart beating steadily behind her. His legs were bent and slightly spread apart to encompass the full width of her body, his powerful arms gathered tightly around her.

She lay her head on his shoulder, just below the crook of his neck, and took several deep breaths while he gently massaged her arms, kissing her lightly from her ear to her throat…from her throat to her shoulder…as he waited for her to settle in.

"Are you ready, my angel?" he asked. His voice was raspy, thick with love.

Jocelyn nodded. "Yes," she whispered. "I think so."

Nathaniel gathered her even closer then and whispered something beautiful in her ears in the ancient language of his people. The words sounded strange and old worldly, thick with an accent from a time gone by. Yet they seemed to flow off of his tongue with a modern grace, like water trickling over a river rock: polished by the hands of time, sculpted through centuries of use.

"You are my *blood destiny*," he repeated, interpreting the words in English, "the other half of my soul. You are the love I have waited a lifetime to find. The gift I will spend a lifetime trying to become worthy of. Your heart was revealed to me beneath the blood moon, your spirit chosen by the goddess Cassiopeia to be honored, cherished, and favored by me—above and beyond all others—for all eternity. Do you accept this as your true destiny?"

Jocelyn smiled. "Yes, I do...if you do."

He chuckled softly. "Jocelyn Levi, do you come to me now of your own free will?"

Jocelyn nodded. "Yes, Nathaniel; I do."

"Will you relinquish your heart, your life, and your body into my care? To be transformed, remade, and reborn? This night, unto forever, to be made immortal?"

Jocelyn weighed his question carefully: She couldn't find the words to answer. Turning to face him, she kissed him gently on the mouth and nodded her head. "Will you always take care of me like you do now?"

Nathaniel's smile lit up his eyes, a beauty to rival the heavens. "Oh yes, *iubita mea*, always."

She turned back around. "I will."

He nuzzled her cheek, slowly exhaled, and then resituated her in his arms. "I want you to relax into me, baby." He gently stroked her hair, then tenderly pulled it away from her neck, tucking it behind her. "I need you to try and let go; do not fight me, if you can help it."

Jocelyn nodded as he gently stroked her neck, the pads of his fingers brushing over her artery again and again in a hypnotic rhythm.

And then he gently tipped her head to the side, urging her ear down to her shoulder. His arms tightened in a viselike grip, the muscles of his legs tensing around her.

"Breathe for me, angel," he whispered, and then he lowered his mouth to her pulse.

He licked the artery with a soft swirl of his tongue, gently scraping his teeth back and forth against her skin. A soft purr escaped his lips. When she was finally, completely, relaxed, like a child who had fallen under a spell, she felt a tiny pinprick, two sharp stings, at the surface of her skin.

And then his teeth sank deep.

The piercing pain jolted her out of her trance, and her body went stiff, her muscles clenching as she waited for the intense sensation of his entry to end.

It felt as if it would go on forever.

The simple act of Nathaniel inserting two razor-sharp fangs into her flesh, piercing through muscle, spearing past tendons, sinking deeper and deeper…until she caught at his arms and tried to pull away.

He didn't let up. He didn't relent. He didn't retreat.

He simply continued to apply steady pressure until his incisors were deeply nestled into her throat, leaving her utterly stunned by the severity of the pain.

Jocelyn struggled for breath, unable to speak. She felt his hands massaging her arms, his thumbs rubbing in soft, caressing circles, a gentle purr rumbling from his throat. And she tried to relax into it, but that was a bit like asking someone to lie down on a razor blade without resistance. It went against her every instinct.

"Shh," he managed to whisper, even with his teeth lodged deeply in her throat.

And then the real pain began…

Tessa Dawn

Poison. Venom. A burning sensation began to swell as toxic fluid poured into her veins…slowly seeping through the artery with tremendous pressure as it invaded her bloodstream.

Jocelyn cried out in misery: What had she expected? A mosquito bite? A bee sting? A flu shot?

The amount of toxin being injected into her vein was like that of a thousand wasps stinging at once, a rattlesnake that wouldn't let go, a 220-pound scorpion, shooting enough fatal venom into her blood to reshape her entire physiology.

What had he said? *Transformed, remade, reborn.* He was *killing* her. He was slowly, insufferably, destroying what she was so that he could remake her as something else.

Panic began to set in.

It was one thing to hold one's breath through a rabies vaccination—or even the insertion of an IV—something one expected to hurt but knew would end soon. It was quite another to try to endure such a thing indefinitely, the initial pain of injection going on and on until every muscle, organ, and tissue in her body was consumed by the searing toxin.

She tried desperately to hold her breath. She shut her eyes. She clutched at his arms. She dug her nails into his flesh, but nothing stopped the torture. It was simply, utterly—and absolutely—unbearable.

There was nothing Nathaniel could have said or done to prepare Jocelyn for the agony she was enduring: Her blood vessels felt as if they were about to burst, the very veins themselves resisting, as if her body were not only rejecting, but downright refusing the foreign inoculation.

And there was nothing left in her constitution that was strong enough to endure such an assault a moment longer.

Jocelyn felt like a failure.

A desperate, suffering, helpless failure. She had wanted this so badly. She had *wanted Nathaniel* so very badly. And the stakes were so *extremely* high, but—

"No more."

Her voice was an anguished whimper. And then she cried

out as a fresh burst of pain racked her body. The blistering venom was really starting to spread out now, flowing downward toward the trunk of her body, approaching her chest and her heart. And it burned like acid.

Tears welled up in her eyes as she began to struggle with much more ferocity. She tried to sit up, to wrench her body free of Nathaniel's iron grip. Her legs kicked and her arms flailed, but he only tightened his hold, his powerful thighs like cords of iron clamping down over hers.

"No, Nathaniel!" she screamed, pleading for mercy. "Stop! You have to stop. I can't do this."

He didn't budge. He didn't panic or even react. He simply continued to inject the painful venom into her veins.

And then the vampire's toxin reached her heart.

A brutal cry of terror ripped from her throat as her body began to shake violently, convulsing in waves of agony until she finally began to seize.

Jocelyn fought wildly.

She clutched at his arms. She scratched and pulled at his hard muscles in a frenzied attempt to break free. She thrashed her head from side to side, trying to dislodge his fangs. She even clawed at his eyes and kicked back at his groin—anything, everything—just to break free, to stop the unbearable pain.

When nothing moved him, when no act of desperation brought her freedom, she at last began to beg and cajole: "Nathaniel, you *have* to stop. Oh God, please...*I know*...I know what it means for you, and I'm sorry. I'm so sorry." Her tears fell like rain. "But if you love me...if you care at all...you will stop."

The seizing continued, and the pain grew worse...as if that were even possible. "Please," she pleaded, her voice hoarse with desperation. "Just let me die. I can die with you; we can still be together. Please, Nathaniel. Don't do this."

She struggled against him with all of her might then, pouring every ounce of energy she had into freeing herself. "Stop it!" she demanded. "Do you hear me? I want you to stop!"

When all of her energy had been spent, she sobbed. "How can you do this to me? Why, Nathaniel? Oh, God, please...*please*...make it stop."

Nathaniel wanted to speak to Jocelyn so badly. He wanted to soothe her, to tell her she was halfway there, to convince her to hold on just a little while longer, but her anguish was so great, her pain so intolerable, he could hardly bear it. He couldn't console her telepathically yet, because his full concentration was required to initiate the conversion.

He knew she felt betrayed, abandoned, and deceived—and it was breaking his heart. But he also knew what stopping would mean for both of them: not only his death, *but hers.*

Her human body could not survive such a lethal injection of vampire venom, and without completing the transfusion, her vampire body would not be strong enough to accept the conversion.

He wanted so desperately to end her pain.

He would have gladly accepted his own death, allowed her to live on without him just to stop her agony, but he couldn't. It just wasn't possible. This was an all-or-nothing proposition that would take life from—or give life to—both of them.

Nathaniel couldn't speak. He couldn't console. He couldn't do anything but restrain the beautiful woman in his arms as she suffered so terribly at his hands. And he didn't dare risk withdrawing his fangs, not even for a moment, because he knew he could never pierce her again.

Nathaniel shut his mind off to the sound of her cries, afraid that she might actually convince him to allow them both to enter the Valley of Spirit and Light together.

He had heard tales of conversion....

The males had been taught all about the powerful transition at the Romanian University: what happened physically, how long it might take, the proper way to administer the venom, how to restrain the recipient...

But nothing in all his long centuries of living had prepared him for what he was witnessing now.

The woman he loved, the *destiny* he had promised to honor, cherish, and favor above all others, was in indescribably agony: *because of him.*

Tears began to well up in his eyes and he struggled to hold them back. Jocelyn was pleading with him now, like a helpless child, begging him for mercy.

She actually used the word mercy.

Nathaniel gently merged with her mind, trying to make sense of what she was going through, to share it, even if he couldn't end it. And what he found was a red cauldron of pain, panic, and confusion, a fear so great it had taken the place of reason. Jocelyn was experiencing nothing less than *torture*, and it had robbed her of her will to live.

Nathaniel could feel the sensation of his own venom pumping into her body as it violently attacked her internal organs, destroying them from the inside out. The assault was merciless on her blood, and the pain was like nothing he had ever witnessed before. No one—male or female, human or vampire—should ever be asked to endure such torment.

Nathaniel held her closer. His hands massaged her arms where he gripped her, even though he knew it was a worthless comfort. As tears streamed down his face, he felt as if his heart might shatter into a million pieces. In all of his centuries of living, he had never felt more helpless.

And so he prayed.

As he beseeched the grace of the Celestial Deities, for the first time in decades, Nathaniel pleaded for an end to Jocelyn's suffering.

Yet time continued to pass. Slowly. Painfully. Until prayers became curses and sorrow gave way to rage. Still, Nathaniel fought to hold it together. For both of them. To keep his fangs securely lodged in her neck...

Tessa Dawn

As he forced the venom to continue flowing.

twenty~six

Jocelyn was too exhausted to fight anymore. The pain had finally won. She felt like death was near now, and she prayed it would come swiftly.

There was no more anger at Nathaniel, no more sense of betrayal or panic, no more begging for mercy. Only the sweet anticipation of an inevitable end.

The transformation obviously hadn't worked.

And curiously, she wondered why...

Why had her body refused the conversion?

As Jocelyn drifted in and out of consciousness—the pain now blessedly causing her to black out—she thought about Nathaniel, how painful his death would be, and she hoped it would be nothing like this.

She thought about Ida, her next-door neighbor, and the family she would never have. And she thought about her fish. Who would take care of them now?

And then all at once, the room seemed to fill with colors, like an iridescent rainbow swirling through the air. Nathaniel seemed to move farther and farther away, slowly drifting out of her awareness, until she could no longer sense the rock-hard arms that held her or the powerful legs wrapped around her.

The jagged teeth embedded in her neck no longer felt as foreboding. Maybe the pain had washed away all of her sins— did she really have that many sins?—so that when she did finally die, there would only be absolution awaiting her: forgiveness, peace, and eternal rest.

She laughed aloud, or at least she thought she did. How silly it all seemed. Maybe it had all been just some sort of crazy dream...

Vampires.

Werewolves.

BLOOD DESTINY

A beautiful, sexy man who lived only for her...adored her...worshipped her.

Immortality.

Now that she thought about it, it had definitely been a dream. Then why did that damn fire in her veins persist on burning?

And then the strangest thing happened.

A bolt of electricity shot through her, like nothing she had ever felt before, and she felt an abrupt, undeniable release, like that of her spirit letting go of her body, moving all at once into a new host. This must be what death felt like: a sudden pop. A simple...letting go.

As the cumbersome weight of her human body seemed to disappear, oxygen poured into her lungs with extraordinary efficiency, and vitality surged through her veins like a flood of new life, invigorating her senses, awakening her mind. Her joints and muscles swiftly came alive: revitalized, energized, rejuvenated. Her heart began to pump fresh blood through her veins like a four-star general sending his elite troops into battle, arousing every organ and tissue to its highest state of renewed health.

Jocelyn felt *perfection* in her body: staggering health and vitality...

And power.

Like she could leap buildings, or fly...run with the wind.

Maybe she was an angel after all.

Jocelyn didn't have to test her newfound strength to know it was there. She felt it in every cell of her body: the complete absence of illness, the total lack of vulnerability to disease, the utter removal of every toxin or pollutant that had been stored in her kidneys or liver for so long.

And mental clarity—

Her five senses were outrageously enhanced. She could hear the wind moving through the trees outside, the individual rustling of the leaves. She heard a robin singing more than a mile away.

Tessa Dawn

And she could smell—

The spoor of cougars in the forest, the rich scent of pine, and the sweet aroma of wet earth beneath the riverbeds. She could even distinguish between the various spices and perfumes in a jar of potpourri that sat on Nathaniel's pine dresser. Pine smelled different than birch. And birch smelled different than aspen. Their needles and leaves made distinctly different sounds. There was a symphony to nature—harmonious, glorious, beautiful.

Now that her fear was gone, Jocelyn could taste its residual evidence in her mouth; she could actually separate the flavors of fight versus flight. And she could acutely feel Nathaniel's body behind her: the perfection and contour of every lean muscle that touched her. She could hear his heart beating in his chest as clearly as if it were her own and she was listening through a stethoscope. And she could identify *his thoughts*. As if *his* electrical impulses were firing in her brain.

Am I dead? She tested the telepathic question.

She heard a huge sigh of relief, although the sound was not an audible vibration but a stimulation of the mind instead.

No, my love.

She felt his joy!

How are you feeling?

Mental telepathy: Holy shit! She could read his mind, and he was reading hers. They were talking without their mouths or ears. Speaking…and hearing…with incredible clarity. And the nuances were far more varied, far more precise than they ever could have been from using the inner ear. It was like receiving sound in high definition.

Am I—

Immortal? Yes, you are.

Jocelyn could still feel the venom pumping into her body, restoring the last remaining cells and tissues, but it no longer felt like poison.

More like the fountain of youth.

Everywhere it flowed it brought health, vitality, and a

powerful awakening.

Jocelyn closed her eyes and began to revel in the warmth and pleasure of the life-giving substance as her pain gave way to ecstasy…a high unlike anything she had ever felt before.

Her head fell back and she moaned, her neck rubbing languidly against Nathaniel's mouth like a cat stroking its body against a leg. She was seeking the immense pleasure of the physical contact now, the sheer ecstasy of his fangs still embedded in her neck. She was drawing him in…wanting…needing…the way he felt: so good. So very, very good.

She wanted more of what he was giving her.

A low-pitched, feminine hiss escaped her mouth as the pleasure completely enveloped her, and she felt Nathaniel's body instantly respond with the same urgency—as a tremendous arousal centered in his groin.

Jocelyn purred like a kitten then, knowing just what buttons to push in order to entice the powerful male vampire behind her. *Her mate.* It was like she was inside of him now—inside of his head, his heart, his skin—and the answering jerk of his sex confirmed that she knew exactly what she was doing.

You are feeling much better, my angel, he drawled.

She could *feel* him smiling.

Jocelyn reached behind her and stroked his glorious hair. *I have never felt this good in all of my life.*

Instinctively, Nathaniel bit down harder, his deep fangs sinking even deeper. Only this time, Jocelyn didn't fight him. She didn't shriek or cry out in pain or try to stop him. Rather, she trembled from the pleasure of it and let out a deep, husky moan of satisfaction.

You like that? Nathaniel purred, sounding pleasantly surprised.

She arched her back and rubbed up against him in answer.

Oh yeah, he whispered, his psychic voice growing hoarse. *You like that, all right.*

Jocelyn's breasts suddenly felt incredibly heavy. Her nipples became hard and painfully erect as desire pooled like a river into her core, flooding her senses with liquid heat. She needed...wanted...with an urgency she had never felt before. And she didn't want foreplay: not now. Not this time. She didn't want to be teased or stroked or fondled. She wanted to be sated. She wanted to feel the full vitality of the ancient male behind her, in his most dominant state. She wanted him to take her like the powerful force of nature he was: to please her, invade her, make her scream...

To give her the full measure of gratification her body was demanding—to ride her hard—without the gentleness she had required as a human.

Sure, she would want that again—tenderness, compassion, slow, erotic lovemaking—but not tonight. Tonight, she wanted to experience her transformation; she wanted to test the limits of her new body, to soar to new heights of pleasure.

She wanted her Alpha male.

And she wanted him now.

Nathaniel read her like a book, their minds so completely merged, as if he had been with her all of his life. He unsheathed his claws and tore at the silk nightgown, shredding it to pieces, a glorious torrent of silk swirling around her.

Her panties went next.

And then a strong, territorial growl of power surged in his throat as he reached around and lifted her by the waist, raising her up and off of the bed with one hard tug, forcing her to her hands and knees, his teeth still deeply embedded in her throat.

Jocelyn purred louder then. Her body felt like it was on fire. She lowered her shoulders and raised her hips in a tantalizing offering.

Nathaniel held her in place with one arm while using the other to free his throbbing erection from his pants. A feral growl escaped his throat as the rock-hard member came free. And then he blanketed her body with all the stealth, power, and domination of a male lion, his jaw locking tight against her neck to hold her in place for his possession: to keep her rigid beneath him as he took her. He mounted her with a fierce groan of pleasure, stabbing deep and hard with one sure stroke, filling her in one smooth motion.

His invasion was rough...powerful...dominant, his possession aggressive. He pistoned wildly, surging deeper and deeper in and out of her heat, taking her higher and higher with every hard, pounding thrust. He ground his pelvis mercilessly against her soft, round bottom with a fierce, relentless lust as he moaned, his voice the husky growl of a predator.

Jocelyn gave herself up to the wild abandon of this new state of arousal. She gave herself up to Nathaniel's commanding, throbbing shaft as he drove her insane with pleasure. She backed into him, pushing hard against each impending thrust, desperate to have more...

Deeper. Harder. Faster.

And he answered her every desire.

Nathaniel drove further and further into her core, taking her passion to a fevered pitch and holding her there. And during those times, when her motion got too wild—when she threatened to dislodge his teeth from her throat—he snarled a low hiss of warning and clamped down harder on her neck, sending a sudden burst of pain and pleasure through her body...a sensation so glorious and primal, she thought she might just die from the ecstasy.

Nathaniel was driving harder and faster now, his hips thrashing with primitive abandon, his wild hair falling down in magnificent waves of silk around her face, his sac slapping against her in a constant, wild rhythm.

Jocelyn sighed and moaned and purred. She thrust her hips back, taking all of him in, needing more of him, still. She had never wanted a man so much in all her life.

This man.

Her man.

His voice was a raspy groan in her mind: *I love you, Jocelyn.*

He whispered the words and then she felt his explosion, a powerful jet of hot, pulsing seed pumping over and over in a

Tessa Dawn

relentless stream of pleasure, spilling deep into her core, filling her sheath, and dripping decadently down her thigh.

Her own orgasm shook them both as her body simply fractured around him, her sex squeezing, milking, and kneading, her womb violently contracting again and again until she thought the orgasm would never end.

Nathaniel held her close, slowly rocking her back and forth, gradually bringing both of them back down to earth.

When they finally stopped, their bodies were covered in sweat, their hearts were beating frantically, and their breath came in short, ragged gasps. Slowly exhaling, Nathaniel removed his fangs, allowing the last few drops of venom to seal the tiny wounds in her neck.

"You almost killed me, woman," he panted, rolling over to lie back on the bed.

Jocelyn spun around and glared at him with a fierce look of astonishment. "*Excuse me?*" she gasped. "Who almost killed who here tonight?"

"Oh yeah," Nathaniel mumbled, offering a sheepish smile. "You almost made me forget."

The light that lit up the vampire's eyes was positively...breathtaking...his serenity so complete that Jocelyn might have almost believed he had sailed through the whole ordeal.

Almost.

Except for one thing...

As sinfully gorgeous as his smile was, it couldn't hide the tracks of his tears.

twenty-seven

Marquis Silivasi lay silently on the bed at the Dark Moon Lodge like a python—an ambush hunter—lurking as still as the night, patiently awaiting his prey.

Giving up control of his body to Nachari had been difficult.

He was not a male who easily relinquished power to another vampire, but it was either that or allow Nachari to make the kill. And Marquis refused to surrender that prize to anyone. Valentine Nistor was his.

Nachari had hidden himself in the small cedar closet just adjacent to the bed, leaving neither sight, nor sound, nor vibration in his wake to alert the enemy of his presence. Like a black widow spider, the talented Master Wizard hovered in the shadows, spinning a deadly web of deceit, orchestrating a fatal plan with the use of Marquis's body.

They were in the same rustic suite Valentine had used to violate—and ultimately murder—Joelle Parker the night of the lycan attack. The room where Joelle had become pregnant with the Dark One's twins. Now, forty-eight hours later, Marquis lay on the same bed, in the same position, exactly as Joelle would still be if she hadn't come to Marquis: if she hadn't found the strength and courage to get out of Valentine's snare.

Marquis could feel his brother's commanding energy as currents of power swept through his body like waves slapping against the seashore. He marveled at Nachari's sheer determination and skill as the young wizard not only cloaked the Master Warrior's presence, but gave him the outward appearance of a pregnant woman.

Marquis looked exactly like Joelle Parker.

He smelled like Joelle.

He moved like Joelle.

He even sounded like Joelle...

BLOOD DESTINY

So that anyone entering the room would see Joelle, a human female in the advanced stages of pregnancy.

They would see the abomination of nature about to take place, the hideous ritual that would ultimately result in the birth of Valentine's twin sons: two more evil souls to expand the house of Jaegar.

And the time was approaching fast now, the hour when the evil spawn would break free from their wretched host, shredding her body and killing without mercy.

With intricate detail, Nachari recreated the illusion of the unborn twins, leaving no stone unturned that might alert their father of the trap awaiting him; he even provided two distinct heartbeats...

And so Marquis waited.

Lying ever still within the body of the murdered woman...anticipating his enemy.

And the son of Jaegar did not disappoint.

Valentine Nistor shimmered into view at precisely fifteen minutes before midnight. He appeared, all at once, standing at the foot of the bed, a wicked smile twisting his gloating mouth, his eyes focused narrowly on his prize as he laughed aloud, almost trembling with anticipation.

Marquis could feel the Dark One's heart racing beneath his iron chest, rising and falling with excitement, as he slowly knelt on the bed, as he crawled over to where the sleeping woman lay...seemingly unaware.

Valentine straddled Joelle's legs just below her pregnant stomach, one huge thigh placed languidly on either side of her body. He stroked her belly and purred a welcome: a fatherly invitation to his unborn children. He closed his eyes and listened to the twin heartbeats, and a look of pure ecstasy swept over his face.

Marquis could smell the pungent odor of Valentine's arousal: a bittersweet spice that stung his nostrils and assaulted his senses, yet he lay perfectly still. Motionless. Focused. As Nachari continued to maintain a steady, resting heart rate in his body.

Every muscle the warrior possessed was twitching in anticipation, the desire to kill rising like the turbulent waters of a flood, a torrent of rage that had been held back far too long behind a creaking, bending dam: a straining vengeance just itching to break free.

There were no weapons hidden beneath the pillows, no daggers or sickles tucked beneath the bed. There was nothing concealed along his body to aid in the battle. Marquis intended to kill the Dark One with his bare hands. And no other pleasure would do.

Marquis could feel the bed depressed on both sides of his waist, sunken where Valentine's knees were burrowed into the mattress, and it felt like an eternity lying still beneath the depraved creature. He measured the vampire's body temperature as it rose several degrees in response to his mounting bloodlust. He could smell the foul odor of the undead's breath as he leaned in closer to examine the human female; yet the Dark One detected nothing amiss.

Resting the bulk of his weight on the back of his legs, Valentine finally called out to his prey: "Joelle, awaken." His voice held a mixture of triumph and anticipation in its deep, gravelly tenor.

Slowly...lazily...the sleeping woman complied.

Feral eyes, the color of blood mixed with molten lava, snapped open, the pupils no more than two tiny slits of menace, their focused glare consumed with rage. A slow, hate-filled smile curved along the corners of Marquis's mouth as his own persona began to deliciously shimmer into view, and then his razor-sharp fangs exploded from his mouth and his dagger-like claws extended from his hands.

"Gladly, darling!" Marquis hissed.

The Ancient Master Warrior lunged forward then, utilizing the full force of his massive body. Valentine shrieked and leapt back, trying to scramble from the bed, but his reaction was way too late. The son of Jadon moved far too fast.

Using the element of surprise, Marquis struck swiftly. He

plunged his fist into Valentine's chest, clutched the undead's heart with a full set of unsheathed claws, and tightened his fingers in a powerful, unyielding grip.

His grasp was like that of a mighty vise: seizing and twisting...but not extracting. There would be no swift death for Valentine Nistor: not this night. The vampire would suffer a slow, agonizing death.

Valentine was stuck.

Frozen in place and unable to break free.

With the powerful Master Warrior's fist clenched tightly around his heart, any sudden attempt at movement would lead to the lethal extraction of the imprisoned organ from his body. Valentine's only choice was to fight, to struggle from a weakened, vulnerable position, hoping to wound his attacker before Marquis detached his heart.

Valentine struck back hard with a powerful counter blow, but the strike never reached its target. A howl of rage and terror shook the room as a bloodied stump made contact with the pillow where Marquis's face had just been. The skilled Master Warrior had evaded the blow with preternatural speed, bobbing his head to the side so quickly the motion was virtually undetectable, even as Nachari stood at the side of the bed, crouched down in a warrior's attack stance, still holding the ivory shaft of a steel dagger in his hand.

The wizard had come out of nowhere, unsheathing the ivory stiletto just in time to make a clean cut across the vampire's wrist, slicing Valentine's hand off before the dangerous claws had a chance to reach Marquis...who had long since moved out of the way anyhow.

Valentine's head snapped to the side, and he hissed at Nachari, his dark eyes burning with black hatred. "You want to join this battle, *wizard?*" It was a clear, unveiled threat, obviously meant to intimidate the younger, less experienced vampire.

Nachari laughed. His voice was a low snarl of contempt and menace. "I'm not seeing much of a battle, Dark One. But no thanks, I'll pass. In fact, I think I'll just sit back and watch the show from here."

He gestured toward a nearby chair. And then his hands began to move in a series of lightning quick movements as he withdrew a shiny, curved sickle from the inside of his coat, spun it around in several smooth circles—like a ninja flipping a pair of nunchucks—and deftly sliced at Valentine's other arm, amputating it right below the bicep with deadly precision.

"Just as soon as I collect this trophy for *my twin!*" He spat the words.

Valentine shrieked in pain and snapped his head back around to look at his foremost enemy: Marquis. And then he released his only remaining weapon—his fangs.

The ancient Dark One was clearly determined to fight to the death with all he possessed. He lunged at Marquis's neck, exerting enormous pressure against the fist still tightened around his heart in order to keep it from dislodging, but once again, Nachari struck from behind.

Using the tip of the sickle in a movement so slight it required no more than a subtle flick of the wrist, he hooked the Dark One's carotid, taking advantage of Valentine's own forward momentum to sever the vital artery.

"I'm sorry," Nachari whispered, "I seem to be completely lacking in impulse control tonight. *Wizards!* We just don't have the discipline of you...warriors."

Marquis caught Valentine's throat in his hand before the creature's fangs could connect with his neck and watched as the Dark One's blood began to shoot out in a pressurized stream as if someone had just unscrewed a fire hydrant. And then he snarled a deep, throaty growl, warning his brother to back off of his prey.

"Nachari, stand down!"

It was an order.

He had allowed his youngest sibling a few acts of retribution, understanding his need to avenge his twin, but the vampire belonged to him. This was his kill. And damn it all to hell, if his little brother didn't stop soon, there wasn't going to be anything left for Marquis to do.

Valentine gurgled and choked on his own blood, a stunned look of disbelief carved on his face. Marquis knew the evil one was trying to call out to his own brothers telepathically, but it was far too late for that.

Nachari Silivasi had graduated the Romanian University as a Master in Wizardry. He now had dominion over the base elements, and he could manipulate the energies of light, sound, and vibration. Nachari had altered the energy field in the room long before Valentine had shown up, creating a static rift in the forces around them, an energetic barrier that made it virtually impossible for thought waves to transmit in or out of the carefully controlled space.

No one would recognize what was taking place in room 423 of the Dark Moon Lodge: not Salvatore or Zarek Nistor…not even Nathaniel or Kagen Silivasi.

"Sorry," Marquis hissed. "Your backup isn't coming."

Valentine howled like an injured animal. He roared his fury like an enraged grizzly bear, his powerful legs beginning to tremble beneath him.

Marquis sat up then, careful to keep his fist tightly clamped around the Dark One's heart, reveling at the sight of Valentine's blood gushing out of him like a leaking sieve, the anguished look of pain stamped deep into his arrogant face.

With a clenched fist, he swung his free hand at the vampire's jaw, connecting dead center with the front of his teeth.

Ivory fangs cracked and erupted, exploding like shattered glass as they shot out of his mouth, leaving the staggered vampire utterly defenseless.

Marquis held up his own bloodied, lacerated hand and turned it over, staring at the jagged teeth marks in his skin. He slowly unclenched his fist in front of Valentine's face, displaying his wicked set of talons…one finger at a time. Extending the claw of his index finger, he engraved a bloody outline around the vampire's eyes—then around his mouth, his nose, and his ears—before slowly etching a harsh line down his chest, across his flat, muscular stomach to his lower pelvis…where he stopped.

He looked his enemy in the eyes. "Pick your poison, Dark One. In what order do you prefer to be dismembered? Eyes first? Ears? Tongue? Or that vile tool you seem so eager to rape helpless humans with?"

Valentine snarled. "Release my heart, son of Jadon, and fight me like a man!"

The words came out gargled and muted, his missing teeth prohibiting his ability to properly form his words.

Despite his sweltering rage, Marquis laughed. "You sound like an imbecile." He turned to Nachari. "I don't know, brother, should I *releath hith heart, tho he can fight me like a man?*"

Nachari shrugged casually. "You might as well; what's he gonna do at this point? *Kick you?* He seems to be running out of options."

Marquis regarded the bleeding, dying monster lodged at the other end of his fist. "Hmm. Perhaps you should remove one of his legs first, at least make the kicking entertaining."

Nachari leapt up from his chair and flew instantly to the side of the bed, his ivory dagger already unsheathed and fisted in his hand.

Marquis hissed. "Sit down, brother. I was kidding."

Nachari frowned and let out a deep-throated grumble. He sauntered back across the room and took a seat by the window next to a stone-top table with a better view of the two warriors. He snapped the dagger back into its holster, leaned back, and crossed his arms, waiting to see what Marquis was going to do next.

Marquis snarled with disdain, took one quick swipe with his claws, and removed the vampire's manhood right through his jeans. "Problem is…" He glared at Valentine. "You're not a man anymore."

Valentine roared in pain and tried to wrench his body backward in a clear attempt to dislodge his own heart into the warrior's fist, to end his own suffering and humiliation. Suicide was clearly preferred to the ongoing torture, but Nachari sprang forward again with preternatural speed and effortlessly held the enemy in place. There would be no escaping justice this night.

Marquis slowly—and vindictively—removed the Dark One's eyes, one at a time. He shaved off his ears and carved out his tongue. He sliced a hundred shallow flesh wounds into his body, ripping off entire sections of skin as he went along.

He scalped the long, thick mane of crimson and black hair from his head and tossed it across the room. He dug random holes into the evil one's skull in a crude, makeshift lobotomy, and then he cut out a long string of intestines and carelessly wrapped them around the vampire's throat.

And still he was not satisfied.

Marquis checked his Rolex. "Four more hours until sunrise." His frustration was evident in his voice.

He gently withdrew his fist from the undead's heart, careful to keep him alive, and then he leapt up from the bed and placed a chair directly in front of an eastern-facing window.

Nachari helped him lug the heavy, unrecognizable heap of what used to be Valentine's body from the bed and place it, along with all of its missing parts, in the chair. Marquis opened the heavy curtains and made his way back to the foot of the bed, where he sat facing the flat-screen plasma television on the adjacent wall.

"Did Nathaniel ever get the cable fixed in this place?" he asked Nachari.

Nachari nodded. "I believe so. I think he hired a new head of maintenance at the beginning of summer."

Marquis sighed. "Good, because we've got a lot of time to kill." He glanced over at the chair. "Do you think you can keep that thing alive until the sun comes up? I'd hate for him to miss the encore."

Nachari nodded. "I'll certainly give it a Viking effort. If not, we can always call Kagen."

Marquis frowned. "Pity he can't hear what we're doing…or even see it coming." He sighed. "Oh well, it should hurt like a bitch anyway."

Despite the resolution…the inevitability…the relief of finally exacting vengeance, there was no satisfaction.

Marquis had lived forever.

He had fought in countless wars, defeated numerous enemies. He was a warrior without equal, save, perhaps, Napolean Mondragon. So there was no sense of pleasure from the kill.

Valentine Nistor was a lesser opponent, and his death would not bring back the ones he loved.

Marquis ripped the bloodstained comforter and sheets from the bed and tossed them in front of the window. He would allow the sun to provide maid service when it came out in the morning, to incinerate the remains and cleanse the room.

He leaned back on the bed, arms folded behind his head, legs crossed in front of him. "Find us something to watch."

Dark eyes turned ice cold and his heart felt like stone, his soul nothing more than a cauldron of black pain and emptiness.

Noiselessly, Nachari sauntered across the room to retrieve the remote control.

twenty-eight

"Jocelyn, I would have you conceive now."

Nathaniel spoke those magical, implausible words on Monday night shortly after her conversion. Shortly after their phenomenal lovemaking. And just like that, her body began to change in answer to his call.

At first, she reported a warm, tingling sensation deep within her womb, a peaceful settling in her soul as the miracle of life began.

But then the changes began to occur quite rapidly.

Her emotions were raw and unpredictable as she vacillated between crying, laughing, and becoming downright agitated with Nathaniel for everything from a lopsided lump in her pillow that he couldn't seem to smooth out, to the annoying way the mattress depressed every time the husky vampire moved his restless body, and the constant drum of the wind against the outside shutters of the bathroom window.

Apparently, he was no longer her supernatural warrior because he did not possess the powers to indiscriminately shut down her senses without putting her to sleep.

She experienced several terrible bouts of nausea that left her kneeling on the bathroom floor, hovering over a black porcelain bowl for at least an hour, only to get up, brush her teeth, enthusiastically return to bed, and immediately send Nathaniel to the kitchen with an odd, inexhaustible list of food she was craving.

For the third time.

Exasperated, Nathaniel had finally called in Alejandra and asked her to make a quick trip to the all-night convenience store. He had apologized repeatedly for the inadequacy, but in all honesty, he just didn't keep corn nuts, tapioca pudding, and spicy V-8 juice in the house.

BLOOD DESTINY

In fact, even if he had, the truth of the matter was that most vampires didn't eat food. They kept it around to appear normal to humans, and they might indulge every now and then if they really enjoyed it—as many human *destinies* chose to do, at least right after their conversions—but over time, the unusual craving usually went away.

By Tuesday night, Jocelyn reported feeling distinct movement in her abdomen. The babies were kicking and straining in her womb as they vied for space in the crowded belly. She insisted that the kicking wasn't nearly as uncomfortable as the incessant pressure against her bladder or the constant itchy sensation she felt as her skin stretched impossibly to accommodate the rapidly growing twins.

Although Nathaniel repeatedly applied moisturizer to the tender flesh, he began to strongly encourage her to allow him to take all physical sensation away; up until then, she had insisted on experiencing as much of the fast-moving pregnancy as possible, short of anything that might cause extreme discomfort or pain.

But by the time she began to experience leg cramps—and let out a string of unexpected curse words in response to being asked whether or not she would like another glass of juice—Nathaniel had decided to take over the pregnancy.

He felt as worn out as she looked.

It was around nine o'clock Wednesday evening, and they only had a few more hours to go before the babies would be born.

"You will sleep now, *iubita mea*." His voice was soft and...exasperated.

"I will not!" she snapped in response, her voice not quite as accommodating.

Nathaniel sighed. "Then what can I do for you, my love?"

Jocelyn looked around the room and shifted uncomfortably on the bed, failing to move the big mass that was now her body more than a centimeter in any direction despite the valiant effort.

Her eyes teared up. "For starters, I guess you could move my legs in a more comfortable position…since I don't seem capable of shifting my own weight anymore!" The tears began to fall. "I look like a beached whale, Nathaniel. Look what you've done to me! How could you?"

Nathaniel smiled, his eyes reflecting only warmth and patience, although deep inside, he was beginning to count the minutes.

He gently moved her legs until she found a comfortable position, and then he leaned over to wipe her falling tears. "Do not cry, angel. It is almost over."

Jocelyn sniffled and looked up at the ceiling. All at once, her eyes became bright with enthusiasm. "More history!" she exclaimed.

Nathaniel visibly wilted. He leaned over the bed and buried his face in his hands. "My darling, I am going to lose my voice. There is no more history. That is all I have lived."

Jocelyn laughed, her hazel eyes becoming a bright, swirling mist. "That is not true, Nathaniel!" She crossed her arms over her enormous belly and cleared her throat. "Let's see; we have already established that you were born at the time of the Holy Roman Emperors, when the Byzantine culture penetrated into the Balkans and Russia…

"You lived to see the Vikings come to America, and you have firsthand knowledge of the crusades, the Aztec and Incan empires. You could tell me more about the plague in Europe. Or how about the Renaissance? Better yet, skip all that; I want to know about the French Revolution…and then the war of 1812."

Nathaniel rubbed his temples and drew in a deep, calming breath. Jocelyn Levi—*Silivasi*—was a total history enthusiast: a complete, utter, and unequivocal book nerd, for lack of a better word. And not your average history buff, either. She was obsessed and fanatical, positively enthralled by anything she considered *living history*. Hearing it. Reliving it. Analyzing it. And hashing it over…and over.

And over.

Finding Nathaniel, a male who had lived over one thousand

years, had been like stumbling over a gold mine for the irresistible human. And the moment she learned he had spent much of his life traveling back and forth between Europe, the Middle East, North and South America, she was determined to relive his entire exhaustive lifespan on earth…

To wring out every last ounce of personal experience and history there was from the immortal being, whether he liked it or not.

Jocelyn was relentless in her quest for firsthand knowledge of people, places, and events, and Nathaniel was a sucker for those beautiful, enchanting eyes and soft, pouty lips. Not to mention the enormously cute belly that continued to expand like a helium-filled balloon right before his eyes.

He had filled up no less than twenty hours of her pregnancy answering questions about kings and emperors, societies and wars, world-changing events. And he was utterly exhausted.

Not to mention, he was beginning to feel…ancient…like some really old geezer who had married a spring chicken he could never hope to keep up with.

Nathaniel Silivasi—an Ancient Master Warrior, a son of Jadon, descendant of the original Celestial Beings—had at last met his match: the one living soul who had finally gotten the best of him.

Jocelyn was becoming quite adept at reading his thoughts, rapidly learning how to tune in and out of the precise frequencies required for smooth, telepathic communication, and she frowned, looking pitiful and disappointed.

"That's okay," she sighed. She started to twiddle her thumbs and turned to look at the clock on the nightstand. "How much more time do we have?"

Nathaniel brushed his hand against her forehead and slowly shook his head. So this was how it was going to be…

He had mated a woman who had somehow wrapped him around her little finger in the space of only a week, and all it took was the slightest hint of disappointment in her voice to get him to jump through hoops to please her.

He rubbed his chin, slightly annoyed with his own lack of resolve. Hell, he was an Ancient Master Warrior, an immortal vampire! "What about the French Revolution would you like to hear, my angel?"

Jocelyn's face lit up. Her brilliant eyes beamed with excitement, and it was worth every ounce of energy he had, all the history in the world, to see that adoring glow coming from those breathtaking eyes in response to something he had said or done.

She smiled and took his hand. "That's okay. I can see that you're exhausted. It's enough to know that you were willing to go there for me...again."

Nathaniel caressed her hand. "Thank you, my love." His relief was palpable. "And of course, I would go anywhere for you. Although, you might want to keep in mind that we have all of *eternity* together. Perhaps you might want to pace yourself." His laughter was rich and full of a peaceful contentment he had never really known existed before.

All at once, Jocelyn's eyes became serious. "There is something I would like to know more about, though, and from what little I can see into your mind, I don't think it's a subject you talk much about."

Nathaniel brought her hand up to his lips and gently kissed the center of her palm. "What's that? There will be no secrets between us."

Jocelyn smirked. "Yeah, ya think? I mean, considering the whole mind-reading thing and all." Her smile was positively elegant, as radiant as her rare, exquisite beauty.

"I want you to tell me about your parents, Nathaniel. Keitaro and Serena, right? What happened to them? If you are immortal beings—"

"*We* are immortal beings," he said.

"If *we* are immortal beings," she repeated, "then that means we can live forever, yet they were not here for...Shelby's burial...and they're not here now. What happened to them, Nathaniel? Where are your parents?" Her voice was a soft, respectful whisper.

Nathaniel put his head in his hand and rubbed his temples, trying to figure out a way to relay the memory without actually connecting to it: without having to feel it.

His parents' death was something he had locked away in that one hallowed place in his heart that held the wounds that would never heal. And opening it, even temporarily, was dangerous.

"Many, many years ago…" He cleared his throat. "When Shelby and Nachari were still children by our standards…they had just turned twenty-one and were about to graduate from the local academy here in Dark Moon Vale, about to undergo their induction ceremony into the house of Jadon—"

"The local academy?" Jocelyn asked, her natural curiosity getting the best of her. "What's an induction ceremony?"

Nathaniel had already become accustomed to Jocelyn's frequent interruptions, and he simply flowed right through the conversation, picking them up as he went. "Yes, the local academy. When a male descendant of Jadon turns five years old, he is sent to the local school here in Dark Moon Vale, as will be the case with our son. It is there that he is taught the *human studies*—math, language arts, science, world history, the culture and concepts of the society around him. When he turns twenty-one, he graduates from the academy. He is considered a *fledgling vampire* then, no longer a child but not yet a master, and he begins to integrate into our society, where he learns our laws and our ways.

"He is taught as an apprentice, learning how to run our various businesses, the details and skill sets that make our society prosperous and independent.

"At the time of his graduation from the academy, he is brought before Napolean to be formally inducted into the *house of Jadon*. It is an ancient and powerful ceremony where he offers his blood as a sacrifice to the people; where he pledges his loyalty, protection, and service for all eternity to our Sovereign, to our continued existence as a species—"

"Somehow, that sounds painful," Jocelyn remarked, her

hand going protectively to her stomach.

Nathaniel smiled. "It is, but it is also an incredible honor and a time of great spiritual awakening for a male vampire." He paused, trying to find the right words. "Napolean Mondragon, our Sovereign, is the only living pure-blood descendant of Jadon; his incarnation dates back to the original Blood Curse. His mother, Katalina, was not a *human destiny*; she was one of the original Celestial Beings. So there is no mixed blood in his veins."

Jocelyn looked momentarily confused. "What kind of blood will be in our child's veins? I *am* like you now, aren't I?"

Nathaniel nodded. "Yes, but you weren't born Vampyr; you were *sired*. Napolean is one of the original Celestial Beings, one of the ancient males who served King Sakarias, who was turned Nosferatu by the Curse."

Jocelyn's eyes grew wide. "Wow. How old is he?"

Nathaniel laughed. "Napolean is ancient."

Jocelyn shook her head. "I'm sorry. I always interrupt. Go on. You were telling me—"

Nathaniel smiled and bent to brush a soft kiss against her mouth. He loved the way she became so engrossed in what she was hearing, the sincere interest she took in learning all she could about her new life. "You are such a miracle to me," he whispered.

Leaning back, he continued. "The male will remain in our society as a fledgling until his one hundredth birthday. It is at that time that he is sent to the sacred homeland of our forefathers, the Romanian University in Europe, where he will study for the next four hundred years in order to master one of the Four Disciplines.

"So as I said, Shelby and Nachari were only twenty-one, about to undergo their induction ceremonies, when the valley was attacked by a large group of vampire hunters, humans and lycans alike, who had joined forces in an effort to extinguish our kind—"

"Why in the world would humans want to kill vampires—yet

accept the lycans?" Jocelyn shook her head.

Nathaniel rubbed his jaw. "Good question. Humankind has an interesting history when it comes to hating anything they fear at the moment, do they not? I think you summed it up well the night of the storm: *The enemy of my enemy is my friend.* The problem is, humans are always changing who and what they fear at any given time period. I have lived to see Christians killing Catholics, only to later join together to oppress the Jews. I remember not so long ago, here in North America, when the Europeans feared the Native Americans and slaughtered them as savages, only to later form alliances with some of the southeastern tribes in order to enslave the Africans. Fear is an irrational council."

Jocelyn frowned. "I bet you have seen a lot of things that don't make it into the history books." She sighed. "So the humans and the lycans attacked the valley together. What happened after that?"

Nathaniel tried to shut down his heart, to simply close his mind to the memory. He spoke the words in a rote voice…like a robot. "My mother was murdered by the Alpha male of the lycans, and my father went mad with grief."

Nathaniel turned away in an effort to steady himself. He was disappointed: He should have been better at this by now. He blinked several times, trying to stay his tears; he would not cry over this loss…again. He had already shed enough tears over the centuries to flood the entire valley.

"We believe Keitaro was either murdered as well or he killed himself…that he followed my mother into the Valley of Spirit and Light. But we never found his body. He simply disappeared one night shortly after her burial and was never seen again."

Jocelyn gasped, her hands coming up to cover her mouth. "I'm so sorry, Nathaniel." The statement was a mere whisper.

Nathaniel cleared his throat. "If my father had lived, we know he would've come back to us after all of this time. So we eventually assumed his death, but we were never able to bury him…to say good-bye."

He took a long, deep breath, knowing his pain was showing

despite his effort to keep it at bay. "I was especially close to my mother, so her death weighed heavily on my conscience as a warrior, one who could not protect her. But Marquis and my father were best friends. I think my father always made an extra effort to connect with him because he was the only one of us boys who did not have a twin. His disappearance almost destroyed my brother."

Jocelyn shook her head. "Well, no wonder he is so…intense…about protecting you guys." She sighed. "Wow, I can't even blame him now for wanting to turn me into a human puppet."

Nathaniel frowned. "Excuse me?"

Jocelyn waved her hand in dismissal. "Nothing."

There was a long moment of silence before either of them spoke.

Finally, Jocelyn reached out, took Nathaniel's hand, and placed it beneath her own, over her belly. "Soon, Keitaro's first grandson will be here."

Nathaniel smiled. "Yes…" He blinked several times. "Have you thought of any names?"

"Actually I have." Jocelyn blushed and drew in a deep breath. "You know, it was the night of that awful storm when I first realized…" She looked off into the distance, a dreamy, contented peace in her eyes.

"Realized what, my love?"

"That I was only running from myself…more afraid of me than you. That I had made a terrible mistake. And that I wanted you to find me. *That I wanted to be with you.*"

Nathaniel felt humbled by her words. "And?"

"And I kind of thought it might be…appropriate…to name our son *Storm.*"

Nathaniel leaned back and tried the name on for size. "Storm Silivasi…I like it."

"Do you?" Her bright eyes lit up with expectation.

"I do."

"Only now," she said, "I think it might also be respectful to include your father's name…if you don't mind…if that kind of thing is done with vampires."

Nathaniel softened. "Keitaro Storm Silivasi?"

Jocelyn nodded. "Yes, but we would call him *Storm*."

Nathaniel splayed his fingers across her belly and bent to kiss the heavy, swelling mound, his eyes misting over. "Hello, Storm." His voice was soft with reverence and gratitude. He looked up at the clock on the nightstand. "Jocelyn, it is time."

Jocelyn's face went flush and she all at once became serious, the merest hint of fear in her eyes. "Should we call Colette?"

They both knew the woman had been at their home for the last twenty-four hours pacing frantically, cleaning the kitchen until the smell of Pine-Sol reeked even on the third floor, and placing beautiful yellow and blue outfits into neat, tidy piles on the antique changing table she had brought for the nursery: a nursery she had anxiously arranged…and rearranged…a dozen times, trying to avail herself of any need the new couple might have and seeming only too happy to do it.

Nathaniel nodded and then he took her hands in his. "Are you ready for what must be done?"

Jocelyn nodded. "I think so. I hope so."

Nathaniel sent a mental call out to Colette, who didn't bother walking the length of the long third-floor hall to get to the master bedroom; she simply materialized beside the bed, her brilliant light-blue eyes wide with expectation.

"Is it time?" she asked, her soft voice almost overflowing with joy.

Nathaniel nodded. "Jocelyn?"

"I'm ready," she said, pulling herself up into a semi-seated position.

Nathaniel closed his eyes, bowed his head, and spoke an eloquent prayer in the old language. Although Jocelyn didn't understand the words, she found them beautiful and hypnotic, mystically rhythmic. And then he gently commanded his sons to come forth from the beautiful human woman who had so capably cared for and created them up to that point.

The bedroom filled with tiny prisms of light, like miniature rainbows swirling through the air in a glistening arc above the bed. An odd sound filled the room, like that of water rushing in a fast-flowing river, and a dazzling halo of luminosity, like iridescent gold dust, began to sparkle all around Jocelyn's stomach…until it finally formed a peak just above the apex of her belly.

The gold dust came together in gradual waves of light, moving faster and faster, even as the rushing sound grew louder and louder, until the outline of a child began to appear.

The first infant materialized slowly, a beautiful angel with blue-black hair and mystical, hazel eyes. He appeared to be just over seven pounds, and he was positively *perfect,* from the flawless color of his honey-gold skin to the faultless shape of his head.

He had strong, healthy arms and legs that flailed about as he shrieked his first full-throated cry, filling the room with the sound of life.

Filling Jocelyn's heart with wonder and awe.

Jocelyn caught her breath, utterly astonished, and her eyes misted over as she reached out to hold the newborn child: her newborn son.

Nathaniel looked positively amazed; the child was a miracle…beautiful. He caught the child in his arms and cradled him gently, turning to hand him to Colette.

Before Jocelyn could protest, he said, "You will hold him soon enough, my love."

Jocelyn knew he was reminding her of…the Dark One. That there was still another child to be born. She took a deep breath and tried to steady herself for what was to come.

When the second child emerged with a full head of crimson and black hair, the thick, wavy tresses bonded in interlocking curls of midnight tinged with wine, she was astonished to see that the curse was actually real.

She had known it, but it was still amazing to witness it.

As Nathaniel reached for the baby, his countenance changed. He held him in a much cooler grasp, not once bothering to look in his eyes, but Jocelyn couldn't help herself—

And she was stunned by what she saw.

The second child had the same vividly beautiful hazel eyes as the first. Jocelyn caught her breath: His skin was perfect. His little hands and feet were...flawless. He was irrefutably magnificent. Absolutely gorgeous.

And the child didn't cry.

He cooed and wiggled about in Nathaniel's arms like any other precious infant.

A series of knots tied in Jocelyn's stomach. This child was not evil. He was not an abomination. And the moment she allowed herself to think the thoughts, the soft little leopard-eyes turned in her direction and locked with hers. They were beaming with...light. Not darkness.

Jocelyn shot up instinctively. Moving with the protectiveness of a mother bear, she wedged her body between Nathaniel and the helpless infant as she snatched him from the vampire's arms and cradled him close to her heart.

Both Nathaniel and Colette inhaled sharply, their eyes wide with shock.

"Jocelyn," Nathaniel called gently, "give me the baby, sweetheart."

Jocelyn covered the child like a running back with a football, her own eyes flashing with such intense sparks of heat she wondered if they might be glowing red.

"Nathaniel, look at him!"

Nathaniel refused, keeping his eyes steadily on hers.

Jocelyn felt a fierce protectiveness swell in her heart. "He has my eyes," she insisted. "He's perfect: something is wrong." She turned to stare at Colette. "He's not at all like Valentine or the Dark Ones...*he's perfect.*"

She glared at Nathaniel then. "Look at him!"

Nathaniel stood in stunned silence, defiantly refusing to look at the child. Instead he stared deep into Jocelyn's eyes with a look that could only be described as a mixture of displeasure, astonishment, and pity. "No, my love, he is—"

"Our son!" she cried. "Look at his eyes. He has *my* eyes!"

Nathaniel shook his head more vigorously this time, and Jocelyn watched as he and Colette exchanged a knowing glance between them.

She could feel the subtle disturbance of energy in the air and knew they were talking to each other telepathically, choosing to use a private bandwidth she was not linked onto.

Jocelyn felt utterly and completely betrayed. She felt cornered and desperate. "Stop talking to each other in private!" she demanded, all at once jumping several feet from the bed in one smooth leap.

She approached the small bassinette Colette had placed in the room for Storm and reached down to grab one of the soft blue blankets folded neatly in the cradle. She wrapped the cooing infant gently in the supple cloth, her back deliberately turned to both of them, and her eyes filled with tears.

"You can't have my son, Nathaniel." She knew she didn't sound rational, but she didn't care. This was a helpless baby. Her baby. And they were going to kill it.

Kill it.

Nathaniel moved with preternatural speed, spinning around to face Jocelyn and the infant, hovering over the bassinette, his large hands going gently but insistently around the child's body.

Both mother and father were locked in the same dreadful moment, two sets of hands beneath the same child.

From someplace deep inside, someplace she didn't even know existed, Jocelyn felt a deep, rumbling sound vibrate within her throat. The harsh growl of warning that escaped her lips was almost as shocking to her as it was to Nathaniel.

Nathaniel stepped back, let go of the child, and squared his shoulders.

Closing her eyes, Jocelyn began to tune into her newfound inner strength, testing her new state of being, awakening the awesome power she now had as a vampire. She was prepared to fight for the child if she had to, and every muscle in her body began to twitch in response to her intention.

Nathaniel immediately grasped her by the shoulders and bared his fangs, like a male lion warning a lioness. "Do not think to challenge me, Jocelyn." He hissed the words. "You may be far more powerful than you were before, but your strength is no match for my own. *And it never will be.*"

His voice was harsh.

Absolute.

Merciless.

"Parents are supposed to *die* for their children," she snarled angrily. "But you...you would *kill* an innocent child so that you could live?" She held the child tight to her breast, and the baby began to cry. "Fine," she uttered, her voice cracking. "Then let me go in his place. Let me trade my life for his."

Colette looked like she had seen a ghost. Her skin turned ghastly white, and Nathaniel stepped back as if he'd been physically struck.

"Jocelyn, my love..." He lowered his voice. "That child is evil." His tone was dark and deliberately mesmerizing, his stare, cold and authoritarian. "He has no soul, and he would kill you the first moment he was able."

He took control of her physical body then, all at once paralyzing her arms, leaving her standing there like a granite statue of Madonna and child as he stepped forward and reached for the infant...

But it was another set of powerful arms that grasped the child.

A tall tower of a man. An intimidating male with flowing black- and silver-banded hair the length of his waist and eyes the color of onyx, with powerful silver slashes in the centers for irises.

The male's voice was like the night sky, sultry and dark,

endless in its depth and power. "You shall relinquish this child at once."

The words were an irrefutable command as he released her from Nathaniel's hold.

Jocelyn felt her body relax. And then she watched herself, as if from a distance, casually handing the baby over into the mighty one's arms. She knew without being told that she was standing before the Sovereign Lord of Nathaniel's people: Napolean Mondragon.

Napolean turned to face Nathaniel. "This night, I will make the blood sacrifice on your behalf. Go to your *destiny* and see to her comfort. I will return later to initiate this daughter of Cassiopeia into the house of Jadon, and to seal the covenant of your child's birth…so that his name and constellation will be known for all time by the Ancients who have come before him…and by all who will come after him."

Jocelyn felt the tears streaming down her face, burning her skin as they fell. Her confusion and helplessness were overwhelming.

Nathaniel nodded in agreement and bowed his head before the towering Ancient whose presence filled the room like a beacon of light and power.

"As you wish, milord."

Colette stood deathly quiet; her head was bowed, her eyes averted to the ground…as if it were some sort of taboo to look upon the Sovereign One's face.

Jocelyn blinked as if she had been in a trance. And then she glared at Nathaniel as Napolean shimmered out of view, taking her beautiful baby boy with him. She covered her face in her hands and cried out, an ear-piercing sob of anguish, too ashamed to look Nathaniel in the eyes.

Nathaniel turned to Colette. "Colette, take Storm out of here…*now*. I will call you in a moment to bring him back."

Colette shimmered out of view with the beautiful firstborn infant, the son of Jadon, cradled closely to her heart, and Nathaniel immediately went to Jocelyn's side.

Jocelyn stepped back, afraid of his anger, dreading the harsh reprimand she knew was coming, but to her utter shock and dismay, Nathaniel bent his head, his glorious dark hair falling forward to cover his face...

And he wept.

Jocelyn stood frozen for a retracted moment, watching the powerful being before her reduced to tears. "Nathaniel," she finally whispered, "I'm sorry."

He gathered her in his arms and held her so tight she thought she might break. "Jocelyn, I would *never* take your child from you. I know he appeared perfect, but do you not remember seeing Valentine? Was he not handsome? Powerful? Physically perfect? Do you not remember how evil he was? How totally depraved and without conscience he was? Don't you know by now that I would die for you, my love? That I would die for our child? That I would trade my life if I could spare you such sorrow?"

His powerful chest was heaving with the weight of his sobs, and she felt disgraceful.

Seeing Nathaniel's pain was worse than any reprimand could have ever been.

Jocelyn's mind began to clear now that the child was no longer in the room. "I think, maybe, the baby did something to me...to my mind." She wrapped her arms around Nathaniel's neck and held him close. "I love you, Nathaniel. Do you hear me? I love you. And I am so, so sorry."

Nathaniel crushed her to him then, kissing her temples, her cheeks, her jaw, her lips. He took her mouth with such absolute abandon it was frightening. The male was hungry...starving...for something much, much deeper than sexual gratification.

The moment seemed to last forever: the two of them locked

in each other's arms, enveloped in each other's love, offering mutual understanding and comfort.

When he finally released her, Nathaniel stepped back and gripped her by her delicate shoulders. "Your true son awaits you, my love. He needs you as much as I do."

Jocelyn brushed a lock of thick black hair away from Nathaniel's face. "As much as I need both of you."

Her eyes met his and she stared at him, just taking him in: loving him more in that moment than she had ever loved anyone...or anything...in all of her life. Nathaniel Silivasi. Her husband. Her vampire.

She smiled up at him, praying he could feel how deeply sorry she was. She didn't understand what had come over her, but she had never meant to strike out at him like that.

She would never wish to hurt him.

They held onto each other again...for what seemed an eternity...and then Nathaniel called Colette back in.

When the pleasant woman shimmered into view with the baby still cradled lovingly in her arms, Jocelyn immediately went to the two of them. "I am sorry, Colette," she whispered, reaching out to take her son into her arms for the first time.

The child looked up at her, and her heart melted with the love and peace that was *her* destiny.

This was her amazing fortune.

Her future.

Jocelyn kissed the baby's forehead and smiled. His impossibly small fingers curled around hers and she laughed with joy.

"Hello, my little angel," she whispered.

Nathaniel gathered them both into his arms, leaned in to kiss his son, and frowned. "I think you mean hello, *my strong warrior*," he corrected.

Jocelyn laughed. "Hello, *my little warrior*."

It was a good compromise.

twenty-nine

Marquis, Nachari, Kagen, and even young Braden gathered around the informal living room on the second floor of Nathaniel and Jocelyn's home waiting to get their first look at Storm.

Napolean Mondragon stood unobtrusively on the far side of the room, next to the large stone fireplace, his silver-black eyes glowing with warmth and pride.

When Nathaniel and Jocelyn entered the room, the brothers all stood to attention, anxiously straining their necks to get a peek at the bundled infant held protectively in his father's arms.

"It's about time," Marquis grumbled, making his way to Nathaniel's side.

Jocelyn intercepted the powerful warrior, placing her body between his and the baby's. "Be gentle, Marquis."

Marquis hissed, rolled his eyes, and pushed her away using a somewhat restrained elbow. "Get out of the way," he grumbled. "Can't you see that this boy has been waiting to meet a real warrior?"

Nathaniel growled a deep, instinctual warning, the territorial instinct of a male animal protecting his young.

Marquis's answering snarl left no room for argument as to who the Alpha male of the family really was...father or no.

"Good Lord," Jocelyn sighed, "there is way too much testosterone in this room."

"Oh, just hand me my nephew," Marquis demanded, scooping the child gently into his arms.

Despite his gravelly voice, his face relaxed the moment he held Storm, and a peaceful, loving smile lined the hard edges of his mouth. "He's so small."

The powerful Ancient Master Warrior sounded amazed. He studied the baby like a scientist with a specimen—as if he were

333

looking for imperfections—committing every line, marking, and characteristic to memory. "Not bad," he snorted, his eyes beaming with pride.

Nachari and Kagen glided over noiselessly, each one taking a position at one of Marquis's sides, inadvertently crowding both Nathaniel and Jocelyn out.

"He has hazel eyes," Nachari remarked in astonishment. He looked over at Jocelyn with approval.

"Yeah, well," Marquis grumbled, "we can toughen him up, make up for that one little...feminine mishap."

Nachari feigned insult. "My eyes are green as well, Marquis."

Marquis shrugged. "Yeah...and you became a wizard."

Kagen chuckled. "He has his father's mouth." He lightly stroked the baby's cheek. When the infant startled in Marquis's arms, Kagen jumped back. "Did I hurt him?"

Jocelyn laughed. "No, Kagen, not at all."

The three large vampires huddled over the baby like a small clan of cavemen warming themselves at a fire, gently touching, prodding, and talking to the child in the old language.

Jocelyn wished she could understand their words, but what was unmistakable, what she could not miss, was the love and warmth in their eyes, the singsong cadence in their voices, and the powerful protectiveness in their postures.

And then Napolean Mondragon stirred.

It was as if all the air in the room shifted into a sudden vacuum, parting like the red sea, making a path for the ancient Lord to approach the child.

Jocelyn shuddered and Nathaniel placed a reassuring hand at the small of her waist.

What is he going to do? she asked, enjoying their newfound telepathic communication.

He is going to accept his name, so it can be recorded in the tome of our people, and then he is going to formally receive Storm's blood, as well as your own, into the house of Jadon.

Our blood? Jocelyn began to feel a little woozy. She tried to hide the fear in her psychic voice but knew that she failed.

Tessa Dawn

Just a little, Nathaniel reassured. *It will only hurt a little. Napolean carries the blood of every member of the house of Jadon in his veins, all those who have come before, and all those who are yet to come. As our Sovereign, he has access to all of the memories, knowledge, and history of each and every soul. He can find anyone living at will, and it is said that if it becomes necessary to protect the people, he can even reach out to those who have moved on to the Valley of Spirit and Light. Once Napolean has your blood, you will always be a member of the house of Jadon.*

Kagen and Nachari stepped back to make room for their Sovereign, who stood directly in front of Marquis and Storm, and Nathaniel ushered Jocelyn forward, positioning her at Marquis's left side even as he stood at his right.

Is Marquis going to hold Storm? she asked.

He is, Nathaniel answered.

Why is that?

Nathaniel smiled at *his destiny*…his mate. *Marquis is the oldest living male of our bloodline, which makes him the head of our family.*

Jocelyn sighed and had to catch herself before rolling her eyes. *Oh great!*

Napolean wore a pair of well-fitted black pants and a white silk shirt, the mixture of black and white drawing out the stark presence of silver in his eyes and hair. His face was like something one might find in an ancient temple—a sacred statue, carved and smoothed to perfection. He was the absolute personification of beauty.

The subtle lines around his eyes were harsh with their reflection of history and timelessness, yet they were equally warm and gentle with wisdom. Napolean was power and nobility incarnate, and he wore a badge of dignity with an air of aristocracy. His eyes held the equal promise of justice and retribution for all those who sought his counsel.

Jocelyn shivered and looked away from the powerful leader of her husband's people…her people. She hoped she wouldn't have too many more occasions to stand before him.

Napolean turned to Nathaniel. "It is with great joy that I greet you this day, my brother, a fellow descendant of Jadon, an

335

BLOOD DESTINY

Ancient Master Warrior, mate to the daughter of Cassiopeia, father to this newborn son of Aquila, the eagle, who makes his home upon the celestial equator. What name have you chosen for this male?"

Nathaniel's eyes beamed with pride. "Should it please you, milord, and find favor with the Celestial Beings, the son of Aquila is to be named *Keitaro Storm Silivasi.*"

Marquis shifted a bit.

His head snapped up and his eyes met Nathaniel's. There was a faint hint of some emotion Jocelyn couldn't quite place before the powerful warrior regained his composure, blinked, and looked away. He bowed his head.

Napolean reached out to take the baby from Marquis's arms. "The name pleases me, warrior, and there is no objection from the Celestial Beings."

Jocelyn's heart began to race as the Sovereign leader bent his head and his fangs began to elongate. Nathaniel sent her a steady stream of warmth wrapped in a subtle warning, commanding her to stay still.

Napolean pierced the child's wrist, vertically, along the vein, and the baby cried out as the powerful leader drank from his arm. After he sealed the wound with his venom, he held the child out in front of him and looked into his eyes. The baby immediately became quiet.

"Welcome to the house of Jadon, Keitaro Storm Silivasi. May your life be filled with peace, triumph, and purpose. May your path always be blessed."

He gave the child back to Marquis, who kissed him lightly on the forehead. "Welcome to our family, Keitaro Storm Silivasi, and to the house of Jadon. May your life be filled with peace, triumph, and purpose. May your path always be blessed."

Kagen took the child then, as the next eldest male relative, and repeated the welcome. Once Nachari had done the same, the child was handed back to Nathaniel, who pulled Jocelyn to his side, sliding her protectively under his arm.

Napolean addressed them both. "By the laws which govern

the house of Jadon, I accept your union as the divine will of the gods and hereby sanction your mating. Jocelyn Levi Silivasi, do you come now of your own free will to enter the house of Jadon?"

Jocelyn swallowed hard, a lump in her throat, and looked at Nathaniel.

I do, Nathaniel whispered in her mind.

"I do," she said.

Hold out your wrist, Nathaniel instructed.

Jocelyn cringed, and then tried to smile, as she tentatively turned her arm over and extended it to the intimidating nobleman.

Napolean's answering smile could have rivaled the moon and the stars for its brilliance. He took her arm with exquisite gentleness and bent his head, long locks of shimmering silver and black falling all around them. And then he pierced her vein cleanly, his teeth sinking deep, his lips forming a tight seal over her arm. His mouth pulled at her vein with a steady drag, but he remained gentle…and oddly, the presence of his lips against her skin flooded her with peace.

Nathaniel stirred, a slight growl reverberating in his throat. He looked down at the ground then, instantly ashamed of the territorial response to Napolean touching Jocelyn.

Napolean released his hold, removed his fangs, and sealed the wound. When he turned to glance at Nathaniel there was an understanding gleam in his eyes, and he laughed softly. "Congratulations," he said to the couple, and just like that, the short ceremony was over.

The brothers crowded in again, trying to get to Storm, and Jocelyn stepped away, allowing them to have their bonding time. No one saw Napolean leave. He was just gone.

And then another voice interrupted the clamor, the sound of a young male repeatedly clearing his throat.

Jocelyn turned to find Braden Bratianu standing at the outskirts of the circle trying to get a look at the baby. In all the intensity of the ceremony, she hadn't even noticed he was there.

"Braden!" she cried, her voice strong with emotion. "I can't believe you're here. It is so nice to see you." She immediately ran over to the young vampire and grasped him by both shoulders, giving him a warm, unsolicited hug of affection.

Braden hugged her back like he wasn't quite sure whether to fully embrace her or duck and run, especially with the older Master Vampires watching, but his eyes revealed his pleasure. And the child looked completely healed: Not a single sign of his injuries remained.

"Kagen!" Jocelyn exclaimed, pleasantly surprised. "You did such a wonderful job taking care of him. Thank you."

Kagen smiled. "Not at all."

Marquis stepped away from the circle then and regarded Braden, looking him up and down several times. The child raised his chin, squared his shoulders, and blinked his eyes, bravely anticipating whatever was coming.

Braden was dressed a little more appropriately than the last time he had been at the house: no more collar, cape, and makeup. However, he seemed to have adopted a new and improved *vampire warrior* look, sort of like a character out of *The Matrix*, complete with heavy black boots; a long, flowing trench coat; black denim jeans; and a thin black turtleneck, as if he were leaning a little more toward being a soldier than a count.

Jocelyn laughed as she watched Marquis slowly circle the child, studying the intense new outfit. And then to her immense surprise, Marquis leaned over, snatched the boy up by the arms, flung him high into the air, and caught him in a great big bear hug. "Now that's more like it, *son!*"

The Master Warrior's voice was strong and proud, and Braden's eyes positively lit up behind the unexpected praise and public show of affection.

Braden laughed with excitement. "I'm gonna be a warrior like you when I go to The University." His eyes were wide, bright, and full of hope.

Marquis set the child down and ruffled his hair. "Excellent choice." He turned to look in the direction of Kagen and

Nachari. "No more sissy healers and wizards in this clan."

Nachari chuckled. "If I recall, I wasn't too sissy to help you orchestrate a *particularly important battle* the other day."

Nathaniel gave Marquis a knowing glance of approval as if the warriors knew something they hadn't shared with Jocelyn.

Kagen chimed in: "And I believe it was my sissy handiwork that patched that kid back together."

Marquis growled. "Whatever." He grabbed Braden by the arm. "Come on, son. I need to catch some fresh air. Care to join me?"

Braden followed the huge vampire out to the patio like a baby duckling following its mother, positively beaming from one ear to the other, while Kagen and Nachari just looked at each other in stunned surprise and shook their heads.

Jocelyn watched as they went.

Marquis had clearly found a new buddy, and it didn't take a psychologist to figure out why: Braden Bratianu had saved Jocelyn's life, and in doing so, he had saved both Nathaniel and Storm. Despite all of his rough edges, Marquis had a heart of gold—and a powerful code of honor. The enormous male was the devoted head of his family.

Her new family.

And she was beginning to wonder how she had ever done without them.

Her life had seemed full before, but it had only been a pitiful imitation of the real thing—

The real thing was right here…

In Nathaniel's dark, loving eyes and his strong, waiting arms. In Nachari's richly textured brilliance. In Kagen's peaceful, expert caretaking. In Marquis's terrifying, overbearing displays of…love. Even in little Braden's bright-eyed wonder and hope for acceptance.

And of course, there was that perfect little miracle she had been given: Aquila, the eagle, her own little Storm.

"Jocelyn!" Nachari's voice interrupted her thoughts. "I think Storm—"

BLOOD DESTINY

"I think he *did something*." Nathaniel grimaced. He was standing next to his brothers, holding Storm out an arm's length away from his body, the child cradled neatly in the palm of his hand.

Nachari wrinkled his perfect nose. "Oh yeah, someone needs to *do something* with him." He took a step back. "Is he supposed to do that already?"

Nathaniel called out toward the hallway, "Alejandra? Colette?" When there was no answer, he tried to pass the baby to Nachari.

Nachari held up both hands in the universal gesture of surrender. "Isn't that kid supposed to drink blood?"

Kagen frowned. "He'll start feeding around age five. Until then, he has to use his digestive system and take nutrients from human food."

Seemingly pleased that Kagen knew what he was talking about, Nathaniel tried to pass the baby to him.

Kagen looked both ways, like maybe Nathaniel had mistaken him for some other brother he didn't know about. When it became abundantly clear that Nathaniel, indeed, meant him, he waved his arm in the air. "Jocelyn!"

Jocelyn rolled her eyes and laughed.

Three large male vampires—one, an Ancient Master Warrior; another, an Ancient Master Healer; and the third, a Master Wizard—all brought to their knees by a one-day-old infant who had apparently soiled his diaper.

"You three are pathetic," she remarked as she took Storm from Nathaniel and cradled the child lovingly against her breast. "And Nathaniel, I would rather you not hold the baby away from your body like a baseball in a glove. You could've dropped him."

Nathaniel shook his head adamantly. "Never, my love."

When she met his eyes, his smile was radiant, his relief apparent. "And that charming smile will get you nowhere."

Nathaniel laughed and all three males began to walk toward the living room.

Jocelyn cleared her throat. "Where do you think you're going?"

Nachari inclined his head in the direction of the sofa. "We'll just wait for you over there."

"We'll be in the living room," Nathaniel concurred.

"No," Jocelyn chastised, "you will not. You will *all* follow me to the changing table. It's about time you big, brave cavemen learn how to change a diaper."

Kagen frowned. "Now that wasn't necessary, little sister." He tried to put a hint of authority in his voice.

Nachari nodded his agreement. "Obviously, Nathaniel needs to learn, but we're…I'm cool."

Jocelyn sighed in exasperation. She glared at Kagen. "It *is* necessary." She rolled her eyes at Nachari. "And you're *not* cool; you're pitiful. You're both coming with Nathaniel to learn how to change your nephew's diaper, and that's that." All of a sudden a wicked smile swept across her mouth. She purposely bared her fangs and snapped.

All three men jumped back, startled.

With a low, feminine growl, she hissed, "Get moving, boys!"

As the three vampires fell silently into line, Jocelyn glanced down at her perfect Storm. The baby's eyes were beaming up at her, his little body wiggling with excitement.

And he was grinning from ear to ear.

Epilogue

Marquis Silivasi stood silently in the shadows. He watched as the last of the humans made their way from the graveside ceremony following Joelle Parker's funeral. He had come to pay his respects but was unable to face the human family whose lineage he had known for centuries. Having to tell Kevin Parker the news of his daughter's death had been one of the worst moments of Marquis's life, and he had lived a very, very long time. His regret was insufferable, his shame for being unable to save her…almost unbearable.

Shimmering out of view, he materialized deep within the Dark Moon Forest at yet another recent grave site—that of his little brother, Shelby. It was the first time he had visited the final resting place since the tragic loss. The first time he had seen the simple white granite marker lying over the desolate plot: *Shelby Silivasi. Honored Brother and Beloved Twin.*

Marquis ran a trembling hand through his thick black hair. The pressing moisture of crimson tears stung his deeply troubled eyes. Shelby had only been five hundred years old when he died, the same age as his twin, Nachari, but the difference was, Nachari had lived to graduate the Romanian University. Nachari had lived to reach his status as a Master Wizard.

Shelby, on the other hand, had stopped just short of receiving an honored distinction because he had found his *blood destiny*: the one human woman chosen by the gods to be his mate. His one opportunity to avoid the ultimate curse of his kind.

Dalia Montano.

And fulfilling the demands of the Blood Curse, securing his future with the human female, had been far more important than completing his studies. Shelby had planned to return to Romania as soon as the blood sacrifice was made, yet the young fledgling had failed at both of his tasks.

Marquis knew he was the one to blame.

He should have been more vigilant.

He should never have let down his guard.

Things had just gone so smoothly—so unbelievably seamlessly—between Shelby and Dalia that no one had foreseen Valentine Nistor's wicked scheme.

It wasn't an excuse. Marquis was an Ancient. He should have known better.

Marquis balled his hands into two tight fists, struggling to contain the rage—the gut-wrenching heartache—that threatened to consume him. The sky above him had already turned as black as night, and the wind was picking up into a fierce howl. He had to keep it together.

He kicked at the cold forest ground, causing a not-so-subtle tremor in the earth beneath him in an effort not to cry out. The vengeance he had finally exacted on Valentine was nothing against the breadth of this loss.

Celestial gods, how could this have happened!

And it wasn't just that Shelby would have been a Master, an achievement born of *four hundred years* of studies; he would have been a Master Warrior…like Marquis. And that meant Marquis would have been in charge of his little brother's ongoing training. It would have been the first time in 479 years—since their father's presumed death—that Marquis would have shared his day-to-day existence with another being.

The first time in 479 years that Marquis Silivasi would not have been alone.

Marquis knelt before the simple white slab of granite, his head bowed in reverence.

So much loss.

He had seen so many warriors needlessly slain over his lifetime as a result of the wretched curse, a pronouncement made upon generations of males for a sin committed so long ago that the fallen warriors didn't even remember the crime. They only knew that when the Blood Moon came, they had thirty days...

One opportunity in an otherwise eternal existence to gain the one human woman who might save them from the ultimate fate of their kind. One month to obtain a chance at life, create the possibility for love, and acquire the blessing of a family.

Thirty days to live or die.

Marquis shook his head. What was the purpose of being a warrior...of being an Ancient...if he couldn't even protect the ones he loved? What was the purpose of surviving this long when his life had been nothing but time, education, endless battles...and loss? And why hadn't that one opportunity to love—to share such a barren existence—ever been given to him?

He was so very weary of living.

Like a slowly boiling cauldron of water, Marquis's body began to tremble with the depth of his anguish. His lungs began to heave, and his heart began to pound from so much rage and injustice, until finally, he could no longer contain his grief, and the pain of a lifetime spilled over.

Hands pressed tight against his temples, Marquis Silivasi threw back his head and shouted all of his rage and grief in one gut-wrenching cry: a lion's roar that shook the very heavens, sending balls of fire the color of blood crashing down upon the earth—hail the size of baseballs battering the valley floor.

As the Ancient Master Warrior's tears fell like crimson raindrops, the rivers overflowed and the heavens shook. Giant boulders perched atop nearby canyon walls crashed to the earth's floor in violent rockslides, even as the side of the mountain itself split open.

And then all was silent.

The anguished cry of the male reverberated through the Rocky Mountains. It echoed through the rising hills, rose to the blackened sky, and stirred deep beneath the cavernous valley, until it finally settled as nothing more than a subtle tremor buried deep within the earth's crust.

Ciopori Demir stirred. Her resting place disturbed.

Deep golden eyes, dotted with amber sparkles like sundrenched diamonds, blinked once…twice…a third time. Heavy, dark lashes fanned her ancient cheeks as eyes that had been closed for centuries fluttered open. Her sleeping mind awakened. Her soul became aware.

The echo of the male's call stirred her heart as she slowly sat up. His anguish penetrated her soul. The cadence of his cry restored her eternal heartbeat. Somehow, his rage reanimated her pure, royal blood…ancient, innocent, and unblemished…even as his grief broke the ancient spell.

Ciopori rubbed her eyes trying to clear her mind. She pushed a heavy lock of her hair from her face and struggled to remember: Where was she? *Who was she?*

The memories came back slowly, one scattered piece at a time. She was the daughter of greatness. The firstborn female child of the Great King Sakarias and his beautiful wife, Jade. She was the caretaker of her youngest sibling, Vanya, and the sister of the royal twins, Jaegar and Jadon. So, what was she doing buried deep within the earth? Surrounded by layers and layers of rich minerals, crusted soil, and clammy moisture?

The ancient princess suddenly felt entombed in the endless layers of evolution. Trapped in a timeless grave. *Think, Ciopori,* she urged herself as the dirt walls of her grave seemed to close in on her. *How is it that you find yourself in this predicament? And what must you do to get out?*

The memories began to creep in incrementally like water through a leaky dam: all the killings, the endless sacrifices, the loss of so many females. The last of their great kind, the Celestial Beings, had been reduced to ashes by the moral depravity of their men and their ravenous hunger for power. Their culture had been decimated by a wicked, insatiable thirst for blood that had become unquenchable.

Ciopori sat up and hugged her knees to her chest, rocking in a smooth, rhythmic motion, trying to calm her mind. Who was the last person she remembered seeing? Ah, of course, *Jadon*, her beloved older brother. Now she remembered.

Jadon had whisked them away—herself and Vanya—at great risk to his own life. In the midst of a violent storm, he had come into their castle bedchamber like a thief in the night, imploring them to flee Romania at once, explaining that they had to get out of the castle immediately if they hoped to live: Jaegar and his warriors were coming for them.

The men had finally crossed the last and final boundary. They had gone mad from their endless bloodlust, and were ready to make the ultimate sacrifice: the virgin daughters of the great king himself, Jaegar's very own sisters.

Determined to see his sisters live and his society survive, Jadon had whisked them across the vast, open countryside, taking them deep into the heart of the Transylvanian Alps, where he had met up with a convoy of traveling warriors, a secret group of mercenaries led by the infamous wizard, Fabian. Eventually, Fabian had secured passage on a ship across the great sea, taking himself, Ciopori, and Vanya to a foreign land far across the ocean, an uninhabited refuge where they would finally be given sanctuary from their own kind.

Sanctuary in the form of a living death.

A deep, dreamless slumber where their bodies would remain alive—immortal yet asleep—until such time as it was finally safe to awaken them again.

Until Jadon came back to get them.

Ciopori wondered what time it was. *What year it was.* She began to thrash around, frantically searching for her sleeping sister in the darkness of the shallow chamber. She must find and awaken Vanya! How long had it been? How many years had they slept? Had Jadon finally come back for them?

And whose anguished cry was that?

Her heart felt heavy from the torment in his voice. Had his sorrow awakened her? Ciopori didn't know why, but she had to find that male.

She had to go to him!

Desperately, she began to claw at the ground, digging in frenzied circles as her body scraped against the walls of the earthen tomb.

"Vanya! Vanya!"

She cried out until her voice grew hoarse, digging...turning...clawing...twisting her body this way and that in a frenzied effort to uncover her baby sister. "Vanya, where are you?"

After what seemed an eternity, Ciopori dropped her head in her hands and started to weep. The earth was suffocating her. She was about to panic. She had to get out of the ground.

Now that she was awake, she could no longer stomach the shallow grave. The smell of damp earth was all around her, the blanket of rich soil encasing her like the burial shroud of a mummy. Ciopori took a long, slow, deep breath and worked to calm her mind. She was a Celestial Being. *Picture the earth. See the sky above you.*

She shifted until she was on her knees: "Ancestors, Great Ones, I humbly beseech you....

From deep within the earth I pray; my tomb as dark as night—
for freedom from this lowly grave; awaken heaven's light.
Place my feet along earth's path; the sky above my head—
where flowers bloom and children laugh; release me from earth's bed."

All at once, Ciopori was standing in a clearing, her feet on solid ground. Towering pines and fir trees surrounded her, and the sky shifted right before her eyes from a darkened gray to a brilliant, aqua blue. Her eyes swept over the land, taking note of the simple granite markers. It was a circular, hallowed clearing. This was sacred earth. A burial ground.

Ciopori stepped backward, reverently removing her shoes from her feet as she paid silent homage to the dead. She wondered who they were. Were these her father's soldiers?

And then she saw him.

The powerful...stunning...warrior.

The one whose cries had awakened her.

He was an enormous male, clearly a fighter, with long, thick hair the color of midnight: the same color as hers.

His eyes were like the depths of the ocean, so black they gleamed blue. And his remarkably handsome face was stricken with sorrow as he knelt before a simple white stone marker. Ciopori knew immediately that he was a warrior of some standing. It was in the proud set of his shoulders, the way he crouched above the ground with both stealth and purpose, the arrogant slant of his chin. There was a hard certainty in his demeanor...in spite of his sorrow.

Ciopori had spent very little time with her father's guard growing up, but she knew enough etiquette to approach the warrior with respect.

She padded silently around the periphery of the grounds, stopping about four feet behind him. Averting her eyes—as was proper when addressing a male of authority—she cleared her throat and awaited his attention.

The male sprang to his feet like a predator, rising and turning to face her in one smooth motion. He looked startled to find her standing there, as if no one had ever snuck up on him before. His face was a hard line of menace as he stared her down with those hauntingly beautiful eyes.

"Greetings, warrior," Ciopori whispered in the old language.

About The Author

Tessa Dawn grew up in Colorado where she developed a deep affinity for the Rocky Mountains. After graduating with a degree  in psychology, she worked for several years in criminal justice and mental health before returning to get her Master's Degree in Nonprofit Management.

Tessa began writing as a child and composed her first full-length novel at the age of eleven. By the time she graduated high-school, she had a banker's box full of short-stories and books. Since then, she has published works as diverse as poetry, greeting cards, workbooks for kids with autism, and academic curricula. The Blood Curse Series marks her long-desired return to her creative-writing roots and her first foray into the Dark Fantasy world of vampire fiction.

Tessa currently splits her time between the Colorado suburbs and mountains with her husband, two children, and "one very crazy cat." She hopes to one day move to the country where she can own horses and what she considers "the most beautiful creature ever created" -- a German Shepherd.

Writing is her bliss.

Books in the Blood Curse Series

Blood Destiny

Blood Awakening

Blood Possession

Blood Shadows

Blood Redemption

If you would like to receive notice of future releases,

please join the author's mailing list at

www.TessaDawn.Com